Praise for Natalie Walters

"Natalie Walters delivers an addictive, fast-paced romcom romp in *Spies, Lies, and Alibis*. You'll be rooting for these complex characters who manage to be relatable even in the midst of espionage and covert ops. It's a refreshing take on romance: funny, tender, and heartfelt but with heart-pounding action and adventure that will keep you reading long past bedtime. A purely delightful read!"

—Emma St. Clair, *USA TODAY*
bestselling author of *If All Else Sails*

"My cover is blown! I'm a die-hard Natalie Walters fan, and if it was too hidden before, now I'm out in the open. *Spies, Lies, and Alibis* is the book to read this year. It's a cocktail of intrigue, wit, action, and romance, wrapped up in a book cover to die for. But don't die for it—that'd be bad—just read it. Now. Before everything implodes and goes sideways. If you didn't know you needed a Natalie Walters spy novel on your bookshelf, now you do!"

—Jaime Jo Wright, bestselling and award-winning
author of *The House on Foster Hill* and
Night Falls On Predicament Avenue

"I love the idea of a romantic story with spies. But make it a romantic comedy with spies? Place in some excellent banter, hilarious internal monologuing, and a hero who is both dashing and adorable? Yes, please! That's what you get with Natalie Walters' newest book, *Spies, Lies, and Alibis*. This interesting, wonderfully romantic, well-paced story pairs the intrigue of the spy-life with the delightful, flirty elements of a second-chance rom-com. What you end up with is a mission impossible to put down."

—Pepper Basham, award-winning
author of *Some Like It Scot*

"This is the novel I've been waiting to read. For those who grew up longing to be a Gallagher Girl or secretly wanting to star in *Mr. and Mrs. Smith,* this book is one you will inhale even as you wonder who can be trusted in this tale of betrayal and secrets. From a Dallas museum to Italy and back to Texas, this book takes readers on an international caper filled with danger, flirtation, and truth. Natalie Walters proves she is one of the top voices in romantic suspense with *Spies, Lies, and Alibis.*"

—Cara Putman, award-winning author
of *The Accused* and *Flight Risk*

SPIES, LIES, & ALIBIS

Also by Natalie Walters

Better Watch Out

The SNAP Agency Novels

Initium (novella)
Lights Out
Fatal Code
Blind Trust

Harbored Secrets Novels

Living Lies
Deadly Deceit
Silent Shadows

Stories

Perilous Obsession included in *Cornered*
Caught in the Crosshairs included in *Targeted*

SPIES, LIES, & ALIBIS

A NOVEL

NATALIE WALTERS

THOMAS NELSON
Since 1798

Spies, Lies, and Alibis

Published in Nashville, Tennessee, by Thomas Nelson. Thomas Nelson is a registered trademark of HarperCollins Christian Publishing, Inc.

Thomas Nelson titles may be purchased in bulk for educational, business, fundraising, or sales promotional use. For information, please email SpecialMarkets@ThomasNelson.com.

HarperCollins Publishers, Macken House, 39/40 Mayor Street Upper, Dublin 1, D01 C9W8, Ireland (https://www.harpercollins.com)

Library of Congress Cataloging-in-Publication Data

Names: Walters, Natalie, 1978- author
Title: Spies, lies, & alibis : a novel / Natalie Walters.
Other titles: Spies, lies, and alibis
Description: Nashville, Tennessee : Thomas Nelson, [2026] | Summary: "They were each other's first love. Now they might be each other's last hope"—Provided by publisher.
Identifiers: LCCN 2025047306 (print) | LCCN 2025047307 (ebook) | ISBN 9781400354535 paperback | ISBN 9780310181088 epub | ISBN 9781400354542
Subjects: LCGFT: Romance fiction | Spy fiction | Fiction | Novels
Classification: LCC PS3623.A4487 S65 2026 (print) | LCC PS3623.A4487 (ebook)
LC record available at https://lccn.loc.gov/2025047306
LC ebook record available at https://lccn.loc.gov/2025047307

Printed in the United States of America

26 27 28 29 30 LBC 5 4 3 2 1

To my readers: Thanks for being the best accomplices
a Sweet & Stabby author could ask for!

CHAPTER 1

Ben

Dallas, Texas
Monday night

The day I walked into school in my Sunday suit, my hair slicked back, and my orange juice in a martini shaker I took from my house, I felt like the coolest kid in school. "Shaken, not stirred," I told Mrs. Connor with a wink. I'm not sure if I earned detention for the wink or when I argued that a spy didn't need to know algebra.

Not that it mattered. When Mrs. Connor asked what I wanted to be when I grew up, I was all about bull riding. Or driving a derby car at the local mud track on a Friday night. Or moving to Australia to wrangle crocodiles like the great Steve Irwin. In sixth grade, the only thing I wanted was a taste of danger—like James Bond.

I scan the interior of the Dallas Museum of Art and feel like I'm in the middle of a Bond movie, but unlike the Ian Fleming plots, the kind of danger surrounding me isn't fictional. And to be honest, the taste of danger isn't as sweet as I'd imagined.

Tonight the art museum is decorated with gold and white balloons and a live band is playing a broad range of music from across the decades. Waiters with trays of appetizers and champagne slip in between the guests.

An older couple around the age of my grandparents is sitting at a secluded table in the sculpture garden. It's corny, I know, and I'd never admit it out loud, but there's something mesmerizing about watching them interact beneath the twinkly lights strung between the live oaks as if they're the only people in the world.

Somehow they've managed to ignore the three hundred other gala guests dancing, eating, and talking loudly around them. I don't know who they are, and my first instinct is to be suspicious, but for a few minutes I give them the benefit of the doubt and believe they are good people—and not Mom and Pop Gambino.

My imagination paints them as a hardworking couple: He invested in the market when he was young and grew his wealth while working his way up the corporate ladder; his wife is a schoolteacher who truly did it for the love of her students while filling their home with love, children, and memories.

I let my mind play out their story, and when I see the husband gently cradle his wife's hand, I can't help but hope my version is right. It stirs a longing for my own story.

"So, no risk, eh?"

My attention is dragged back to the man standing next to me at the outdoor bar. Charles Rinault's brown eyes are a little glassy but not enough to hide his interest in my answer. "Low risk, low reward. High risk . . ." I smile. "Well, with your success you must know the rest."

Mr. Rinault's expression lights up with pride. He's a restaurateur, and from the story he's fed me for the last twenty minutes, he started from nothing except a fat inheritance from his French great-grandmother he never knew. He took that money and opened two French nightclubs that also serve food, hence why he calls himself a restaurateur rather than what he truly is—a shady, criminal club owner.

It's so cliché. Burlesque club owner? Sometimes I wish criminals would be a little more imaginative, but their lack of creativity makes my job easier. At least most jobs. My gaze slides back to the older couple again, and tonight my job feels . . . taxing.

Eighteen months ago my real life was put on hold when the FBI assigned me to go undercover as a financial advisor working for AJ Finance, a fictional boutique investment firm that requires interested clients to have a financial portfolio in the high millions to even be invited to a concept meeting. But I'm only interested in one man's accounts, and that man isn't Charles Rinault.

"It's my job to leverage the risk so that your *investment* remains clean." The band has chosen a slow number, allowing the volume of the conversations around me to pick up, so I lower my voice. "I'm not here to convince you to use my service, Mr. Rinault. My client list is quite full, and honestly, I'm not even sure I can take another—"

"No, no." Mr. Rinault slaps his glass of whiskey on the bar top and then throws a sloppy smile at the couple on the other side of him. "I want to invest. Just tell me what I need to do."

A tall brunette enters my line of sight, her green eyes locked on me as her slender frame saunters in my direction. Her appearance at my side steals Mr. Rinault's focus, turning it envious when her hand grazes the sleeve of my tuxedo. "I've been looking for you." Her gaze shifts to Mr. Rinault and then back to me. "Are you going to be here all night?"

Her tone isn't flirtatious, which matches the tight smile she gives me. She wedges her way between me and Mr. Rinault to order a drink from the bartender. Her eyes flash with a message. *It's time.*

The move is intentional and gives me the chance to look over my shoulder in the direction my partner, Ruby Knight, alluded to. I scan the area searching for anything that seems . . . suspicious. Anything that stands out among the lavish show of wealth on parade by the guests who have all congregated in the name of philanthropy. *And crime.*

It's not lost on me that some of these individuals hiding behind their overly bright veneer smiles are slimy snakes with hushed-up criminal histories. Or, like Charles Rinault, they believe laundering money with *me* is worth the risk. I should feel out of place given the net worth surrounding me is in the millions, billions for some. Meanwhile, I spent last night budgeting for a summer fishing trip and debating whether a three-star motel is better than a two-star hotel.

In my notch lapel tuxedo—the same one James Bond prefers (I checked)—no one should suspect I'm not who I say I am, which means my meeting tonight with a crime boss shouldn't draw any extra suspicion.

Especially when I disappear.

After a minute, my eyes catch on a familiar face—Lorenzo Ramirez—and every nerve in my body goes on alert.

Ramirez owns Enzo Coal & Oil, a family-run business started by his grandfather that deals in the extraction, refinement, and sale of fossil fuels. But beneath the façade of a legitimate business, Ramirez engages in illegal activity that includes money laundering and arms trafficking, which has put him under the scrutiny of federal prosecutors for Racketeer Influenced and Corrupt Organizations (RICO) charges. However, it's the brutal murder of Special Agent Daniel "Danny" Morales that has me and the entire Dallas field office targeting Ramirez.

Morales was looking into the death of an undercover DEA informant, and somehow he got caught in the crosshairs of Lorenzo Ramirez. We intercepted an encrypted message to Ramirez indicating a "problem was solved," and a bullet recovered from the scene was traced back to a cartel he's worked with, but it wasn't enough to convict.

That's where I come in.

The one thing all criminals want to protect more than their freedom? Their money. And for my role as AJ Finance's most proficient financial advisor, the FBI made sure I had a thick portfolio of clients who paid me to keep their money as starched as their white-collar shirts.

But Lorenzo Ramirez isn't dumb, and he's had enough experience being investigated by law enforcement, federal or otherwise, to keep his circle tight. And his mouth shut.

I couldn't just saunter up to him, hand him my business card, and hope he'd call me and tell me how he ordered the death of a federal agent. The only way to get access to Ramirez was to make him want to meet me more than I wanted to meet him.

It was a long shot, but he took the bait. Through his personal attorney, Jimmy Rook, I was invited to help Lorenzo Ramirez manage a financial deal that involves a private meeting this evening.

"If you'll excuse me." I push my untouched glass of champagne across the bar. "Mr. Rinault, this is my assistant, Isabella McAllen. If you give her your information, we'll see what we can do about getting you through the doors of AJ Finance."

Mr. Rinault's glassy gaze settles on Ruby. He sizes her up and smiles like one of those cartoon wolves who see their prey. "I've never had a problem getting myself through doors."

The man is disgusting. I don't believe he's a threat—especially not to Ruby—but am I comfortable leaving her here? Ruby must read my mind because the edge of her lip curls into a smirk. I hold her gaze a second longer to make sure she'll be okay. I'm rewarded with a hard stare that says she knows a dozen ways to kill me.

Leaving them at the bar, I wind my way through the crowd and head toward the stairs. A quick look reveals no one is paying attention to me. I take the steps two at a time to the second-floor mezzanine area. There are fewer guests up here and their attention is focused on the dancing below. Easily enough, I slip around the velvet rope barrier keeping guests from the third and fourth floors.

At the top of the third floor, I tug at my tie while I catch my breath. This mission has kept me in more penguin suits than I care for. As eager as I am to hang up the tuxedos and slip back into my trusty pair of jeans and boots, I'm even more eager to watch Ramirez trade his pinstripe suits for a prison-orange jumpsuit.

"I didn't deserve that."

The words snap in my ear and I can't help my smile. I glance down the empty hallway filled with Asian art. The music echoing from below is just loud enough to cover my low response. "How'd you get away from him so fast? I'm impressed."

"Don't be."

It isn't Isabella McAllen's syrupy tone speaking through my earpiece now; it's all Ruby. And I'm concerned. Making my way down the hall, I take a few seconds to appreciate a woodblock print called *Hara: Mount Fuji in the Morning* just in case someone happens to catch me up here. "What did you do?"

"Why do you always assume I *did* something?"

I walk quietly toward my destination at the end of the hall. There's a door marked Employees Only, and with a quick glance over my shoulder I turn the knob and let myself through. Behind the door, I feel less exposed and continue my conversation with Ruby as I take another set of stairs back down to the second level. "*Did* you do something?"

She hums in my ear all innocent, but Ruby Knight is one of the FBI's best agents, with a nearly flawless résumé. Nearly. There are three things that Ruby hates, which have caused some issues on the job. One, having to prove herself as a female agent; two, people touching her food; and—

"He called Tucker Reid a hack. Said the Cowboys would have a more consistent running back in a turtle."

And people who dis the Dallas Cowboys. Ruby is very sensitive about football. I close my eyes briefly, unsure if I want to know more. "Please tell me Mr. Rinault is still walking."

"He's walking." I can hear the spark of unapologetic mischief in her voice. "But with a limp." I imagine her giving an innocent shrug. "What can I say, I'm a little clumsy in these heels."

Lies.

"You've got eyes on Ramirez?"

"Yep," Ruby answers. "What time is your meeting?"

"Fifteen minutes," I answer after checking my watch. With caution, I slowly push open a door that leads me into another gallery room. Just like on the third level, a velvet rope cordons off this section of the museum from guests. Soft lights illuminate the artwork on the walls and the Latin American sculptures on pedestals.

Tonight's meeting is going to take place in the Mayer Library. It's private, quiet, and off-limits to everyone but Lorenzo Ramirez and whoever he's supposed to be meeting to discuss a deal with great financial opportunity. My role was to come with a plan to manage the profits of the deal and, as advised by Jimmy Rook, "prove my worth."

Oh, I have a plan. I double-check my pocket, ensuring the cigarette lighter containing the Raspberry Pi Zero is secure. The human interface device will act as a covert back door, allowing the FBI to remotely intercept network traffic and access Ramirez's laptop as soon as he logs in. If he opens any accounts or sensitive files, we'll see everything. All I need to do is get inside the office and plant it. I pull out my Lishi lock-pick tool and start toward the locked door.

I'm careful not to let my confidence lure me into complacency. Ruby will alert me if Ramirez moves, but there are still museum security employees making rounds. I need to tread carefully. I can't risk exposure of any kind. Lorenzo Ramirez might not pull the trigger, but his hands are as bloody as the ones he pays to do it.

CHAPTER 2

Cybil

Dallas, Texas
Monday night

The Dallas Museum of Art buzzes with excitement over the surprise headliner, country star Bart Jennings, but my attention keeps sweeping to the hunk of muscle who could be Vin Diesel's stunt double. I'm hoping he's more furious than fast—I'm confident I can outrun furious. But the way his right arm hangs, I know there's a gun beneath his tuxedo coat, and the scars on his knuckles tell me he's not the type to rely solely on the weapon at his side to take down an adversary.

It's weird the things I notice now since working for Earl Edmond. Like how someone stands and walks a little differently when they have a gun tucked against their body. Or how someone can donate millions of dollars to a charity with one hand and pay off arms dealers with the other. Or that secret conversations don't always happen in shady nightclubs or in dark Italian restaurants over a plate of spaghetti like they do in the movies.

Sometimes they happen in law offices, on a park bench, at a child's birthday party, and surprisingly—more frequently than I ever imagined—at charity galas.

Like tonight.

Bart Jennings kicks off a rousing song that electrifies the crowd, and it's my cue to sneak away. I check my left where my boss, Earl Edmond, and his son Sebastian are talking with the hosts of tonight's fundraiser to support the South Dallas Community Center. I glance around at the A-list of affluent guests interspersed with professional athletes, actors, and musicians, all gathered in the name of helping those less fortunate. The cynical part of me wonders if any of these people would be as philanthropic if they couldn't just write a check.

Not tonight's problem.

No. Tonight's problem is a six-foot-something bald man who is armed and standing between me and the third-floor bathroom. There's no way he's museum security, which means he's not here to protect the art.

I toy with the ring on my thumb, locking onto my target. With a silent *Sorry about your night,* I time my move perfectly—elbowing into the path of a server balancing a tray of freshly poured champagne. The poor guy doesn't stand a chance. The tray tilts, the glasses fly, and a symphony of shattering crystal cuts through the noise. The music drowns most of the chaos, but the mess still pulls the attention of the nearest staff—and, more importantly, Faux-Diesel.

Not wasting a second, I slip around him while his back is turned and hustle up the stairs to the third level. At the top, a flash of movement makes me pause and press into a corner. A handful of museum security guards are on patrol tonight—two of them prowling the roped-off levels. No weapons, but they don't have to be armed to ruin my night. I check my watch, marking the time. When I peek around the corner again, both guards have vanished toward level four.

I slip into the women's restroom at the end of the hall, checking the stalls before ducking into the third one. The black floor-length gown I borrowed pools around my feet as I wriggle out of it. It's not as flashy as the low-cut, glittery numbers floating around the gallery, but that's the point. I'm not here to stand out. Blending in? I've had a lifetime of practice. It used to bother me. I used to feel like I was fading. Now? Now it's survival.

Now it helps me work as a *covert asset*—to collect intel on corrupt individuals and businesses that prey on the innocent. *Another thing I'm painfully experienced in.* I twist the ring, grounding myself in the promise I made a long time ago never to be powerless again.

The bathroom walls vibrate with a twangy anthem about a man, his pickup truck, and a lifetime of questionable decisions. I'm counting on the charity gala's headliner to distract my boss long enough that he won't realize I'm gone. My elbow clips the side of the cramped stall, sending a sharp jolt through my arm, but I grit my teeth and focus—carefully draping the gown over the edge of the stall. Underneath, I'm squeezed into shapewear—supposedly more practical for movement than a ball gown. *Breathing, apparently, is optional.*

I rip a few squares of toilet paper and layer them across the seat. Stepping out of my heels, I climb up, balancing on the questionable surface like a very determined circus performer. On my toes, I press up on the ceiling panel and start feeling around. After a few seconds of swiping at—and collecting—a truly gross amount of dust, I find no sign of the backpack.

I wobble on the toilet seat, and the confidence I had two minutes ago—when I seamlessly snuck away from Mr. Edmond and the gala—is melting into panic. Did I pick the wrong stall? The wrong bathroom? Sweat slides down my back as I mentally replay Athena's instructions.

Third-level restroom. Conservation Gallery. Third stall.

Check, check, check. So where's the stupid—ah! My fingers catch on a nylon strap and I tug the bag down. Hopping to the cold tile floor, I unzip the backpack and yank out a pair of black leggings and a matching top. I'd tried to convince Athena that it would look *way* less suspicious if I was caught wandering the halls in a gown instead of dressed like a cat burglar. Shockingly, she disagreed.

And really, who was I to argue? Athena—definitely not her real name—was my handler. The woman paying me to spy on my boss. His employees. His business. And business associates who might be engaging in illegal practices. The same woman I'm pretty sure would pull a Houdini if I ever got caught.

"Just don't get caught," I mutter under my breath, tugging the shirt over my head. Or as my mother used to say, "*Don't write a check you can't cash.*" As a kid, I thought she meant it literally. I'd watch her scribble checks for rent, groceries, or utilities—only to come home to our stuff packed in boxes on a porch, or to have our heat cut off in the middle of winter, or to be escorted out of the grocery store empty-handed.

It wasn't until middle school that I understood what she *really* meant. By then, we'd moved more than a dozen times. I'd finally made a real friend who invited me into a world of home-cooked meals, parents who asked about homework, and the security of having a permanent address. I begged Mom not to move us. Even promised to get babysitting and pet-sitting jobs to help with the bills. My mom wrote me a check she couldn't cash—and six months later, we were gone. In college, I understood what ADHD had stolen from her—how her symptoms weren't just quirky or forgetful, but the kind that lived at the far end of the spectrum. How it wasn't neglect or malice. It was chaos she couldn't outrun. But by then, all I craved was the safety and security of a permanent address.

I still do—just preferably not at the state penitentiary, if I get caught.

There's a lull in the music rattling the museum's walls, and I catch my breath. My pulse pounds a staccato against my ribs. I check my watch. Time's slipping. I carefully fold my gown into the bag along with my heels, swapping them for a pair of black flats, and then pull a tube of Chanel lipstick from my silver sequined clutch. It slides easily into the pocket of the small gear pouch strapped to my wrist.

With the backpack stashed back in the ceiling, I give myself a quick glance in the mirror. For a second, the woman staring back at me doesn't even look familiar. I shove down the anxious pinch twisting in my gut and force a small, reassuring smile. The nerves always show up in the minutes before the job, but they don't stick around for long.

I'm ready. I've already walked the museum twice this week, logged the security patterns, and marked the blind spots. Now, it's time to do my job.

"*Find out why Earl Edmond is meeting with Lorenzo Ramirez.*"

That, along with the instructions about the bag, were the only directives in Athena's text. I don't know everything about the company she works for, but I know enough to trust I'm working for the good guys. My job isn't to understand what they plan to do with the information—just to get it and get out.

I step out of the bathroom and into the darkened hallway. Faux-Diesel should be back to guarding the stairwell, keeping curious guests away from this floor. If my timing's right, the museum's security guards should be busy one level up. That gives me just enough of a window to break into the office, plant the lipstick recorder, slip back into my dress, and make it back to the gala before the meeting starts. Just another night of light felonies and no arrests. *I hope.*

Beneath my feet, the floor thrums with the bass of the drums, and I time my steps to match. Under the dim glow of the gallery lights, it feels like every painting is watching me. Judging me. I hurry to the door of the Mayer Library and test the handle. Locked. "That would be too easy," I mutter under my breath.

I slip the tension wrench and hook pick from my wrist pouch and drop to my knees. There are nights like tonight when the irony of my life feels almost laughable. A mountain of college debt for an education in how to *protect* the law—and here I am breaking it. They don't teach you this kind of thing in any LSAT practice test. How to spy on your boss. Or one of his associates who . . .

"He's killed for less."

Two days ago, I overheard Mr. Edmond snapping at Sebastian behind his office door. Gruff words. Raw fear. I hadn't caught much else—but the look in Mr. Edmond's eyes when Sebastian stormed out told me everything I needed to know. This man they were meeting tonight was dangerous.

My hand slips. The hook pick scrapes against the metal, the sharp noise slicing through the quiet like a blade. I freeze. Below me, the rhythm of the music has shifted into a slow, mournful ballad. No heavy beat left to hide behind. The paintings are still staring. Especially the one closest to me. I squint at the tiny placard: *Desperate Man* by Gustave Courbet. It's a portrait of a man clawing at his own hair, wide-eyed with pure, unhinged panic.

Relax, buddy. I'm the one committing the felony here.

Exhaling slowly, I refocus on the lock. It's a simple pin tumbler. Easy. Except—

A prickle runs down my spine. Every muscle in my body locks up, and I go statue-still, lungs fighting to stay quiet. I don't know what triggered it—sound, movement, instinct—but something's wrong.

Sliding the tools back into my pouch, I rock to my feet and press into the wall. My gaze sweeps the room. Past the paintings, the sculpture stands, the roped-off displays, until it lingers on the empty shadows between them. The ones too deep. Too still. A chill scrapes across my skin. No one else is supposed to be here. And yet . . . The feeling won't shake.

Something—or someone—is hiding in the dark.

If it's the latter, I've made a critical mistake.

Maybe even a deadly one.

CHAPTER 3

Ben

Dallas, Texas
Monday night

My eyes narrow on the figure dressed in black. I don't move. I can't. From where I'm tucked against the wall, it doesn't look like they've spotted me—but they know someone's here. At least that's my guess based on how fast they stopped trying to pick the library door's lock.

Whoever it is, they know what they're doing. Their movements are clean, practiced, and efficient enough to make my gut tighten.

The museum is full of priceless art, and a clever thief might choose a fundraiser to pull a job while everyone's distracted by a country star and free champagne. But this one? They're not interested in art. They're focused on that door. Who else besides me would be trying to break into the very room where Ramirez's laptop is sitting?

My mind spins. Nearly two years deep undercover with Operation Shadow Broker, and my team combed through every one of Ramirez's potential enemies, looking for anyone who might want to take him down. The list was long, the task tedious, but in the end, nobody was reckless—or suicidal—enough to go after Ramirez head-on. At least no one we knew about.

So who is this mystery figure in black?

My pulse hammers in my ears. Time's bleeding away and soon Ramirez will be up here. I have two choices. Both will expose me. But one might give me the upper hand. Maybe.

"Who's there?"

My voice echoes off the gallery walls. I brace, expecting the figure to startle, run—something. They don't even flinch. The complete lack of reaction feels deliberate. A power play I wasn't ready for.

"You're not supposed to be here," I say, keeping my position tight against the wall. My tone sharp. Steady. "This area is off-limits to guests."

A scuffling sound pulls my attention a few inches left of where I've been looking. That's when I realize they are moving. Blending into the shadows. I thought I had them pinned—but with tiny, imperceptible steps, they've been shifting just enough so that I'm mostly talking to a wall.

Unease coils through my muscles. Every instinct I have is screaming to go on the offensive, to drag whoever's lurking into the light. But I can't blow my cover. So I lean into the part.

"Museum security. You need to leave now."

There's a noise—small, so small I almost miss it—but unmistakable. A snort.

I blink. The moment of confusion barely has time to register before another sound cuts through the air: voices. Footsteps. I risk a glance over my shoulder. Two museum security guards are heading straight for me.

The shadow figure must hear them, too, because they bolt—slipping deeper into the darkness and disappearing toward the back hallway. Instinct kicks in and I follow them. Not because I want to give chase. I *don't*. As much as I'd like to unmask whoever's screwing with my mission, getting caught up here isn't an option. And I'm pretty sure "I was stopping a mysterious cat burglar" won't hold much weight when the museum calls the police.

Ahead of me, the door to the stairwell clicks shut. I reach it just in time to catch a flash of black darting up the stairs. I hesitate, heart hammering.

Down is safer.

Down is smart.

Down is how I stick to the plan. But the figure in black just blew my mission—and when Special Agent Katherine Scott demands an explanation, I want a name.

I make my choice and go up.

If there's even a small chance I can ID whoever ruined eighteen months of undercover work, I'm taking it.

Slowly, I pry open the door and peek into the fourth-level gallery. I have no idea if the person I'm chasing is armed. Whoever's lurking is probably just as ticked off at me for interrupting their plans as I am at them.

I slip inside. Technically, I should have the advantage. I was just here. I know the layout. But whatever ease I felt minutes ago? Gone. Now, every dark corner between the sculptures and display cases looks ready to strike.

Turning back isn't an option. If museum security catches me skulking around, I'll have to explain, and there's no version of that conversation I like. The only way out is across the gallery, through the stairwell door on the far side. And the only thing standing in my way is the figure in black.

Movement by a window snaps my attention left. I pick up my pace, careful to stick to the shadows. A display wall stands between us, and as I duck past a spotlight shining down on an abstract piece, my shoulder brushes the frame.

I freeze. A soft red glow pulses behind the painting—a motion alarm. One wrong move, and this place will light up like a Christmas tree. Exhaling slowly, I ease back.

Behind me, the stairwell door bangs open. Male voices echo across the gallery. The guards. *Fantastic.* My time's up.

I pivot toward the stairwell, moving fast but quiet, rounding the corner—expecting my quarry to be long gone—only to find them less than ten feet away. They're facing me. Or at least, I think they are.

Darkness cloaks them so thoroughly, all I can make out are the whites of their eyes. Something about the way they're standing, the tension vibrating off them, feels . . . wrong.

There's no time to puzzle it out. The guards are getting closer. I spin toward the stairwell—only to hear footsteps coming up fast.

"I'm heading to the fourth level now," a voice says, followed by the sharp burst of static from a radio.

Backing up a few steps, I realize I'm pinned. Two guards behind me and one about to cut me off in front. I glance at the mounted security cameras. Someone on our tech team had better be awake at the wheel tonight.

My gaze cuts left—to the figure in black. They're edging toward the window. If they try opening it, the alarms will make both our lives harder. But they stop. And the wall beside them shifts. Not a wall—a door. One hidden so well it even has fake crown molding and a painting hung on it. In the space of a blink, the figure slips through and vanishes.

I start for the door—it's my only shot out of here—but when I get to the wall, there's no knob. The first two guards are only a room over now, and the third guard is calling out to them. Only a wall and this door separate me from getting caught.

My fingers scrape along the molding until I find the latch. I twist it and wedge the door open just enough to slip through into a low-lit hallway. Crates and frame boxes line the walls. This must be where they move the pieces in and out of the gallery. The hallway only leads one way, so I follow it, quick and silent, until I hit a service elevator and another set of stairs. No sight of the figure in black. Doesn't matter anymore. Saving this mission is the only priority.

"What are you doing?"

Ruby's voice crackles in my earpiece, making my heart spike. If she's checking in, I've already burned too much time. Ruby doesn't do patience. If I don't answer her fast, she'll come looking, and that's the last thing I want.

I can't drag another agent into this mess.

Sweat beads along my collar as I jog down the steps. I don't know where this stairwell exits, but I can't take the risk of popping out in the middle of the gala. The guards are clustered on the fourth level. The third level should be clear.

I ease the door open and step into a narrow, dark hallway. It takes a second for my eyes to adjust. Then I spot the easels and half-restored paintings. The oily chemical smell hits me a second later—linseed oil, varnish, solvents. Conservation studio.

If I'm here, then—

I crack open the next door and confirm it. Across the hall sits the Mayer Library. Only now, I'm out of time. Ramirez and Rook could show up any second—or Ruby will. Neither option ends well.

Frustration tightens in my gut.

Movement across the gallery catches my eye. The figure in black, slipping between the exhibits. They don't know I'm here. Yet. So I take advantage. Moving swiftly toward them, I keep the pedestals holding sculptures between us.

"Stop." The word rumbles out, half growl, half command. To my surprise, they do.

It feels like déjà vu. Shadow against shadow. Facing off. Only now, they have two choices—run upstairs toward the guards or downstairs toward the gala.

I take a step forward, feeling like the tables have finally shifted in my favor. Until I see their hand move. Quickly, I shift left, putting a marble bust between me and whatever they're about to pull. Gun? Blade? Something worse?

But they're not aiming at me. Their hand presses against the wall, right next to a portrait of a woman reaching from a boat to rescue the shipwrecked.

I freeze, confusion cutting through the adrenaline. Then it clicks. The motion sensor. One nudge of that frame and the alarms will go off and chaos will descend. But—what about them? They'll be caught too. Unless . . .

They have a plan.

Who are you? The thought barely forms before they tap the frame. I brace for the shriek of alarms, the explosion of red lights, the pounding boots of security. Nothing.

I glance wildly around, heart hammering, but all I hear is the honky-tonk twang drifting up from the gala. *Silent alarm.* By the time the realization hits, the figure in black is gone. *This would never happen to Bond.*

CHAPTER 4

Cybil

Dallas, Texas
Monday night

This cannot be happening.

I skirt around a corner and dart into the women's bathroom, slamming the third stall door shut and twisting the lock. I attempt to jump onto the toilet seat—but my right foot skids across the slick plastic. I hear the splash a second before cold toilet water soaks my foot.

Welp, these shoes are going into the fire.

Swallowing a gag, I fight the urge to scream and extract my foot from its questionable bath. My pulse hasn't stopped battering my throat since I got caught at the door, and now I'm standing in some knockoff version of Karate Kid's crane pose on a public toilet, trying to figure out who the heck that man was.

At first I assumed he was museum security. But he didn't call for backup. Didn't reach for a radio. Which means . . . something is wrong. Was he private security for Ramirez? A friend of Faux-Diesel?

All I caught was a glimpse—tall, broad shoulders, black tux. Absolutely zero identifying features that could separate him from the sea of overpriced cologne and cuff links roaming the gala tonight.

I wait—counting out ninety agonizing seconds—before stepping off the toilet and unlocking the stall door. I pause with every movement, holding my breath to listen, but all I hear is the pounding of my own heartbeat. And the occasional drip of toilet water sliding off my toes.

I can't hide here forever.

Mr. Edmond has probably noticed my absence by now. With any luck, claiming I was in the ladies' room won't raise too many questions. But if I'm going to pull this off, I need to leave. Now. And not get caught.

I grab for the toilet paper to mop up my foot and find . . . one ply? *Of course*. It takes half a roll of the transparent stuff to dry my foot before I shimmy back into my gown, hide the bag again, and slip the lipstick recorder back into my clutch. First attempt: botched. But I don't give up.

No matter what messes I get myself into, it's hard to complain when the money hits my account. I need this paycheck to pay my rent and my student loans, to help my mom, and if I'm lucky, to maybe finally replace the underwear I've owned since college. *It's the little things*.

I crack the door an inch. No one's waiting for me.

Instead of risking the main stairs and a collision with Faux-Diesel, I opt for the side stairwell. There's still a chance I'll run into museum security, but back in my gown, I feel armored. One thing Mr. Edmond has taught me: Money buys invisibility. Nobody questions a well-dressed woman.

Moonlight spills through the windows, casting a silver glow over the gala. Bart Jennings is dancing across the stage, the crowd singing along, the whole place vibrating with energy. I should be focused on getting back to Mr. Edmond. But instead, it's the server carrying a tray of chocolate desserts who captures my full attention.

Surely I have time for one little choco—

"He won't die. But he'll wish he had."

The harsh whisper halts me in my heels, pulling my attention to a door that's been left slightly ajar. I glance back over my shoulder, knowing I should get back to Mr. Edmond. Instead, curiosity wins. It always does. It's what keeps the bills paid.

"Just one or two drops. I promise he'll never put his hands on you again."

I ease the door open and find two female servers crammed inside what looks like an oversized broom closet. The brunette spins around, shielding the blonde behind her. I catch a glimpse—smeared makeup, teary eyes.

"What's going on?" I ask.

The brunette's eyes flash. "A guy out there got handsy with her. She asked him to stop. He took it as a challenge."

I shift my focus to the blonde. Her chin is tucked as if she's embarrassed.

"Are you hurt?" I ask.

Her head snaps up. "No, ma'am."

She's all professional polish. Neat uniform, tasteful makeup, blond hair twisted into a chignon, though some strands have escaped. Her makeup, or what's left of it, is tastefully done, giving her that girl-next-door look.

"I wasn't flirting," she blurts. "I swear."

Anger tightens in my gut. Why is the first instinct always to blame ourselves?

"Who was it?" I press.

Both girls hesitate.

"The man who put his hands on you," I clarify. "I need to know."

It takes a minute of coaxing, but finally the blonde describes him—a creep holding court at the bar. I don't hesitate.

Yes, I'm late getting back to Mr. Edmond. Yes, this is probably dumb. But letting this slide isn't an option.

It doesn't take me long to find the man the server described. White tuxedo. Smug grin. Half perched on a barstool, pawing at a woman in a red cocktail dress and flashing his watch like it's some kind of mating call.

"You like what you see?"

Ew. I step up, flashing my brightest smile and thrusting my hand in his face. "I don't think we've met. I'm Cybil Langford."

His gaze bounces off Red Dress and lands on me. I don't miss the relief that washes over her face before she slips away. He doesn't seem as grateful for my interruption.

"Gee, that's a nice watch." I squint at it. "Is it a Casio?"

He looks genuinely scandalized. "Baby, it's a Rolex."

Baby. Kill me now.

"Wow. I bet it cost a lot." I run my manicured nails lightly along his wrist. "Mind if I take a closer look?"

He grins. Then yelps when I twist his thumb back at a painful angle—a useful move my uncle taught me when I started dating. "Wh-what are you doing?" he stammers.

"Shh." I lean in, sweet as poison. "We don't want to make a scene."

Around us, the crowd begins singing loudly with a familiar song. Perfect cover. He tries to squirm, but with the bar at his back, he's stuck.

"Listen, John Revolta, when a woman tells you to back off," I hiss, "you do it." I push harder, until I feel the joint shift. Fear finally flares in his eyes. "Got it?" I whisper.

He nods, sweating. I start to release him—when he lurches and clamps onto my wrist, yanking me closer. "Who do you think you are?" he spits.

I smile, all teeth. "I already told you. Cybil Langford."

He keeps my wrist low and tight, trying to make it look like an intimate conversation. Cute. Except now I'm thinking about how best to break his nose without splattering blood on my dress—

"Cybil."

The deep voice behind me freezes us both.

Sebastian Edmond steps into view, cool and lethal. His presence causes the man to drop my wrist like it burns. Irritation flares in my chest that it's Sebastian who scares the man, but he probably saved me from an assault charge.

"Mr. Edmond," he croaks.

Sebastian doesn't bother acknowledging the greeting. He signals to security with a flick of two fingers.

As security closes in, I rub my wrist. "I didn't need your help."

"You never do," Sebastian says dryly, flagging the bartender for a drink. "Where were you?"

It doesn't completely surprise me that Sebastian noticed I was gone. He pays attention when it serves him—whether out of habit, suspicion, or that Edmond instinct to catalog threats and assets. He's like the big brother I never asked for—the kind who'd absolutely rat me out to Daddy if it aligned with his agenda.

"Chasing down a waiter for more of those chocolate desserts."

Sebastian arches a brow. "And that guy?"

"He got handsy."

"With you?" There's a sharp edge to his voice now.

I shrug. "Not me."

His shoulders ease slightly, but suspicion still lingers in his watchful stare.

"Where's Mr. Edmond?" I ask, shifting the subject.

"With George Washington."

"What?"

Sebastian collects his drink. Sniffs it. Then takes a slow sip. "The museum has an oil painting of George Washington." He tips his head in the direction of a hallway. "Dad wanted to see it before the meeting."

Mr. Edmond might love America's history, but he has a more . . . flexible relationship obeying her laws. At least, according to Athena. But he hasn't been arrested for anything yet, which only feeds into my belief that the rich and powerful don't get booked; they get buildings named after them.

"Has the meeting started?"

Sebastian tilts his glass, studying me over the rim. "Not without me."

There's always been an edge between Sebastian and his father. Part of it's generational. Part of it's a power struggle—one man unwilling to let go, one unwilling to wait his turn.

I'm reminded of the heated argument between Sebastian and his father. *"He's killed for less."* Those four words bring me back to my failed mission—and the man behind it. I search the sea of men in tuxedos around me. Maybe there'll be some hint of recognition: a mole, a crooked nose, anything that will help me identify the person who hid behind a marble bust.

My gaze sweeps the crowd and stops on the security staff. Maroon jackets, badges, hovering at the edges of the room. Bored and inattentive. Nothing about their posture suggests they're on alert and looking for me.

Which means . . . the man upstairs *wasn't* museum security.

My mind replays the earlier events. *Someone* caught me trying to break into the Mayer Library. Any decent guest in attendance tonight would've assumed I was a burglar and reported me, right? But he didn't. He chased after me, but only when the real museum security showed up.

Which tells me he didn't want to get caught either.

The thought rattles through my brain almost as loudly as the drumbeat from the band. The man upstairs wasn't supposed to be there either. So why was he? Who was he? My questions shudder to a stop when the next question comes: Did he see *me*? Like really see me? Enough to identify me?

My fingers fly to my hair, yanking loose bobby pins until the tight chignon falls over my shoulders and curtains my face. I'm no longer annoyed with Athena for forcing me to change out of my dress. If the man from upstairs is looking for me, I'm hoping the clothing change will throw him off. Still, I feel vulnerable. Exposed.

I'm *not* as invisible as I want to be.

"I think I'll go make sure your father has everything he needs," I tell Sebastian, already moving before he can stop me.

CHAPTER 5

Ben

Dallas, Texas
Monday night

The alarm spreading through me is shifting into panic. Every worst-case scenario barrels through my brain. Did someone make us? Has our mission been compromised? My pace quickens as I shove through the stairwell door and round the corner—straight into a server. With deftness, he quick-steps to the side and manages to keep all the champagne flutes upright on his tray.

I apologize and lift a glass from his tray. I'm not about to drink it, but I need something to keep my hands from clenching into fists. Heat radiates under my tux, my pulse pounding against the stiff collar. I resist the urge to rip the bow tie from around my neck. *Did James Bond ever have this much trouble with formal wear?*

Forcing a tight breath through my lungs, I seamlessly melt into the crowd on the second-floor mezzanine. I need to look natural. Casual. Like a guy just enjoying the concert, not a guy who nearly got caught by some—what, exactly? Thief? Avid enthusiast of eighteenth-century literature?

Something doesn't add up.

An art heist during a gala is brazen, but as far as I know there's no art *inside* the Mayer Library. Just books, magazines, and a few of Winston Churchill's writings. All the valuable pieces are displayed *outside*, lining the halls. And if someone wanted those, why trip the motion alarm? Why risk drawing attention to both of us?

I scan the crowd, instincts sharpening. A museum security guard leans against the wall nearby, looking . . . bored. Not like someone who just got an alert about a silent alarm going off. Another quick sweep of the room confirms it—no tension, no crackling radios, no urgent chatter. Nothing but casual disinterest.

My confusion sharpens into realization.

The alarm wasn't triggered—it was a distraction.

I was played.

The truth hits like a sucker punch. Whoever that was, they weren't after priceless art. They weren't reaching for the painting to steal it. It was a distraction. A threat. They weren't trying to shake the museum security. They were trying to shake *me*. They knew the painting was protected by a silent alarm and they banked on me reacting exactly the way I did. Like an amateur. I took the bait and probably left them upstairs, free to do the one thing I needed to do—get inside that library.

My jaw tightens. I check my watch. I need to figure out how to salvage this mission—and fast. I wait until Bart Jennings hits the chorus, the crowd singing along loud enough to cover my voice, before speaking low into my comms. "We have a problem."

It takes a second before Ruby responds, her voice tight in my ear. "You see him too."

Him? The first thing that flashes through my mind is the figure in black. I didn't have a chance to communicate with Ruby when it all went sideways, but if anyone could spot a deviation in our mission plan, it's her. If she saw someone before I did, maybe it's the guy who just blew apart my op.

"Who?" I ask, already sweeping the mezzanine for any familiar threat.

"Below. At your nine o'clock."

My gaze moves around the room, trying to spot where Ruby's watching me from. I've learned to stop being surprised at Ruby's ability to see things and yet remain unseen. When I don't find her, I shift my focus left, searching the crowd like I'm expecting to see the figure in black from upstairs. I don't. The face I *do* see turns my blood ice cold.

Sammy Pawson.

What's he doing here?

He's leaning against a column, popping shrimp into his mouth like he's tailgating, not crashing a black-tie gala.

"What are the odds," Ruby says dryly in my ear, "that a man who enjoys firebombing businesses also enjoys two-stepping?"

Her irony jolts me into motion. I hit the stairs fast and weave through guests and servers, heading toward where I saw Pawson standing. He's already gone. A discarded shrimp tail glistens in an empty champagne glass nearby—lazy evidence he was ever here.

I pivot in a full circle, searching the room for the man who once used a tire iron to rearrange the bones in another man's face for parking in the wrong spot.

Instead of getting five to ninety-nine, Sammy "The Paws" Pawson walked out of the courthouse a free man. The victim decided not to testify, and the prosecutor couldn't prove the coercion. Now Pawson's back on the street, rumored to be doing contract work for Lorenzo Ramirez—which likely included killing Agent Danny Morales.

His presence at the gala immediately has me on edge. There's only one reason a guy like Pawson shows up at a gala like this. And it means my night has just gone from bad to worse.

"How'd it go upstairs?"

Speaking of bad. "Not good."

"Meaning?"

"Someone else was there."

The music's too loud for anyone nearby to overhear, but I keep moving in the direction of Ramirez's table, hoping Pawson might be there too. Then I'll find out why.

"Who?"

"No idea."

Now's not the time to get into the details. When I reach a corner tucked near a marble statue of Lady Godiva, I slow enough to add,

"They were trying to break into the library. Took off before I could see who it was."

"Did they see you?"

"Not well enough, I don't think."

"You don't *think*?" Ruby's tone sharpens. "What do you think they were after?"

I hesitate for half a second. As far as I know, there's nothing valuable inside the library. *Nothing except Lorenzo Ramirez's laptop.* Ahead of me, I spot Ramirez and Rook posted at their table, drinks in hand, laughing with the gala hosts. Who else would be gunning for Ramirez's laptop? And what happens if they get there before me?

Maybe it's not too late.

"I need to get back up there."

"The meeting's about to start."

I catch a glimpse of Ramirez and Rook pushing up from their seats. I'm already backtracking toward the stairs leading up to the third floor.

"I know." My eyes scan the crowd as I move. It's pointless because I don't know who I'm looking for, but I'm convinced the figure in black is still in the museum. "I just need a few minutes."

"What about Pawson?"

The man with bricks for fists is nowhere in sight, and apprehension shoots through me. Was it Pawson upstairs? No way. Pawson would rather bash your face in than run.

"Send a message to tech. See what they can find on the cameras," I say.

"Got it. Don't be stupid."

"Got it." The rote answer slips from my lips. I learned early on that Ruby's version of affection is all stickers and thorns—pep talks sound like death threats, and encouragement comes in the form of exasperated sighs, but after a failed mission in which her partner almost died three years ago, she doesn't fool around with chance.

And I won't either.

I reach the stairwell, relieved to find the door still unattended. I slip inside and take the stairs two at a time, confidence growing with every step. This time, if anyone questions me, I can tell the truth. Or at least my version of it. I'm expected for the meeting with Ramirez.

The gallery lights are brighter now, illuminating all the nooks and corners where someone could hide. My anger at being played flickers back to life, fueling my pace. I round the corner—and smash straight into a woman. Her purse hits the marble floor with a clatter as she stumbles backward. I instinctively reach out, steadying her with a hand to her arm.

"I'm sorry, I didn't see—"

The words catch midair. My gaze locks onto a pair of brown eyes. And for a second, the world tilts. *No.* It can't be. A strange wave of familiarity crashes over me—raw and visceral. I know those eyes. And I'm *absolutely* not ready for the impact. I brace a hand against the wall to steady myself. Of all the places, all the nights, all the impossible odds—there's no way *she'd* be here.

Yet here she is.

In a blink, I'm back to summers long gone, when those same brown eyes belonged to a girl who stole a piece of my heart—and maybe shaved a few years off my life. With no thought on my part, the name rips from my mouth. "Cybil Langford?"

Her eyes widen just a fraction. Recognition flickers—and then vanishes behind a wall of ice so fast, I almost doubt I saw it. Almost.

My gaze sweeps over her. Not in a lewd way, but in a *can this woman really be the same girl whose shirt I used to stick worms down?* way. When my eyes meet hers again, I realize my mistake.

Was I admiring the way her dress accentuates her curves beautifully? Sure, but I can't help it. A lot has changed, and the years have been good to her. But the real mistake—the fatal one—is that I showed I know her. And if I know who she is . . . she knows who *I* am. The *real* me. Not the alias I need to protect at all costs. *Me.*

"No," she says sharply.

I blink. "What?"

"No," she repeats, twisting away from me as she crouches to scoop up her fallen belongings.

No? Confusion churns through me like a slow, heavy fog. A tube of lipstick is next to my foot along with a snack-size bag of M&M's. I reach for the lipstick just as she does—and instinct kicks in first. I snatch it up before she can. Her hand freezes in midair. Honey-brown eyes snap to mine, sharp and clear. And this time there's no mistaking it.

It's her. *My* Cybil. Okay, not *mine*—but the Cybil of summers spent at her cousin's ranch in Cypress Creek with my best friend, Rex.

"I need that back and you need to leave," she says coolly.

The iciness in her voice makes me second-guess everything. I straighten to my full height, handing back the lipstick. "I'm sorry. You just look . . . familiar?"

"Do I? Must be my chin."

Her chin? I glance at it automatically—yeah, it's a nice chin—but that's not what's pulling at some deep, frayed memory inside me. It's *her*.

And if it *is* Cybil, she doesn't recognize me.

Rather than feeling grateful or relieved that my cover and the last eighteen months of undercover aren't blown, I feel . . . *offended?* Insecurity buzzes under my skin. Sure, I'm older. I've let my facial hair grow a little. But—

"This part of the museum is closed off to guests."

Leave. The smart move would be to walk away. She doesn't know who I am. Or maybe I'm wrong. It's been, what—ten, twelve years? I could be mistaken, but I know I'm not. There's a familiar tension thrumming in my chest that has only ever occurred around one woman.

I don't walk away. I belong here. She does not.

"I'm sorry?"

It takes me a second to realize I spoke the thought out loud. "You said this area is closed to guests. But *you're* here."

She arches a single brow. "I'm working."

I lift an eyebrow right back. "Here? In this hallway? By this door?"

"You really need to leave." She pulls out her phone and gives me a dismissive look, twisting away.

Unfortunately, my foot's on the hem of her dress.

There's a rip.

Annnd she's falling.

My timing is good. My execution? Not so much. I lunge for her but misjudge the distance. My hands land at her hips just as we both collide into the door. My shoulder hits first with a thud, but her head lands safely against my chest.

I'm still trying to rebalance our tangled bodies when the door swings open under our weight. We stumble forward—a graceless, flailing mess. My gaze drops to the hem of her dress, now ripped past anything PG-13 and heading north.

A heavy hand lands on my shoulder. I look up into the chiseled, scowling face of a man who looks like he was carved from anger and gym memberships. And judging by the bulging tension in his jaw, he's two seconds from knocking me out cold.

He snarls. An actual snarl. And it makes me the tiniest bit jealous I've never been in a snarling situation myself. When I track his gaze downward, realization slams into me. My hand is still resting on Cybil's hip, fingers grazing the exposed skin where her dress tore.

I jerk my hand away fast and straighten, stepping clear of the man's bruising grip. My gaze slides down the length of the table—to the older man seated at the end of it. Across from him, Ramirez's laptop sits, practically glowing like the Holy Grail of incriminating evidence.

Behind me, the elevator dings—and the stakes grow. Lorenzo Ramirez steps into the room, Rook at his side. Everyone is eyeing us with suspicion. I need an excuse. Fast.

"Cybil?" the older man at the table says, his voice low and curious.

My attention swings to the woman at my side. She's glaring at me. Oh, it's *absolutely* her.

"I'm sorry for the interruption, sir," she says smoothly, stepping around me and tugging at her hem with impressive dignity. "I was coming to see if there was anything you needed before your meeting."

His meeting?

Her earlier words—*"I'm working"*—echo in my brain as I watch her move into place beside the older man, all composed professionalism. Meanwhile, my heart is hammering against my ribs, trying to process *why* Cybil Langford is working for anyone associated with Lorenzo Ramirez.

The snarling man looks at me and growls, "Who are you?"

"No one," Cybil answers crisply, before I can even open my mouth. The conviction in her voice stings worse than it should. "Just some guy I bumped into in the hallway."

"Looked like a little more than that," he answers back, and I immediately hate him.

"Please, Sebastian." Cybil gestures vaguely at me. "Him? Give me some credit."

My pride is taking hits like I'm in the ring with Mike Tyson. I don't know why it bothers me that she doesn't recognize me, but it does. And the irony of our worlds colliding again, right now, when everything's at stake? I'll have to unpack that later. Right now, if I want to protect my cover and keep Cybil safe, I need to play along.

"My apologies," I say stiffly, glancing at Ramirez. "She tripped on her dress."

"You stepped on my dress," Cybil corrects without missing a beat.

"Semantics."

She cocks her head, sweetly savage. "Is it?"

The challenge I see in the glare she's sending excites me. I want nothing more than to accept, but not here. Not in present company. I glance at Lorenzo Ramirez. "My apologies for the delay, sir."

"A real knight in shining armor, huh?" I don't miss the sarcasm or the suspicion in Pug Face's words. "How about you rejoin the party, Mr. . . ."

In for a penny . . .

"Craig," I answer smoothly.

At the edge of my vision, Cybil's eye twitches. It's the smallest tell—but I catch it. And my face cuts into a wide smile. *There's no going back now.*

"My name is Craig Miller."

CHAPTER 6

Cybil

Dallas, Texas
Monday night

Craig Miller? It takes everything in me to keep my jaw from unhinging. *Craig freaking Miller?* I must've heard that wrong. Had to. But when I spare a glance in Ben's—not *Craig's*—direction—he's flashing me a smile.

And. Then. He. Winks. *Winks!*

Does he think this is a game? Some kind of joke? Probably, and unfortunately, I recognize the infuriating glint of humor dancing in his eyes. There's only one reason he'd use *that* name. He's caught me in my pretense and knows that I know *exactly* who he is.

Shock doesn't even begin to describe what I felt the second my eyes landed on Bennett Bradley in the hallway. I thought fatigue was playing games with my brain. No way was my cousin Rex's best friend, and the tormentor of my summers, standing in the same hallway, at the same gala, in all of Dallas—*in all of Texas*—as me.

But here he is, barely resembling the boy in torn jeans, dusty boots, and T-shirts that I remember. He's grown into a man who fills out a tuxedo like a Hemsworth, and dang it if the way he's looking at me doesn't stir up something I'd left abandoned near the old oak tree at my aunt and uncle's ranch twelve years ago.

I thought I had him almost convinced he was wrong, especially when I saw a flash of confusion settle into the fine lines around his eyes, but like a tick on a bloodhound, he won't shake loose. Just like when we were kids.

And now he's standing in front of my boss, sending me what probably looks like a flirtatious wink—and lying.

But I don't react.

I can't.

Not here.

Upbeat country music hums in the background, but the air between us is thick with suspicion. Mostly aimed at Ben. Except for the two men I don't recognize standing across from Mr. Edmond—their attention is zeroed in on me.

The first man, tall and broad, looks to be in his late sixties. His dark features, sharp eyes, and tailored tuxedo emphasize wealth, power, and a ruthless intelligence compared to the man next to him. The other man has a lean, wiry frame and a beaked nose that gives him the look of a vulture.

These are the men Mr. Edmond and Sebastian are here to meet. The kind of men who don't leave witnesses when things go sideways. The kind of men whose attention I don't want. Not when I have a listening device stashed in my clutch.

I cannot get caught.

Clutching the torn slit of my dress, I blow out a slow, measured breath. I'm trying to look casual while my heartbeat goes into overdrive for reasons I really don't want to unpack right now. The only thing I like unpacking is a box of chocolates—sweet, reliable, and never out to ruin someone's life. Unlike Ben, whose sudden reappearance is about five seconds from blowing everything up.

Focus. I force my attention to Sebastian, noting the suspicion furrowing his forehead. I need to get Ben out of here before his juvenile sense of humor gets us both in trouble.

"I'm very sorry, gentlemen," I say, injecting just the right amount of fluster into my voice. I turn to Ben and grit out, "*Mr. Miller* and I didn't mean to interrupt your meeting."

Before I can herd Ben back to the gala where I can demand answers from him, the first man's voice cuts through the room.

"Are you leaving, Mr. Miller?"

It's deep. Authoritative. Clear. It takes me a moment to realize—he thinks he's talking to Ben.

"No, sir, Mr. Ramirez," Ben answers smoothly. "I'm ready when you are."

I nearly flinch at the name. Ramirez. *The* Ramirez.

Sebastian hesitates for a second before giving Ben a clipped nod and stepping stiffly aside. "Follow me, Mr. Miller," he says, his voice flat, before leading Ben to the conference table.

Wait. What? Ben knows these guys? And they know him? No—*not* Ben. *Craig Miller.* The confusion must be plain on my face, but if Sebastian notices, he doesn't show it. He just turns to me, cool and dismissive.

"You should return to the party, Cybil."

Heat surges up my neck. Dismissed. Under any other circumstance, I wouldn't think twice about Sebastian's power play. I'm not part of this meeting. I'm not even supposed to be up here. But tonight's different—and Sebastian's words slice through old scars I thought I had healed. Vulnerability I haven't felt since the last time I saw Ben lances through me, sharp and unwelcome.

Before I can move, Mr. Edmond speaks up, smooth and unbothered. "Cybil, would you mind finding Margot Stanton downstairs? She's handling the Edison project, and I'd like to set up a meeting as soon as my schedule allows."

His is a polite dismissal, wrapped in an assignment. But the weight of too many old memories pressing against my chest makes his request sting. I answer in a voice that barely sounds like mine. "Yes, of course, Mr. Edmond."

Sebastian shifts his attention to Ben and Mr. Ramirez. "Shall we begin?"

I have no choice but to leave. Doing anything else would only raise flags and bring more unwanted attention to myself. Who am I kidding?

More flags are waving now than when the marching band takes the football field for the halftime show. But I'm the only one who sees them.

Panic swells inside me. What is Bennett Bradley doing here? Why is he in a meeting with my boss, Sebastian, and a man named Mr. Ramirez? And why do they believe he's Craig Miller?

I need answers.

With a shaky breath, I subtly unclasp my clutch and offer a polite, empty smile to the room. Then, as I step toward the door, I let my heel catch the edge of the rug. I stumble forward, grabbing at a side table while my clutch spills across the floor. Again. Wallet, phone, bobby pins, and the tube of lipstick scatter like confetti. Perfect.

"I'm so sorry," I say, trying to sound mortified.

Mr. Edmond moves to help, but I wave him off. "I've got it," I insist, crouching as gracefully as I can manage in this dress.

Ben doesn't move. He just watches, hands in pockets, like he's enjoying the show. And it's a harsh reminder of exactly why I never wanted to see him again. I scoop up my things—everything but the lipstick—and shove them back into my bag. Mr. Edmond stretches his hand to help me up.

"One too many glasses of champagne, I guess." I give a sheepish smile as he pulls me to my feet.

I haven't touched a drop of champagne. But between nearly getting caught earlier and Ben's unexpected reappearance, I feel drunk on stress.

Ben's eyes track me, a tiny frown pulling between his brows. I ignore him and the rest of the men watching me as I back out of the library. The door closes behind me and I exhale for the first time in minutes. Finally, something went right.

I slip my phone from my clutch. With one tap, I activate the recording device hidden inside the lipstick. Wherever I am in the museum, it'll transmit the audio and upload it straight to Athena's server. I don't have to be anywhere near that room. Or Ben. Ever again.

A small, smug smile tugs at my lips. *Mission accomp—*

"Cybil."

I freeze.

Sebastian stands in the doorway, holding the lipstick between his fingers. "You forgot something."

Ice floods my veins. I walk back and take the lipstick from him, forcing a tight, casual smile. "Thanks. That's my favorite lipstick."

Suspicion gleams in Sebastian's eyes. I meet his stare without flinching. After a beat, he smirks and closes the door on me. Annoyance churns in my gut. My night—my mission—has been ruined twice.

I retreat down the hall, my heels clicking over the polished floor. Once I reach the elevator and get inside, the doors close and I let myself slump against the wall. This night cannot get worse. I dig through my clutch, find my emergency stash of M&M's, and rip the packet open with my teeth. I pour in a mouthful directly from the bag, letting the sugar calm the rising tide of humiliation and panic.

I'm not supposed to feel this way anymore. Small. Left out. Forgotten. The girl who wasn't enough. I twist the ring circling my thumb. *I'm not that girl anymore.*

The elevator dings, and I swipe at my eyes before the doors slide open. The gala is still in full swing—laughter, music, champagne. It all feels overwhelming, and I need space. I make quick work of locating Margot Stanton and scheduling a meeting before I weave my way through the glittering crowd to escape into the cool night air of the sculpture garden and sink onto a bench near the exit.

It's nearing midnight, but only a few guests are trickling out, collecting their cars from the valet or catching a rideshare. I envy them. I'd love nothing more than to exchange this dress for pajamas and crawl into bed. I look at my empty M&M's bag. *With more chocolate.*

But no. Upstairs, Ben Bradley is sitting in a high-stakes meeting, under a fake name, and I'm here with an empty bag of candy and no new information to give to Athena—

Except . . . that's not true.

I have names.

Ramirez and—Ben.

Something doesn't feel right. What's he doing in there? Lying?

I pull out my phone and hover over a text to Rex. They were best friends once. Maybe he knows something. But it's late—dragging Rex into this mess feels wrong. He's nosy. He'd want answers I can't give. Definitely not a good idea.

Instead, I google Ben. And get—nothing. Full name? Nothing. Facebook? Dead end. Instagram? Ghost town. I even check *DateDash,* the cursed dating app Joy signed me up for after my coffee shop date with a guy whose idea of fun was showing me his vintage dental tool collection. *In what world is tooth extraction romantic?*

But the app gives me nothing. Apparently, glowed-up Bennett Bradley doesn't need a dating app to meet women. And I doubt he'd be dating women who think flossing is a love language. Not that I care. *I don't.* And to prove it, I shove my phone into my clutch just in time to spot movement across the courtyard.

Ben.

He's walking alongside Ramirez and the vulture-faced man, heading toward the valet. The meeting's over? That was fast. Too fast.

I fumble to pull my phone back out and open my camera app, trying to snap a photo. The glare of the lights makes the image fuzzy. Ramirez and the vulture slide into a black Mercedes. Ben shifts and I can't get a clean shot of the license plate.

I scramble forward, ducking behind a potted tree to try again, but before I can snap a photo, the Mercedes peels away. Ben lingers for a moment—and then a woman in a black dress approaches him. They talk. Or . . . it *looks* like they're talking. It's weirdly stiff. Not flirtatious—but not casual either. A black SUV pulls up and Ben takes the keys from the valet.

The woman melts back into the gala. And I'm left wondering who she is—and why she's making my stomach twist. *And why didn't I get a photo of her?*

I hate how distracted I am because of *him.* Ben's already getting into the SUV. Before I can overthink it, I hustle after him—but the torn hem of my dress catches under my heel and I nearly face-plant. It's like my wardrobe has a personal vendetta against me tonight. Regaining my balance, and a smidge of dignity, I glance up in time to see Ben's brake lights flash red—and then he's gone.

"Excuse me, ma'am." A thin man with a pencil mustache steps around me, pointing to a blue Prius with an "I Brake for Speed Bumps" bumper sticker. "That's my Uber."

"Sorry," I mumble as I step back, but when the door opens, a flash of inspiration hits. Or at least that's what I'm going to call it as I watch the man fold himself into the back seat of the Uber.

And before I can talk myself out of it, I climb in after him.

"Hey! What are you doing?" he squawks.

"Howdy, folks. My, what a handsome pair you are," the Prius driver chirps. She's a white-haired woman with thick glasses and enough tie-dyed bear stickers on her dashboard to qualify for Grateful Dead sainthood. "Fun night?"

Fun? I snort. "If running into the guy who excels in being a major pain in my side counts as fun, then yes. Totally fun." I open my clutch and pull out all the cash I have. "I'll pay you"—I count it fast—"one hundred and twelve dollars to follow that black SUV."

"No," the man beside me whines, shoving his phone in my face. The Uber app glows accusingly. "I've already paid forty-six dollars for Debbie to take *me* to my apartment. Get out of my Uber."

"Y'all are gonna have to speak up," Debbie says, cupping her ear. "I gave up my hearing for Jerry Garcia." Her car smells faintly of peppermint and cats, and there's a collage of tabbies dangling from her rearview mirror. "If you two wanna get cuddly back there, I won't hear a thing," she adds brightly.

"Ew," I blurt. The guy next to me gives me a look like I'd be lucky. I roll my eyes. Though, if he doesn't have a finger dental drill from the 1870s, he's a step up from the last guy. Barely.

I point at Ben's SUV, desperate. "Listen, my brother's in that car and he's about to propose to the wrong girl. She hates cats, doesn't recycle, and drives a Hummer." I shove the money forward. "Please. I have to stop him."

"This is ridiculous," the man groans. "Get another Uber."

"Hold on, honey," Debbie says.

Yes. I brace myself against the seat, expecting a fast and furious chase. Instead, Debbie flips on her blinker and *eases* out of the parking lot at roughly the speed of a tortoise on Benadryl.

What is happening? My heart's racing faster than Debbie's Prius. Heck, Jerry Garcia's probably rotting faster in his grave.

The guy next to me snorts and crosses his arms, settling in for what is clearly not his best night. That makes two of us.

"Um, Debbie." I lean forward. The light's green and we're three cars back. "Can you catch up?"

"I've got you," Debbie promises and hums along to the radio as she *casually* accelerates.

Ben's SUV is already pulling ahead, changing lanes.

"Can you drive any faster?" I plead.

"Of course," she beams. "But these electric cars only get good mileage if I stay just under the speed limit."

My foot is practically pressing through the floor mat, as if sheer willpower could make this Prius fly. "Debbie," I beg, "I'll give you another hundred dollars if you catch up to that SUV."

There goes my grocery money for the week. I'm going to be living off ramen and a prayer—but I *have* to know what Ben is doing here. Why he lied.

"Please, Debbie," I add, desperate. "Can you go *any* faster?"

Her eyes flash at me in the rearview mirror and she gives me a sympathetic nod. "I can try."

The guy beside me is tapping away on his phone. "Maybe you should've Uber-hopped into a Corvette."

"Maybe you should've asked your mommy to pick you up."

"That's ridiculous," he huffs. "Mom never misses *The Late Show*."

How is this my life?

I scoot forward, gripping the front passenger seat as Debbie's Prius picks up a whole seven miles per hour. Ahead, Ben's SUV is at a yellow light. This is our chance to catch him—but at the last second, Ben veers right.

"Right lane, Debbie! Right lane!" I yelp.

Debbie flinches, and I instantly feel guilty, but we can't lose him. She inches toward the turn, painfully slow, and I'm clenching my jaw so hard I'm one stress fracture away from a dental bill I *definitely* can't afford.

By the time we round the corner, Ben's car is gone.

"Where to next, honey?" Debbie asks, doing a little dance of excitement in her seat. "I feel like one of them NASCAR fellas."

I don't have the heart to tell her she'd be lapped by a riding lawn mower. "Looks like he's up at that Starbucks," I say instead. "You can drop me off there."

Debbie beams, pulling into the parking lot. "Save him from himself, dear."

Save him? The only thing Ben needs saving from is his own juvenile antics—and I didn't sign up for that circus. "Yes, ma'am."

The guy in the back seat leans forward. "This isn't going to affect my Uber rating, is it?"

I roll my eyes and climb out of the Prius. Debbie gives a proud little rev of the engine before zooming away at the breakneck speed of five miles per hour.

Making my way to the outdoor seating, I sag onto a chair, the adrenaline crashing hard. This night has gone from bad to worse. I failed to record the meeting. I have nothing but names. And I'm stuck eating ramen for a week. Which I can live with—I'm not afraid of the sodium. But Bennett Bradley popping back into my life? That was a whole other level of heartburn I wanted to avoid.

CHAPTER 7

Ben

Dallas, Texas
Tuesday morning

The sun yawns across the blue Texas sky and I-30 is already bumper to bumper. I suck down the last dregs of a coffee I probably should've avoided. My nervous system is already keyed up and the caffeine is just throwing kerosene on it. But I needed the routine.

Wake up, work out, take a shower, get dressed, drink coffee, go to work. The monotony tricks my brain into believing everything is still normal. That my world hasn't tilted off its axis in a way I never saw coming.

The longer I work for the FBI, the more I crave stability in the ordinary. Like walking through the glass doors of the Henderson Building, riding the elevator, nodding at strangers talking about sports and weather before peeling off onto our respective floors like it's any other day.

But nothing about my job is ordinary, and last night proved that.

My brain hasn't stopped replaying it. Cybil Langford. The girl who once gave me a black eye for putting frogs in her boots. Now all grown up—and somehow tied to the very company Ramirez wants to work with.

At the twenty-second floor, I step off the elevator and into the familiar façade of AJ Investments. The polished reception desk. The sleek sign. The friendly agent greeting me with a "Morning, Mr. Miller" as I scan my badge. The illusion of normalcy.

The floor is divided into large conference rooms that overlook the city on one side and individual offices on the other where members of the forensic accounting team are working other cases. On the surface, anyone who happens upon our floor would see what we wanted them to see—an *ordinary* investment firm.

I'm halfway to my office when my phone buzzes with a message that has me pivoting to a stairwell. I take the stairs up to the twenty-third floor and scan my ID card again to unlock the door to enter what was once the offices to Dallas's number one real estate company. Right now, it's the FBI headquarters for Operation Shadow Broker.

I walk past empty cubicles to a corner office with a view of the Dallas skyline and find FBI Special Agents Ruby Knight and Seth Jackson waiting.

"You look . . ." Ruby gives my navy suit a once-over. "Like *you* were the one up with a sick child."

Ruby, perfectly polished in a gray pantsuit and ponytail, looks about as fresh as the morning news anchor. I sink into the seat between her and Seth. "Good morning to you too."

I glance over at Seth, whose exhaustion is hanging in the circles beneath his eyes. "Long night?"

Seth, senior to me by a few years, one wife, two kids, gives a tired grin over his coffee mug. "Spent the night sucking snot out of a squirmy—"

"Stop," Ruby gags, holding up a hand. "Don't finish that sentence."

Seth just chuckles. "Hey, kids are just tiny criminals. Sticky fingers. Loud demands. Suspicious odors. Training ground for this job."

"At least criminals are predictable," Ruby mutters.

I suppress a grin, but my focus shifts back to Seth and why I asked him to meet me this morning. As one of the best forensic accountants the Bureau has, he's been pivotal in the behind-the-scenes role of making my alias as a financial advisor believable. "Would you mind looking into something for me?"

Like a button has been pressed, Seth shifts, focused. "What've you got?"

"Can you look into a company called VerityCrypt?"

"VerityCrypt," Seth repeats. "Looking for anything specific?"

"Not sure yet," I say. "Ramirez mentioned it to Rook last night, but if it's important, I want to know."

"Got it." Seth nods.

Our boss, Special Agent in Charge Katherine Scott, steps into the room with a smile that doesn't quite reach her eyes. She sets down a laptop and a handful of files, surveying us with that hawklike precision that makes me sit up straighter.

"Morning," she says, before glancing at Seth. "How are the girls?"

"Flu's hit the Jackson household," Seth says with a yawn. "My mom's at the house to help keep it contained."

Ruby wrinkles her nose and squirts hand sanitizer into her palms like she's preparing for chemical warfare.

Seth rises from his seat. "I'll dig into VerityCrypt's filings first. See if anything's twitching under the hood."

"Appreciate it," I say, meaning it. If he can juggle sick toddlers and federal takedowns, maybe there's hope for me to have a life outside of the job one day too. The image of Cybil flashes through my mind—Cybil in my arms, Cybil looking at me like she'd seen a ghost. I shove the thought aside. One crisis at a time.

Seth leaves us with Katherine, who sits in her chair and pins me with a look that churns the coffee in my gut. "Let's talk about last night."

The memories rush back. Someone attempting to break into the museum library. Sammy Pawson appearing—and disappearing. Cybil. How the meeting was cut short unexpectedly when Earl Edmond questioned Lorenzo Ramirez about someone interfering in his business in Italy.

I included all of this in the report I sent to her late last night—everything except my personal connection to Cybil. Because if I revealed that, I'd have already been pulled from the mission. And I can't leave. Not now. Not when the collateral damage has a name, beautiful brown eyes, and a smile that could either jump-start a heart . . . or crush it.

"What do we know about Edmond Developments?"

Katherine's question snaps me back to the present.

Ruby flips open a file. "Luxury real estate, high-end commercial and residential properties. Earl Edmond built it from nothing, transforming underdeveloped areas into prime real estate developments. His son, Sebastian Edmond, is the CFO but also has a cryptocurrency company on the side. Cybil Langford graduated from University of North Texas with a political science undergrad and started working for Edmond." She closes the folder. "I've got an agent digging for more information on her."

I shift in my seat. It won't take long to connect the dots from Cybil's life to mine. I open my mouth to say something when Katherine continues.

"And Sammy Pawson?" she asks.

I shake my head. "After the initial sighting, he disappeared. Ramirez and Rook didn't mention him."

"I lost him," Ruby says flatly, clearly still annoyed. She was circling the museum while I was trapped in the world's shortest meeting. "What about the museum surveillance?"

Katherine's fingers fly over her keyboard. She frowns. "Jammed."

"By us?" I ask.

"No," she says. "Not our people."

Ruby frowns. "So no footage of whoever was trying to break into the library before us?"

"Not at this time." Katherine shakes her head. "Any theories on who might be behind that?"

"I wouldn't rule out Ramirez," I say. "He hates leaving a trail, and the timing fits. The meeting hadn't even started before Earl Edmond questioned Ramirez about his interference with a supplier in Italy."

Ruby crossed her arms. "I'm surprised Ramirez didn't lose it."

"I was too." I sit forward and my focus sharpens. "But here's the strange part. While Ramirez didn't deny it, he also seemed caught off guard by the accusation. He seemed suspicious."

"Of whom?" Katherine asks.

"Earl Edmond. Earl's son. Something wasn't right. Ramirez mentioned something to Rook about VerityCrypt afterward. I looked it up last night. It's a cryptocurrency company owned by Sebastian Edmond. I've asked Seth to check it out and get back to us."

"Maybe that's why Sammy 'The Paws' Pawson showed up," Ruby says, arms still crossed. "You said Ramirez needs Edmond to secure some kind of property overseas, right?"

I nod. "Yeah, something about an old manufacturing site in Italy."

"If Edmond's stalling, Ramirez might've invited Sammy to apply pressure. A little reminder not to get cold feet."

The theory makes too much sense. And if Ramirez was worried enough to bring muscle to a gala full of witnesses, then Cybil—standing right in the middle of it—was already too close to the fire.

Katherine's brows pinch. "Do you think the deal is going to get squashed?"

I don't hesitate. "If it does, we're dead in the water. The only way we nail Ramirez is through that laptop—and the only way I get near it is if this deal stays alive."

Ruby leans back in her chair and smirks. "Simple. Keep the deal alive to stay alive—our new motto for the mission."

The words hit harder than they should because I know exactly what can blow this deal, and the weight of it is pressing down on me. I glance at Katherine. "There's something you should know about Cybil Langford."

Ruby's smirk fades. Katherine just waits, patient.

"I know her," I say. "We spent summers together as kids. She's the cousin of my best friend growing up, but I haven't seen her since she left for college."

Katherine folds her hands. "You're still friends with her cousin?"

"I am," I sigh. "We don't see each other often, but we keep in touch."

Katherine sits there quietly, thinking. And then she looks at me. "Did she recognize you?"

I nod once. "She knows I'm lying about my name. She didn't call me out . . . but she knows."

"And the mission?" Katherine asks. "Has it been compromised?"

My shoulders drop with the weight behind that question. We've all been working for the last eighteen months to get me into the inner circle of trust with Ramirez. Thousands of hours spent building my alias to entice Rook into trusting me so he'd introduce me to Ramirez as someone they could trust to help hide their money and get rich at it.

Up until last night, I'd played the role flawlessly.

"I can't be sure," I finally answer. "Everything happened in a matter of minutes."

Ruby narrows her eyes. "If she talks to the wrong person, everything we've built goes up in smoke."

The truth stings. I know Ruby's angry—and she has every right to be. I should've said something last night, but I was still trying to wrap my head around the whole situation. This mission isn't just about RICO charges. It's about Danny Morales. And making Ramirez pay for what he did. I owed Ruby the truth and I can't let her down. I can't let any of them down.

"Pull me from the mission," I say.

"What?" Ruby snaps, shocked.

"I'll come up with something. Make an excuse why I can't help Ramirez. Another client needs me, and we'll send in Seth. He's been walking me through this anyway—he knows the mission."

"He's an accountant, Ben," Ruby answers first. "He's not trained for undercover ops. Ramirez is already suspicious. If you pull out now, you think he's just gonna hand over the laptop to whoever walks through the door next?"

She's right. I know she's right. But I don't want to let this mission fall apart because of me. I look to Katherine for guidance.

"You stay," she says without hesitation.

My chest tightens. "What?"

"Ruby's right," Katherine says, steady and unflinching. "You're already in, and pulling you now might not just cost us the operation—it could tip off Ramirez. If he thinks he's being investigated, he'll disappear. New name. New face. New empire. We'll lose him for good."

She leans back, leveling me with a look that carries the full weight of what she's asking. "Unless you want to call it."

Time slows. Calling a mission is serious. It means we're out of options. It means signing a death warrant on everything we've built to put Ramirez away. On everyone Ramirez might hurt next. Including Cybil.

I rake a hand down my face, the reality settling like lead in my gut. If I walk away now, there's no reaching back for her. No way to warn her. She becomes just another casualty Ramirez leaves in his wake. I force my voice steady. "What do you want me to do?"

Katherine tilts her head slightly, eyes sharp. "You convince your childhood friend to believe your story." Her gaze holds mine like a dare. "She's a liability. Turn her into an asset."

CHAPTER 8

Cybil

Dallas, Texas
Tuesday afternoon

"You sure you're not just stalking your childhood boyfriend because you secretly want to marry him?"

I glare at Joy Lockhart, who's slouched dramatically in the passenger seat of my car, one leg kicked up on the dash like we're not parked on a busy street mid-stakeout.

"Not boyfriend," I say between gritted teeth. "*Friend*. And that's being generous."

Joy pops a chocolate-covered almond in her mouth, unbothered. "Is he cute?"

My body betrays me. Heat creeps up my neck as the memory of Ben in a tuxedo flashes back—broad shoulders, sharp jawline, a smirk that, against all logic, still felt a little like home.

"Irrelevant," I say, turning my attention back to the towering glass and steel building I've been staring at for almost an hour. It gleams in the sun, a futuristic monster among the older brick buildings on Elm Street, promising luxury, power, and bottled water that probably costs twelve dollars. And within this fortress of wealth is AJ Finance and its villain—Craig *freaking* Miller.

"So . . . not cute. Hot," Joy teases, elbowing me.

"Maybe bringing you was a bad idea."

"Aw, come on." She holds up the bag of candy. "I brought snacks."

"And not enough caffeine for this conversation," I grumble, covering a yawn. "Hand them over."

She pours a handful of candy into her palm before handing me the bag like I'm two seconds from setting the building on fire. Honestly, I might.

Is sleep deprivation a reasonable excuse for arson?

This is why I dragged my most loyal and sarcastic best friend here. Because after four miserable hours of sleep, there's no telling what I might convince myself to do without adult supervision.

"How long did you google him last night?" Joy asks, chewing thoughtfully.

"Too long," I groan, letting my head thump against the headrest. "Searched social media. Court records. Even considered paying one of those creepy 'find anyone' websites."

"And?"

"And nothing. Nada. Zilch. It's like he doesn't exist."

"Hot, mysterious finance ghost," Joy says, voice chipper.

I ignore her. If I wanted the truth about Bennett Bradley, one call to Athena would give me everything I needed. But I'm not ready for that conversation. Not until I get some clarity on why the boy I used to know is lying about who he is.

It's the question that kept me up all night. The question that had me spending hours digging through the old photo albums my aunt Renee gave me after every summer spent on the ranch.

Growing up, moving constantly with my mom, we didn't have much that couldn't be crammed into the back of a car or borrowed pickup. Those albums were my proof that, at least for a little while, I belonged somewhere.

It surprised me how quickly the images made the memories come alive—and the emotions too. Especially the memories of Ben. How I didn't like him. Until . . . I did. Until *like* turned into a hopeless teenage crush that had me believing, for one stupid second, that maybe he felt the same way.

It's been more than a decade since that last summer, since that night.

Ben asked me to meet him there—at the oak tree, the one in the west pasture, where he first teased me about falling off a fence post and then offered his hand like it meant something. That day, I thought he was going to tell me he liked me. That our childhood teasing had somehow turned into flirting and that maybe it meant we could be something. I wore my nicest sundress, the one with little blue flowers that I was saving for graduation the following year. I was two seconds away from believing in a different future.

But then I overheard him.

Ben laughing with Rex, saying something stupid. Something careless. "*You think I'm into her? Come on, Rex. She's a mess. Reckless.*"

It was so long ago, but I remember everything about that moment—where I was standing, the ache in my chest, the heat behind my eyes. I didn't go to the tree. I told myself it didn't matter. That he would've broken my heart eventually anyway. And since that night, I let his words fuel my focus.

So no—Ben Bradley is not my childhood boyfriend. He's the boy who taught me that love is something you have to earn. And it's why I don't trust him.

Somewhere around three in the morning, after too many memories and too many feelings I thought I had buried, I stuffed the albums under my bed. Out of sight, out of mind.

Or so I told myself.

I woke up this morning, went to work, organized Mr. Edmond's schedule for the day, including two investor meetings and a site inspection, and flagged contracts for his lawyer to look over. And then Mr. Edmond handed me a file with financial service authorizations he wanted me to scan and archive. Nothing revealing. Nothing criminal. Except for Craig *freaking* Miller's name listed as an outside consultant. And here I am.

"Craig *freaking* Miller," I say again.

"Maybe he's in WITSEC," Joy says deadpan, like she's already planning to testify at my competency hearing. "New identity. Terrible name. Very on-brand for you."

"He's not in witness protection." I roll my eyes. "And if he was, he wouldn't be living in Texas, and he certainly wouldn't pick Craig *freaking* Miller as his alias."

Joy hums, unimpressed. "I mean, if the goal was to sound aggressively boring, mission accomplished."

"He did it to annoy me," I mutter, glaring at the glass revolving doors, willing Bennett Bradley to dare step a foot outside. "And I hate him for it. And who does he think he is"—my voice jumps an octave—"posing like some big-shot financial advisor, schmoozing the wealthy, and then looking at me like *I'm* the one who doesn't belong?"

Joy flicks an almond at my lap. "You're spiraling. Eat that before you start quoting Taylor Swift lyrics."

I stuff the almond in my mouth. It doesn't help.

"I just— He was never the corporate type," I grumble. "Why *finance* of all things?"

We sit quietly, watching people hustle in and out of the building. My lunch break is ticking away fast. Another five minutes pass. Ben still doesn't appear.

I slump lower in my seat and mutter, "Maybe he doesn't eat lunch."

Then Joy straightens with a wicked grin. "I've got it," she says. "Order Uber Eats to the lobby under his name. He'll have to come down to get it. And you"—she points dramatically at me—"you intercept the delivery. Instant confrontation."

I blink at her. "That's . . . brilliant."

She shrugs. "I know."

Excitement surges through me. I open the app, order a sandwich under "Craig Miller" from the closest restaurant, and sit back, heart thundering. This is it. This is how I get answers. Not feelings. Not clarity on why Ben's infuriating smirk still makes my pulse jump. Nope. Definitely not thinking about him. I'm cool. Calm. This is peak professional focus. I'm like a Bond girl if she had student loans and an overactive conscience.

"It's kind of cute," Joy says. "You know—classic enemies-to-lovers story."

I wrinkle my nose. "If by cute you mean the time he released my aunt and uncle's deranged rooster in my bedroom, then yes. Total fairy tale."

A sharp laugh bursts from Joy's lips, which to her credit she quickly covers with her hand across her mouth, but the laughter is swimming in her expression.

"It's not funny," I grumble, fighting my own smile at the memory. "Kentucky Fried showed no mercy coming after us kids. He—"

"Kentucky Fried?" Joy squeaks between her fingers, and that's it. She doubles over in laughter and it's contagious. I'm laughing, too, even though nothing about my aunt and uncle's deranged rooster is comical. I still have nightmares, but it feels good to laugh.

"Have I told you about my new book?"

Relief washes over me. Books are a safe subject. One I'm happy to discuss as opposed to the unsafe topic of Ben. Ben *freaking* Bradley. Yep. It works that way too.

"So this book . . ." Joy's lip quirks and I recognize my mistake immediately. She doesn't give up that easily. "It's about jungle warfare and there's a section on psychological methods for information extraction."

"Fascinating," I deadpan.

She stares at me. I stare at her. It's a showdown and I refuse to bend.

Joy shrugs. "Fine. If you don't want to tell me that Ben was the love of your life. The one who got away. The one who broke your heart. The one you've been praying about . . ." Her eyes sparkle and mine begin to twitch. "The one you thought you lost forever but who has now returned and—"

My phone buzzes with a notification that the Uber driver is arriving—perfect timing.

"It's time," Joy says, her tone flat like a mafia boss giving final orders. "Ready?"

"Yes. No," I say, suddenly unsure of the plan. "I don't know."

A chocolate-covered almond hits my forehead.

"Hey!" I rub the spot and then grab the candy from my lap and pop it into my mouth. "We don't waste chocolate."

She turns to me, voice low and dead serious. "March over there. Be polite. Be direct. Be the reason he needs therapy."

I huff out a laugh. It's wildly irresponsible advice. It's also exactly what I need. I get out of the car, square my shoulders, and march toward the building like I have a plan. I'm crossing the parking lot just as the Uber driver pulls up to the curb.

Or attempts to. A man in a yellow vest waves him forward, giving me a chance to push through the revolving doors and get inside the building first. A minute later, the driver walks in, brown paper bag in hand, and heads toward the security directory desk.

I'm at a safe distance not to be noticed but close enough to catch bits of the conversation. A phone call is placed by the security officer, and he frowns. *Not expecting lunch, Craig?* A back-and-forth conversation takes place between the security guard and the driver before the driver sets the bag on the desk and leaves. The security guard nods and hangs up the phone, and I hope that means *Craig* is on his way down.

The elevator opens with a ding. And out walks Ben. Laughing. With a woman. Not just any woman—a beautiful woman. Polished. Confident. Looking like everything I'm not.

Ben says something and they share a laugh like they've done it a thousand times. My stomach sinks. Hard.

Abort mission. Abort now.

I spin around quickly, ducking my chin and heading straight for the revolving door. And this is where the universe decides to humble me. I misjudge the timing—completely—thinking I can slip through without waiting. I can't.

The revolving door smacks me square in the shoulder, spins me backward, and traps me inside one of the glass compartments like a very confused hamster. I panic and push. Too hard. The door lurches. The person behind me yelps. The entire mechanism shudders on its axis and *stops moving*.

I'm stuck.

Inside a clear, spinning tomb of shame.

Through the glass, I see Ben turning at the commotion—brows furrowed, steps slowing, *definitely* noticing.

"No," I hiss under my breath.

Panic kicks my adrenaline into overdrive. I wedge my shoulder into the frame and shove the door manually with everything I've got. It moves inches—but it's enough. With one final, desperate twist of my body, I squeeze through the tight space and hurl myself out of the revolving door. I stumble onto the sidewalk, breathless, hair sticking to my forehead, dignity shredded into fine confetti.

"Cybil?"

Nope. Nope. Nope.

I bolt.

"Cybil!"

Ignoring Ben's voice calling after me, I fix my gaze on Joy. She sees me and frantically waves her hands in big slicing motions warning me, *Don't come back here!* And immediately slides down in her seat like she's trying to pretend she doesn't know me.

"Cybil, wait—"

Ben's voice carries, confused and way too close. Panic fires through me. I need to get away from here. I take off down the sidewalk, narrowly missing a man carrying a tray of iced coffees, and duck into the first place I see—a busy restaurant, packed with lunch-hour chaos.

Heads turn. Silverware clatters. I jolt to a stop, paste on a smile, tucking a loose strand of hair behind my ear. Calmly, I breeze past the hostess stand, radiating the energy of someone who definitely has a lunch reservation and is definitely not fleeing the scene of her own public humiliation.

Behind the bar, I spot a hallway, the blessed Restrooms sign, and make a break for it. I push through the swinging door into the women's restroom. A quick scan of the open stall doors and I slump back against the cool tile wall, gasping for breath.

This is fine.

Everything's fine.

This was all part of the plan.

CHAPTER 9

Cybil

Dallas, Texas
Tuesday afternoon

"What was I thinking?"

I should've stayed at work. Skipped lunch. Or at the very least, taken my lunch at the bookstore like I always do. But no, I had to do a stakeout. Like some low-budget spy movie heroine with a bag of chocolate-covered almonds and a best friend who was supposed to talk me down—not double-tap the Like button on my bad idea.

Now I'm hiding in a restaurant bathroom like a deranged woman running from a bad Tinder date. I check the stalls again, making sure they're empty, then brace both hands on the counter. My reflection is a mess of panic and regret. My hair has half fallen out of its twist, my blouse is wrinkled from trying to wedge myself through the revolving door, and I'm pretty sure I pulled a muscle in my calf.

"This can't be happening." Twenty-four hours ago, I was focused. Undercover. Strategically feeding intel to Athena about my boss's shady business associates. My mission was clear—track leads, stay invisible, gather evidence. Now? Now everything is tilting sideways because Ben Bradley popped back up in my life like the devil in cuff links, threatening every ounce of emotional stability I thought I had left.

Well done, Cybil. Really crushing the adulting thing.

My nerves are fraying. I spin the ring around my thumb, trying to ground myself before I, as Joy so politely pointed out earlier, spiral. *Breathe, Cybil.* The ring pops off with a soft *ping* and clatters across the tile.

"Seriously?" I hiss, dropping to my hands and knees to scramble after it.

The door creaks behind me.

"You okay?"

My gaze jerks upward to find Ben standing in the women's bathroom, arms folded across his chest, staring down at me with that aggravating smirk.

I shoot to my feet, ring clutched in my fist. "What are you doing here?" I whisper-scream. "You can't be in here. It's harassment. Trespassing. Emotional distress—none of it felonious *yet,* but give me time."

"It's a misdemeanor at best," he says, unfolding his arms and slipping his hands into his pockets. "And if we're talking crimes, I could argue *you're* the one committing them. Stalking me? If you wanted to grab lunch, you could've just called my assistant and set up an appointment."

"I wasn't stalking you," I say immediately, slipping the ring back on my thumb. "I was—on my lunch break."

He doesn't even try to hide his grin. "In the revolving door?"

I lift my chin. "Getting steps in."

"Weak alibi."

"I don't need an alibi because I *wasn't* stalking you."

"Okay, okay." He raises his hands in mock surrender. "I believe you."

Then he winks—and I swear, *swear,* if looks could kill, the DA would already be filing paperwork.

I glare at him. "I forgot how annoying you are."

I wash my hands, hoping Ben will take the hint and leave. No such luck. I glance at the mirror. He's still there, leaning casually against the wall like he's not breaking rules of social decorum by being in here.

"What are you doing?" I ask again, quieter this time.

"I told you," he says, voice gentle. "I wanted to check on you."

The sincerity in his voice brushes too close to something I've tried hard to bury—the version of us that almost existed, once. I snap the faucet off, needing the sound to stop, needing him to stop being so . . . *him*.

"No," I say, too sharp. I grab a paper towel. "What are you doing, *Ben?*"

He exhales and rubs the back of his neck. "I didn't know you worked for Earl Edmond."

I blink, caught off guard. "What does that have to do with anything?"

He doesn't answer fast enough.

"You said your name is Craig Miller," I say through gritted teeth. "Craig *freaking* Miller."

One corner of his mouth lifts. Smug. Always smug.

"It's not funny," I growl. "Do you even know who you're lying to?"

His smile fades. "I'm not lying."

My mouth opens to argue, but he holds up both hands.

"Not entirely," he amends. "I work with high-net-worth clients. Privacy is everything. The alias protects them."

I blink. "You're serious?"

"People like discretion more than dividends. My clients can't have their names tied to certain deals—lawsuits, regulators, rivals. So we use aliases. Trusts. Shell corps. It keeps them off the radar. Think of it like a celebrity checking into a hotel under an alias. Same principle." He shrugs. "My alias allows me to manage their finances with anonymity."

I stare at him, processing. And the thing is . . . it tracks. I've seen plenty of contracts come through Edmond's office with third-party names on them. Half the properties he owns were bought under holding companies. This, I learned, is how the rich protect themselves.

Ben steps forward, his chin dipping so he's looking directly into my eyes. "Cybil, I know this seems like an unusual request, but it's imperative to my job and to my clients that you use my alias." His voice lowers. "*Craig Miller* is the wall between me and the kind of people who would do anything to protect their assets."

It sounds like a warning. And suddenly, I don't know whether to believe him . . . or report him. For the first time, I wonder if Ben is in deeper than I thought. Not just with Mr. Ramirez, but with the kind of people Athena watches—criminals who use their wealth like camouflage.

It leaves me unsettled. I want to warn him. But I don't. Because I can't. Because if I do, I risk everything—my mission, my paycheck, and the small chance I still have at law school.

He's looking at me like he can read the hesitation on my face, and I hate that. Hate that he still knows how to press every emotional pressure point like it's muscle memory. Hate that a single glance from him has me doubting every line I've drawn between right and necessary.

Then—like a switch—he smirks and adjusts his tie in the mirror. The return of that smug grin is both wildly annoying and unfairly attractive.

"Besides, *Billy girl*, you wouldn't want me to lose my job. I'm the one handling the finances of the deal between your boss and Mr. Ramirez."

My jaw drops. "Did you seriously just—"

Maybe it's the arrogance. Maybe it's the fact that he used the worst nickname known to mankind, gifted to me by him and Rex one unfortunate summer. Either way, I swallow down my warning and force my expression back to neutral.

There's a line being drawn that only I can see. On one side? Ben handling the finances for the deal is the exact kind of intel Athena needs. It's why I took this job. Why I agreed to spy. Why I can't afford to quit until I can drag myself out of debt and into law school.

But on the other side?

It's Ben. And I don't know if he's just the wrong guy, hired at the wrong time by the wrong people, or if there's something more to his involvement. Something criminal.

The idea makes my chest tighten. He *sounds* like he's just doing his job, but there's something too polished about his explanation. Too smooth about the way he waltzed into the meeting last night. I've seen men lie before—seen how easily truth slips into fiction when money's on the table.

If I blow the whistle too early, I could ruin his career for no reason. But if I don't, and he *is* involved, then I'm giving him a front-row seat to a crime that will have his name all over it.

So maybe for now, I don't move. Maybe I just watch. Take notes. Send Athena what I can. And if it gets too risky . . . I'll warn him. Somehow. But until then, I'll play along.

Because I need this paycheck. And maybe—just maybe—I need to know who Ben Bradley really is and why after all these years, and against every ounce of logic, my heart is doing that ridiculous, traitorous skip when he's near me.

"It'll be like old times," Ben says, stepping into my line of sight again. "You and me, hanging out. Playing games."

Something sparks behind my ribs. Something I don't like.

"Why *Craig*?"

He pauses, surprised. "What?"

"Why use the name Craig Miller?"

His smile returns, full wattage this time. He shrugs. "It's a forgettable name for a forgettable guy."

I narrow my eyes on him. "Really? All these years and you're using the name of my high school ex-boyfriend. Seems like the only one who hasn't forgotten about him is you."

Ben's eyes light with a fire, and before I'm drawn to it, I brush past him, hand on the door. "Let me check the hallway. Make sure no one sees you walking out of the women's restroom."

I'm halfway out when he calls softly, "Cybil."

I glance back.

"You were way too good for Craig Miller."

My heart stutters. I force a smile. "Still am."

Then I slip into the hallway without looking back, weaving past two ladies heading toward the restroom. I *should* warn them. But instead, I smile. *Game on, Craig.*

CHAPTER 10

Ben

Dallas, Texas
Tuesday afternoon

Well played, Billy.

I crack a smile, stepping out of the busy restaurant and into the humid press of downtown Dallas. Sunlight glints off passing traffic, and I give another wave to the women who marched me out. Not one but two ladies caught me in the women's restroom seconds after Cybil left, and I can't be sure it wasn't a planned assault. A solid one given the Southern scolding one lady gave me while a tiny hurricane of a woman waved her hands and shouted in Spanish—something about chanclas and cabezas, which translated roughly to: *You're about to regret your life choices, gringo.*

And I did what any grown man trained by the FBI would do: apologized like my freedom depended on it and made a tactical retreat before anyone could call security. I half expected Cybil to be waiting in the hallway with popcorn and a scorecard. But she wasn't.

Now, as I walk the few blocks back toward my office building, dodging sun glare off car hoods and construction noise, I find myself hoping—really hoping—that she bought it. The alias. The explanation. The whole carefully packaged version of Craig Miller I delivered with a straight face and a pounding pulse.

Not in a million years would I have expected to find her here—older, sharper, still full of fire. And I definitely didn't expect to feel seventeen again just from the way she looked at me. Like she was remembering too.

Back then, she could outrun me on foot and outsmart me with a dare. Cybil Langford was all elbows and sarcasm and never backed down from a challenge—especially if Rex and I were the ones issuing it. I used to drive her nuts on purpose just to see how far I could push her before she snapped—and it usually involved a threat of duct tape and a permanent marker.

But that's the problem.

The fact that I spotted her at my building tells me exactly what I should've remembered—Cybil doesn't let anything slide. I knew she was going to call me out on the lie. On the name I chose. Katherine wants me to turn Cybil into an asset, but I'd forgotten she was more likely to flip the script than play along. If I'm going to make this work, I need to figure out how to use her with as little contact as possible.

Which means I need to stay away from her. Spend as little time as possible around her. One, for her safety, two, for my safety, and three because apparently I have a death wish and think flirting with someone who could expose me with one wrong word is a *great idea*.

It's not. Obviously.

Just because she still makes me laugh. Just because I remember how her hair used to smell like coconut in the summer. Just because her smile hits like a sucker punch. None of that means anything.

It's nostalgia. Hormones. Proximity. *And totally manageable.*

My building rises ahead, all mirrored glass and steel edges. My focus needs to be on the mission. On Ramirez. He's who I'm working for, so there shouldn't be any reason Cybil and I cross paths again.

I'm a few feet away from the entrance when one of the security guards—Manny—calls out and jogs over with a brown paper bag.

"Hey, Miller! You forgot your lunch."

I squint at it. "I already told you, I didn't order lunch."

He shrugs. "Delivery said it was for you. Name's on the order."

I take the bag, already suspicious. Manny's right. My name *is* on the order, but when I peek inside and see the fish sandwich, I know it's a mistake. I'd rather eat a stapler than fish. I'm about to hand it back when a black Mercedes G-Wagon glides up to the curb like it owns the street.

The passenger door swings open, and Jimmy Rook steps out like we're old friends meeting for coffee. "Craig, you got a minute?"

He doesn't wait for an answer. Just opens the back door—removing any illusion of choice. My pulse jumps. This is out of the ordinary. And in my line of work, *out of the ordinary* has a nasty habit of turning fatal.

Lorenzo Ramirez is in the back seat, calm as ever. I climb in beside him, keeping my expression neutral, like this is all part of the day's agenda and not a potential prelude to getting buried in a ditch off I-35.

I settle into the leather seat, and if the surprise meeting wasn't enough to spike my blood pressure, the sight of Sammy "The Paws" Pawson behind the wheel finishes the job. Crime bosses don't bring their muscle to a lunch meeting unless it comes with a side of cement shoes.

Ramirez glances down at the paper bag still in my hand. "Lunch?"

I look down at the bag. "It's not mine."

Before I can explain, Sammy Pawson reaches back from the driver's seat and snatches it out of my hand.

"Be my guest," I mutter, watching him peel open the bag and pull out the sandwich. He bites into it like he hasn't had a meal in . . . well, at least since the shrimp last night at the museum. *Punching people probably burns a lot of calories.*

When we don't pull away from my office, I breathe a little easier that maybe I'm not about to meet my Maker. There are too many witnesses. But still, I understand the tango of power has begun. Him showing up unannounced demanding my attention is all about control. And the only way not to let someone like Ramirez think he has complete control is to limit his access to what he wants—me. I check my watch. "I have a few minutes between clients, Mr. Ramirez. What can I do for you?"

He gives me a practiced smile. "You're familiar with international banking, yes?"

I know *nothing* about international banking. That's why Seth Jackson is on the team. It's taken months to set up *Craig Miller*'s portfolio of wealth-building for clients who are powerfully, politically, and *criminally* connected. And quicker than a rumor can spread through junior high, the FBI made sure word got around until Jimmy Rook "stumbled" upon the not-so-secret ways I was making my clients wealthy. But rumors aren't everything if you can't back them up. The FBI had to filter hundreds of thousands of dollars into Rook's investment account to prove I could deliver before he finally introduced me to Ramirez.

Or rather, introduced *Craig Miller*. He's the expert and it's his persona that I shift into effortlessly. "Intimately. I've handled foreign accounts from Dubai to the Caymans. I know how to navigate international compliance laws and move money to where it needs to be."

"What about Italy?"

"Sì, sono preparato," I say, assuring him I'm prepared. *And grateful for taking Italian in college to impress Cassidy Jo, who dropped out after two weeks.* "Just have your banker in Italy send me the documents, and I can make sure your accounts are ready."

"Oh, we won't be leaving that to email, Craig." Ramirez adjusts the cuff of his sleeve, casual as ever. "Italy can be tricky. Beautiful, yes—but it has a habit of chewing up amateurs and leaving their bones on the beach."

Was that a threat of scenic dismemberment?

"This requires a face-to-face meeting in Lagoverde." He studies me. "To ensure there are no miscommunications and transactions stay clean."

This is why Lorenzo Ramirez has never been arrested. Because he knows exactly what to say and what not to say in case anyone is recording. When I first met him, I suspected I'd be patted down, possibly given a cavity search, to look for a recording device. But no one touched me. That didn't mean there wasn't an underlying threat of it, and we weren't going to take any chances on trying to get Ramirez to say something that his attorneys—the ones smarter than Rook—would somehow get thrown out of court before the ink dried on charges.

"You want me to go with you to Italy?"

"Is that going to be a problem?"

Sammy crumples the sandwich wrapper and looks back at me. If I were really a financial advisor to the criminally nutso, I'm sure I could charter a jet and be sipping espresso in Lagoverde by dinner. But the FBI doesn't work that fast. I meet Ramirez's gaze. This isn't a request.

"It shouldn't be," I answer. "But I'd need to check my schedule. When would I need to be there?"

"Day after tomorrow."

"Thursday." I school my expression, hoping it looks like I'm mentally rearranging my schedule instead of trying to show how much that date complicates everything.

"That's . . . quick," I say. "Is there a reason for the urgency?"

"Edmond's concerns require our immediate attention in Italy." He flicks a glance at Rook. "And I'm afraid time is what we don't have, Mr. Miller."

Edmond. My muscles tense and Cybil's face flashes to mind, nearly snapping me out of character. That's the difference, isn't it? I'm *playing* a part. But Cybil? She's in the middle of this for real. And if Earl Edmond is involved with Lorenzo Ramirez, that makes him dangerous.

Does she even know who she's working for?

I'm second-guessing Katherine's directive now. Turn Cybil into an asset. Great. But how do I do that without putting her in more danger? How do I warn her without blowing my cover? I can't. I saw the look in her eyes in the bathroom. A harbored distrust of me. But I can't sit here and do nothing. I have to try . . . something.

"I understand," I say carefully, "but if I'm going to do my job right—keep everything tidy—I need time to do my due diligence."

Ramirez waves a dismissive hand. "Don't waste my time, Miller. If you can't handle my business, I'll find someone else who can."

I know I'm treading a fine line. Getting to Italy, working alongside Ramirez's bankers—that'll put me close enough to his systems to find what I need. His files. The accounts. Maybe even the hit order to take out Danny Morales.

I nod slowly. "Time is money, Mr. Ramirez. I never waste either. I'm here to make you a very rich man—and protect your money while I'm at it. If that means Italy, I'll make it work. But . . ." I pause long enough to make him lean in. "It's important I know who I'm working for. That I can trust them."

"And you don't think you can trust me?" Ramirez gives a hearty chuckle. "Is that it?"

"You've had me fully vetted," I say, glancing at Rook, who nods. Then I look back at Ramirez. "I'd like the same courtesy. Mutual trust. That's how my business works. I know nothing of Earl Edmond."

Ramirez watches me for a long second and then smiles, slow and satisfied, like I just passed a test I didn't know I was taking. "I appreciate your instinct, which is why I know you're the right man for the job. You can trust Edmond. Just like with you, Rook's made sure we won't have any issues there." He flicks his eyes to his lawyer. "Right?"

Rook smiles. "We won't have any issues from Earl or Sebastian Edmond."

Not sure I like the way that sounds. I keep my voice level. "So they'll be joining us in Italy?"

"Yes."

"Hope he brings that assistant of his," Sammy says with a smile.

My spine locks. I don't know if it's the way he says it or the way Rook smirks beside him, but every alarm in my head goes off. Cybil. It's her sass, her smarts, her looks—she draws attention like a match draws oxygen. And attention, in this world, is a problem.

My hand tightens around my knee. Any chance I had of getting Edmond out of this deal evaporates. So does the chance of getting Cybil out clean.

Ramirez slips a pair of sunglasses over his eyes, the meeting apparently finished. This time Rook doesn't open the door for me. I let myself out of the car. "I'll see you in Italy."

There's a reason why Ramirez hasn't been caught. If anything in his plan goes south, he knows how to protect himself. Just like Katherine said, he'll disappear. The FBI has contingencies in place to protect me—

make *me* disappear so it looks like I'm sitting on a beach somewhere without an extradition agreement. But what about Cybil? Who's going to have her back? Who is going to protect her?

My sixth-grade teacher said there's no such thing as a dumb question, but that's not true. The only thing dumber than asking who's going to protect her is pretending the answer isn't me.

CHAPTER 11

Cybil

Dallas, Texas
Wednesday morning

I slap my hand down on the alarm clock before it goes off. Not like I needed it. Sleep and I broke up somewhere around four in the morning. Probably because my brain won't shut up. I still haven't heard back from Athena. I've left two messages—one about the gala and another about the unexpected Ben-shaped complication. But nothing. And now before I can even recover from the emotional whiplash, I get to add jet lag to the list.

When I got back to the office yesterday, Mr. Edmond informed me I'd be accompanying him and Sebastian to Italy. Meetings with suppliers, he said. Routine. Nothing I haven't sat through before—except this time, Ramirez's name came up. Briefly. Casually. Just long enough to let me know this trip is important.

Mr. Edmond and Sebastian were locked in meetings the rest of the afternoon, which left me with too much time to spiral. If Ramirez is involved, then it's possible Ben is too. Which means there's a very real possibility I'm not just walking into a tense business trip. I'm walking into a distraction in a tailored suit.

"Craig *freaking* Miller." I glare at the water stain on the ceiling over my bed. It's starting to morph into something between a sloth and my emotional stability. I close my dry eyes and exhale all the breath from my lungs. "This cannot be happening."

I need chocolate. And caffeine.

I kick at the sheets tangled around my legs, roll to my side, and squint toward the kitchen. The hum of the refrigerator calls to me like a beacon of hope. *Chocolate cake.* Dragging myself out of bed, I pad barefoot toward the fridge.

Last night after work, Joy insisted we go out for dinner. I think it was her attempt at redemption for abandoning me in my hour of need—aka getting trapped in the revolving door like a malfunctioning Roomba.

When I finally made it back to the car, still trying to unmelt my brain, she took one look at me and wordlessly handed over a bag of M&M's from my glove compartment emergency stash. She at least had the courtesy to look apologetic . . . in between the hysterical laughter.

My bank account wasn't exactly on board with eating out, but Joy declared the day officially worthy of chocolate cake. And who am I to argue against chocolate? We splurged at a steak house where everything is à la carte. It's not the kind of place I'd ever drop sixty-five dollars for a piece of meat, much less eighteen dollars for mashed potatoes, no matter how deliciously creamy they claim to be. It is, however, the place I'd allow Joy to order a fifteen-dollar piece of chocolate cake that melts in your mouth and makes all your problems disappear.

Unless your best friend insists on bringing them up. Again.

"What are you going to do if Ben goes to Italy too?" she asked as casually as someone commenting on the weather and completely unaware of the emotional earthquake she'd just triggered.

I didn't have an answer. And because nothing pairs with chocolate like unresolved teenage drama, I didn't finish my cake. *Tragic.*

Italy. With Ben?

Only it's not Ben. It's *Craig Miller*.

"'A forgettable name for a forgettable person,'" I mutter in a mocking tone as I yank open the fridge door. "'You were way too good for Craig Miller.'"

There was a moment—just a flicker—when he said those words that I almost believed there was something deeper behind them.

Nope. Not going there.

If there's one thing I know about Bennett Bradley—he's a schmoozer. It didn't matter if he and Rex were filling my boots with mud or setting off firecrackers outside my bedroom window—Ben knew exactly how to flash that crooked smile and get away with everything.

And no one was immune. Not my aunt Renee. Not the server at Dairy Queen.

Not. Even. Me.

I pull out the leftover cake, start the coffee, and fall into the morning routine—showering, brushing my teeth, getting dressed for work—trying not to think about Italy. Trying not to think about Ben. Or what it'll mean if he goes to Italy.

The scent of brewing coffee fills the kitchen. My stomach grumbles. I pour my coffee into a travel cup and take a bite of the cake.

Joy's words echo in my head: *"Breakfast of champions."*

"Or the financially burdened," I murmur around another bite.

My circle of friends is tight. I have two. Joy and Marcos. Joy is the unassuming public librarian who took actual joy in challenging our professors—usually just to prove she could outsmart them before lunch. She doesn't talk much about her family, but I'm starting to think her family tree has deeper roots in espionage than in the Dewey Decimal System. Her lockpicking skills, knack for cloning key fobs, and casual ability to vanish from security cameras weren't exactly covered in Legal Ethics. Most of what I know about novice spycraft, I learned from Joy.

Those skills have come in handy with our friend Marcos Delgado. After graduating, he took over his uncle's business, ProSecure Investigative Group, and occasionally outsources the legwork on some of his insurance fraud cases to Joy and me. It's not glamorous, but with student loan bills looming, I'm not picky. I'm grateful.

Marcos and Joy don't know everything I do for Athena, but they've known about my financial mess since college—back when they caught me utilizing the campus food pantry. They didn't say a word, but the next week I had an anonymous grocery delivery at my apartment that included several party-size bags of M&M's, and it pretty much sealed my loyalty to them.

My gaze drifts to the suitcase I pulled out for Italy. I groan. There *has* to be a way out of this. I touch my throat. Is that a tickle? Yes. I think I feel something. I cough. It's pathetic. But I've got sick leave saved up. Mr. Edmond wouldn't force me to go to Italy if I'm not feeling well, right?

And if Mr. Edmond and Sebastian were out of the office, I'd have full access to snoop. I could go through their files, emails, accounts. I don't need to fly halfway across the world to find intel for Athena, do I? I mean, sure, I'd *love* a business trip to Italy. I'd just really prefer more of a gelato and gondolas vacay than a guns and cannoli one.

A sharp knock breaks into my thoughts.

I'm halfway to my door before I realize something isn't right. It's not even seven in the morning, and I'm not expecting anyone.

My pulse ticks up. I glance around my apartment. For what, I don't know. But after the last few days, my nerves are on edge.

Another knock. "Maintenance."

I frown. Maintenance? I peek through the peephole and see a person wearing a hat with a maintenance company logo, but the brim is pulled too low to see the face.

"I didn't put in any service requests," I say.

"A neighbor reported a leak in the apartment above you," the voice says. "It's sewage."

Ew. I think about the water stain over my bed. I unbolt the door and open it—only to find Athena standing there. Wearing a blue maintenance shirt. A hat. A patch that says her name is "Bob."

"Morning," she says breezily, walking past me like she owns the place. She drops a tool bag on the floor without breaking stride.

"Come on in?" I close the door behind her, stunned.

This is not protocol. Athena has never come to my apartment before.

Our meetings have always been in public—casual drop-ins at a coffee shop or library. Places where the exchange of information can pass unnoticed.

But this? This isn't casual. This is a flag on fire.

Especially since I'd messaged her *twice*—and got radio silence in return.

"Sorry to surprise you," she says, scanning my cramped apartment with those sharp, assessing eyes.

The scrutiny of my meager furnishings makes me feel uncomfortable. My apartment is mostly essential. Items collected at garage sales and thrift stores. There are only two things I purchased absolutely brand-new, my mattress and couch. Somewhere around the age of ten, after my mom and I had moved eight times, I learned the value of sleeping on furniture that didn't host a colorful display of stains and odors.

Her gaze lingers on the stack of bills by the microwave. I swipe them into a drawer, suddenly unsure if I'm embarrassed, annoyed . . . or just alarmed.

"What are you doing here"—I raise an eyebrow at the fake name tag on her shirt—"Bob?"

"I wanted to catch you before you left for work," Athena says, moving to my window like she's casing the street. "We need to talk about your trip to Italy."

"I don't think I'm going."

Her head whips toward me. "Why not?"

"I was thinking I'd get more done here. With Mr. Edmond and Sebastian out of the office, I could go through files. I overheard Sebastian and his father arguing over finances. Sounded like it might have something to do with Sebastian's crypto company. It felt off. I can dig around, see what's going on—"

"You're going with them," Athena cuts in. Her voice is calm but firm. "There's been a development."

She shifts the blinds again. I cross the room, more uneasy than before. Outside, a neighbor is tossing trash into the dumpster. Totally normal. Which only makes this weirder.

"What kind of development?" I ask.

"We lost the museum lead," Athena says, crossing her arms. "Whoever stopped you from getting into the museum library the other night stopped us from getting the information we needed about the deal Ramirez is making with Edmond."

Guilt scrapes the back of my throat. If I'd gone upstairs sooner, figured out a better way to plant the listening device. If I hadn't been distracted by . . .

"We're still working to identify them," Athena continues. "But based on other intel, we're working under the assumption that someone else wanted access to that office for the same reasons we did—for information about the deal. That's your assignment. We're not just interested in Ramirez. We already know he's a criminal. We want the details behind the deal. What it is. What Edmond and Ramirez's role is. And who else might be involved."

It didn't surprise me that she had more intel than I did. As a covert asset, I wasn't looped in on the full scope of a mission. My original assignment was simple: Find out who Edmond was meeting with. But now it sounds like the focus is shifting—from tracking Ramirez to dissecting the actual deal. Which means this isn't just another financial scheme. It's bigger. The stakes higher.

Who else might be involved? Ben's stupid smug face pops into my mind. He's involved. But *how* involved? "I don't think it's a good idea," I say slowly. "Because of—"

"The financial advisor, Craig Miller," she finishes for me.

Even just hearing the name makes my stomach knot.

"Or should I say Ben Bradley," she adds, and that name punches harder.

I swallow.

"He said he uses aliases to protect his clients," I offer apologetically.

Athena shrugs, too casual. "That's not unusual with his clientele. Politicians. CEOs. Oil magnates. He's built a career helping the wealthy, powerful, and criminally connected hide their money."

Hearing her describe what Ben does sounds a lot different than the way he described it to me yesterday in the restroom. He's a financial advisor, which in and of itself is a solid career choice, but then you add in his clients . . . and that's where it gets confusing.

The Ben I remember was always jumping headfirst into whatever scheme he and Rex came up with, without a thought to the consequences that might follow. More than once, their tricks on me earned both of them extra chores from Uncle Buddy.

"There are still some things we're working out." Athena's gaze goes distant. "But for now, we think Craig Miller might be useful."

My jaw tightens. "Useful how?"

"Given your history, I think he could be an . . . asset."

The word lodges like glass. An asset? I glance down at the ring on my thumb—my dad's ring. When we were twelve, the chain I wore it on snapped while I was playing near the edge of a ravine behind Aunt Renee's house. I watched it tumble down, hitting rock and brush before disappearing into the undergrowth.

I didn't move. Couldn't breathe. That ring was all I had left of my father.

Before I could even react, Ben was already scrambling down the slope. No rope. No plan. Just a twelve-year-old boy with dirt-crusted sneakers and zero survival instincts. He came back bleeding from a cut above his brow, covered in scratches, and grinning like he'd just won a medal.

Ben earned two stitches, a lecture from Uncle Buddy, and a week-long grounding. "Worth it," he told me.

Back then, I thought he did it to show off. That he was seeking attention by doing something risky, but it was just his personality. He's always been the kind of person who jumps straight into the ravine and doesn't stop to wonder if he can climb back out.

Is that what's happened here? How did he get tangled up with Lorenzo Ramirez? Does he see the edge to pull himself out?

"You want me to use him?" I ask, still looking at the ring. "To get information?"

"We want you to do exactly what you've been doing," Athena says.

"Stay close to Mr. Edmond. He's your alibi. But keep your ears open. Ben—Craig Miller—doesn't make his money working for the good guys. He's working directly with Ramirez on this deal. If he trusts you, he might let something slip. That's the information we need."

My stomach churns.

Athena watches me carefully, like this is some kind of test. I peek at the drawer holding my bills. This is a test I literally cannot afford to fail.

"On these kinds of trips, I'll be coordinating meetings and managing paperwork," I say, trying to keep my voice steady. "Is there something I need to be looking for specifically?"

Athena exhales, just long enough to let me know she doesn't have all the answers either. "We're still working to confirm a few things, but at this point, just be yourself. Watch. Listen. Do what you've been doing and there shouldn't be any problems."

My throat tightens. No problems? There's already a problem, and he's tall, dark, and exactly the kind of handsome that ruins your common sense.

I twist my father's ring again and let out a slow breath.

Ben doesn't belong in this world—but what if I'm wrong? What if the boy who once climbed down a ravine to rescue a piece of my heart has climbed into something darker . . . and stayed?

I look at Athena. "Can I trust him?"

She doesn't even blink. "Trust is optional. Results aren't." She grabs her tool bag and heads for the door. "If it helps, we don't trust anyone."

That doesn't help, but I keep it to myself and watch Bob the maintenance worker walk out of my apartment, leaving me to pack a suitcase, chase down intel on a criminal empire, and possibly stab a childhood friend with a dessert fork.

Two days in Italy.

What could possibly go wrong?

CHAPTER 12

Ben

Dallas, Texas
Wednesday night

"What do you mean you're packing heat?"

I press my cell phone closer to my ear, hoping I misheard my gran's declaration. Her cackling on the other end confirms she's not taking this nearly as seriously as my mom, who just called asking me to talk some sense into my grandmother.

"Isn't that what you law types call it?"

"No, Gran, it's not." I glance up as Ruby walks into the office holding a coffee cup like it's the Holy Grail. I hold out my hand. She stops midstep, eyes wide, and clutches the cup like I've just asked her to hand over her firstborn.

"Who told you to buy a gun?" I ask into the phone.

Ruby's eyebrows shoot to her hairline before a smirk creases her lips and she reluctantly hands me her coffee. One sip and I nearly gag on the sugar level before handing it back.

"Toby," Gran says cheerfully. "He's that good-looking fella Martha Jane's granddaughter used to see. You know who she is, right? The pretty girl who takes photos of the dead?"

Photos of the dead? I stare at the wall like it might help my brain catch up. Gran's words echo in my head, and I start to seriously question whether she's finally lost her marbles. Not that any of us Bradleys would dare say that out loud. Not if we valued our lives. Dorothy Bradley might be in her seventies, but she can still take down a full-grown man with a glare and a rolling pin.

"She's the girl who came out after Glory thought she found a human bone in the park."

There's not enough caffeine in Texas to jolt my day back to order. I'm about to have Ruby call my mom back when it clicks. "Wait. Do you mean she's a crime scene tech?"

"Yes, yes. That's the one. She dated Toby for a while, but I think he spent too much time at the gym. Nice muscles, but what're you gonna do with a bunch of muscles if you don't have a nice wife to show them off to? Stop it, Bernie," Gran says, scolding her best friend and fellow geriatric criminal comrade, Bernice. "Bernie has the hots for Toby and isn't one bit sad he's single now."

Aspirin. I need aspirin. "Gran, the gun? Did you buy a gun?"

Ruby drops into the chair across from me and props her boots on the desk. She's clearly enjoying the conversation that's causing my brain to pulse against my skull.

"Well, honey, I tried, but the man at the store said I needed to have i-dent-if-ication." The word crawls out, dripping with Southern sass. "'Course I don't have a driver's license anymore and he wouldn't take my Magnolia Hill resident card. Or the extra twenty I tried to bribe him with."

"You tried to bribe him?"

Ruby's feet drop to the ground as she leans forward, her eyes sparkling. "Speaker," she whispers, gesturing at my cell phone. "Put it on speaker."

I shake my head and frown at the very clear amusement she's getting from my grandmother trying to invoke her Second Amendment rights.

"He didn't take it," Gran continues. "Good fella, that one. Said I can't buy a gun until I bring back my state-issued ID."

I exhale, relieved that, at the very least, someone out there is following the law. "Gran, you don't need a gun." I'm already mentally drafting the text that sends my mom to Magnolia Hill on a covert mission to confiscate Gran's ID. But first things first. "Why is Toby telling you to buy a gun?"

"Oh, he's not, honey." I hear *Wheel of Fortune* blaring in the background. Gran raises her voice to compete with the TV. "He teaches self-defense, and Bernie asked if we were too old to own guns, and he said no. So Bernie and I got to thinking—we should get a pistol. You know, kind of like as a mascot for our club."

Ruby snorts. Loudly. I glare at her. She grins and mouths, *I love her.* I toss a pen at her head, which she dodges like she trains regularly for this kind of abuse—just as SAC Katherine Scott walks into the office.

"Gran, I've got to go," I say quickly. "But you do not need a gun for your club."

"But we've already got the pearls."

Ruby is practically choking on her laughter now, and Katherine gives me that *do I need to be concerned?* look.

"Gran," I say, fighting the headache pulsing behind my eyes, "do not buy any guns from anyone—at least until I can go with you and help you pick one out."

Katherine raises an eyebrow. Ruby blinks at me in surprise. I shake my head quickly—absolutely *not* happening—but it's easier to let Gran think I'm on board than to start a whole new argument. I wrap up the call, making her promise—twice—that she won't buy any weapons without checking with me first.

"Weapons?" Katherine settles into her chair. Behind her, the Dallas skyline flickers to life against the velvet dusk. "Is this the part where I start worrying?"

"With my gran? Always."

"How do I join her Pistols and Pearls club?" Ruby grins. "I don't own pearls, but I have a pistol."

"You're about fifty years too young," I say, rolling my eyes. "And I'm texting my father to make sure no one at her retirement community is, as Gran put it, 'packing heat.'" I throw up air quotes for good measure.

Ruby chuckles. Katherine still looks like she's debating a background check on my grandmother—and honestly, based on the stories Dad used to tell me about her, it's probably overdue.

But the humor fades as my mind shifts back to the reason we're still at the office after hours.

"That was . . . enlightening," Katherine says, arching a brow as she sets a folder on the table. "If you're sure your grandmother isn't going to end up on a federal watch list, let's see if we can end this night before the cleaning crew gets here."

I toss my phone onto the desk and reach for the folder Seth dropped off earlier. "Let's talk VerityCrypto." I flip it open and slide matching documents to them. "Seth's done a preliminary pass. On the surface, it looks like a textbook crypto startup—fast growth, strong branding, media spin. But there are a few things that make him uneasy."

"Like what?" Ruby asks.

"Timing inconsistencies. Certain wallet addresses rerouting through strange exchanges. A couple of offshore registrations that look clean, but the time stamps don't match up with the press releases," I say, recalling the way Seth explained it to me. Like I was five. There's a reason I didn't go into forensic accounting. Numbers. "He says there's nothing solid yet, but he's flagging it for further review once OSB is done."

Katherine nods. "Operation Shadow Broker is the priority. We can't dig too deep—not yet. Too much noise and we risk Ramirez catching wind. And we still don't have enough for a RICO indictment." She looks to Ruby. "What do we know about Earl Edmond?"

Ruby opens her own file. "Interestingly enough, Edmond's real estate company has had its own questionable dealings. In the early days of his company's growth, there were inflated valuations, kickbacks, a few red-flagged contractors. Our white-collar crime division tagged Earl Edmond early on for public corruption and financial crimes, but it never turned into a case."

"Why not?" I ask. If Earl Edmond had been charged, Cybil wouldn't be working for him and she wouldn't be caught in the middle of this mess.

"Not sure," Ruby answers. "There aren't any notes in the file. But I did a little digging, and what's interesting is that it looks like he's tried to clean up. His wife died six years ago, complications from pneumonia. That's about the same time he started bringing in compliance experts and streamlining operations, but it cost him. Nearly thirty percent revenue drop, causing contractors to walk and investors to pull back."

"So either grief made him grow a conscience," Katherine says, "or he's playing the long game."

"Which could explain why he's entertaining a deal with Ramirez." Ruby looks between us. "Ramirez offers big cash. A fast return. Edmond might be desperate to recover losses."

My stomach tightens. If Edmond's that close to the edge, that means Cybil's standing in the middle of his crumbling empire, and she doesn't even realize how fast it could fall on top of her.

Katherine nods. "That brings us to Italy." She pulls out a travel packet and slides it across the desk to me. "US Attorney General Fritz personally signed off on a limited travel directive. The FBI director fast-tracked your clearance. You leave tomorrow."

I glance through the documents. Passport, flight details—private jet. Another part of Craig Miller's financial fairy tale.

"Fritz believes we're close," Katherine says. "Close enough that a controlled risk is worth it. If this trip gets us the kind of evidence that ties Ramirez to extortion, wire fraud, obstruction—"

"Murder," Ruby adds, her tone flat. "Danny Morales didn't get shot for fun."

"—then we'll have what we need for a RICO indictment," Katherine finishes. "Do you anticipate any issues?"

Ruby opens another folder. "We pulled the flight manifest. Sammy Pawson's on it."

My pulse spikes. Ramirez's muscle. His fixer. His silent threat. He doesn't leave the country unless Ramirez expects trouble . . . or plans to handle it. If he's going, this trip isn't just business—it's enforcement. But for whom?

"Ramirez is hosting the trip. I received the details on the villa—where we'll be staying. He wants me positioned as his point of contact for all financial transactions during the negotiation. I've done a cursory check on the banker he's introducing me to, Alessandro Moretti—he's old money, operates several offshore institutions in Switzerland and Malta. Seth's prepared me with all the documents I'll need and Ruby's taken care of the tech."

Ruby meets my eyes with a nod. "Your laptop's been embedded with a network packet analyzer. It's passive surveillance and less risky than direct access. Looks and acts like standard accounting software and will sniff for unsecured connections whenever Ramriez or anyone else logs onto the villa's Wi-Fi. If his laptop syncs with any financial accounts or opens unprotected files, the sniffer will mirror the data, and we'll grab it in real time from our end."

I nod. "And if Ramirez uses a secure VPN?"

"You'll have to get close enough to plug in or air-drop a decoy file," Ruby says. "We've baked a few document bugs into your USBs—if one gets opened, we'll get a full path to the host machine."

"Just get close enough without setting off his suspicion." I tap the edge of the folder. "No problem."

"And Ms. Langford." Katherine watches me carefully. "Is she going to be an issue?"

I shift in my seat, thinking about the restroom incident yesterday—her eyes, cautious but curious, like she couldn't decide whether to trust me or report me. "I can manage her."

Ruby whistles. "Top ten things to never say to a woman."

"I don't mean it like that," I add quickly, annoyed at Ruby's insinuation that I'm that kind of man. "If she's the same girl I remember, she'd punch me for even trying."

Ruby grins. "I respect her already."

Honestly, the idea of Ruby and Cybil becoming friends sounds . . . weirdly good. Like something that shouldn't matter but does.

Katherine presses again. "Is she a risk? To your cover? The mission?"

I hesitate. "I don't know."

I think of Cybil at the museum—how quickly she switched from recognition to indifference. The way she said *Craig* like she was choking on the word. When I chose the name, it wasn't like I did it to hurt her. I never imagined our paths would cross, and now that they have . . .

"It's been twelve years," I say finally. "I think I can trust her."

"People change in less time." Katherine raises an eyebrow. "Some for better. Some . . . not."

I know what she's implying. We don't get to assume the best—not in this job. But when I think of Cybil, I don't see a threat. I see the girl in the torn jean shorts and her uncle's flannel shirt, chasing after me and Rex with murder in her eyes after we dumped chicken feed in her purse.

Except now she's a woman. And that memory has been hijacked by the way she looked at me yesterday, her mouth set in that stubborn line, her eyes calculating. Unaware that her presence was messing with my pulse in a way that was entirely unhelpful.

And she's walking a line she doesn't even know exists, and I can't shake the feeling that if she slips—just once—she'll land right in the crosshairs. I won't let that happen.

"I need you to keep your head in the game," Katherine says. "There's a lot riding on this mission."

I nod, my thoughts shifting to Danny Morales. His family. The cold precision of Ramirez's operation. And now Cybil, tangled in the middle of it. This mission was already high risk. But now? It's personal.

"Understood," I say, the word thick on my tongue.

Katherine leans back, folding her arms, eyes steady. "Good. Because if she's the one who exposes you—even by accident—we lose everything."

CHAPTER 13

Cybil

Lagoverde, Italy
Thursday night

"Missing. Luggage."

The very beautiful Italian woman—Fiorella, because of course she has a name that sounds like a perfume ad—keeps nodding at me, but the lost look in her equally beautiful eyes says she has no idea what I'm saying.

I step back and check the sign above my head. "Bagaglio aereo Lagoverde." That's the name of the tiny airline that delivered me to the Lagoverde airport. There's a picture of a suitcase next to it, so logic suggests I'm in the right place to find my missing luggage.

I set my cappuccino on the counter and point to the tag the gate agent in Rome handed me when she decided my "American-sized carry-on" was too big for the overhead bin. "My bag is on this flight," I say, then point to the empty luggage carousel behind me. "Not there. Missing."

Fiorella—who, let's be honest, looks like she stepped off a runway, not into a baggage claim job—gives me a placating smile. If this were America, travelers would probably *hope* to lose their luggage just to talk to her. Assuming they spoke Italian.

Which I do not.

She glances at my cappuccino like it personally offends her, so I slide it off the counter.

"La tua, borsa non è qui," she says.

I have no idea what that means.

This is what I get for choosing the high road and not accepting Mr. Edmond's invitation to fly private with him and Sebastian. A "moral superiority" is what Athena calls my refusal to accept a paycheck from Mr. Edmond. I refuse to take money—or travel perks—from a man who profits off shady deals. No matter how generous he tries to be. My income comes directly from Athena and the side jobs I do for Marcos—covert tasks wrapped in nondisclosure agreements and plausible deniability. It's enough to pay my rent, feed my chocolate habit, and keep my conscience mostly quiet.

So here I am: moral superiority rerouting my paycheck from Edmond to a victims' advocacy group, and me wedged in a middle seat on a regional airline—because apparently, my conscience prefers turbulence and a complimentary side of missing baggage.

"Signora, per favore, compili il modulo."

I take the form and fan myself with it, searching the mostly empty airport for anyone who might be American—or at least capable of speaking English. No such luck. Unlike the bustling airport in Rome, this one is a tenth of the size, maybe smaller. A handful of gates line one side, and a private terminal sits behind a wall of glass, shielding the wealthy and powerful from the rest of us commoners.

The only thing open when I arrived was a tiny coffee kiosk where I managed to secure a true Italian cappuccino to steady my nerves. Barely. The barista kept shaking his head at me, offering espresso instead. But a straight shot of caffeine this late at night would be the sprinkles to my already disastrous sundae.

"Signora?"

I turn back to Fiorella, still annoyingly flawless in her polyester uniform. Who am I kidding? This is Italy; it's probably Versace. She holds out a pen. I take it with a muttered *grazie*—one of three Italian words I know. *Buongiorno, ciao,* and *grazie*. I also know *macaroni* and *fettuccine*, but that's not going to help me right now.

Pen in hand, I twist to grab my shoulder bag off the floor—but catch my heel in the strap. There's that moment when you can *feel* the fall happening, when time slows just enough for you to register the person who's about to witness your descent into humiliation.

So whose broad frame and crooked smile do I see right before my cappuccino baptizes the front of my shirt?

Bennett Bradley.

Aka Craig *freaking* Miller.

The noise that escapes my lips is somewhere between a yelp, a groan, and a cry as lukewarm liquid drenches the only outfit I possess in Italy.

"Whoa." Ben rushes toward me, hands flailing in that useless gesture people make when they want to help but have absolutely nothing to offer. It's somehow making everything worse.

Until he turns and flashes that crooked smile at Fiorella—and starts speaking in fluent Italian.

Fluent. Italian.

I just stare at him, jaw unhinged, while my cappuccino-soaked shirt begins clinging to all the wrong places.

Fiorella nods at whatever he says and disappears into the office behind her.

"Did you burn yourself?"

"No."

He eyes me like he doesn't believe that for a second, and for a moment, I forget I'm not supposed to like him. "Let me take that." He takes the empty cup from my hand and tosses it into the trash, then gently pries the pen and form from my fingers. "You're sure you're okay?"

I realize I'm staring. "Yeah. No. I mean—they lost my bag. You speak Italian?"

Ben's smile tilts humble. "A little."

Fiorella returns with paper towels, which she passes to him with a flutter of dark lashes. He says something else to her—something that makes her blush—and my own cheeks burn, but for entirely different reasons. Even without wearing a cappuccino and looking like I've traveled for twelve hours, standing next to Fiorella is a humbling experience. She's all polished elegance. I'm a hot, soggy mess.

And just like that, I'm seventeen again, standing in the Texas heat, hoping I might someday be enough for a boy like Ben Bradley.

"Here."

Ben passes the paper towels to me and I blot the stain, but it's pointless. "It looks like I've been stabbed by a cappuccino."

"It's artistic," Ben says, his lip quirking. "Espresso-nist art."

He waggles his eyebrows at me, clearly impressed with himself. And there's a tiny traitorous tug in my chest that wants to give him the win. But Athena's voice cuts through the fog—her warning, which already feels like a lifetime ago. *"Ben doesn't make his money working for the good guys."*

Whatever charm he's working with—crooked smiles, smoldering brows, espresso puns—it's just camouflage. And I can't afford to get distracted by camouflage. No matter how good he looks speaking Italian.

"Thanks, I've got it from here."

"You're staying at the Villa Serendipitá?"

I scrunch the paper towels in my hand. "Yes." The word comes out slow, cautious, as I scan his face. "How do you know that?"

"We're all staying there."

"Wha—"

Before I can finish, Ben turns back to Fiorella and launches into more of his maddeningly fluent Italian. In the blur of their rapid-fire exchange, he scribbles something on a piece of paper while she rummages through a cabinet. A moment later, they make a trade—the paper for a rolled-up ball of fabric—and somehow he's slinging my shoulder bag over his own.

"Ready?"

"For what?"

Ben gives me a look like I've lost it. Maybe I have. Sleep deprivation and time zones are conspiring against my brain. "To the villa?"

"I'm not going—" I glance at Fiorella, who's now flipping off lights and locking up for the night. "I still need to find my luggage. The form—"

"All filled out. Fiorella has the villa's address, the phone number there, and mine. She'll call when they find your bag."

Oh, I bet she has his number.

"I can get to the villa on my own." I try for confidence, but based on how well tonight has gone, my tone is lacking. The way Ben's eyes crinkle at the edges, he hears it too.

"Put this on." He hands me the ball of fabric, and I realize it's a sweatshirt. But the second I catch the writing across the front, I shove it right back into his hands.

"No."

He frowns. "What's wrong?"

I snatch it back, flatten it out, and hold it up like evidence. His mouth twitches and his Adam's apple jumps before he clears his throat with exaggerated innocence.

"I don't see the problem."

"'I'm sexy and Italian—got meatballs?'" I deadpan. "Did you do this on purpose?"

"I simply asked Fiorella if she had something you could change into so you're not wearing a sticky shirt."

I glance toward the counter, but Fiorella is gone—probably halfway into a group text about the American girl who can't handle her cappuccino. "I'm not wearing this."

Ben shrugs. "Okay, but your blouse is see-through."

"What?" I press the sweatshirt to my chest and peek down. My eyes snap back to him, but all I catch is his back as he strolls toward the exit with my bag. "It is not."

But I slip the sweatshirt over my head, just in case, and hurry after Ben.

"I can get a taxi," I say, reaching for my bag.

"Just say thank you."

"What?"

He holds open the glass door, eyes steady. "It's okay to say thank you and accept help."

His tone is kind, but it still lands like an admonishment. I wasn't *trying* to be ungrateful. And if Ben hadn't shown up when he did, I'd probably still be at the counter, waging war with my limited vocabulary and Fiorella's painfully polite pity.

At the curb, a sleek black BMW with dark-tinted windows glides up to the curb. The driver steps out, takes my bag, and loads it into the trunk. Ben opens the back door and waits.

I hesitate. *Accepting help always comes at a cost.* Sometimes it's monetary. Sometimes it's physical. Sometimes it costs everything. When you grow up without the means to pay the price, you learn it's safer to rely on yourself. But tonight? I'm too tired to negotiate the emotional fine print.

"Thank you," I say quietly as I slide into the back seat.

Ben climbs in beside me, setting a leather bag on the floor by his feet before loosening the top button of his shirt. Then he rolls up the sleeves—and I instantly regret looking. Forearms should not be allowed to be that distracting. The driver shuts the door, and the car eases away from the curb.

I look at the bag by his feet. "Is that all you brought?" I ask, needing to fill the air with something other than the heat crawling up my neck.

"My luggage is already in the trunk." He settles back, perfectly at ease.

I glance at him, trying not to look like I'm comparing. But I am. He looks like he just strolled out of a spa—not a transcontinental flight. His shirt isn't even wrinkled. Meanwhile, I'm one wrong move away from smelling like a milky espresso for eternity. I sweep my hair into a topknot and will my pride to recover. "I thought my flight was the last one in."

"It was."

I frown. "Then how—?"

"Private jet."

Of course. I look away, jaw tight. There has to be a middle road somewhere between coach and criminal luxury. Maybe a semi-ethical economy plus with no champagne but just enough legroom for the morally superior? I push the envy down and sit straighter. I need to remember who I'm talking to—who he *works* for.

If I'm stuck in the car with Ben, I might as well try to learn something useful for Athena. "So," I say casually, "you must do pretty good business to afford flying private."

"It's the company's jet."

Not helpful. "Do you travel out of country a lot for work?"

"Not really." He shifts and his knee bumps mine. A little zing dances across my skin, and I pretend it didn't happen. I subtly move my leg away. "What about you?" he asks. "I thought you were flying in with Mr. Edmond and Sebastian."

I shrug, slouching deeper into the seat. "I had some work to do at the office," I lie.

He nods, then reaches for his bag, unzips it, and pulls out a pack of M&M's. He opens it and holds it toward me. "Still your favorite?"

My stomach tightens at the sight of them—comfort food, sugar therapy, and one of my oldest coping mechanisms. I want them. Badly. But I shake my head. "No, thanks."

His brow lifts. "You're turning down chocolate?"

"I don't like it."

Ben cocks his head, skeptical. "The girl I remember stashed bags of these like a chipmunk stocking up for hibernation. You kept bags stashed in your—"

"Maybe I'm not the girl you remember," I say, cutting him off.

He studies me for a beat, like he's not sure whether that makes him disappointed or just more intrigued.

I fidget with the ring on my thumb. Spinning it, then tightening it against my knuckle. It's loose, maybe from the flight. Or nerves. I glance at him, and his eyes catch on my hand.

"It fits," he says softly.

My throat tightens. The memory of him climbing into the ravine flashes back to mind again. The boy who, without hesitation, went after my ring to save it. A boy I thought I knew.

But that was before . . . Before now, when I know he works for someone like Ramirez. Before everything about him—his charm, his smile, the way he remembers my favorite candy—might be nothing more than a carefully constructed lie. I slide my hand into my lap, away from his view, and turn back to the window.

I can't afford to forget why I'm here. And I definitely can't afford to fall for the boy I *used* to know.

The car winds up the circular drive of Villa Serendipitá, headlights sweeping across gravel and stone. It's late—so late that the town of Lagoverde is nothing but shadows and scattered golden windows dotting the hills. I press my forehead to the glass, trying to catch a glimpse of Italy beyond the night, but the darkness swallows it whole.

When the driver opens my door, my jaw drops at the beautiful Italian villa. Even in the muted glow of exterior lights, it's stunning.

Honey-colored stone catches the warm glint of lanterns. Green shutters hug arched windows. Ivy and bougainvillea stretch like lazy arms up the walls. I catch just a glimpse of the terra-cotta roof and the lemon trees in the courtyard, and in this moonlit version it looks like a fairy tale.

I want to absorb every bit of it—because places like this don't happen to me in real life. They happen to people with trust funds or criminal ties.

"The key to your room."

Ben's voice pulls me back to reality. While I've been admiring tile and inhaling the soft citrus scent, he's already grabbed his suitcase and collected our room keys from the concierge. He hands me mine.

We cross the courtyard and step into a wide foyer with vaulted ceilings and wrought-iron chandeliers. Everything smells like citrus and polished wood and old money. Or stolen money. Villa Serendipitá is the kind of place you book for a wedding—*Godfather* style.

"There's no elevator," Ben says as we reach the bottom of a grand staircase. "It's just one floor."

We climb the stairs and are halfway down the hallway when a man steps through an arched doorway that looks like it's attached to a veranda. He's tall, sharp-jawed, and doesn't look like someone who belongs in this beautiful villa. His gaze slides over me with cool disinterest, but Ben's body goes stiff. Just a blink of tension that makes me notice the twitch of his jaw.

"Friend of yours?" I ask, nodding toward the guy who's disappeared back on the veranda.

Ben doesn't look directly. "No."

But there's something about his answer that has me making a mental note. The way Ben shifted—yeah, he knows that guy.

My room is across the hall from Ben's. He hesitates at his door.

"Do you want to switch rooms?" he asks.

I blink. "Why?"

He shrugs. "The sun rises on that side of the villa. I know you're not a morning person. Thought you might want the one that stays darker longer."

My jaw twitches. I hate how predictable he still thinks I am. I plant my hand on my hip and smile sweetly. "Actually, I *love* the morning now. Nothing better than waking up to the sunlight on my face."

Ben stares with a look that says he doesn't buy the lie I'm trying to sell him, but I refuse to let him think he still *knows* me. He shrugs. "Suit yourself."

"I always do." I slide my card key across the reader, and the light blinks green. The door unlocks. "One more thing," I glance at Ben over my shoulder. "Will you let me know if Fiorella calls about my luggage?"

"I will," he says. "But for the record, that sweatshirt's growing on me."

I roll my eyes. "Good night, *Mr. Miller*."

He smiles, lazy and smug. "Good night, *Billy*."

He says it just low enough to float across the hall before his door clicks shut. Three words. A stupid nickname. And just like that, I know—Bennett Bradley is going to make this job very, *very* complicated.

CHAPTER 14

Ben

Lagoverde, Italy
Friday morning

Morning light filters through the archways and spills across the terracotta tiles of the veranda, warming the spot where I've planted myself after a quick breakfast and an even quicker meeting with Ramirez and Rook. Beyond the balcony, the sunlight glints off the lake that gives the quaint Italian village, Lagoverde, its name. Cicadas hum. Birds chatter from the branches overhead. And down the sloping hillside, the town is waking up.

I could die here.

The irony isn't lost on me. Especially after the conversation I just had with Ramirez. My plan this morning was simple. Outline how I'd manage his accounts for the deal. Ask strategic questions. Propose a few layered shell options. Talk off-ledger asset routes and how I plan to clean up overlapping ownership trails. You know—normal criminal enterprise things.

But Ramirez wasn't interested.

He said he wouldn't be joining me for the meeting with Alessandro Moretti. Told me he trusted me to handle the details. That was surprise number one.

Surprise number two was the YubiKey clipped to his key chain, resting beside his espresso like a casual afterthought. Small. Harmless looking. But lethal to my entire plan.

The device generates a new encrypted passcode every day, required to access his files and accounts. If he's using it to log in, the sniffer hidden in my laptop won't capture anything useful. No data. No evidence.

So whatever he's hiding? It's locked behind a blinking piece of plastic now sitting in his pocket. Which means I need a new plan. One that doesn't get me killed.

Lagoverde is a beautiful place to die. But I'd like to keep that off the plan.

I've already sent an encrypted update to Ruby, looping her in on the new complication. Not exactly the wake-up call I wanted to give her, but if we're hoping to salvage this mission, she needs to know the facts—fast.

For now, I act like everything's fine. Like my mission didn't just hit a wall. Like I'm not thinking about the brunette sleeping across the hall from me.

I stretch my arms overhead, trying to shake the tension I woke up with. Last night after I'd stepped into the suite, it took everything in me not to cross the hall and knock on Cybil's door—just to check on her. Make sure she was okay.

If it were just the two of us here, I might've done it. But with Ramirez, Rook, Mr. Edmond, and Sebastian scattered through the villa like land mines, the risk of exposing our connection wasn't worth it.

So instead, I grabbed one of my clean T-shirts, set it outside her door with a quick knock, then ducked back into my room like some idiot teenager pulling a stunt at summer camp.

I watched through the peephole like a stalker, unsure if she'd take it or toss it back at my door. But when she opened her door, I swear I caught the hint of a smile tug at her lips. I didn't think about what the image of her sleeping in my shirt would do to my pulse—until it did.

And then Ruby ruined it with a single text message.

Remember who Cybil is working for and what they are willing to do to protect their interests. If she slips up, it's your neck. Watch her, but don't get distracted. She may not be an innocent bystander, and you can't afford to forget that, no matter how much you think you can trust her.

I'd chalked up seeing Cybil at the airport as coincidence. Ruby's message made it clear—it wasn't. The FBI orchestrated this. Made sure our paths crossed last night.

She may not be an innocent bystander. Yet that's exactly who I believe her to be. No way is Cybil anything more than someone working for the wrong man at the wrong time and certainly in the wrong place.

I rise from the table and head inside. I have a meeting with an Italian banker in an hour. A man who's definitely not innocent and is maybe the only thread I have to pull if I want to unravel Ramirez's empire from the inside.

I take the long way through the hall, instinct or something like it tugging me away from the direct route. That's when I see her.

Cybil.

She's midstep in the hallway, pausing just long enough to peek inside one of the doors. Her hand rests lightly on the knob before she lets it ease closed.

I approach, keeping my steps quiet. She doesn't hear me until I'm behind her. "Looking for a minibar, or plotting your escape route?"

She startles—slightly—but recovers fast. Her arms cross. Eyes narrow. "Coffee," she says, dry as ever. "If I don't find caffeine soon, I will become a public safety issue."

I nod down the hall. "Breakfast is set up on the veranda."

"Thanks," she mutters, brushing past me.

She's wearing my T-shirt, knotted at the hip over the slacks she had on last night. Somehow, she's made the ensemble fashionable. My clothes have never looked that good—or that off-limits. She glances at the folder in my hand. "Spreadsheets in the morning?"

"I always start my day with coffee and a side of numbers."

Her brow arches. "You seem more like a Lucky Charms kind of guy."

I go still for half a second, scanning for anyone who might be close enough to hear. No one here would know that about me—my favorite childhood breakfast. No one but her. She's playing a dangerous game and doesn't even know it. One wrong comment, one curious ear, and suddenly it's not just a joke between us—it's a crack in the armor. A reason for someone like Ramirez to ask questions I can't afford.

I should go back to my room, then head out to my meeting, but I find myself walking with her to the veranda. Her eyes light up when she sees the buffet table set up with fresh fruit, eggs, and pastries. She zeroes in on a croissant and starts to reach for it.

I get there first.

"Hey?"

"Sorry," I say, taking a big bite just to prove the point. I rotate the pastry so she can see the chocolate layered between the buttery pastry. "You don't like chocolate."

She glares and steps around me, grabbing coffee instead. With a mug in hand, she walks to the railing, her profile framed by the lake in front of her. "It's almost too beautiful to be real."

"Sure is," I reply before I can stop myself.

She glances back, eyes catching mine. And for a second, it's not a game.

"Will you have time to sightsee while you're here?" I ask, trying to shove the moment back into the box where it belongs.

"A little this morning," she says. "Mr. Edmond gave me the morning off to sleep and grab some clothes in town before our meetings."

The breeze lifts a strand of hair, making it dance against her neck, and I swallow. Hard.

I need to leave. I need to prep for the meeting. I need to stop looking at her like she's anything but a potential liability.

Then she turns those eyes on me. "How long have you been working for him?"

I rock on my heels. "Who?"

"Mr. Ramirez, the man who paid for all of this."

"Not long," I say.

"And yet here you are. Private jets and views for days."

"Just a day and a half," I correct her. "But yeah, the job comes with perks."

"I bet it does," she mumbles into her coffee.

"Sorry?"

"Nothing." She smiles, but it doesn't quite reach her eyes. I want to ask why, but before I can, she's already moving.

"You're not having breakfast?"

She eyes the buffet table and the plain croissants. "I'll grab something in town. Thanks for letting me borrow this," she says, tugging the hem of my T-shirt. "I'll get it back to you today."

"No rush," I say—because I mean it. I shouldn't. But I do.

She disappears through the archway, and I catch myself watching her go. Truth is, I like seeing her in my shirt. More than I should. But leaning into that now? That's a one-way ticket to disaster.

Because Cybil's not the only one working the wrong job in the wrong place at the worst possible time.

I let that sobering thought follow me into town to meet Alessandro Moretti. Lagoverde is already buzzing, prepping for the Festival of Masks. Stalls are going up along the piazza, their striped awnings unfurling like sails. Paper lanterns hang from the second-story balconies, strung between buildings like garland.

My burner buzzes in my pocket.

I duck into a narrow alley between two pastel buildings—shuttered windows overhead, drying laundry swaying like flags. Quiet enough to take the call.

"Miller."

"I've got Seth on the line," Ruby says.

"Hey, man," Seth adds, voice rough around the edges.

I check my watch, do the math. "It's not even four in Dallas. Please tell me you didn't get up just for me."

"Nah, it's fine," Seth says. "Jess caught whatever the girls had, so I've been up all night on dad duty. It's fine. I'm dead inside."

"Sorry, man."

Ruby cuts in. "Focus, boys. I think I've got a way around the YubiKey."

I relax against the concrete wall. "Tell me."

"First, you're lucky we didn't try anything at the museum," she says. "If you'd used the device on Ramirez's laptop without knowing about that key, it would've flagged an intrusion attempt instantly. He would've burned you on the spot."

My guts twists. Sammy Pawson had been at the museum. I don't want to think about what he would've done if I'd been caught. But . . . now he's here. In Italy.

Last night, seeing him in the same hallway as Cybil—I nearly reached for her. Instinct. One I had to bury fast. I don't want her anywhere near that man, but I can't react without blowing my cover. And that kills me. There has to be a better way to keep her safe.

The memory of Edmond questioning Ramirez returns and a new fear wriggles its way into my brain. "Do you think Ramirez suspects something?"

Ruby's quiet for a beat. "We haven't picked up on any chatter. Nothing on our end indicates you've been made. But that doesn't mean you're in the clear. He's suspicious of everyone—assume yourself included."

"Noted."

I scan the street. Tourists wander past with shopping bags, ducking into cafés and boutiques. A woman in a linen dress laughs with her friend. It's all so normal. But I half expect to see Sammy's face in the crowd, staring back from some shadow.

"You remember that air-drop decoy I loaded on the drive?" Ruby asks.

"Yeah."

"It'll work if Ramirez opens it. Doesn't matter if he's got a YubiKey—if he's already logged in, the file will piggyback off the session."

"But you've got to be close when it happens," Seth adds. "Bluetooth range. The decoy doesn't transmit over Wi-Fi, so you're the receiver. You miss the window, you miss the data."

"So I just need him to open up a file while I'm in range," I mutter. "Sounds easy."

"It's not," Ruby agrees.

"Ramirez isn't exactly my email buddy," I say. "Everything goes through Rook."

"You're meeting with the banker, right?" Seth asks.

"Yeah, in about ten minutes."

"Good. When it's finished, go to Ramirez. Tell him there's a revised document—something new, something time-sensitive. He opens it while you're nearby, the bug does its thing."

"And if he pushes back?"

"Tell him the update is critical," Seth says, yawning. "Say the changes address a compliance issue. International regulations, cross-border transfers—whatever sounds annoying enough that he believes you. If he delays, you can mention that it's the kind of oversight that flags regulators. SEC, foreign banks—and that's the last thing he wants."

I nod to myself, already forming the lie. "A revised shell corp draft."

"Exactly," Seth says. "Once he opens it, you've got twenty minutes. If he scrolls through anything suspicious, you'll have it."

"And if he doesn't?" I ask.

"Then we pivot," Ruby says. "But this gives you your best shot without needed access credentials."

My phone buzzes again—calendar alert. Time to meet Moretti.

"Thanks," I say. "Both of you. I'll update you later."

I end the call and pocket the phone, stepping back into the sunlight and toward the café. The morning crowd thickens, voices rising, vendors hawking espresso and festival masks in bursts of color. I weave between them, trying to focus on Moretti and the mission with Ramirez.

But my thoughts won't settle.

Even if this works—even if Ramirez opens the file and gives us what we need—I need to make sure Cybil doesn't get caught in the middle.

Applause erupts ahead, drawing my attention to a street performer spinning in a white costume, a colorful mask hiding his face. Music spills from a nearby café. Locals cheer. It's the kind of picturesque chaos tourists love to post about.

I skirt around the crowd, eyes sweeping the faces—out of habit more than intent. But I catch myself looking for her. It's stupid. Reckless. I know that. Especially after the call I just had. Especially with Sammy Pawson somewhere out there. I didn't see him this morning, but that didn't mean he wasn't nearby. Watching.

The last thing I want is for Cybil to be anywhere near him or me while I'm working this case. And yet . . . some traitorous part of me hopes she'll be standing at a corner, holding a coffee, smiling like we're just two people on vacation. Like this is a moment instead of a mission.

Get your head straight, Ben. Remember who Cybil is working for and what they're willing to do to protect their interests. She may not be an innocent bystander . . .

I don't know what Earl Edmond is capable of—but I know what Ramirez is. He's the kind of man who doesn't send emails. He sends Sammy Pawson.

I stop in front of a busy *panetteria,* and the scent of warm bread and sugar perfumes the air. But it's not the smell that holds me still.

A man in gray slacks and a black shirt leans against a post across the street. Fedora pulled low over his brow. Not monitoring the bakery. Not paying attention to the crowd. Watching *me.*

My pulse spikes. I search my memory. Nothing. I don't recognize him. And that's a problem.

I cross the street, moving casually, as if I haven't clocked him. Ten feet later, he follows. Not a coincidence—I'm being tailed.

How long? And by whom?

It's not Pawson. But it could be someone who works for him. Someone paid to watch. Or worse. I wouldn't be surprised if there's a network here—men in suits with local accents and clean knives.

Guys who don't ask questions.

They just find you.

And make sure no one ever does again.

CHAPTER 15

Cybil

Lagoverde, Italy
Friday morning

"Bellissima."

Beautiful is the last word I'd use to describe the disaster blinking back at me in the mirror. The villa concierge gave me a list of nearby boutiques, but after converting euros to dollars and realizing my budget was more suggestion than substance, I ended up here—in a shop that sells international calling cards, Pope-themed knickknacks, and a deeply concerning assortment of anatomically suggestive pasta. And, unfortunately, the only clothes my bank account can afford.

The airline still hasn't found my luggage. The concierge offered to send my coffee-stained blouse to be cleaned, but it wouldn't be back in time for my meetings with Edmond. So here I am. Desperate. But not *this* desperate.

"Bellissima, sì?"

The sweet, elderly shopkeeper tries again. Wispy gray hair frames her weathered face, and she gestures to me with the kind of hopeful smile that could probably sell sand to a Sicilian.

I glance down at the very . . . patriotic outfit she convinced me to try on. I'd hoped for some designer-inspired pantsuit or trendy wrap dress, but instead I'm standing under buzzing fluorescent lights in a royal blue tracksuit with the word *ITALIA* blazing across my chest like a tourist beacon. The stripes down the sleeves and pant legs? Red, white, and green. Naturally.

"Kardashian," she says proudly, gesturing at me like I'm ready for the runway. Or a car commercial.

I try to chuckle. "More like Joey Tribbiani in a tracksuit," I mutter.

And that's the problem. I cannot show up to meetings looking like Italy's unofficial mascot. The goal is to *blend in,* not become a walking souvenir.

The bell over the door jingles, and she shuffles off to help a new customer. I send up a silent prayer they're bilingual and can help me communicate that I don't want to look like a knockoff reality star. My hopes are dashed when I hear them break into enthusiastic Italian.

I duck back behind the curtain and stare at my reflection again. This can't be my life. And yet—here I am.

My options are limited. If you love Ferrari, this place has an entire section. Fancy aprons featuring Michelangelo's *David?* You're covered. They even have T-shirts with quippy puns and jokes, like "Fuhgeddaboudit" and "Grab life by the meatballs." I already have one of those—thanks to Ben.

Speaking of Ben, where is he when I need him?

No, I don't need him. I need his Italian. That's it. Just his language skills. Not his smile. Or the way he looks at me like he still sees the girl I was. I just need the Italian.

The tracksuit itches. Probably polyester. Or regret.

Ben's T-shirt lies on the bench. It's buttery soft and still smells like him—clean soap, something citrusy. Something . . . dangerous to my emotional stability.

I shouldn't have worn it today. Last night, I shoved it in the armoire and put on the complimentary robe instead, pretending it didn't matter that he left the shirt outside my door. But it did. And I hate that it did.

The gesture caught me off guard. Just like everything else about him lately. I keep trying to categorize him: the boy I once knew, the potential threat Athena warned me about, the man who stole my chocolate croissant. Still kicking myself for that lie.

Twelve years I've carried his voice like a splinter under my skin. *"She's a mess. Reckless."* His words chased me through college, into a job and a life that didn't unravel every time someone let me down. And now Ben's here, unraveling everything.

This morning was already a close call. I thought I was being careful, tiptoeing down the hallway to check the villa's study where the meeting is supposed to take place this afternoon, only to practically run into Ben.

I panicked. Blurted out something about coffee, which technically wasn't a lie. But Ben's casual demeanor, his smug smile, the way he keeps acting like he knows me—it's throwing me off.

My phone rings, yanking me back to the present. It's my mom.

"Hey, Mom." I check the time in Michigan. Five a.m. "You're up early today."

"Hi, honey! Quick question—do you know how to unfreeze a bank account?"

I close my eyes and sigh. "What did you do?"

"I may have flagged the autopay for my electricity as fraud again. The logo changed."

Of course it did. Mom has come a long way since showing up on my doorstep with a suitcase, a loose grip on reality, and a promise to do better. But ADHD doesn't vanish with good intentions. It still sneaks up on her—disguised as impulsive decisions, forgotten bills, and, yes, fraud alerts on recurring charges that help her stay on top of her payments.

I couldn't trust her then—not when I was working two jobs and drowning in student loans I took out to support us both—but I couldn't turn her away either.

With Joy's help, we found the Lighthouse Sanctuary, a structured living community with job support and staff who understand ADHD. It's been a godsend. But it's not cheap. A sponsor covers a third of the residency program and I cover the rest. Mom takes care of her day-to-day bills.

I miss her. I just don't miss the chaos.

My fingers play with the thin gold band on my thumb. How different would our lives be if my dad was still here? Or if my mom's attention span was long enough to see between the lies that stole the settlement money right from under her nose?

"How far behind are you?"

"Just a few months," she says like it's nothing.

But it's more than nothing. It means I'll have to move money around to figure out how to cover the unexpected expense. It also means I'm stuck wearing this atrocious outfit.

"Okay," I say. "I'll take care of it."

"Thank you, sweetie. I owe you."

That's always how it goes. I love her, but she's always going to be one unpaid bill away from a first-name basis with debt collectors.

I hang up and fork over ninety-eight euros for the tracksuit and walk out of the store with my pride slightly more impoverished than my bank account. Any hope I had of flying under the radar in this outfit dies the moment I step outside.

An old man with thick eyebrows and no sense of boundaries wolf-whistles. I lift my chin and try to channel Kardashian energy. "I'm confident. I am cool. I am—oof!"

I'm crashing into a line of rental bikes. Just when I thought it couldn't get worse, three of them fall noisily to the ground.

"Sorry," I say to the teen who comes to help.

"You want bike?"

"Absolutely not," I say—just as I spot Ben across the piazza.

He's seated at a café table with a man who at first glance I thought was Rook. But moving around the bikes, I get a better look. And it's not Ramirez's lawyer. This man is tall. Expensive looking. Mafia vibes. His hair is slicked back, his suit sharp, and those eyes? Cold. Calculating. And tracking the movement around him like he's watching for someone.

I inch toward a rack of masks strung up in front of a gift shop and duck behind it. My heart's thudding so loud I worry he'll hear it across the street. Ben turns his head.

"Signora?" I spin and face the shop owner, a man with a bright smile and wearing a bright red Ferrari shirt. He waves a feathered mask at my face. "Maschera?"

"Uh, no, grazie."

"It's okay." The owner picks up another mask with bright ribbons and lace. "You try?"

Ben's back to speaking to the man, but I don't want to take a chance of him catching me watching him. So I take the mask from the store owner.

"Okay," I say, slipping it over my face.

From behind the mask, I take a couple of photos with my phone, trying to zoom in as much as I can, and send them to Athena. I continue to observe Ben and the man talking. They're looking at papers, but I'm too far away to see anything.

Is Ben really financing money for criminals? I don't *want* to believe it. But it's hard not to let my imagination put the pieces together.

My phone pings with a message from Athena.

Alessandro Moretti. President of Italia Sovereign Bank. Suspected ties to multiple criminal organizations.

I knew he was mafia. My smug satisfaction at being right is short-lived. This isn't some random person meeting with a mafia banker—it's Ben.

Get as much information as you can.

Ben and Moretti stand. A sleek black car pulls up. Another man gets out and shakes Ben's hand. Who's that? I lower the mask, setting it back on the rack, and then slip into the crowd. It's much thicker now, the pre-festival events filling the streets with vendors and tourists. I try to push my way through, but before I can get a good look or take another photo, the car is gone.

"Bike?" the teen from earlier asks again, holding out a neon pink number with a basket.

I'm about to tell him no when I see the car with Ben inside stopped by a parade. Maybe I'm not too late. I shove a crumple of euros into the boy's hand and hop on the bike. He says something in Italian as he hands me a helmet, but I'm already pedaling after the car.

Except this isn't a normal bike.

"What the—" It surges forward with power. I look down at the black box. A motor?

I'm weaving through people, the wind slapping my cheeks, the handlebars shaking in my sweaty grip. How do I slow this thing down? I dare a quick glance at the handles and there's not one of those squeezie brake things.

A horn blasts and I look up in time to narrowly miss a pedestrian who gives me a hand gesture I can understand. I try to slow down, stop pedaling, drag my feet on the pavement, but it's no use. The car turns. I turn. The alleyway narrows. Another car nearly clips me as it cuts me off.

There's traffic, and like a true Italian, I navigate through the tight space between cars until I'm just close enough to look inside the windows. When I do, I meet the confused looks of an older man and his wife.

I've lost him. Great.

I pedal back toward what I *hope* is the square, only to realize every street here looks the same. The winding alleys, the cobblestones, the charming shutters and balconies—it's a maze disguised as a postcard.

Panic nudges me to pedal harder. Huge mistake. This thing launches like it's in a race. I'm rocketing downhill, the square up ahead, tourists scattering as I blow past.

"Brakes. Brakes. Brakes." I press everything—pedals, grips, prayer.

Finally, there's a clearing ahead. But I'm still going too fast. The closer I get to it, the more people begin waving at me, warning me to slow down. All I can do is grit my teeth and pretend like I'm in control. A few people yell. I yell back, "Sorry!"

I round the curve just in time to see the cart. Up. Close. And personal.

I slam into it, crashing into a pile of flowers, fruit, and . . . is that a fish? A bucket of water tips, soaking me from head to toe.

People rush over. I sit up slowly. There's more Italian I can't understand. And the absolute humility of sitting in a puddle of water with lettuce in my hair and tomato stains on my tracksuit, looking like a Mediterranean salad.

CHAPTER 16

Ben

Lagoverde, Italy
Friday morning

I'm elbowing through the crowd to get closer to the commotion, and when I do, my heart nearly crashes through my rib cage. *Cybil.* "Mi scusi, mi scusi."

She's sitting on the street, surrounded by bruised produce and stunned pedestrians. She blinks up at me like I dropped out of the sky.

"B—"

"Are you hurt?" I cut her off, dropping to my knees. Her hair's a mess, tomato smeared on her shirt, cheeks pink with embarrassment. I reach out, fingers brushing her leg to check for injury, but she swats my hand away.

"Does it hurt anywhere?" I press. "Head? Limbs? Cracked ego?"

"Besides my pride?" she mutters, glancing around at the gawkers before narrowing her eyes on me. "What are you doing here?"

Her tone is sharp enough to draw blood. But I don't answer—because I can't. Because the real reason involves the man who was following me. I'd spotted him watching us during the meeting. I needed to know who he was, so I declined Moretti's offer to join him and Marcello Vieri for lunch and circled back to the last place I saw the man.

I couldn't find him and was on my way back to the villa. Then I heard the scream. The crash. Now I'm here, facing Cybil's misdirected agitation.

"Cybil," I say, steady and low, "I need you to hear me. Does anything feel broken?"

Before she can answer, the produce vendor storms over, Italian flying fast and furious. His precious tomatoes didn't survive her crash landing. I stand, pull out my wallet, and negotiate a peace treaty with euros.

"Puoi schiantarti e pagarmi," he grumbles, counting the bills.

The crowd trickles away. Cybil's already back on her feet, shouldering her purse and giving me the full view of her outfit. The bright blue tracksuit is giving nineties rapper vibes, but the way she's eyeballing me, I know to keep that to myself.

"Just . . ." She exhales, shoulders sagging. "Don't."

I grab the bike. "I wasn't going to say anything."

"Your face speaks without words, *Craig*." She looks herself over. "All I need is mozzarella and I'd be a caprese salad."

My alias sounds wrong coming out of her mouth, and I suddenly hate hearing her say it. Especially after she almost said my real name. "I like caprese salad."

She lifts her gaze to mine, and instead of annoyance, I catch something heavier—defeat. "Are you sure you're okay?"

"I'm fine." She takes the bike from me. "The kid didn't mention this stupid bike has no brakes."

I eye the handlebars, then reach over and twist the grips backward. "They're right here."

"Great." She steers it toward the sidewalk. "But I won't be riding again."

I fall in step beside her. She stops.

"You don't have to follow me."

"I'm not." I tip my chin toward the main road. "I'm heading back to the villa. Same direction. You?"

Her sigh is all the answer I need. We walk in silence until we hit the piazza. Pedestrian traffic squeezes us to the edge. I scan for the man I saw earlier, but he's nowhere in sight.

Then I glance at Cybil.

She's tugging at her tomato-stained jacket, head ducked to avoid the curious looks. I've seen this posture before—shoulders curled in like she's trying to disappear. She wore that same look the first summer I met her at Rex's ranch. Showed up in jeans too short and shoes with holes.

It wasn't hard to spot poverty in Cypress Creek, but it wasn't the worn clothes that burned the memory into my brain. It was the way she wore the abandonment. That and the black eye she gave me when I looked at her with pity.

I'm not looking for another.

I scan the street. Spot what I need.

"Will you do me a favor?"

Cybil pauses, eyeing me with suspicion. "What?"

"Wait here. Just one minute. Please?"

"Why?"

I sigh. "Can't you just trust me, woman?"

Her brows lift. "I don't know, *Craig*. Can I?"

I step close. The move catches her by surprise, and I can see she wants to step back, put space between us, but she doesn't move. Just glares.

I lean in, close enough to feel her breath catch. "Keep saying my name like *that* and you're going to blow my cover." She shivers and I pretend I don't feel it straight to my chest. Pretend my pulse isn't suddenly pounding in my ears. I reach up, pluck a piece of lettuce from her hair, and twirl it between my fingers. "One minute. Don't move."

I jog across the street to a clothing store. A quick conversation with the clerk and I'm back out, scanning for her. She's still here. Tucked in the shade of an alleyway. *She stayed.*

But my smile vanishes when I spot him. Same guy from earlier. I *am* being followed. *Except . . .*

Slowing my pace, I weave through the congested sidewalks, keeping the man in my peripheral vision. And that's when I notice—he's not watching me. He's watching her. Cybil.

My stomach knots. Ramirez doesn't trust anyone. I expect to be watched. Followed. It's why I cut off all connection with family and friends outside of our FBI office for the last eighteen months. But Cybil? She's not supposed to be a part of this. Not really. Not like this.

I waste no time jogging back to meet her. "Thanks for waiting." I lift the bike. "What do you say we ride this back to the villa?"

Cybil gapes at me. "Are you crazy? I nearly died."

"That's because you didn't know how to drive it. I do." I glance toward the man still watching. Every second she hesitates makes me more anxious to get her off the streets. "Don't you have a meeting to get ready for?"

Resignation pinches her brows together and she groans. "Fine."

I snap a quick selfie, ignoring her protests, and hope Ruby can ID the guy in the background as I shove the phone in my pocket.

"Hold tight," I say over my shoulder.

Her hands hover around the seat, clearly searching for something to hold on to that doesn't involve touching me. With a sigh, I grab her hands and wrap them firmly around my waist.

I push the pedal, bringing the engine to life, and pull into traffic. Her grip tightens. It's familiar and new all at once, and as I leave the man behind us, I'm forced to remind myself that this can't mean anything.

A few hours later, the sun slants low in the sky, casting long shadows across the villa's white oak floors as I finish buttoning my shirt. I haven't seen Cybil since we got back to the villa. She jumped off the bike and bolted inside before I even had a chance to turn it off.

The concierge handled returning the bike to the vendor, leaving me with nothing but the echo of her arms still wrapped around me. That memory had me distracted through my next meeting with a compliance officer, a guy willing to fast-track the shell companies Ramirez wants, no questions asked.

And now I'm suiting up for round two with Ramirez and Rook. This is my shot to deploy the air-drop device. If I can get Ramirez to open the embedded file, we'll find what we need to shut this whole thing down. And maybe, just maybe, I'll figure out a way to get Cybil back in my arms without risking her life or mine.

There's a knock at my door, and I check my reflection before opening it.

Cybil stands there, fuming. "Did you do this?"

I blink. "What?"

"This." She gestures at the black dress she's wearing. She looks incredible. "It was delivered to my room after we got back to the villa."

"Was it?"

She grabs my shirt and hauls me down the hall to the veranda like I'm a misbehaving child, then checks over both shoulders before turning on me. "Did you buy this dress for me?"

My face must give me away.

"I don't need your pity," she snaps, poking my chest.

I gently take her hand. "I remember your right hook, Billy."

"Don't call me that." She snatches her hand back, looking around. "Someone could hear you."

She's right. I know. But that nickname—there's an intimacy in it that makes the risk worth it. Almost.

No ID on the man. No connection to Ramirez.

If anything could keep my focus off Cybil's touch, it's the text message from Ruby about the picture I sent her. If he's American, he should've popped up in the system. So who is he? Ruby is going to run him through Interpol next.

Until I have an answer, I need to make sure anything that happens between me and Cybil is professional. At least to anyone watching . . .

I shrug. "It's nothing."

A fiery spark lights her eyes. "It's expensive."

"It's a gift."

She stands there, hair clipped back, a breeze catching the faint scent of her perfume. Her makeup is light, but she doesn't need much. Her natural beauty always had a way of driving my pulse crazy—especially when she's staring me down.

"An expensive gift," she says.

"I was trying to help," I say, shrugging like I didn't put way too much thought into a black dress I picked out in under ninety seconds. "If it makes you feel better, you can pay me back."

She gives me a long, flat look. "Says the guy who probably keeps a Swiss bank account in his sock drawer."

"You know," I say, fighting a grin, "if the dress hadn't worked out, you could've rocked that blue tracksuit at your meeting. It had a real 'I just wrestled a produce truck' vibe."

Cybil's face goes completely blank. "If you ever bring up that tracksuit again, I will end you."

I smirk. "Is that a threat or a promise?"

"This is Italy, Craig. They don't just make pasta from scratch. They make problems disappear."

The smile freezes on my face.

I think she's joking.

Probably.

Maybe.

She walks to the railing, her heels clicking with purpose. The sun throws a soft gold across the villa's balcony, and for a second, it's almost peaceful. Instinct and years of training tell me the best time to gather intel is when someone's guard is down.

"So," I say casually, leaning beside her, "how'd your meetings go?"

"Fine," she says with all the enthusiasm of a TSA agent confirming I'm not smuggling an extra ounce of liquid in my carry-on.

"You done for the day?"

"One more." She glances sideways, eyes cool. "And you? Meeting another billionaire who believes paying taxes is a suggestion?"

I force a smile, but it doesn't reach. I should be relieved. It means she's bought the cover. That I've done my job—convinced her I'm exactly who I say I am. But it still lands like a gut punch. The way she's looking at me like I'm the kind of man she's spent her life avoiding.

"I'm just doing the job I was hired to do," I say quietly.

She lifts a shoulder. "Whatever helps you sleep at night, Craig."

My jaw tightens. I should let it go. But I don't. "You mean the same kind of men as your boss?"

That gets her attention. Her head turns sharply. For a beat, neither of us says anything. The silence between us is thin, stretched taut.

Then she smiles—a dangerous, diplomatic thing. "Meet any interesting people in town today?"

"Just an old friend," I say, letting it land.

She narrows her eyes slightly, then smirks. "Oh? Must've made quite an impression—you're still alive."

"Day's not over and she did just threaten to have me erased from the Italian countryside."

"I stand by that."

We fall quiet for a beat, and I wonder if she feels it too—that old zing, the one that used to spark between us like a live wire when we were too young to know what to do with it. I try not to stare, but something in the curve of her mouth or the way she shifts her weight makes me think she remembers too.

A pair of doves coos somewhere overhead. Music and chatter drift up from the piazza. She exhales slowly, her fingers absently spinning the gold band on her thumb.

"Thank you," she says softly.

"You don't have to—"

"Please." She cuts me off with a glance. "Just let me."

I do because something in her voice tells me this isn't just about the dress.

"After my dad's accident," she begins, her tone measured, "his company paid my mom a settlement. I don't know how much exactly. But

I overheard my aunt and uncle talking once . . . said it should've been enough to take care of us."

She's still spinning the ring. The gold flashes in the sunlight like it wants to say more than she does.

"My mom trusted this woman—Celeste Harlowe. Called herself a financial advisor. Told my mom the best way to protect the money, to make it last forever, was to invest it. Said we'd never have to worry again."

I already know where this is going. My stomach knots anyway.

"She disappeared," Cybil says, voice flat now. "Took everything. Every last cent. It was a scam. *She* was a scam."

She turns to me then, not angry, just matter-of-fact. "Do you know what people with money have that people without money don't?"

I hold her gaze, already bracing for the answer.

"Security. Stability. A permanent address that anchors them in an unpredictable world."

And just like that, I see her—really see her. Not just the beautiful woman in the black dress. Not the assistant with a sharp mouth and a sharper mind. But the girl who showed up every summer, shoulders pulled in like armor.

I never knew what to say back then. I still don't.

"Is that why you work so hard for Mr. Edmond?"

Her throat bobs as she swallows. She meets my eyes for a second, then looks away toward the lake. "Working for Mr. Edmond allows me to make sure I'm never taken advantage of again."

There's a bite in her voice. An edge that wasn't there a second ago. And I hate that it's real. That someone hurt her family like that. That my alias is a reminder of the pain.

I open my mouth to say something, but a throat clears behind us, and I turn.

Edmond stands a few feet away. His eyes land on me, sharp and assessing, before softening when they shift to Cybil.

"Are you ready, Cybil?"

She nods and follows him back into the villa without another word.

I stay where I am, gripping the balcony railing, frustrated. Ruby warned me to be careful. To keep my distance. Stick to the mission. But it's not just my mission anymore. If we take Ramirez down, and if Edmond's part of it—even on the fringe—we take him down too.

Cybil will lose everything. Again. And this time, I'll be the one responsible for breaking her.

CHAPTER 17

Cybil

Lagoverde, Italy
Friday, late afternoon

"There will be no delays!"

Ramirez's voice slices through the tension that's been building since the start of the meeting. I tighten my grip on the pen in my hand and force myself to stay still as he picks up a gold letter opener and drives the tip into the desk he's sitting behind.

Across from him sits a man named Giancarlo. His English is clipped and a little broken, but the gist of his explanation is clear—there's been a delay in the build-out of a new manufacturing facility.

It feels like everyone in the room is holding their breath.

Or maybe it's just me?

I'm still a little shaken from my conversation with Ben on the veranda. The dress, simple but beautiful, and perfectly my size, might not have seemed like a big deal to him, but to me it is more than *just a gift*.

Ben doesn't owe me kindness. He doesn't owe me anything. Not after the words I overheard all those years ago—words that shaped the very foundation of insecurities I apparently still carry.

I run my fingers across the hem of the fabric—so different from the blue monstrosity of the tracksuit currently crumpled in a sad heap on my bathroom floor. This dress feels . . . safe.

So safe, in fact, I told Ben about my dad. About Celeste Harlowe. Things I never talk about. But the words just slipped out like some kind of accidental confession.

"We have an agreement," Ramirez says, his voice snapping me back to the moment. "And there are consequences I'd hate to enforce if the terms of our contract aren't met." He twirls the letter opener between his fingers. "I hear the quality assurance protocols in Italy aren't as thorough as they are in America. If the terms of that agreement aren't met"—his gaze hardens on Giancarlo—"accidents happen here, yes?"

My pulse quickens. That doesn't sound like business. That sounds like a threat. Giancarlo doesn't flinch. He's built like a man who carries bricks for fun—broad, solid, and definitely not the kind of guy who backs down easily. His hands look like they've been used to pour concrete—or break jaws.

His jaw twitches as he gives a shallow nod.

"We'd hate to see that, right?" Ramirez smirks, eyes flicking to Sebastian and then Mr. Edmond.

Sebastian shifts in his seat, glancing at his dad. Mr. Edmond stays stoic, but there's a flicker of unease in his eyes that makes me nervous. As long as I've worked for Earl Edmond, he's embodied power, wealth, and control. I've seen him bulldoze billionaires without smudging his cuff links. But since this meeting started, that confidence has been . . . diluted. Like someone swapped his espresso with weak decaf.

Before we left Dallas, I caught wind of the issue that cut Edmond's meeting with Ramirez short at the museum. An issue with one of Edmond's longtime suppliers in Italy—a guy named Marcello. Apparently, shipments of a specialized concrete additive stopped without warning. Ramirez blamed port delays. But after our meeting this afternoon, Edmond's not buying it.

Now Giancarlo's the one in the hot seat. He's Edmond's trusted project manager in Europe, but now it looks like Ramirez has commandeered him, the way a mafia boss might borrow your favorite contractor—with threats and a smile.

Mr. Ramirez stabs the letter opener into the desk, and I flinch. His gaze darts to me, an icy smile playing on his lips. I straighten in my chair, refusing to cower even as a chill skirts across my skin.

"If Marcello needs a reminder how important this deal is, I'll make sure the message is loud enough every man from here to Rome will hear it."

Giancarlo gives another tight nod, and with a flick of Ramirez's fingers, he's dismissed. *Yeah, I'm pretty sure Marcello's getting a horse head in his bed.*

I shudder at the visual. This is *not* how I imagined the meeting going. But I should've known it wouldn't involve quick notes and cappuccinos the second Ramirez instructed us to leave our cell phones and laptops in our rooms. Sebastian looked ready to argue, but Mr. Edmond placed a hand on his arm and gave the slightest shake of his head. That was enough. We followed orders.

Maybe Ramirez made the request to protect the deal's confidentiality—but my gut says otherwise. This smells like suspicion. So when he handed me a pen and paper, asking if I needed to take notes, I smiled and accepted out of courtesy . . . then didn't write down a single word. I don't trust him not to cross-reference my bullet points with a bullet.

If I'm passing anything along to Athena, it'll be from my memory. So far, what I've got is shaky at best: Something called Aurelite-X is being imported into Italy for manufacturing. Of what? No clue. The conversation kept switching between English and Italian like a cursed Duolingo challenge. Maybe that's the point—keep everyone off balance. Keep us guessing.

Ramirez rises from his seat and buttons his suit jacket. The meeting is over and I release the breath I've been holding.

I wait until Mr. Edmond and Sebastian stand before inching toward the table where the paperwork sits. If I can get a glimpse of what's on it, just one detail, it might be enough to satisfy Athena. But Ramirez sweeps the documents into a folder and locks it in the desk.

"And everything is set for the transfer of funds?" Sebastian asks, voice light but a little too eager.

Mr. Edmond shoots him a look—less reprimand, more resignation.

Ramirez claps Sebastian on the shoulder like they're old friends, and Mr. Edmond's sharp gaze tells me he doesn't like it. "Money is the last thing you need to worry about. Craig Miller will ensure every dollar is accounted for and protected. All one billion of them."

One billion dollars.

My stomach drops. What exactly is Craig *freaking* Miller going to do to protect that kind of money? For the last forty-eight hours, I've been slowly rebuilding a version of him in my mind—piecing together the boy I used to know with the man who ordered me a dress so I wouldn't feel humiliated. The guy I just confided in about my dad and why I'd never let anyone make me feel powerless again.

And now? He's working for a man who just threatened someone with a smile and might be moving blood money through this deal.

Athena was right. I need to stop romanticizing him and remember who Ben's working for—and why I'm here.

Ramirez ushers us out of the office. "The villa staff has prepared a beautiful meal for our final evening here. Let's go and enjoy it."

Yeah, because nothing says "Bon appétit" like veiled threats.

I glance back at the desk, pulse quickening. I don't know what Aurelite-X is or what kind of deal Mr. Edmond and Sebastian signed on to, but I know Athena's willing to pay. And tonight I'm going to get into that locked desk.

I leave my room with my phone and key pick set stashed in my clutch. Just in case the perfect opportunity comes for me to sneak into Ramirez's office.

The scent of garlic and herbs drifts from the kitchen, curling through the villa's ancient halls and reminding me I haven't eaten since my sad excuse for breakfast hours ago. My stomach growls in anticipation as I follow the corridor toward the dining room.

I turn the corner, then stop.

Ben's voice. It's faint but unmistakable, coming from a small room just off the hallway. The door is mostly closed—but not all the way.

"If it has to be done tonight, I'll handle it," Ben says, his tone calm.

"I don't want any loose ends," Ramirez replies, and there's a bite to his words. "It's not personal. It's just damage control."

"Understood," Ben says, his voice lower. Measured. "I've never let a liability interfere with a deal. No matter who it involves."

The words land like a punch to the chest. A liability? What liability? Who?

Marcello? It has to be Marcello, right? Something about Ben's tone sends a shiver down my spine. Calm. Authoritative. But there's an edge to it—too confident, too practiced. Like he's not just familiar with Ramirez's messes . . . he's cleaned them up before.

This is not the boy I remember. Or the man who bought me a dress like he still knew who I was. In this moment, with the low timbre of his voice threading through the door and the warning in Ramirez's tone still hanging in the air—I'm not so sure of anything.

I back up a step, careful not to make a sound, heart pounding against my ribs like it's sending me Morse code to get the heck out of here. But I don't. I stay. No, I take a step closer, barely breathing, trying to make out more—just one more word, one more breadcrumb. But it's silent.

Not the natural kind. The unnatural kind that only happens when you're eavesdropping and suddenly remember that people eventually stop talking and walk out of rooms. A chair scrapes, then I hear steps and the click of a door handle. Panic surges, sending my brain into full alert. They're coming out. I spin on my heel, heart launching into my throat as I consider which is more suspicious—hiding in a closet or running.

"Cybil?"

I jump so hard I nearly knock over the decorative vase behind me. Sebastian stands a few feet away, looking at me like I've grown a second head.

"You okay?"

"Nothing!" I say way too quickly, and he frowns. "I mean—"

The door behind me opens. Ramirez steps out first, followed by Rook and Ben. Ben's gaze locks on mine instantly, and something in his expression flickers—surprise? Concern? Mild murderous intent?

I slip my hand around Sebastian's arm. "I was just on my way to find you for dinner."

Sebastian glances between me and the room behind me, then gives me a weird little nod like he's decided just to go with it. Bless him.

Ben, on the other hand, gives me a dark look. Jealousy? The thought of that should not delight me the way it does as I watch him walk away.

Ramirez's eyes narrow slightly, then drift to Sebastian. "We'll see you both at dinner."

And with that, they walk past us. Rook gives me a lingering look that makes my skin crawl. Ben's gaze lingers too—but there's something else in his eyes. Something I can't afford to trust right now.

I smile wider. This is fine. "Should we go?"

Sebastian begins to lead me away when I spot someone standing at the back of the hallway. The same man from last night when Ben and I arrived at the villa.

"Who's that?" I ask Sebastian quietly.

He glances over, then shrugs. "Ramirez's security."

"Security? He looks like a guy who buried the last person who called him security."

Sebastian snorts. "Yeah, well. Don't make eye contact."

It's moments like this when Sebastian gives off an older-brother energy—equal parts protectiveness and smart-aleck commentary—that I almost forget he's also up to his neck in this mess. I don't know how much he's in on, but I know he's not clueless.

The dining room exudes a kind of rustic elegance that fits the picturesque countryside stretching beyond the open arched windows. We're seated around a stunning white oak table set with fine china, crystal glassware, and a centerpiece overflowing with fresh-cut roses, lilies, and sprigs of lavender. Ramirez and Mr. Edmond take their places at opposite ends of the table, while Ben and Jimmy Rook sit directly across from me and Sebastian. The only one missing is the creepy guy from the hallway, and I'm afraid I'm too hungry to be concerned, but a part of me wonders if he's on his way to visit Marcello.

Ben catches my eye, holding my gaze just long enough to make me wonder if he knows I overheard him. Then he smiles. Easy. Charming.

I break eye contact when the chef arrives. He introduces the menu in elegant Italian, then switches to English with a reverent grin. The first course is bruschetta with heirloom tomatoes and basil oil, followed by hand-rolled pasta in a truffle cream sauce, veal osso buco with gremolata, and wine pairings that probably cost more than my car.

"And for dessert," he announces, practically glowing, "a decadent chocolate hazelnut torte with Italian cream."

Ben doesn't miss a beat. "I'll take hers."

I blink. "Excuse me?"

"You don't like chocolate, right?"

I narrow my eyes at his smug face. "Right."

Sebastian chokes on his wine. "You don't hate—"

I stomp on his toe under the table.

He yelps. "What the heck, Cy—"

"I'll be skipping dessert tonight, thank you," I say through gritted teeth, not missing the look Ben sends me.

Dinner service starts immediately, and while the bruschetta is fresh and bursting with flavor, the table conversation is as stale as expired crackers. You'd think, considering someone named Marcello might be eating his next meal with a knife in his back, there'd be a little more spark.

But maybe that's just the anxiety still twisting my stomach into knots. Ramirez's threat plays on a loop in my head—right alongside his oh-so-casual assurance that Craig Miller would handle the billion-dollar deal. And Mr. Edmond? He's been off all night. Odd behavior for someone about to be a billion dollars wealthier.

I keep stealing glances at Ben, sharp in his tailored suit, a single curl falling over his forehead like it's been placed there for the sole purpose of screwing with my focus. Who *is* Bennett Bradley now? The man who brushes shoulders with criminals like it's no big deal. Is that just part of his job description?

"Did you enjoy your time in town, Cybil?" Mr. Edmond asks.

My cheeks warm. "It was . . . eventful," I say, reaching for my wine like it might erase the memory of this morning's crash landing into a veggie cart. "I wish I had more time to explore."

"You should rent a bike," Ben says smoothly.

My gaze snaps to him. He's hiding a smirk behind his water glass.

"Bikes aren't really my thing," I say through a tight smile. "Too unpredictable."

Ben sets down his glass. The gleam is unmistakable—and infuriating. "Shopping more predictable? I heard blue tracksuits are in style."

I want to stab him. Just a little. Nothing fatal. Maybe something in the arm. But I settle for stabbing my pasta instead. I've already given up chocolate—he's not worth giving up carbs for too. *Maybe if it were brussels sprouts.* The veal arrives next, tender and rich, but I'm too busy skewering Ben in my head to appreciate it.

"I like your dress," Mr. Edmond says, tossing me a kind smile. "You look lovely tonight."

"Much better choice than a tracksuit," Sebastian adds, throwing Ben a look.

Ben's eyes remain on me. "I agree."

His voice is low, steady, and aimed like a dart to my sternum. I pretend to be fascinated by my plate, but not before I catch the slow curve of his smile. My pulse thuds in my ears, and I force myself to breathe. Why is it so easy for him to rattle me? This—whatever this is—has to stop before someone notices.

Someone like Ramirez.

I glance down the table to find him watching us. Not smiling. Not speaking. Just watching.

"So, Cybil . . ." Ramirez says, swirling his wine. "What's your background? How long have you been working as Earl's assistant?"

"Executive assistant," Mr. Edmond corrects him smoothly. "But not for long, right, Cybil? One day I hope to promote her to in-house counsel."

Ben's eyes cut to me, brows lifting. "You're a lawyer?"

"Not yet." I force a smile, hating the flush I can feel rising. "I'm studying for the LSATs and working to save money for law school."

Ben's watching me. And for one dizzying second, he looks . . . impressed?

"Cybil here is a rare gem," Mr. Edmond adds, lifting his glass. "Understands the value of hard work. Refuses to accept help—even though she's an asset to me and my company."

"My father would be lost without her," Sebastian says deadpan. "Isn't that right, Dad?"

Mr. Edmond ignores him. I wish I could ignore the guilt crawling under my skin. Because he's not wrong. I *have* worked hard. Paying back loans. Taking care of my mom. Pushing myself every day to outrun the chaos I was born into. But I'm also sitting at a table with a man who has no idea I'm spying on him. Who thinks I'm loyal. Who doesn't know I've been feeding information to a private agency in exchange for money I desperately need.

I glance away and toy with the ring on my thumb, a subtle reminder of what I need to do—find an excuse to get away from here and into that office.

I just need a little distraction. The servers remove our empty plates and bring out the chocolate dessert that looks so decadent it might be worth killing for. I glare at Ben. This is his fault.

Unfortunately, it's Sebastian who's going to take the brunt of my frustration. He lifts his glass of wine, and before I can talk myself out of it, I "accidentally" bump his elbow with the grace of a toddler learning to use a spoon.

The timing is chef's kiss—his arm jerks, and a glorious wave of red wine arcs straight into my lap. Silverware clatters as I shove back from the table with an exaggerated gasp. Everyone is watching me, and even though I'm the one who orchestrated the mayhem, heat creeps up my neck.

"What was that, Cybil?" Sebastian stares at me, holding out a napkin like it might rescue my dignity. "Why'd you hit me?"

"I was reaching for the uh . . . knife." I dab at my lap, but there's really no point. Ten out of ten for spectacle, zero for subtlety. "I should clean this up," I say, already pushing back my chair.

"There's a restroom around the corner," a server offers.

"Perfect, thank you." I hand him the wine-soaked napkin and grab my clutch. "If you will excuse me."

I don't wait for permission and hurry out of the dining room like I can't outrun my embarrassment fast enough. Once I round the corner, I pause. Wait. Listen. Conversation in the dining room resumes, forks clink, and I'm mad all over again about missing out on that dessert.

There's laughter—probably at my expense. Good. Let them. If they're too busy enjoying my clumsiness, that means I can do what I need to do.

I walk past the restroom and head straight for the office. One quick look over my shoulder and I try the doorknob. Unlocked.

I slip inside. The office is quiet and dark, save for moonlight slipping through the French doors. It's almost pretty—if I weren't about to commit corporate espionage in a merlot-soaked dress.

At the desk, I check the drawer. Still locked. I remove the key pick set from my clutch. A chill skitters over my skin as Ramirez's voice echoes in my head. *"Accidents happen here, yes?"*

I can do this. I *will* do this. My fingers move to my thumb out of habit and freeze. The ring's gone. My heart seizes until I remember I moved it after my little veggie-cart crashing incident. Right thumb to left thumb. I slide it back where it belongs. It's still loose, but the weight of it on my right thumb steadies me. I can do this.

And no one needs to wake up with a horse head in their bed—not even Marcello. Hopefully.

With quickness, I pop the lock on the drawer and quietly slide it open. There it is. The folder. I pull out my phone and flip it open, spreading the manufacturing plans across the desk. Everything's in Italian except for a few diagrams that might as well be IKEA instructions.

I start snapping photos. One page. Two. I'm halfway through when—

Footsteps. Heavy ones. Someone's coming.

My gaze flicks down to the papers on the desk and blood rushes to my ears. If I'm caught in here, there's no excuse Ramirez will buy that doesn't end with me in a pair of cement boots at the bottom of the Lagoverde lake. *Does Prada make a cement boot for their mobster clients?*

I freeze, heart racing as a shadow blocks the light under the door. Someone's coming in.

Nope. Nope, nope, nope—

I scoop up the papers, shove them into the folder, and close the drawer—except I don't, because I catch my thumb in it. Pain rockets up my hand. Tears spring to my eyes—pain? fear? Probably both—but I bite down on a scream.

I stumble toward the French doors that open onto a private veranda overlooking the manicured lawn and sparkling pool—one story up and absolutely not designed for emergency escapes. I wrench open the door, slip outside, and reach back to close it when—

Clink.

No.

My ring. My dad's ring. It slides off my thumb, hits the floor, and disappears into the dark. I drop to my knees, but it's useless. I can't see a thing, and I don't have time.

The office door creaks open.

I don't have a choice.

My heart shatters as I leave the ring behind.

CHAPTER 18

Ben

Lagoverde, Italy
Friday night

"Close the door," Rook says as he leads me into a wood-paneled office. He heads straight for the decanter on the sideboard. "Drink?"

The door closes with a soft click that sounds a lot more final than it should. Halfway through my dessert, I caught Ramirez sending a look to Rook, and suddenly I was asked to follow him here. A breeze wafts in from the cracked French door. The scent of cypress and old stone mixes with something far more familiar—tension. It's practically baked into the walls.

"I prefer the chocolate torte," I answer as Rook gestures for me to sit as he pours himself a splash of something amber. I sit in the leather chair across from the desk. "Is there a problem?"

Rook sniffs his drink before taking a sip, then nods. "You had a chance to review Edmond's holdings?"

I keep my expression neutral. Seth Jackson is the one who's been reviewing Edmond's account and feeding me the script I need to sell that I know what I'm talking about. "Some. Why?"

"You find anything . . . concerning?"

Not unless Seth missed something. A quick analysis showed Edmond cleaning house with his finances. Liquidating assets. I shrug, offering a tidbit of intel Seth has fed me. "Some of his shell structures are outdated, but nothing that would jeopardize a transfer." I pause, watching him. "Is there something I should be concerned about?"

Rook swirls his glass like it might hold answers. "I think there's a chance Earl is second-guessing the deal. Maybe looking for a way out. The last couple of years he hasn't been the same. I thought Sebastian might be enough to keep him focused, but it seems like he might have his own agenda—and that's making Lorenzo nervous."

I nod slowly. That tracks. Ramirez was wired tighter than a coiled spring earlier. Whatever happened with Edmond and Giancarlo had him distracted. Rattled. Paranoid. When I tried to show him the embedded files, he barely let me get past the login screen before brushing me off. Ending the only window I had to access his accounts. Strike two.

"Lorenzo won't tolerate anyone compromising the deal, which is why he wants to make sure we have a backup plan. In case any unforeseen changes happen with the deal."

Unforeseen changes? Backup plan? In the criminal dictionary, those words are synonymous with *start digging and don't ask questions.*

Before I can ask questions, I catch a flicker of movement out on the veranda. Just a rustle between trees, a shadow slipping past moonlight. Maybe it's nothing. Maybe it's paranoia. Or maybe it's the growing dread twisting in my gut that everything about tonight—about this trip—is off.

"In Lorenzo's line of work, he believes it's best practice to eliminate issues before they become issues, wouldn't you agree?"

I immediately think of Danny Morales and grind my molars. This is why I have to play my part, complete the mission, so I can eliminate the real issue—Ramirez. "Sure."

"We're wondering if someone close to Earl Edmond might have insight into his next move."

I don't like where this is going.

He leans forward. "It seems like Earl really respects his assistant. Almost admirably."

Every muscle in my body tenses, but I don't say a thing.

"And you two seem to have a . . . connection."

My stomach drops, blood running cold. I've been careless. I've allowed old memories and renewed feelings to blur the lines, and it may have just compromised everything—including Cybil's life.

I school my features into something neutral. "I grow my network to grow the bottom line. That's not a connection. It's a calculation."

Rook studies me like he's trying to weigh the truth of my words. He shrugs a shoulder. "Call it what you like, but we want you to find out what she knows. What Earl's planning. If he's out—or working some kind of side deal. We don't need surprises."

My spine straightens. "You want me to dig."

"Casually," Rook says. "Friendly. See what you can find out. We need to know if Edmond's planning to cut Lorenzo out. Or sell access to someone else."

And put Cybil dead center in Ramirez's crosshairs.

Every part of me wants to tell him to back off. But I can't. Not without blowing my cover. But is it possible that Ramirez's suspicion of Edmond might be the very thing that saves Cybil? If Edmond's out of the deal, so is Cybil's proximity to any potential blowout.

I force a thoughtful frown. "If Earl Edmond is the variable, why not just exclude him from the deal?"

"We still need him—for now. His logistics teams have federal clearances in three key regions. And it's his suppliers that will keep alarms silent as product moves across the border."

The hair on the back of my neck stands up. Operation Shadow Broker has been about securing the evidence needed to put Ramirez behind bars for RICO charges. The details—vague as they are—from Rook are the kind of evidence we can use against him. But it's not enough. I need more.

I hesitate. Careful of what I say next. "If Edmond really is pulling away, if he becomes a liability to Ramirez, that makes him a risk—to my clients and their assets. It's my job to protect them, and I won't compromise my reputation."

That catches Rook off guard. His glass stills in his hand. "You're walking away?"

"I'm offering a solution," I say, leaning in. "Right now, Edmond has exclusivity to the deal, which gives him leverage. The kind, as you said, that's making Ramirez nervous." I push gently. "What if you sideline Edmond? I've got clients with land along the Gulf, private security clearances, and no sentimental ties to any of this. They don't ask questions—they just move product. If you're looking for reliability without the risk, maybe it's time to reevaluate your partnership. Bring in outside investors. Remove Edmond's exclusivity and dictate the price, the players, the pace—you have all the leverage."

Rook tilts his head, considering. It's no accident I'm pitching this to him first. Ramirez needs ego stroking and theatrics. But Rook? He's the gatekeeper. If I can sell the plan to him, he'll carry it straight to Ramirez—and take credit for it, which only sweetens the deal.

His gaze sharpens. "Would this affect the accounts?"

"Absolutely," I lie smoothly. "In a good way. You open things up, the valuation increases. You set the price. You control everything."

He leans back, letting that sink in.

Just then, the breeze shifts—and the French door creaks open. Rook stands and walks toward the door, peering out onto the dark veranda. As he steps away from the desk, I spot something glinting on the floor.

A glimmer of gold catches the moonlight. I walk to the foot of the desk and crouch down. My stomach drops. A ring. *Her* ring. Cybil's.

The one she never takes off. Wore it on a chain when we were kids, keeps it on her thumb now like it's a piece of armor. It's like a breadcrumb in a wolf's den. Why is it here? Where is she? She was in a hurry to leave the table after the spilled wine. Did she go straight to her room? Or did she take a detour?

Dinner wasn't normal—unless you're James Bond making small talk with the people packing heat under the linen napkins. The wine spill, Sebastian's twitchy reaction, Cybil's rush to leave the table. The way the whole scene played out was . . . awkward. I thought maybe I was the only one who noticed, but now I'm not so sure.

Would Edmond really use Cybil to get out of the deal? I scan the office, but nothing's out of place. Except the ring. I rise slowly, trying to keep my face unreadable as I slip the ring into my pocket.

Rook pulls the door closed and latches the lock, not noticing I'm rattled. He downs the rest of his drink and nods. "I'll talk to Lorenzo. In the meantime, see what you can learn from the assistant."

Ice water runs through my veins. "She seems pretty loyal. Doesn't seem the type to open up."

"Then get creative," he says, leaning forward. "If Edmond's pulling out or playing a second angle, she'll be the first to know. Maybe even be a part of it."

The thought of Cybil tangled deeper in this mess makes me want to put my fist through the mahogany desk. But I follow Rook out of the office and catch sight of Sammy Pawson standing in the hallway with a forkful of chocolate torte in his mouth.

I can feel him watching me as I head down the hall, ignoring the way his presence makes my blood run cold. If they're circling Cybil, I've got to get to her first.

CHAPTER 19

Ben

Lagoverde, Italy
Friday night

The urge to knock on Cybil's door is overwhelming. But I have a shadow—Pawson. I expected him to leave with Rook and find Ramirez. But I can feel him tailing me as I walk past the dining room, empty of Sebastian and Mr. Edmond, and head to the kitchen. I secure another piece of chocolate torte and head back to my room. My eyes flick toward her door, just for a second. Just long enough to hope she's safe behind it.

Rook's voice echoes in my head. "See what you can find out from the assistant."

It's not a request. It's an order. One I have no intention of following—at least not for Ramirez. But pretending like I will? That's going to get tricky. How do I look like I'm gathering information without putting more of a target on her back?

Instinct has me sweeping my room the second I step inside. Before dinner, I left the French doors to the balcony open. Nothing looks disturbed, but the weight of Cybil's ring in my pocket—and Rook's command to use her—puts me on edge.

I set the slice of chocolate torte on the table and check the bathroom. The wardrobe. Sweep a hand under the bed. I run my fingers along the dresser, lamps, and bedside table like I'm expecting something to bite back. A pair of reading glasses sits on top of *Catcher in the Rye*. I pick them up, angling the hinge to confirm the tiny red light is still blinking. Good. The feed's live.

I open the app on my phone and scrub through the grayscale footage. No one's been in or out since I left for dinner. Still, I don't relax.

I remove my jacket and drape it over the chair. Loosen my tie. Under any other circumstances, I'd welcome the chance to get closer to Cybil. That's not a chore. It's a dream I didn't know still burned inside of me. The story she shared with me on the veranda this afternoon—that little slice of her life felt like something sacred.

But now? If I could go back and undo everything since that night in the museum—including not having our lives reconnect—I'd do it, if it meant keeping her safe. That's the kicker though. If I hadn't been there, she'd still be working for Mr. Edmond, and Ramirez's suspicions would still put her in danger.

I drag a hand down my face, exhaustion and jet lag setting in like cement. How long do I have to wait before I can cross the hall and check on her without looking obvious? The chocolate torte sits where I left it—my flimsy excuse if someone catches us talking.

If I was concerned about the man following me in town today, I need to be extra mindful of the ones watching me inside the villa. One wrong move, and I won't be the only one who pays for it.

A muffled yelp breaks through the quiet. My head snaps toward the balcony, and I'm on my feet instantly, pulling the door open. Jasmine fills the air as I scan the darkness. It's too thick to see anything clearly, but something's out there.

Another sound—scuffling. And a . . . whimper?

I move to the edge of the balcony railing with light steps. There's a scraping noise, and then I see her. Cybil. Pressed against the other side of the railing, half buried in vines and trying very hard not to look guilty.

"What the heck are you doing?" I hiss.

She exhales hard, like a kid caught mid–cookie theft. When she finally looks at me, the guilt's gone—just pure, unfiltered annoyance. "Oh, you know, just enjoying the night air."

I assess her position—arms flexed tight on the railing, heels firmly planted on the cement ledge, dress wrinkled, twig in her hair like a fashion choice gone wrong. She's not in distress. Just busted.

My fingers close around the ring in my pocket. I shouldn't engage—not with Ramirez already suspicious and looking for cracks. But this is too good to pass up. Cybil's one part chaos, two parts pride, and I've always been just dumb enough to poke a hornet's nest.

I glance around. No witnesses. "It *is* a nice night."

She glares, her face flushed. "Do you *mind* helping me before I fall to my death?"

"Oh, you won't die if you fall. Just broken bones, probably." I lean casually over the railing. "Make sure you aim for the bushes."

She huffs. "Are you going to make me beg?"

I lift a brow. "Will you?"

"No."

"Well, then." I tap the railing and take a leisurely step back. "Enjoy yourself."

She mutters something under her breath and starts shimmying sideways—until her foot catches on a vine.

Her yelp is the only warning I get.

I lunge, grabbing her arms just as she slips, my upper body yanked over the railing. My heart slams against my ribs as I strain to haul her up. "Seriously, Cybil?" I grunt.

She kicks, trying to help. All that does is shift her weight—and send us both crashing backward onto my balcony.

I hit the tile flat, air knocked from my lungs. She lands squarely on top of me.

For a second, we just lie there, both breathing hard.

Then she smirks. "I don't beg."

She's impossible. And I like it. Way too much.

The realization hits like a jolt—sharp and unsettling. Or maybe it's something worse. Doesn't matter. *This* is exactly what's going to get me in trouble. What Rook noticed at dinner and what I need to shut down.

"Your elbow's in my liver," I wheeze.

Carefully, I lift her by the arms and roll her off me. The second the weight's gone, I feel it—this weird unmoored sensation, like she was an anchor I didn't know I needed. And that right there? That's the problem.

I roll to my side, push to my feet, and offer her a hand. She takes it. That's a surprise. And it feels . . . good. Like maybe her guard's finally down.

But with Cybil, I'm not betting on it. I need to tread carefully.

"So as much as I love playing the hero," I say, brushing off my shirt, "you want to tell me what you were doing out there?"

She avoids my eyes, smoothing her dress like it personally offended her. No answer.

I reach for her hand—lightly, a brush of my thumb over her palm—and she flinches. Pulls her hand back.

That's when I notice her hands are raw, skin red and scraped. How long was she clinging to that ledge? And why? That last question simmers, but I dismiss it—for the moment—to take care of her.

"Come on," I murmur, gently tugging her into my room.

She resists.

"You're welcome to try the ledge again, Billy."

"Don't call me that." But the nickname does its magic. Always does. She storms past me like she's in charge but makes a beeline for the door.

"No, you don't."

I catch her momentum, my hand on her elbow, giving her a little spin like it's a dance. Her hands land softly on my chest, and for a second, everything stops. Our eyes lock. She starts to pull back, but I don't let her.

My gaze drops to her right hand. The missing ring. This is my shot.

"You didn't answer my question," I say quietly. "What were you doing on that ledge?"

Her fingers twitch against my shirt. If she had the ring, she'd be spinning it right now. She's stalling. Buying time. Reaching for a story.

And I already know—it's not going to be the truth.

So I decide to help. "You weren't trying to break in somewhere, were you?"

Her eyes go wide. "Are you feeling okay?" She presses the back of her hand to my forehead like she's checking for a fever.

A beat passes.

Her hand lingers a second too long, then she yanks it back like I burned her. Like she felt the same current of electricity I did.

"Stop raising your brows like that," she snaps.

I lift them higher. "Like what?"

"Like that." She scowls at me, cheeks flushed.

"You're mad at my eyebrows?

"Only because you know how to use them."

"Use them?"

She lets out a dramatic sigh and steps back, swatting the air between us like she's trying to shoo away a swarm of bees—or maybe just the crackling chemistry we're pretending not to notice. "You're insufferable," she mutters. "Of course you don't get it. I raise my eyebrows and look like I'm being electrocuted. You do it and it's all . . . smoldering."

I let one brow dance up again. "Smoldering, huh?"

"You're *so* annoying."

"I'll take that as a yes, you were breaking in."

She crosses her arms. "I was *not*—"

She exhales hard, like I'm the one being ridiculous, and pushes away from me. "I was trying to help a cat."

I blink. "A cat."

She nods, straight-faced. "Yes. It was stuck on the ledge. Terrified. I couldn't just leave it."

"A cat."

"Yes."

"You hate cats."

She falters—just a flicker—but recovers quickly. "I do not."

I fold my arms. "You used to carry a water bottle on your hip like a gunslinger just to keep the barn cats away."

"They were vicious."

"They were *kittens*."

I stare at her. She stares right back.

"Where is it now?" I gesture toward the balcony.

"Where's what?"

"The cat?"

She hesitates. "It . . . ran away."

I exhale through my nose. "Right."

She's lying. Cybil has hated cats since the day a feral barn kitten got tangled in her braids and took a fistful of hair with it. But it's not just the lie—it's the anxiousness beneath it. My hand slips into my pocket and I close my fingers around her ring. I should give it back. But I don't.

If she was in Ramirez's office looking for it, why lie about it? Rook's words from earlier circle back, sharp and unwanted. Is there truth in Ramirez's suspicion that Edmond's going rogue? And where does that leave Cybil?

A knot twists in my gut. "Are you sure everything's okay?"

She meets my eyes, but her smile shows up late. "Yes, it's just been a long day, and I wasn't planning to end it stuck out on a ledge."

"To save a cat."

She lets out a breath. "Yes, *Craig*, to save a cat. Now, if you don't mind, I'd really like to go to my room and forget this day ever happened."

My posture softens at her tone. I want answers, but something about the way she won't look at me keeps me from pressing further.

She's halfway to the door when she freezes. Her eyes lock on the slice of chocolate torte sitting on the table.

I notice. Of course I do. "You can have it," I offer.

"I already told you—"

"You don't like chocolate," I finish. "But I thought maybe this would change your mind. I know you—"

"Why are you so determined to prove you know me?" She folds her arms tight across her chest.

The words hit harder than I expect. My voice is quieter when I say, "Why are you so determined to prove I don't?"

The tension between us turns electric again, crawling under my skin and buzzing like a live wire. All I can think about is what Rook asked me to do. *If Edmond is playing Ramirez, maybe she's in on it too.*

But that doesn't track. Not with the girl I remember. Not with the woman standing in front of me. "I know you," I say, softer now. "Or I did."

Her arms fall to her sides. "I'm not the same girl."

The words slice through me.

She turns to go, and I step ahead of her.

"Wait."

"Be—Craig," she corrects herself, and the exhaustion clings to her voice. "I'm sure your mind is spinning with all the ways to tease me, but please—let this night end with a smidge of dignity."

Guilt rips through me. Is that what she thinks I'd do? Tease her? Sure, I used to. When we were kids. But tonight it felt like slipping back into something comfortable. Familiar. Like I just wanted her to look at me the way she used to—fiery, unfiltered. With just enough teasing to give me hope.

Her posture is stiff, like she's already bracing herself—against me. It hurts more than I want to admit. I open the door and glance down the hall. It's empty except for a carry-on suitcase parked outside her door. I step back and gesture. "I wanted to make sure you were safe to leave my room." I meet her eyes. "Integrity and dignity intact."

There's a pause—just a breath—where I think she's going to say something. But her expression shutters and she walks out.

"Good night," she says over her shoulder and disappears into her room, taking her suitcase with her.

I'm about to shut my door, but I see the cake. I'm not going to eat it, so I grab the plate and step into the hallway. I set it on a table and go inside my room.

I shut the door, lean against it. The weight of her ring presses into my palm. I turn it over in my fingers.

Cybil's lying.

Keeping secrets.

And secrets get people killed.

Pulling my cell phone out, I type a message to Ruby:

Get me everything you can find on Cybil Renee Langford.

CHAPTER 20

Cybil

Lagoverde, Italy
Saturday morning

I've lost a lot of things in my life—my sense of direction, self-control around chocolate, and recently, my dignity in more ways than I want to remember. But losing my dad's ring? That feels like I'm drowning in a lake of poor choices made worse by the fact that I can't stop my heart from betraying me with every stubborn, foolish beat for Bennett *freaking* Bradley.

Last night was not my finest moment. I was nearly caught snooping in Ramirez's office and figured climbing over a second-story balcony was marginally better than ending up in a car trunk. That plan unraveled—naturally—when someone locked the office door, leaving me trapped on the balcony ledge with exactly one option: shimmy along the narrow ledge to the first open door not being guarded. Of course it would be Ben's room.

The morning sunlight streams through the lace curtains, painting a delicate pattern on the hardwood—the same floor I crumpled to after sneaking off early this morning to search the office. The door was open, giving me the perfect chance to retrieve the ring. But after crawling around like a B-list burglar under desks and furniture? The hard truth hit me square in the chest—the ring is gone.

Heartache is currently in a cage match with fear, and fear is winning by a knockout. If someone found that ring—someone like Rook or, heaven help me, Ramirez—would they believe me if I said, "Oh, I just dropped it while doing absolutely nothing suspicious"? That feels like the kind of excuse that gets you a first-class seat on the next missing persons documentary.

It's not like I can report it missing without also filing for witness protection. Or, you know, faking my death and moving to a goat farm in Wales.

I rub the bare spot on my thumb. My ring. The one thing I've held on to through every life detour, heartbreak, and late-night identity crisis. I need to find it. I need it back. And I need to figure out how to do that without tipping off the criminal network sleeping down the hall.

Someone must've found the ring. But who? And would they believe I lost it during the meeting? Mr. Edmond is my safest ally. Hopefully.

I push myself off the floor. I spent half the night trying to forget the smug look on Ben's face when he caught me midfall like some action hero. Or the way his eyes glimmered with concern, confusion, and something deeper. Something dangerous. Something I used to dream about before I knew what it meant to lose.

"Are you sure everything's okay?"

He asked it like he meant it. Like if I told him the truth—told him *everything*—he'd fix it. Just like he did with the butterflies.

The memory surfaces uninvited. Rex and Ben had invited some classmates to the ranch, and I spent the day avoiding them, wandering the fields, chasing butterflies. One boy thought it would be hilarious to catch one and kill it. I stood there horrified, my chest tight with something raw and awful. And then I cried, which only led to teasing—but not from Ben or Rex.

It was the first time I could remember that they came to my defense. Ben shoved the boy hard enough to put him on the ground. Rex told everyone to leave. And I was allowed to deal with my emotions privately.

The next morning, I woke to the sound of shovels scraping dirt. Outside my bedroom window, I found Ben and Aunt Renee kneeling beside a fresh garden bed. They planted flowers, carefully chosen ones with bright petals and sweet nectar that would draw the butterflies back to me.

Ben never said a word. Never asked if it helped. But every summer when the butterflies returned, I knew the answer.

My heart flutters like a traitor, and I drop to the edge of the bed with a groan. The sun pierces the space like it's on a mission to personally offend me. I should've taken Ben up on his offer to switch rooms when he offered. But that would be admitting that he knows me. My gaze slides to the empty plate where a piece of chocolate torte once sat. It was divine. And so what if Ben knows me—it doesn't mean anything.

No. Nope. We are *not* doing this. Falling for Ben is as dangerous as falling off that ledge—and at least with the ledge, I only risked a broken neck. With Ben? It's my heart. My mission. My whole existence.

And if Ramirez finds out I'm spying on him? I won't need a ledge—I'll get an underwater tour of Lake Lagoverde.

My phone rings. Caller ID says "Daylight Donuts."

That can only mean one thing. "Hello."

"Good. You're up." It's Athena.

"Good morning to you too."

"Yeah, yeah, drink a cappuccino for me."

"You know it's surprisingly difficult to order a cappuccino in Italy."

"What do you mean?"

I grab my outfit from my suitcase and head to the bathroom. "The baristas look at me like I'm asking for a unicorn latte."

She pauses. "What time are you ordering the drink?"

"What does that have to do with anything?"

"Italians don't drink cappuccinos after eleven."

There it is. Humor. That's what I hear in her voice, and I'm glad she can't see the blush blooming across my cheeks. Every cappuccino I've ordered was well after eleven. "You couldn't have told me that before?"

"Sorry, I should've added 'coffee etiquette' after teaching you how to pick locks and encrypt your emails."

"First rule of coffee etiquette—no sarcasm before the first cup."

"Sorry. It's been a long night."

That grabs my attention. "You're still at work?"

"Yeah, but it's fine. The couch in my office is comfier than my bed."

That sounds like a lie, but I'm too tired to argue. I shove in my earbuds to keep getting ready. "I'm guessing that's my fault."

"Not entirely."

Excellent. Just enough guilt to season my already amazing morning. I sent Athena a message last night after I got back into my room. I told her about the photos I'd taken with my phone of the Aurelite-X plans, omitting the part where I was dangling off a balcony rail or the way Ben still makes my stomach flip.

I'm pretty sure it's bad form to fall for the guy working with the enemy. Though, in my defense, it seems to work out for James Bond.

And while Ben has the James Bond look going for him, I'm the furthest thing from the debonair secret agent.

"I've set up an exchange for you today," Athena says. "In an hour, go to the Bottega del Caffè. Order a caffè corretto alla lavanda—"

"Corretto alla lavanda," I repeat.

"Yes, it's a lavender-spiked espresso—"

"Spiked?" I squeak. "I can't drink that."

"You don't need to *drink* it, just order it. The courier will recognize the order. Set your phone on the counter when you pick up your drink. He'll do the same and swap them."

"He's taking my phone?"

When I first started working for Athena, I assumed I'd get one of those burner phones like in the movies—something preloaded with encrypted apps and absolutely zero *Candy Crush*. But she told me carrying two phones would be suspicious. So instead, she taught me how to encrypt my texts and cloak my browser history. Which is why this freaks me out. Because if I know how to keep a message safe but she still wants my entire phone swapped, that means the risk isn't just digital—it's physical. "Why?"

The pause is long enough to make my stomach do backflips. "The information you've given us is . . . valuable."

My brain, like the little capitalist it is, immediately translates her comment into dollar signs. I'm not proud of it, but rent is due, and charity doesn't pay off student loans or cover my mom's spending habits.

"I can't say more, except we need the information on your phone. It takes precedence over everything else."

It's not the first time Athena has kept the details to herself, but it's the first time it has felt like there's more hanging in the balance of the nondisclosure. "How serious is this?"

"The less you know, the better. For now," Athena quickly adds. "You're not in any immediate danger. We've got eyes on you."

I immediately look around my bathroom like someone might be crouched behind the shower curtain with binoculars and a croissant. "You do?"

"Of course, Cybil. We know who you're dealing with. We don't take chances. Our man has been watching you."

My eyes flick to the soggy blue tracksuit on the floor, and mortification curls my toes. "So you, um, know about yesterday in town?"

"Yes."

I groan. Fantastic. Was an image of me looking like an Italian salad being passed around the agency group chat? *Last night with Ben.* "Do you have someone inside the villa?"

"No one but you," Athena answers, but leaves it hanging like she has more to say.

"What is it?"

"There might be . . . another issue," Athena says carefully. "After you told us what you overheard last night between Ramirez and your *friend*, we're looking into him. And what we've found—or haven't found—is concerning."

I freeze. The other thing I told Athena about was the conversation I overhead—or the bits and pieces of it—between Ben and Ramirez. "Concerning how?"

"Craig Miller's identity is shallow. That's expected. But Bennett Bradley? What we *can* find feels generic. A little vanilla."

"What does that mean?"

"It means that until we know more, you need to be careful. Don't trust him."

Right. No trusting the maybe-criminal with the world's best jawline. Got it.

"Just get your phone to the courier. We'll do the rest."

"Got it."

Athena hangs on the line for a few seconds. "Is everything okay?"

Define *okay*. If I don't count the unresolved feelings for Ben, then yeah, I'm just dandy. "Yeah. Just . . . need to get moving."

"Cybil?"

"Yeah?"

"You're doing a great job."

That sticks. Not just because it's kind, but because it feels real. Athena never says things she doesn't mean.

"Thanks."

We end the call. I get dressed—choosing wide-leg trousers, a cropped blouse, and low-top tennis shoes. I check my reflection in the mirror, and for the first time since landing in Italy, I feel more like myself. Fashion meets "flee the scene on foot" practicality.

I swipe on lip gloss, zip my suitcase, and grab my purse. Phone in hand, I square my shoulders with a renewed sense of confidence. I can do this.

I've got this.

I open the door—

Confidence takes a nosedive faster than my willpower around chocolate.

Ben's standing in the hallway, all swagger and sex appeal, like James Bond had a fling with a Calvin Klein model.

I'm in so much trouble.

CHAPTER 21

Ben

Lagoverde, Italy
Saturday morning

I've seen fugitives facing federal prison look happier to see me than Cybil does right now. I set aside the blow to my ego, because as much as I'd love for her to look at me the way she did last night when she was tucked into my arms, I need to focus on why she lied to me.

She freezes midstep in the hallway like I just suggested we elope.

"Heading out?" I ask casually.

Her eyes dart like she's considering jumping through the nearest window. "Just into town for a coffee."

"Perfect. Me too."

Her smile is the kind you give a dentist holding a drill. "Okay, have fun."

She sidesteps around me like she's evading a land mine. I let her reach the bottom of the stairs before I follow. Not because I'm polite—because I'm strategic. She's hiding something. I pat the ring in my pocket, confident I know just how to make her talk.

If I can catch up to her. She's out the door like she can't get away from me fast enough, and it fuels my determination to know why.

"Why are you following me?" she snaps over her shoulder once we hit the cobblestones.

"I'm not. I'm going into town."

Her hair swings off her shoulders as she tosses a scowl back at me. "Shouldn't you be working?"

"Shouldn't you?"

Her jaw twitches. One point for me.

Lagoverde is a riot of color and chaos today. The Festival of Masks has turned the quaint town into pure chaos. The narrow streets are a sea of people navigating street vendors, shopping at market stalls, and snapping photos of the curated displays of ornate masks in every color and style imaginable.

Cafés have spilled out on the sidewalks, their tables clustered together under awnings providing shade from the bright sun. We pass another coffee shop and Cybil isn't slowing down. In fact, she's weaving through the crowd like—*she's trying to lose me.*

I pick up my pace just in time for a street performer in a bone-white mask to block my path and wave glittery ribbons in my face.

"Mi scusi," I say.

He twirls. I step left—he blocks. Right—he follows.

"Come on, buddy."

He points to his hat. I toss in some coins. He bows like I've knighted him. When I look up, Cybil's gone. Classic misdirection. Rookie mistake.

I start scanning the storefronts and cafés, ignoring the gnawing déjà vu. I've chased Cybil before—usually with a snake in one hand and a lasso in the other—but this feels different. This chase has stakes. Real ones. I'm not giving up until I know why she lied to me last night . . . and why I found her ring in Ramirez's office.

Maybe it's completely innocent.

I want to believe that. Especially after Ruby called this morning.

She sent me a full dossier on Cybil—everything from her birth record to her credit history to the list of guys she's dated. I deleted it without opening the file. Told Ruby I wasn't interested in digging through Cybil's life unless there were actual red flags.

There were two.

First, she was hired by Earl Edmond two weeks before she graduated from UNT. Second, she once dated a guy with a user account on a dark web forum called *The Extraction Room*. Handle: Toothbutcher.

Honestly, the first one barely qualifies as a red flag compared to the second. And I don't know what unsettles me more—the fact that she dated a guy called Toothbutcher . . . or that I'm jealous of a guy *called* Toothbutcher.

I have no business poking around in Cybil's dating life, but I felt a little better when Ruby told me she flagged Toothbutcher's IP so the bureau could monitor his online activity. That should've been the end of it, but I haven't stopped wondering what it would've been like to date Cybil myself.

I mean, if she was willing to date a demented dentist, I've gotta be at least one notch above that on the romantic food chain, right?

I'm about to turn around when I spot her. She's perched on the patio of Bottega del Caffé. The old-world coffee shop is all old stone and rough-hewn beams that look a thousand years old. There's a stone archway entry, but beyond that the entire sitting area is uncovered except for the trees and umbrellas.

She's pretending not to see me as I walk over, but I know she does. Her gaze flicks to mine, and her face drops like she just found out I'm her blind date.

"Is it your life's mission to aggravate me?" she mutters as I sit.

"Some people climb Everest. I choose you."

She shoots me a glare that could blister paint. Her eyes flick to her phone. Then to the street. Then to me. "What are you doing here, *Craig*?"

"I appreciate the way you spit out my name. Delivers believability."

She starts to push back her chair, and instincts kick in. I reach across the table and gently touch her hand. "Wait."

She looks down where I'm holding her hand, then pulls away like I've burned her. "I don't have time."

"Please." I catch the quick flick of her eyes to her phone. She's stalling. Scrambling for a way out. "It won't take long. And you haven't had your coffee."

Her lips press into a tight line as she stands from her chair. She's searching for an excuse, but I'm already pulling the last card I've got. I reach into my pocket and hold up the ring.

"And I found this."

She freezes. For a second, her whole body goes still, her eyes locked on the ring like she can't believe it's real. A flash of emotion passes across her face—something raw and real—but it's gone in a blink, replaced with a look sharp enough to draw blood.

"Where did you find that?"

I nod to the chair she just vacated. "Why don't you tell me?"

She swallows, eyes darting like she's one second from bolting—and I'm pretty sure the only thing keeping her here is the fact that I'm still holding her father's ring. When she opens her palm to me, I know I'm right.

"First"—I hold it up between my fingers—"tell me how you lost this."

"It slipped off." The answer comes quickly—too quickly. "Happy?"

"Where?"

"The same place you found it." Her dark brown eyes flicker with a challenge, a spark of the fire that used to scare me but that I've recently found attractive—which scares me too. "May I have it back?"

There's a wobble to her voice, and as much as I want to use the ring to my advantage, I can't. I know how much it means to her, but that doesn't mean I won't push. There's too much at stake.

"On one condition."

She exhales sharply. "What?"

"Answer three questions."

On the street, a parade marches past, filling the café with music. Customers clap and sing in Italian, but all I can focus on is Cybil—on how she keeps sneaking glances at the door like she's ready to bolt.

"Three questions," I repeat when the noise quiets.

She crosses her arms. "Fine."

"First—do you have a thing for dentists?"

Cybil's forehead creases. "What?"

"Yes or no?"

"Are you considering a career change?"

"Maybe."

She rolls her eyes. "No, I don't have a thing for dentists."

"What were you doing in Ramirez's office?"

She doesn't answer right away. And that tells me everything.

"I was there for a meeting with Mr. Edmond and Mr. Ramirez. I must've dropped the ring then." She lifts her chin.

If she's telling the truth, why wouldn't she go back for the ring immediately? Why leave it there? Because she's lying. The frustration returns. If she's covering for her boss, she has no idea what kind of danger she's in.

"And the cat?"

Her brow furrows.

"You said you climbed out on a ledge to rescue a cat."

"Oh. The cat." Her tone is about as convincing as a toddler with frosting on their face saying they didn't eat the cake. "It was cute."

"You don't like cats."

"I'm evolving."

"But you got distracted by a cat on the ledge."

She glares at me, but before she answers, her attention snags on something over my shoulder. When I go to look back, she speaks up. "Why does that bother you so much?"

My jaw clenches. "Are you serious, Cybil? You could've fallen and broken something—or worse." My voice is sharper than I intend, frustration bleeding through. "And I don't believe for one second that you'd risk your life for a cat." I hold up her father's ring. "But for this? I'd believe that."

Her eyes flick to the ring and then back to my face. "So what if I did? What business is it of yours if I went back to find my father's ring?"

My stomach tightens. Cybil has no idea that her being here—working for Earl Edmond, who's tangled up with Lorenzo Ramirez—is very much my business. But I can't tell her that. I can't tell her anything.

So I lean in and drop my voice. "Because it was reckless."

That hits her. Her shoulders snap back like I've struck a nerve—and I think I have. For a split second, something flickers across her face. Raw. Wounded. It guts me more than I expect and I immediately regret my words.

"Cybil . . ." The truth is sitting on the edge of my tongue, but I bite it back. If I say too much, I risk everything—including her safety. I can't do that. "You're smart. Too smart to be working for someone like Edmond."

Her fingers rub the bare spot on her thumb. Then she shifts—just slightly. A barely there shake of her head, like she doesn't believe me. I want to make her believe, but then I catch her eyes drifting toward the counter.

A man stands there now—light blue linen shirt, clean haircut, scanning the space like a guy who's trained to notice exits. Posture's wrong for a tourist. All awareness, no chill.

Every instinct in my body buzzes.

My mind flashes back to yesterday—to the man watching me in the piazza. The one I caught watching Cybil later. I couldn't get a good look at him then, so I can't tell if this is the same guy.

Rook said they didn't have anyone tailing me. Maybe it was the truth. Maybe it wasn't. After last night's conversation, I'd be an idiot to think I've mitigated his suspicions. Which means this guy might not be here to watch me. He might be watching Cybil.

The barista behind the counter calls out an order. Cybil stands. So do I.

But she holds up a hand, stopping me. Her cheeks are flushed now, pink and guarded. "May I have my ring back, please?"

I hesitate—but only for a second. Then I press it into her palm.

Her fingers close around it tightly. Like she needs to feel the weight of it. Like it's more than a ring. She doesn't say anything else. Just steps past me and picks up her order without a glance back.

I watch her go, shoulder brushing mine as she passes, and it takes everything I've got not to follow her out right then.

Five seconds later, the man at the counter leaves.

I wait two more, then follow.

CHAPTER 22

Cybil

Lagoverde, Italy
Saturday morning

This is a nightmare. No, really. Hundreds—maybe thousands—of people are swarming the streets in elaborate masks. It's a Tim Burton movie come to life. Carved smiles, vacant eye holes, all popping up around corners like some kind of twisted Renaissance-themed jump scare.

I look over my shoulder and groan. My real problem isn't the masked crowd surrounding me but the tall man with dark, dangerously tousled hair and a smile that could melt gelato faster than the Italian sun. He just ruined the exchange with the courier, and now he's following me. *Again.*

Ben and his sharp eyes, his quiet interrogation, the way he tilts his head just so—like he can still see through me after all these years. He questioned why I was in the office, why I wasn't chasing after my ring, and then—*then*—he hit me with that offhand remark about working for Earl Edmond.

"You're too smart to be working for someone like Earl Edmond."

It wasn't just a compliment. It was a *loaded* one. And for a split second, I wanted to believe that Ben had changed, that maybe he was finally seeing me as more than the girl I was all those summers ago.

But like clockwork, he ruined it.

"Finding you out on that ledge was reckless."

The cold prickle I felt when that word left his mouth runs down my spine again. I know exactly what it means and I'm right back there. Young, naïve, waiting under the oak tree, holding my breath, heart too full of something hopeful—until I heard his voice.

"Come on, Rex. She's a mess. Reckless."

I exhale sharply, shoving aside the sting of his words. Maybe he's right—maybe I am reckless. But not in the way he thinks. Letting myself believe he's changed, that I can afford to feel anything for him, *that's* reckless. And I don't have time for it.

I have a job to do.

Lose Ben.

Find the courier.

Give him my phone.

And leave every stupid, lingering feeling for Ben in the dust where it belongs.

Unfortunately, Ben spots me like he has some kind of built-in-tracking radar, and my annoyance doubles. I weave through the crowd, determined to shake him. Why is he following me? Why does he have to make everything complicated? And why, for the love of all things sane, is there still a stupid soft spot for him in my heart?

I'm so tangled up in these questions—in *him*—that I completely miss the curb and nearly wipe out a children's puppet show. A marionette loses an arm, a kid screams, and an Italian grandmother levels me with a side-eye so sharp it could cut pasta. I give an apologetic wave and try to melt into the crowd.

"Cybil!"

Nope. Not turning around.

"Wait!"

Too late. His voice catches up with me, all warm and golden and inconvenient.

I whirl around. "Why are you following me?"

He lifts his hands. "Because I want to apologize." He sighs. "And because you just amputated a puppet. Statistically speaking, you're due for another near-death experience."

I glare at him. "Do you have some kind of hero complex? Finance not thrilling enough, so now you moonlight as a disaster chaperone?"

"I'd prefer if you keep both feet on the ground and maybe stay away from motorized bikes," he says, way too sincerely. "Besides . . . I just got you back in my life. I'd rather not lose you to a marionette-related homicide."

Oh, come on. I will *not* swoon at that. I will not. I can feel my heart caving—

Cybil Langford, do not give in to his words. Or the way he's looking at you. Stay strong, girl.

"I'm not in your life, Ben. Our paths crossed because of our jobs. That's all."

His face flickers with something—regret—but it's gone before I can confirm. "Even so, I know what it's like, working for men like Earl Edmond. I just hope he appreciates what you've given up for him."

I stop. Turn. "What's that supposed to mean?"

"Exactly what I said." His voice is casual. Too casual. "High-powered clients make high-powered messes. Sometimes they ask the impossible. And sometimes we say yes without realizing we're selling off little pieces of ourselves."

"Mr. Edmond is good to me." I hold his gaze. "I have no regrets."

He studies me like I'm an equation that doesn't quite add up. His words stir something unwelcome in my chest, but I shove it down. I can't afford to let him get in my head or work his way deeper into my heart. I don't wait for more. I turn on my heel and slip into the crowd—because I have a job to do.

Lose Ben. Find the courier. Make the drop.

I don't look back. I don't need to. I can feel him there, trailing me like a shadow I can't shake.

"I know you're following me." He's close enough that I know he can hear me over the noise of the crowded street.

"I'm not."

"That's not what it looks like."

"I'm walking back to the villa."

"You can walk on the other side of the street."

"It would be easier to cross the Red Sea. On foot. Carrying a donkey."

My lips twitch against my will. *No. Don't smile. Don't you dare smile.* But it's impossible. I've missed this—missed him. The thought sneaks in before I can stop it, and I shove it down just as fast.

This is not the time for nostalgia.

My phone buzzes in my hand. A text from Athena.

Keep walking. Courier will find you.

Sure, no problem, Athena.

Just as soon as I lose Ben.

I pick up my pace, weaving through the crowded streets, past tourists snapping photos and vendors waving masks in the air. I just need a clear path. A distraction.

Taking a corner, I'm stopped by an explosion of confetti in my face, temporarily blinding me. When my vision clears, I'm surrounded by a mob of overly enthusiastic Italian women fawning over me like I'm their long-lost daughter—and honestly, I'm scared.

"La sposa! La sposa!"

The women cheer and one of them puts a delicate white veil over my head and another shoves a bouquet into my hands. It doesn't take a degree in Italian to figure out that *la sposa* sounds a lot like *spouse*—add the veil, the flowers, and the sheer enthusiasm radiating off this crowd, and it feels like I'm being swept into the Italian version of a shotgun wedding . . . probably with a side of cannoli.

I try to back away, but another woman in a "World's Best Nonna" shirt—who has the biceps of a retired wrestler—clamps onto my shoulders and pushes me forward.

"Wait, I'm not—"

"Shh, tradition," Wrestler Nonna insists, patting my cheek before beaming at the onlookers. "Che bellissima!"

I don't know what's happening. I don't know how it's happening. All I know is that within seconds, I'm being thrust into the enthusiastic crowd. I have a death grip on my phone.

I risk a glance over my shoulder and see Ben trying to get to me, but the crowd is too thick and blocking his every advance. He angles his attention to me and mouths, *What is happening?*

I can't help but laugh. It's not funny. Well, it kind of is, but how in the world is the courier going to find me?

A deep, theatrical voice suddenly bellows over the noise: "Dovè la mia bellissima sposa?" And then in English, "Where is my beautiful bride?"

The crowd parts, and striding toward me—towering over the revelers like some kind of Venetian god—is a man in a massive wolf mask.

The fur-covered monstrosity is intricately detailed, a fusion of elegant craftmanship and straight-up horror movie. His deep crimson cloak flairs dramatically behind him, exposing a very well-toned chest.

The mask's golden eyes lock onto mine, and for one horrified second, I think the guy might be some unhinged romantic lunatic about to whisk me away to his underground lair. Before I can back away, he sweeps me into an over-the-top dip, my veil fluttering dramatically as the crowd goes wild.

"Bacio! Bacio!"

I have no idea what they're chanting, but the hungry look in the wolf's eyes has me nervous. "Bacio?"

"Kiss," he growls and delivers a wolfish smile that tells me how he got this role.

I choke.

"Bacio! Bacio!"

This was definitely not part of the plan.

I spot Ben pushing through the crowd, but a group of men in elaborate animal masks—foxes, ravens, and a particularly menacing boar—hold him back. His jaw tightens, his shoulders bunch, and the death glare he's sending to the wolf-masked man gripping my waist practically crackles with rage.

A warmth spreads through me. Oh yeah. He looks very much like he's jealous. I like it.

The wolf-man grins, winks, then twirls me straight into a swirling mass of identically veiled festival brides. Their masked partners sweep in, linking arms as we're spun into a choreographed procession down the street. One of them—tall, steady—catches my wrist before I can break away.

Behind me, Ben is trying to push past the animal-masked men, his sharp exhale carrying all the way to me. I can *feel* the frustration rolling off him even from here.

This wasn't my plan, but it's working.

Now, to escape my dance partner.

"Excuse me." I try to pull my arm free, but he holds on, guiding me smoothly through the steps.

"I heard you like caffè corretto alla lavanda."

Oh. *Oh.* My pulse kicks up. *The courier.*

"Yes," I murmur.

He smiles, spins me under his arm, and as our hands meet again, I feel something cool press into my palm. A cell phone. In one seamless motion, I slip him mine. Another twist, another turn, and just like that—he's gone.

A slow, smug grin spreads across my face. With a casual flick of my wrist, I toss my bouquet into the air and vanish into the festival.

Better luck next time, Ben.

CHAPTER 23

Ben

Dallas, Texas
Friday morning

There are a lot of ways to lose a woman. Apparently, standing still for five minutes while an Italian parade stampedes past you is one of them. I still don't know how she pulled it off. One second, Cybil was in my sights. The next? Gone. Whisked away by some wolf-masked Casanova like she was the start of an underfunded Venetian soap opera. He dipped her, the crowd shouted "Bacio!" and I'd be lying if I said I didn't want to rip off that guy's papier-mâché snout and flatten him.

But that was six days ago. Now I'm back in Dallas, tucked inside the four beige walls of my fake office, where I shouldn't be thinking about a guy in a wolf mask—or how close his lips got to Cybil's neck. I need to be focused on how I'm going to keep Cybil from getting crushed in the middle of whatever power play Ramirez is orchestrating against Earl Edmond.

Cybil's lying. I'm sure of it. I just don't know why. The conversation on the veranda about her father's settlement money getting stolen has me convinced she's the same girl I remember—one who wouldn't let anyone use her. But people change. Life wears them down. My heart wants to believe she's still that girl. My brain reminds me I can't afford to be wrong.

Ruby walks in and drops into the seat next to me. "Thought you might want to know—your gran's background check was approved for a missile launcher."

Katherine looks up from her computer, clearly concerned about the direction of the conversation.

"That would be funny, except you don't know my gran. She found a guy selling a cannon on Facebook Marketplace and talked him down to fifty bucks and a blueberry pie."

Ruby laughs. "Which is worse? A grandma who's into black-market artillery or one who keeps trying to marry me off?"

"Okay," Katherine says in a tone that sobers the mood. "We didn't get into Ramirez's account with the airdrop device, so that puts us back to square one."

She says *we*, and I appreciate it. Katherine has always made this feel like a team effort instead of a one-man mission. Doesn't make the sting of failure any less sharp though.

"Let's focus on what we do have," Katherine says, refocusing our conversation.

"What about the guy in Italy—the one at the coffee shop?" Ruby asks.

I scrub a hand through my hair. "I thought he might've been following me, but when he left the café, he went the opposite direction as Cybil—Ms. Langford," I correct, a little too quickly. "After my meeting with Ramirez, maybe I was just being paranoid."

"Don't do that," Katherine says.

"Do what?"

"You're trained to spot anomalies. Is this the guy you saw?"

She swivels her monitor around so I can see. A grainy security still. I lean forward, squinting. The guy's build matches. Hair color too. I'm about to say *maybe* when I spot the background—the café. And just behind the suspect? Cybil. Standing close. My hand on hers. It's the exact moment I tried to stop her from leaving. But from this angle, it looks . . . intimate.

I shift in my chair. Clear my throat. "Yeah, that's him. Who is he?"

"No idea," Katherine says. "And apparently, nobody else does either."

"What do you mean?"

She leans back, crossing her arms. "No matches on facial recognition. Not in our system, Interpol, or Italy's internal records. We're working with our liaison in Florence, but for now, we're dealing with a ghost."

"Think he could be the guy from the museum?" Ruby asks.

I stare at the screen. The possibility clicks. "Could be. If it's the same guy, then he's targeting Ramirez. Or at least his deal."

"And that makes him a variable," Katherine adds. "One we need to be prepared for before the cocktail party tomorrow night."

Right. Back to the plan.

"Seth will be going in as a high-level crypto investor with a few aggressive global partnerships. The Bureau's been building out his cover for the last few days—contracts, offshore accounts, a fake website that makes him look like *Forbes* forgot to name him their 'Next Tech Billionaire.'"

Ruby lifts an eyebrow. "And Seth's ready to mingle with sharks now?"

"He's ready," I say. "And he's already practicing how to sip champagne without choking."

The joke lands flat. Because the truth is, I'm worried. The last thing I want to do is put another innocent person in the crosshairs of Ramirez. But we don't have any other options.

"Seth may not have operative experience," I admit. "But he's great with the numbers. He understands the language of deals. If Ramirez starts pushing, I think he'll be able to hold his own. And if not, I'll be there."

Katherine nods slowly. "And Mercer too."

"Right." Julian Mercer is our fail-safe, but he's also a loaded gun. If he gets involved, things can escalate quickly, so I'm hoping we don't have to use him. "Ramirez wants to feel like he's in control. The cocktail party gives him that. He gets to 'interview' new prospects, test the waters, and send a message to Edmond without lifting a finger. Seth only needs to keep him occupied enough for us to clone the YubiKey."

"Without getting killed," Ruby adds as if necessary. She flips through a file on her tablet. "Anything new on Edmond?"

"Still quiet." I glance toward the whiteboard at the front of the room. Edmond's name is up there in all caps. "He's either planning his exit or trying to go around Ramirez."

Ruby pauses. "Why does Ramirez think Cybil will turn on her boss?"

"Maybe he thinks she's easy bait," I say. "A pretty face he can use to get to Edmond. But if that's the plan . . ." I shake my head, jaw tightening. "Then he clearly doesn't know the girl I know."

There's a beat of silence. Ruby and Katherine look at me.

I clear my throat. "Or used to know."

"She's got several thousands of reasons why she might be an easy target," Katherine says.

When I got back from Italy and faced the debriefing with Attorney General Fritz, Katherine made me go through Cybil's dossier. And the debt Cybil is in is staggering. In my job, I've learned crime has a price and people in need of money are usually willing to cross lines they wouldn't have otherwise. But Cybil?

It's the question that keeps me up at night. And it doesn't change the fact that she's still dodging questions like she's got something to hide. But if Ramirez thinks he can use her to get to Edmond, I need to get to her first.

"So far it doesn't appear like Ramirez has made any attempts to get to her," Ruby says. "Outside of you."

I glance at her. "You're tracking her?"

"Light surveillance. Public-facing feeds only," Ruby says, tapping her screen and then handing her tablet to me. "Working for someone like Earl Edmond, she really ought to vary her routine. Way too predictable."

I study the screen. Ruby's right. Cybil's schedule for the last week is mapped out in clean, clinical detail. Surveillance time stamps. Locations. My eyes land on an address she visits every afternoon, right around this time.

"We're also watching to make sure Sammy Pawson isn't circling," Katherine adds.

My jaw tightens. The guy was a menacing shadow in Italy, and if Cybil's schedule is this predictable, she's an easy target.

"If Ramirez is watching her," Katherine says, "we need to get ahead of this. You need to find out if she's either an asset we protect or a liability we neutralize."

The words land with a dull thud in my chest. Asset. Liability. She's more than a bullet point on a threat assessment sheet. She's Cybil.

The meeting ends. I tell myself I need some air. But five minutes later, I'm in my car, punching the address into my GPS. I'm just going to drive by. I'm not stalking her. I'm protecting her. And—minor technicality—I can't stay away.

Twenty minutes later, I walk past the bookstore. For the third time. I'm not here because I've missed her. Her smile. Her sass. The way she glares at me like she's already planning where to bury the body. I'm here because Cybil Langford might be compromised.

And—fine—because I care. A lot.

I push open the bookstore door and step inside. All right. Just in and out. Quick visual confirmation. Zero interaction. Nobody has to know.

It takes me a minute, but I spot her—tucked into a corner chair near the Reference section, sipping something iced with a thick book resting on her lap.

From a perfectly normal spot behind a rotating wire rack of greeting cards, I watch her. She taps a highlighter on the corner of the book, completely focused, her forehead creased just slightly in thought. Her fingers twitch on the page when she reads. She marks things with her highlighter. And I don't know what it is about girls who read, but it's incredibly attractive. And dangerous to my heart. I want a closer look.

I skirt around the perimeter of the store, keeping shelves and tables stacked with books between us. I'm trying to see what she's reading—because apparently, now I want to be a part of the thing that has her so locked in.

I lean just a little too far to the left . . . and knock over a carefully balanced tower of "Staff Picks for Sensitive Souls." The pastel paperbacks go down like a literary Jenga game. I freeze. Cybil looks up. I duck behind the nearest bookshelf.

And immediately regret it.

"Why are you hiding?"

I freeze.

Slowly, I turn my head. A toddler—small, sticky, and deeply suspicious—stares at me. His eyes narrow. He's got jelly smeared across one cheek, *Dragons Love Tacos* in one hand, and a half-eaten graham cracker in the other.

I'm surrounded by picture books and plush dragons wearing tiny sweaters. I grab the closest book—something about a pigeon who doesn't want to share his sandwich—and whisper, "I'm not hiding. I'm reading."

Before I can shoo him away, he plops down directly on my foot and shoves the taco book into my hands.

"Read it."

"Not today, buddy."

His blue eyes well up. Chin trembles. And I'm one wrong word away from detonation.

"No, no, no—don't cry," I whisper in a panic. "I'll, uh . . ."

I look around. I spot a stuffed dragon and grab it.

"Here. Why don't you read the story to the dragon?"

He accepts it solemnly, like we struck a truce. I silently pat myself on the back for a successful toddler negotiation.

And then . . . she appears. Stylish. Flustered. Latte in one hand, diaper bag in the other. Her eyes lock onto me.

"Charlie, did you make a friend?" she asks brightly, smiling in a way that makes me suspect this is what a rat feels like right before a cat pounces. "What's your friend's name?"

Friend?

I try to shake Charlie off my foot. No luck. Kid's got the grip of a barnacle. "I was just, uh"—I rise slowly—"looking for a book."

"In the children's section?" Her tone lifts like I've just proposed. "You have kids?"

"No." Too fast. Too loud.

So loud that Cybil's head lifts across the store. She turns. Sees me. I duck. Hard. In the process, I knock Charlie over.

"Whoops, buddy, you okay?"

"Yeah!" He grins and—naturally, as boys do—interprets the fall as an invitation to wrestle. He launches at me. I catch him midair just before he collides into a shelf of board books.

"You're a natural." Charlie's mom beams. "Are you here every Friday? Because this place could use a few more knights in shining armor."

I offer a strained smile and dare another glance over the top of the bookshelf. Cybil's at the counter now, talking with an employee. If I don't get out of this preschool rom-com subplot, I'm going to lose her again. And after Italy, I'm not ready for round two of the vanishing act.

"It was nice meeting you." I look from mother to child. "Charlie."

She steps in front of me and blocks my escape. "This might be a little bold, but Charlie doesn't usually take to people. If you're single, maybe I could get your number? We could meet here again? Or at the park? Or my—"

"Excuse me, sir." A store employee appears beside us, holding a large book with the caution of someone handling nuclear material. "Here's that book you asked for."

She hands me a hardcover with the title *Surviving Incurable Fungal Infections*.

My cheeks flame and I try to shove the book back at her. "I didn't ask for this," I stammer.

From the corner of my eye, I see Cybil watching. Smiling. Smug.

"We don't have the one on rashes," the employee adds helpfully, "but we can order it for you."

Charlie's mom blinks. Looks at me. Then the book. Then me again.

"Good luck with that," she says, scooping up her son like I'm radioactive and speed-walking toward the exit.

The employee leaves me with my book and my publicly diagnosed fictional fungus, and when I look to find Cybil, she's gone.

CHAPTER 24

Ben

Dallas, Texas
Saturday night

There's an art to schmoozing criminals. You don't want to look too eager, or they'll think you're an informant. Too aloof, and they'll think you're a cop. The trick is to be just corrupt enough to belong but not so corrupt someone assumes you're a threat and you end up in a ditch.

Which, considering the crowd and Ramirez's growing suspicion, might be a very real possibility.

So here I am wearing my best "definitely not a federal agent" smile and nodding through another conversation about hedge funds, offshore accounts, and the best way to "protect" assets in Singapore.

Oh, and in a charcoal gray suit that has the vibes of Daniel Craig's Bond in Spectre*—taste matters too.*

Excusing myself from the conversation, I lift a glass of overpriced bourbon from a passing server's tray and survey the crowd. Ramirez has spared no expense tonight. Blackwood Prime isn't one of those overhyped places where people take pictures of their food. The steak house is tucked into a nondescript corner of the city, the kind of place you only know about if someone invites you. No flashy signs, no glowy entrance. Just a single brushed-steel door and a valet who knows your name before you even step out of the car.

Inside it's modern and intimate. Low amber lighting, dark mahogany paneling, and black leather seating. It's a place built to look unassuming, but the handpicked wine list, not to mention the temperature-controlled wall-length glass case displaying rare dry-aged beef like museum pieces waiting to be sacrificed, screams money.

Since the restaurant is closed to the public tonight, I have no doubt that every server, every chef, and every bartender is either hand-selected or paid off to keep their mouths shut. The guest list is impressive—enough financial corruption in one room to give the SEC a heart attack.

But none of that matters to me. The only criminal on my radar is Ramirez. He's not leaving anything to chance tonight—security is stationed around the restaurant, with a team at the door scanning every guest. I give my breast pocket a quick pat, reassuring myself that the hollowed-out pen hiding the YubiKey duplicator is still there.

"Gym socks and Doritos."

Ruby's voice crackles in my ear and I find a quiet corner. "What?"

"The smell." She gags. "It's like I'm stuck in my little brother's bedroom circa his high school days."

Tonight Ruby's running surveillance in a van parked down the street. She wasn't happy about being behind-the-scenes, but we were left with little choice. There isn't one person in this room who doesn't have a wealth portfolio in the multimillions. Ruby attended the museum gala as a colleague, and her presence tonight would have risked raising questions we didn't want to spend time answering. Instead, our focus became introducing Seth Jackson as "Grant Holloway"—a high-risk, high-reward investor who owns Holloway Global Holdings.

A live jazz trio plays in the corner, and I find Seth holding up the wall near a hallway that leads to the restroom. Dressed in a sharp suit and gold Rolex, our forensic accountant showed up tonight looking the part of interested investor who's rumored to have skirted regulations when it comes to projects he's backed in energy, tech, and defense contracts.

Just the kind of guy Ramirez should spare a conversation with long enough to put our plan into action . . . if he didn't look suspect.

At six foot something, Seth usually has a commanding presence, but tonight his normally sharp eyes look glassy, his posture stiff.

"You got eyes on Holloway?" I ask Ruby.

"Yes."

I keep watching him. "Does he look okay to you?"

"Sure."

Ruby's tone suggests that might not be entirely true. "What do you know that I don't?"

She sighs. "He's not feeling great. Kids had the flu, remember?"

I do, and my stomach twists. Ramirez already suspects Edmond of betraying him, and we can't afford for anything to tip that suspicion to our mission. "Why didn't he say something to Katherine?"

"Would you?" Ruby countered. *Okay, that's fair.* Katherine Scott's reputation within the agency is built on success, and if an agent has the chance to work for her, it boosts their career. No one wants to be the one who let her down or messed up her stellar track record.

I make my way to Seth, careful to monitor anyone watching us. "Hey, man, you good?"

Seth's jaw tightens like he's holding back a cough. "Yeah."

"You look like you're about to keel over. I can't have my rich investor passing out in front of Ramirez."

"If you really want to take someone down, make them drink after a sick toddler," Seth deadpans, and I can't tell if it's the low lights or if he actually looks green. "I'll be fine."

I want to believe him, but I'm unsure. Do I pull him off the mission? Can I do this without him?

A burst of laughter pulls my attention to a man chatting like he doesn't have a care in the world. Julian Mercer is all wiry muscle and quick reflexes and is here on behalf of the FBI, thanks to years of practice lifting everything from pocket squares to state secrets.

He's our ringer—the reformed criminal who cut a deal with the government for a get-out-of-jail card. Tonight our co-opted asset gets to prove his worth by swiping the YubiKey off Ramirez—preferably without getting us all killed.

And right now, he might be my only hope of pulling off this mission if Seth is too sick to continue. I check the time.

"Shouldn't be too long." I give Seth another once-over. "I'll be back to introduce you to Ramirez."

"Feel better?" Ruby asks.

"Not even a little."

"Well, don't shoot the messenger, but Edmond and Langford have arrived."

At the entrance, Cybil walks in, looking like a force of nature in a sleek black velvet dress that hugs her figure like it was made for her—classy, striking, and gathering far too much attention from the men in the room. Her arm is tucked into the crook of Sebastian's elbow, her posture the perfect balance of elegance and control . . . and confidence. It's like she knows she belongs here among this crowd, and I'm unsure how to assess what that means.

Something tightens in my chest. *Protect her.* That's what my racing heart is telling me, but my brain is warning me to be vigilant. As much as I don't want to follow Rook's directive to "find out what she knows," I *need* to know. Is Cybil working on behalf of her boss to double-cross Ramirez?

As if on cue, Ruby is there to make sure I don't forget. "How are you going to handle this?"

I slip into the crowd but keep my eye trained on Cybil. Her dark hair falls effortlessly in waves down her back, and the desire to run my hands through it has me feeling restless. Like I'm chasing something I can't have. I should be thinking about the mission, about Ramirez, about not getting killed—but all I can think about is how much I want to touch her again.

Is there any chance we come out of this and find a future together?

Behind them, Edmond enters, looking every bit the self-assured businessman. Would he really risk Cybil's life to, what—make more money? Destroy Ramirez's deal? There's nothing worth more than Cybil's life, but I'm not Earl Edmond, and maybe to him she's expendable.

My eyes flick back to Cybil as she moves through the crowd with ease. Anger pulses hot under my collar. I'll find out what Cybil knows, if for no other reason than to figure out how to keep her from being Edmond's pawn. *Protect her.*

"I'm going to do my job," I answer.

"You ready?"

Reluctantly, I drag my gaze away from Cybil and focus on Ramirez, who's holding court at a private booth, cycling through investors in tight fifteen-minute conversations. Just enough time to lure them in with promises of wealth so obscene they'd never spend it all—even if they tried.

My pulse kicks up a notch. Time to introduce Grant Holloway to Ramirez. I signal Seth, who heads my way, and I'm immediately worried. There's a slight hesitation to his step, and he looks like he's about two seconds away from face-planting into a tray of beef tartare.

I turn to catch Julian Mercer's attention, but he's momentarily preoccupied—entirely captivated by a woman dripping in diamonds. Or maybe it's the other way around. We were warned about his habit of making casual while pulling off something highly illegal, like discussing fine dining while lifting a security pass. But with the way she's batting her lashes, I can't tell if he's charming her or if she's the one reeling him in.

Am I watching my whole plan go up in smoke?

Rook waves me over, and I don't know if I need to stall, improvise, or start praying.

"We have a problem," Ruby speaks into my ear.

Seth pauses, gives me a shake of his head, turns, and makes a beeline to the restroom. *Not good.*

"You're seeing it too?"

"How does she know him?"

It takes me a second to realize she's not talking about Seth. Her? I glance over at Julian. He's either working his magic or about to get himself engaged, but I don't recognize the woman. "Is she a threat?"

"Isn't that what you're there to figure out?"

The man Ramirez was meeting with is leaving his seat. I don't have time for Ruby's sass. "I've never seen her before."

There's a second of silence before Ruby asks, "Who are you talking about?"

"The woman with Julian. Who are *you* talking about?"

"Your old girlfriend."

I don't bother correcting Ruby as I scan the room for Cybil. I find her talking to an older man in a nearly black tailored suit. His posture is rigid, shoulders broad, and he's carrying a little around the middle, but something warns me the man isn't out of shape. He's built like someone who spends more time giving orders than throwing punches.

"Who is he?"

"Milosh Kamarov. Former Russian intelligence turned private security consultant."

From the van, Ruby is running facial recognition through an exterior camera we installed on a light post the day before. I still don't know who was following me in Italy and/or if they're connected to whoever was digging into my alias.

"Should I be concerned?"

Ruby's voice crackles in my ear, low and grim. "Remember that intel op in Moscow a few years back? The one where three agents went in and never came out? Milosh's name was all over it."

"Awesome. A KGB David Copperfield." Rook looks over at me and I acknowledge him, but I move in the opposite direction. *Yep, definitely time to pray.*

"What are you going to do?"

"Try to salvage this mission."

Cybil and Milosh. The more I think about it, the less sense it makes. Does she even know who she's talking to? If I wasn't already questioning her taste in company, I sure am now. I don't know which is worse—her having no clue the danger she's in or me pretending I'm not already halfway in love with her and willing to risk everything to protect her.

CHAPTER 25

Cybil

Dallas, Texas
Saturday night

If this is how I look at chocolate, I owe the cocoa bean an apology.

Milosh—with a Russian last name I didn't quite catch the first time—has been staring at me like I'm tonight's main course. Or maybe the way I stare at a tray of freshly made brownies.

Again, my apologies, chocolate.

I'm pretty sure it wasn't my amazing personality that had him ogling me in a way that had my skin crawling. His eyes didn't just wander—they lingered, practically tracing every inch of me.

Yeah, I'll never look at chocolate the same way again.

I'm pretty sure I'm using chocolate to keep me emotionally disengaged or from being icked out so that I can do what I need to do tonight—get the names of investors involved in Ramirez's deal. Athena made it crystal clear that something big and dangerous will be going down. I have to finish this job no matter how many uncomfortable moments it brings.

From the moment I arrived at the steak house, my focus was to mingle with as many people as possible and collect names. So far I have three. And a half.

"Milosh, is that a family name?"

"It mean . . . beloved." His breath is all vodka. "Very, how you say . . . caring."

His icy blue eyes are predatory as they follow me, like he knows exactly what I'm up to, that I'm fishing for information. The discomfort in my chest grows, warning me it's time to move on to my next target.

I glance around the restaurant. The air smells like seared meat, truffle butter, and expensive cologne, but beneath that there's a quiet tension. Everyone is here for a reason, invited by the man holding court at the back table. Ramirez.

The jazz band isn't playing loud and brassy music, but the slow, smooth kind that makes you think of deals being made in whispers. A few couples sway on the dance floor, but one pair catches my attention. They're maybe in their late fifties or early sixties—around the age of my aunt and uncle—elegant, polished, moving in the kind of rhythm that reveals years of practice. They look like the kind of couple who hosts backyard barbecues, coaches their kids' sports, and gives practical anniversary gifts. So how did they end up in this viper's den of criminals? Are they here to invest in whatever the Aurelite-X deal is? Do they know what it is? Or why Athena is worried about it?

Maybe they don't know.

I think back to my mom and how naive she'd been to trust Celeste Harlow. Celeste sold her this great story of increasing my father's settlement so that we would be taken care of for the rest of our lives—no worries. Did Ramirez target this couple for their wealth? What lies has he fed them?

I'm ready to excuse myself to go meet them when Ben is suddenly standing in front me in a suit that fits him so perfectly, I momentarily forget to breathe.

"Cybil, I don't think I've met your friend."

Ben's words are directed at me, but it's clear from the way his sharp gaze is locked onto Milosh that he's not just making small talk. There's something in his expression, something dangerous simmering beneath the surface, that instantly puts me on edge. I don't think it's jealousy—after all,

Milosh is at least thirty years older than me—but there's definitely tension between the two men that makes my skin prickle.

A full breath finally fills my lungs, along with relief. Ben doesn't even know he's just helped me. "This is Milosh . . ." I press my lips together, looking embarrassed. "I'm so sorry, I don't remember your last name."

"Kamarov," Milosh responds, barely giving Ben a passing glance. "You are?"

"Craig." Ben extends his hand, but his gaze slides to me for a fraction of a second, and I swear I see a small smirk tugging at the corner of his mouth. "Craig Miller."

Milosh ignores Ben's offered handshake as though it's beneath him, but Ben remains unbothered, hands slipping casually into his pockets before he turns his full attention to me.

"Do you have a minute?"

"Actually, I was about to—"

"Dance," Ben interrupts smoothly, his voice low and commanding. Before I can react, he reaches for my hand, his fingers warm against my cool skin, his gaze never leaving mine. And unlike the repulsion I felt with Milosh, my body gravitates to him.

But I don't have time to dance. I try to pull my hand back, but he's already got a firm grip. Then he winks at someone behind me.

"Right, Mr. Edmond?"

Mr. Edmond, who has been in a separate conversation nearby, steps forward with a smile. "I think I'm going to have to agree with Craig. There's always time for a dance."

Not when I need to get names in a room full of criminals.

Mr. Edmond holds my gaze, leaning in. "Besides, I'd like to chat with Mr. Kamarov."

My senses perk at this. I glance at Kamarov, and he's watching the exchange with an interest that removes any chance to reject Ben's offer. I don't know how Mr. Edmond knows Kamarov, but their conversation could be crucial to Athena. I have no choice but to let it happen, hoping I can find out what it's about later.

"Fine."

Ben's lips tip up, and I see way too much satisfaction in his blue eyes. He thinks he's won, but he hasn't seen my dance moves yet.

I let him lead me to the dance floor as the band picks a peppier number, drawing more couples in. He tugs me against his chest, his smile vanishing the second my heel finds his foot.

He winces but recovers, attempting to glide me across the floor. I yank hard to the right, sending his shoulder straight into another couple. Ben apologizes, then tightens his grip, challenge flashing in his eyes.

"I took you for a better dancer, Billy." He spins me out and pulls me back in hard enough I crash into his chest, sending a rush of heat through me that has nothing to do with the dance.

I will *not* romanticize this—no matter how much my heart wants to.

"Your mistake, *Craig*." I stomp on his toe again, satisfied when his jaw twitches and his eyes water. "We don't make good partners."

Ben raises a brow, and my traitorous heart flutters like a communist sympathizer.

"You don't think so?" His hand settles firmly against the small of my back, guiding me with smooth, deliberate steps. We move in perfect sync—too perfect—twisting and turning as the room blurs around us. His eyes never leave mine, and after a few more spins, I can't help it. I laugh. Deep, soul-renewing laughter that I haven't experienced since . . . the last time I was with Ben. He smiles back appreciatively, like I just gave him a gift, and there's an undeniable and unexpected spark—a mix of comfort and something fragile—that makes my heart beat a little faster.

He spins me again, and for a moment, it's like we were made for this, like that older couple with years of practice, and suddenly all the emotions I buried years ago come rushing back with a single, undeniable thought—I'm still in love with him.

Gazing into his blue eyes, I see the boy who made me feel safe. Wanted. *Worthy*. And now he's here, making me feel all of it again.

The music slows, but Ben doesn't let go. His fingers skim my waist as we sway, his eyes searching mine like he's fighting a war I don't understand.

"What are you doing talking to Milosh Kamarov?"

The question snaps me out of my Ben-trance, and just like that, I'm reminded of the dangerous game Ben might be playing. My chest tightens, and the warmth that lingered between us evaporates in an instant. This isn't a fairy tale. Ben is involved in something I barely understand, something dark and risky, something that has Athena worried, and I have to remind myself why I'm here—why I can't afford to get too close. Ben knows exactly how to use his charm to disarm me, and I can't let that happen. But if he's playing me, I'll play him right back. *It takes two to tango.*

I raise a brow. "You dragged me to the dance floor to ask me about my conversation?"

He grins. "It works for James Bond."

"You're not James Bond."

"Come on." Ben tilts his head. "I'm *kind of* like James Bond." He twirls me out and reels me back in, our bodies colliding. I scowl at how annoyingly good he smells. "I got you safely out of the spilled cappuccino debacle, then rescued you from the dangerous fruit cart, and let's not forget the cat that nearly got you killed on the ledge. *All* very Bond-like, if you ask me."

I roll my eyes at him. "Newsflash, 007—I don't need rescuing. Not from coffee, produce, or a charming billionaire."

Ben's eyes widen. "You find him charming?"

Not even a little bit, but you don't get to know that. "Jealous?"

"Maybe." His answer catches me off guard. "He doesn't seem your type."

I scoff. "And you know my type?"

Why am I letting him get to me?

"It's not Russian oligarch." His gaze smolders. "Or an Italian in a wolf-man mask."

So that *was* jealousy I saw on his face. "I don't know. Did you see his clavicles?"

Ben's jaw muscle tics, eyes narrowing. "No, can't say I noticed his collarbones."

"Your loss. They were *amazing*," I purr, thoroughly enjoying the turmoil I see brewing in Ben's baby blues. "Why are you so interested in Kamarov?"

"He's got great clavicles." Ben surprises me with a low dip, and I let out a small yelp, my fingers instinctively gripping his solid arms. His lips hover dangerously close to mine, and for a brief moment, I think I'd have a better chance resisting chocolate than I would pushing Ben away right now. As he lifts me back up, he leans in, his breath warm against my ear, and whispers, "I'm more curious about why someone as sharp as you is working for Earl Edmond."

"Why do you care?" I whisper back, my voice betraying the way my heart races at the question. I'm unsettled—not by the words, but by how badly I want to hear his answer.

But before Ben can answer, I catch Sebastian's gaze. His eyes lock onto mine, an unspoken question in them that sends a chill through me. I've made a mistake. I've let Ben distract me. *Again*.

"I need to go."

"Cybil—"

"Have a nice night, Mr. Miller." I force a smile and back away, my feet moving quickly, but Sebastian's watchful, suspicious stare follows me.

I turn sharply, making my way off the dance floor and heading straight for the only place I know I can escape the tension—the ladies' restroom.

A man bumps into me, his body swaying dangerously before he reaches out, attempting to steady himself against the wall but missing the mark. He stumbles into me instead, his breath coming in shallow, ragged gasps. "S-sorry," he mutters, his voice strained.

I steady him, pushing his shoulders back with more force than I intended, and that's when I notice it—his eyes a dull, glassy green, staring at me with a vacant expression. He looks unsteady. There's no odor of alcohol on his breath, but something's off.

"Sir, are you okay?"

His eyes shift slowly, focusing on me beneath heavy lids. "Bathroom?"

Frowning, I point to the door behind him. "Right there."

"Thanks," he mutters, barely making eye contact before he turns away and trudges slowly toward the restroom, each step heavy like he's fighting just to move.

I stand there for a moment, watching him enter the restroom. Concern creeps into my chest. Should I get him help? I'm about to go find a server to check on the man when I catch a murmur of a conversation drifting toward me from the kitchen.

Ramirez. His voice is low but sharp, his words clipped, urgent. "This is the final move. We can't afford any more delays."

I instinctively press my back against the wall as my pulse quickens. This could be my chance to gather the information I need—if I can get close enough. But then I hear Ben's voice, deep and steady, joining the conversation. My stomach tightens.

My mind is warring with the urge to find out what they're saying and the reality that I might learn how deeply Ben is involved—that he might not be the man I keep wanting him to be.

The thought grips me like a vise, and for a moment I'm paralyzed. If I take one step closer, I might shatter the fragile hope I've been holding on to. But if I walk away now, I'll never know the truth.

CHAPTER 26

Cybil

Dallas, Texas
Saturday night

Hearing Ben say my name a few minutes ago would've sent a thrill through me, but hearing him say it now—to Ramirez—sends a bolt of pure panic through my veins.

"Ms. Langford is—"

I jump when a clattering of pans drowns out the rest of Ben's words. What is he telling Ramirez about me? I scoot closer to the kitchen's doorway, desperate to hear what he's saying.

"Somebody's feeding them information."

This sounds like Ramirez's lawyer, and my heart jackhammers against my ribs. *They know about me. How?*

"I don't like loose ends," Ramirez says, his voice ice-cold. "Make the problem go away."

Blood drains from my face. My brain kicks into overdrive, scrambling to remember every conversation, every question I've asked, every step I've taken. *What did I do wrong?* If I was going to get caught, I thought it would be by Mr. Edmond—not Ramirez. Not Ben.

My breathing shallows. I take a quick step back and crash into a server. The tray of empty plates tilts—then crashes to the floor with a deafening clatter.

The server swears, and I mutter a frantic apology, my hands shaking as I move around the mess, desperate to disappear before anyone sees me. But it's too late.

A door swings open and heavy footsteps bring Ben and Rook into the hallway, their gazes scanning the wreckage before locking onto *me*.

Ben's expression stops me cold. It's not the gentle gaze I got lost in minutes ago when I was dancing in his arms. His jaw is tight, lips pressed together. His eyes are dark and unreadable and sending me a warning that coils tight in my stomach. He knows I heard something I shouldn't have.

My breath shudders. I need to get out of here.

Backing away from the mess, I leave Ben and Rook in the hallway and step back into the main restaurant. The glow of the chandeliers, the murmur of conversation, the clinking of glasses—it all feels like a cruel illusion of normalcy.

But there is nothing normal about what's happening around me. I'm surrounded by a roomful of individuals who have the power, money, and connections to make me disappear. I scan the room, my eyes darting from face to face. Every look lingers too long. Every whisper sounds like my name. My fingers tingle with the need to grab my keys and make a break for it.

Just act normal. Get your purse. Get out.

The jazz trio is playing something slow and brooding, the kind of tune you hear in a mob movie right before someone ends up in an oil barrel. The ominous melody curls around me like smoke, seeping into my already frayed nerves. *So this is the soundtrack to my death—awesome.*

Sliding between guests, I weave my way toward the coat check. Every few steps, I steal a glance over my shoulder, expecting to see Ben, Rook, or—worse—Ramirez closing in. But they're nowhere in sight. Instead, I notice something even more unsettling—Ramirez's men.

They're everywhere—*like a mafia flash mob, except their only choreographed move is tossing people into the back of a van.*

And if they suspect me, if Ben or Rook has put them on alert, that's exactly what they're going to do to me.

"My bag, please," I say, handing my ticket to the clerk. My palms are damp, and my pulse is pounding so hard I feel it in my throat. Unfortunately, the clerk doesn't sense my urgency and moves at a glacial pace.

The moment she hands over my purse, I turn—only to crash into a solid wall of muscle.

No. Not a wall.

Milosh.

His hand clamps around my arm, his grip hot and unsteady. "Leaving so soon, beautiful?" His breath reeks of alcohol, his words slurred but his hold firm. "Stay a little longer. Dance with me like you dance with little man."

Under normal circumstances, Milosh referring to Ben as "little man" would've made me laugh, but his tightening grip on my arm has my stomach twisting. I try to step back, but he follows, backing me against the wall.

"I really need to go," I say, putting as much authority in my voice as I can.

He doesn't let go. His fingers curl tighter, his other hand drifting lower, brushing along my arm. My skin prickles with fear.

"Let me go," I say sharply.

Milosh's lips curl wickedly like we're playing a game he's always won. Sweat breaks out on the back of my neck. Marcos made sure I had self-defense training, but Milosh is at least a hundred pounds heavier than me, and if I engage him, it'll ruin my attempt at a quiet escape.

Hmm, quietly accept a handsy Russian oligarch or take him out and accept my fate in a woodchipper?

A smooth, authoritative voice slices through the tension and my decision. "Are you okay, Cybil?"

Mr. Edmond.

Relief rushes through me as I turn my head. He stands a few feet away, his presence steady, unmoving. Behind him, Sebastian watches Milosh with the kind of detached boredom that barely hides his disdain.

Milosh hesitates, sways slightly, then releases me with a muttered curse.

I step away fast, my skin crawling. "I'm fine," I lie, forcing a grateful smile. "I just don't feel well."

Mr. Edmond studies me, his expression unreadable. "Go home, then," he says simply.

I nod quickly. *Almost there.*

Clutching my purse, I leave Milosh with Mr. Edmond and Sebastian and head down the dark hallway leading to my escape. I'm nearly there when a shadow steps into my path.

Rook.

"Leaving already?" His voice is casual, but his gaze pins me in place. "I was hoping we could chat."

My stomach clenches. I look over my shoulder to where Mr. Edmond and Sebastian are down the hall. I should've stayed close to them. Is the saying "It's safer to stay with the enemies you know than the ones you don't"?

"Just a few moments."

I'm trapped. If I refuse, it'll only make me look more suspicious. I paste on a smile even as my pulse races. "Of course," I say, turning to head back the way I came. Maybe if Mr. Edmond or Sebastian sees me, they'll get me out of this situation too.

"This way."

Rook gestures to another hallway. It's dark, quiet, and I'm pretty sure if I die back here, no one will know. So like the professional spy I'm pretending to be, I fall into step beside him.

"Should I get Mr. Edmond and Sebastian?" I thumb in their direction over my shoulder. "They're just down—"

"No, no," Rook assures me. "Lorenzo would like to speak to you alone."

Alone. Yep, that equals death in every mob movie.

We take a corner, and I hear voices and kitchen noises. Another turn and I realize we've circled the restaurant and are back at the hallway where I was caught eavesdropping. Hope flutters in my chest that if I scream now, someone will hear. Doesn't mean they'll do anything about it—I have no doubt every one of these employees can be bought off with a gym bag full of cash.

Think, Cybil. Think.

We pass a door with an emergency exit light shining like a beacon of freedom. I slide a glance at Rook. He's lanky, thin. I might have a fighting chance if I catch him by surprise.

But not him.

Ben exits the kitchen, his eyes catching mine before moving to Rook. "What are you doing?"

"Lorenzo asked to speak to Ms. Langford."

There's something in Ben's gaze that looks nervous, but then it's gone and in its place is hard steel. He's looking at me like I've betrayed him, and I don't think he's coming to my rescue this time.

I can't even assess how that makes my heart feel before loud commotion echoes from the kitchen. There are shouts and Rook immediately leaves my side to investigate.

There's a whistle. Sharp. Familiar. Instinct draws my gaze to Ben. He's leaning against the wall, unbothered by the chaos. The low light catches on the curve of his mouth—a fraction of a smirk, like he knows something I don't.

Then he pulls the alarm.

The shriek of sirens pierces the air. Kitchen workers and staff pour into the hallway, shouting about a fire. The acrid smell of smoke fills the air—the proverbial match that sets off the chaos.

I don't wait. I turn, slip into the crowd, and move with the rush toward the nearest exit. The emergency door swings open, emptying the frantic crowd into the parking lot behind the building, where my car is parked.

The air is thick with panic as more people evacuate, including residents from the condos above the restaurant. When they catch sight of the smoke, their anxiety ratchets up. I push through the growing mob, making a beeline for my car, but then my heel catches on a crack in the sidewalk.

In my scramble to steady myself, I collide with a man.

"What's happening?" he asks, his voice laced with confusion.

I'm about to apologize when I recognize him—the same man I saw earlier in the hallway. He's swaying, looking even worse than before. "Sir, there's a fire in the restaurant. You need to get somewhere safe."

"Safe?" His eyes glaze over, and he mumbles something about not feeling well.

I glance around, searching for anyone who's missing the guy, but no one seems to be looking for him. My eyes spot Ben and his narrowed gaze *is* on the hunt for someone—me?

I can't waste any more time.

"Sir, you need to get to your car," I urge him.

He nods, still dazed, and points to a nearby car. Whatever. I just need to go.

I reach my car and freeze. Sitting on the hood, with piercing yellow eyes fixed on me, is a cat. I didn't admit it to Ben in Italy, but he was right—I hate cats, and they all seem to know it. I press my key fob, hoping the sound will send the cat running. It doesn't.

"I don't have time for this." I walk around to the back door, hoping slamming it will scare the cat away. It doesn't budge.

"Shoo!" I yell at the cat. It stares at me like I'm the nuisance, and then it moves—right under my car. "No, you stupid cat!"

A small, irrational part of me wants to jump into the car and just drive away, but I can't risk running over the stupid thing. As much as I hate cats, I can't bring myself to do that.

Grumbling, I kneel on the asphalt, the pebbles biting into my skin as I search under the car. There he is, perched near the tire. I rise and move to the other side of the car to chase him away.

The sound of fire engines blaring nearby makes my pulse spike. Behind me the crowd is thick, cars clogging the lot as people scramble to leave. I don't know if it's fear of the fire or fear that when the police arrive, they'll be suspicious of the crowd of criminal guests.

I return my attention to the cat. The last thing I need is to get stuck in this mess. I squint under the car. Nothing.

Relief washes over me as I stand and rush to the driver's side, sliding into the car and slamming the door behind me. I start the engine and inch my way through the parking lot, maneuvering carefully around the cars and people, keeping my head low just in case Ben's not the only one looking for me. Once I'm a few blocks away and my heart rate finally begins to slow, I pull my phone from the console and dial Athena.

When she picks up, all I can manage is, "I'm in trouble."

CHAPTER 27

Ben

Dallas, Texas
Saturday night

Smoke clogs the air, thick and acrid, burning the back of my throat as I push through the crowd. The wail of sirens bounces off the buildings, red and blue lights slicing through the night like a crime scene in the making—and I'm at the center of it.

The trick to starting a fire in a commercial kitchen isn't accelerants—it's timing. A grease-soaked rag, a conveniently unattended stove, and a fire small enough not to cause actual damage or put anyone in immediate harm, but big enough to send every sous-chef into a panic.

Adding arsonist to my résumé wasn't on my bingo card, but desperate times call for Bond-level improvisation—minus the gadgets, martini, and British accent. I didn't see another option after my conversation with Rook and Ramirez inside the kitchen.

"One of Edmond's offshore holdings accounts has been flagged for review."

"Who flagged it?" I asked, trying to keep my tone casual, unconcerned, even though I was very, very concerned. If someone had flagged Edmond's account, it meant people were watching and any transactions would immediately lead back to Ramirez, forcing him to tighten his security on his accounts. We needed to get access to the YubiKey now more than ever.

"It didn't come from internal compliance," Rook answered for Ramirez. "Somebody's feeding them information."

Ramirez stared me down. "If Edmond's people are drawing attention to their crypto accounts, the deal is compromised."

Rook exhaled sharply. "We can't afford loose ends."

The suspicion on Edmond had doubled, and caught in the middle was Cybil. "I can investigate this. Give me a day, two max, and I'll have answers for you."

Ramirez's gaze darkened. "Make the problem go away."

I didn't know who was behind the flagged account, but it just jeopardized my mission—and Cybil's safety. Catching her in the hallway outside the kitchen was a problem. It looked suspicious—even to me. What was she doing? Listening? For Edmond?

I needed answers—and time.

I needed to buy us time so I can figure out how deep Cybil is in this mess and how I can help her out of it without blowing up my entire mission.

Outside, the parking lot is a mess—horns blaring, people shoving, everyone convinced they should be the first to get out. I don't see Cybil.

Good.

Now I need to move before the fire department extinguishes my chance. I push back through the chaos, into the restaurant that no longer resembles the elegant den of criminals it was minutes ago. White tablecloths are askew, some stained with spilled wine. Silverware and shattered glass crunch underfoot, and abandoned chairs sit at odd angles. Smoke curls from the kitchen, hazy tendrils creeping into the main dining area where I find a man in a dark suit speaking in low, clipped tones to Ramirez and Rook. His posture is rigid, his expression severe—the kind of authority that comes with being the one in charge. Security? The restaurant owner? Whatever they're discussing is more important than evacuating the restaurant.

I don't know how much time I have, but I need to salvage this mission. I spot Julian, helping the woman he'd been charming earlier to retrieve her purse from beneath a table. As he straightens, our eyes meet, and I catch that calculating glint—the kind that makes me wonder if he's focused on my mission or just working the odds in his favor.

He murmurs something to the woman, flashing that easy grin, before she passes him a card and exits the restaurant. Julian pockets the card before his gaze moves from me to Ramirez, the message clear—he's ready.

Firefighters enter the building and begin barking orders at us to vacate the restaurant even against the protests of the man talking to Ramirez.

"You have a plan?" I mutter to Julian when he's close.

He smirks. "Thirty seconds of distraction is all I need."

On an ordinary evening, distracting Ramirez for half a minute would be easy, but given that the night has gone up in smoke, I need to play this right. I need Seth.

Back outside, I scan those lingering. Most of Ramirez's guests have left, and the people remaining in the parking lot are residents of the building and surrounding buildings watching the commotion.

But I don't see Seth. The last time I saw him, he was circling back to the restroom looking awful. He wouldn't still be in there, would he?

"You have eyes on Mr. Holloway?"

Ruby doesn't answer me, and I don't like the way that makes me nervous. I tuck my chin and try again, hoping the noise prevented her from hearing me.

"Ruby?"

"Sorry." Her one-word reply is breathless. "Had to move because of the fire trucks."

"I haven't seen Mr. Holloway in a while. You?"

"No. And my camera angle's blocked by a ladder truck."

"There are security cameras facing the parking lot. Check those."

"Give me a second."

I spot Ramirez near a curb, Rook at his side, both moving with purpose toward a sleek black car idling along the street. Julian crosses my field of vision, heading toward Ramirez.

"I don't have a second."

I push through the stragglers lingering outside and call out, "Mr. Ramirez." He slows just enough to glance over his shoulder. "Unfortunate way to end the night."

He turns fully, expression unreadable. "It is."

I take the opening, "I'm sorry you didn't get the chance to meet Mr. Holloway. I know he's very interested in meeting with you. I could reschedule a—"

Ramirez holds up a hand, stopping me. "That won't be necessary." He casts a glance at the scene unfolding around us. There's an inscrutable look in his eyes. "You were right. Bringing everyone together gave me a clearer picture of what I have." He glances at Rook, then back at me. "I've been undervaluing my deal."

My stomach tightens. If he's reevaluating, that means changes—lockdowns, more security, fewer access points. We don't have time for this. If we don't get the YubiKey now, I don't know if we'll get another shot.

Julian slides through the crowd with effortless grace, his movements smooth and deliberate. He weaves closer to Ramirez, careful to appear unremarkable, a shadow among shadows. He gets within arm's reach, and my pulse races with each step. This is it. We have to get the YubiKey before all of Ramirez's account details vanish behind an impenetrable wall of security measures.

Julian prepares to make his move—but Ramirez unbuttons his suit coat, slips out of it, and tosses it into the back seat of the car.

Julian's eyes flicker with the briefest flash of frustration, but he recovers instantly. Slipping past Ramirez, he seamlessly rejoins the flow of people, his casual demeanor never breaking. But as he moves, I catch Rook's sharp gaze locking onto Julian, his eyes narrowing with quiet suspicion. It's subtle, but it's there.

I grind my teeth, forcing my expression to stay neutral as a sharp wave of frustration knots in my chest. Sweat gathers at my collar, and I have no idea how Daniel Craig wore this in the sweltering heat of Morocco. "I can't speak for Mr. Holloway, but I'm sure he'd appreciate whatever opportunity you're willing to offer to get him into the deal."

Ramirez tugs at his cuff, his gaze sharpening. "Before all of this"—he gestures at the scene around us—"I spoke with a broker, Samuel Baird. Have you heard of him?"

I shake my head. "Can't say that I have." I try to recall the faces of those I saw talking with Ramirez before I was pulled into the kitchen. "Was he the gentleman you were speaking with before we met?"

Ramirez nods, his eyes narrowing slightly. "He was. Like you, he's got a diverse clientele—international, and all of them, he believes, might be very interested in the deal."

That sends a spike of unease through me. The FBI's focus has never been on the deal itself—it's always been about getting close enough to Ramirez to gather intel for the RICO charges that could finally put him away. He's untouchable for the murder of Danny Morales, but if we could nail him on his financial crimes, it would give Danny's family some sense of justice. But now . . .

Samuel Baird has just added another level of complication. I can only hope that Ruby is already doing her magic and finding out who this broker is and what his angle is before the night gets worse.

Ramirez steps back toward the car, giving me one last glance. "If Mr. Holloway is still interested in my business, tell him to come with his checkbook. I've decided"—he pauses, a slow smirk curving his lips—"I'm opening the deal to the highest bidder."

That's worse. A lot worse.

"What about Mr. Edmond?" I ask, keeping my voice steady. "Is he still involved?"

Something crosses Ramirez's face, but all he offers me is a shrug. "Up to him."

I don't know how to take that. "Will you still be needing my services? If you're talking different countries, I'll need details to get the appropriate paperwork prepared for the transactions."

"Don't worry, Mr. Miller." Ramirez slides into the back seat of the car, his voice flat. "You'll have everything you need."

Something twists inside of me. This isn't good. I need to find Seth, get back to Ruby, and call Katherine Scott in to regroup. But before I can move, my comm crackles to life in my ear. Ruby's voice is tight with urgency.

"We have a problem."

CHAPTER 28

Cybil

Dallas, Texas
Saturday night

As I speed away from the restaurant, gripping the steering wheel like it's the last solid thing in my life, two things are abundantly clear—I am *not* a spy, and I should've passed on the fettuccine ravioli appetizer.

I swallow back the nausea and repeat myself to Athena. "I'm in trouble."

Athena's calm voice comes through my speaker. "What happened?"

The words spill out, rushed. "I think I've been compromised. Ben was questioning me again and I needed to get away from him"—*and the feelings he was stirring up in me.* "I went to the bathroom, but there was this guy and—"

"Take a breath, Cybil."

I suck in a breath. "I overheard something, just a few words, but it was Ben talking to Ramirez and Rook. They said my name. And then they caught me."

My pulse pounds in my ears. I can still feel the weight of Ben's stare when he found me in the hall, the way his expression shifted. Like he *knew* what I was doing.

"*Who* caught you?"

"Ben. And Rook, Ramirez's lawyer." My mind was spinning, replaying every second of the night in an endless, stomach-churning loop.

"Athena, what if he sold me out?" My voice cracks. "What if Ben figured out what I've been doing and he—"

"Breathe," Athena reminds me again, her voice steady as ever. "Where are you now?"

I blink. I've been so consumed in getting as far away from the restaurant as possible, I haven't paid attention to where I'm driving. The city lights have faded behind me, replaced by dimly lit streets lined with aging brick buildings and low-rent office spaces. A few neon signs flicker overhead, casting eerie glows onto the cracked sidewalks. Most of the storefronts are dark—insurance agencies, bail bond offices, a payday loan place with bars on the windows. Exactly the kind of place where no one asks questions if they hear gunshots. My paranoia spikes. "Somewhere near downtown."

"How far are you from your apartment?"

I open my mouth to respond when something shifts behind me. A faint rustling that causes the hair on my arms to stand.

"Athena," I whisper. "Something's wrong."

Another noise—heavier this time, like a shuffle of weight against fabric. I twist my head, looking at the back seat, and my breath catches in my throat. A *man* is in my back seat.

I scream. The car swerves violently, tires screeching. My seat belt locks as I yank the wheel, barely managing to keep my car from crossing into the opposite lane. My tires smash against the curb with a jump and I throw the car into Park.

"What's happening?"

I can't get out of the car fast enough . . . but my stupid seat belt is determined to keep me trapped. "There's someone in my car!" I shout, still clawing at the buckle.

"Right now?"

Her confusion incites me. I finally wrench myself free and scramble out of the car, nearly strangling myself with the seat belt. I don't need to fear Ramirez after all—seems like automobile safety will be the thing that kills me.

"Yes, right now." Should I be running from my car? Screaming for help? Calling 911 instead of explaining to Athena that there's a freaking man in my car?

"What's he doing?"

My car was just hijacked, I'm on the verge of puking my guts out or having a heart attack, and she wants to know what the man's *doing*?

"Cybil, what is he doing?"

Heart hammering, I spin around and yank open the back door, fully prepared to run for my life.

But the man doesn't lunge at me with a knife or point a gun at me. His slumped-over form doesn't move at all. I stare at him, my brain short-circuiting. "Uh . . ." I swallow. "He's not doing anything."

"What? I can't hear you."

I retrieve my phone from where it slipped between the seats and change it from my car speaker to my phone speaker. "He's not doing anything. He's not moving."

"He's unconscious?"

"I don't know."

"Is he breathing?"

My heart stalls as I stare at the unmoving man. "He's dead?"

"I don't know, is he?"

"Athena!" I hiss. "What do I do?"

"Stay calm."

"Are you serious?"

"Listen, I'm assuming you don't normally keep spare bodies in your car to save on tolls, right? So let's just take this one step at a time. I need you to check for a pulse."

"Do I have to?"

"Dealing with a drunk man is different than dealing with a dead man."

"Fine." I lean into the car and gingerly reach toward his wrist. His skin is hot against my fingers, but relief rushes through me when I feel proof. "He's alive."

"Good. Now describe him."

"Describe him?"

"What's he wearing?" Athena's voice is unshakable like she's walked a person through this type of scenario before, and for some reason that does not make me feel better. "Does he look like a homeless guy who took advantage of your unlocked door or—"

"No. He's wearing a suit. Nice shoes. Wait . . ." My hands are still shaking, but I lean into the car again and look at his face. "I think I recognize him. Yeah, he was at the restaurant. I thought he was drunk—he staggered outside right before I left." My mind is racing, piecing things together. "Oh no. I told him to get to his car, but he must've gotten into my car by mistake."

Athena snorted. "That excuse won't hold up in court."

I jump back. "What?"

"Check his pockets for ID."

I make a face. "Um, no."

"We need to find out who this guy is, Cybil. Someone could be looking for him—maybe Ramirez?"

My eyes flash to my surroundings. Dark, isolated, perfect spot to kill me. I look back at the unconscious man and groan. "Sir, I'm just going to check your pockets for identification," I say in case he can hear me. He lets out a snore and I jump, smacking my head against the car frame. "I hate this."

"You're doing fine."

"You're not the one groping an unconscious man." I decide to check his suit jacket pockets first. Sliding my hand between his jacket and chest, I'm not prepared for the heat radiating off his body. It's like I stuck my hand inside a sauna. I quickly search the first interior pockets and find nothing. My gaze slides to his pants pockets.

Just do it fast.

With a deep breath, I reach for his back pocket and squeeze my eyes shut as I pat them down. "I'm so sorry, sir."

"Cybil, can you hurry instead of apologizing?"

"I'm going as fast as I can." I grit my teeth and give his front pockets a G-rated patting. "He doesn't have a wallet."

"Cell phone?"

I back away from the car. "Nothing."

"Take a picture of his face and send it to me."

I snap a quick photo, send it, and begin pacing. If I've ever had any delusions about being some kind of elite undercover agent, this disaster has just smacked me upside the head with reality. Hard. *There's an unconscious man in my back seat.*

How has my life gone so completely sideways?

I was just supposed to get names. That's all. Simple. Easy. Or at least it should've been—until Ben showed up. Ever since his perfectly smug face showed up at the museum, my carefully laid-out plan has turned into a chaotic mess of close calls, unexpected complications, and *way* too much eye contact for someone who's working for the enemy.

Have I been duped?

The question sends bile into my throat, and I don't feel well.

"Cybil, I need you to listen to me and *not* panic."

"*Why* would you say that?" My voice shoots up an octave.

"Because I need you to stay calm."

My heart is racing. "You don't tell someone with an unconscious man in their back seat not to panic unless there's a *really* good reason to panic."

Athena exhaled. "He's an FBI agent."

The world around me tilts, my knees turning to jelly, and I lurch for the back of my car, puking. *I will never eat fettuccine ravioli again.* Who am I kidding—they don't serve that in prison. I'm going to prison. I heave again, emptying what's left in my stomach on the side of the road.

"Cybil, you're going to be okay."

Tears sting my eyes. "I kidnapped an FBI agent, Athena. Nothing is going to be okay."

"Technically, *he* got into your car," she says dryly.

"That won't hold up in court," I say, repeating her earlier words. "I'm going to jail. This is it. This is how I go down. They're going to put me in handcuffs, a jumpsuit. I don't even look good in orange—"

"Cybil." Athena's voice cuts through my spiral. "You're not going to jail. Focus. Why would an FBI agent be at the cocktail party?"

I wipe my mouth and lean against the car, feeling unsteady. "How would I know?"

"Think. You were at a cocktail party with a curated guest list. You got names, right?"

It takes a few seconds for my brain to focus on what Athena is asking. "Yes, a few."

"Give me their names."

I press my fingers to my temple, willing my brain to work, but it's useless—muddled by adrenaline, exhaustion, fear, and the *freaking unconscious FBI agent* sprawled across my back seat. "I don't know," I rasp, trying to force clarity through the haze. "Baird, that's his last name. I can't remember his first name. And Milosh." I squeeze my eyes shut, grasping for his last name, but instead, *Ben's* face flashes in my mind, smug and unreadable. My chest tightens. "Kamarov." I exhale. "Ben . . . Ben was questioning why I was talking with a Russian oligarch."

"Okay," Athena says, followed by the rapid clacking of a keyboard. "Milosh Kamarov is former Russian intelligence with a rumored history of torture. Definitely not a good guy."

I'm past the part where I should be freaked out that almost being accosted by a Russian supervillain is not the worst part of my night. "What does that have to do with me not going to jail?"

"Ask yourself what an FBI agent is doing at the same party as an ex-KGB officer with ties to arms dealers and money launderers and who could write a book on how to make his enemies disappear without a trace."

My panic pauses just long enough for reason to creep in. "They wouldn't be at the same party unless the FBI is investigating someone *at* the party."

"Exactly."

I frown. "But who? Ramirez?"

"I don't know."

For the first time, Athena sounds . . . uncertain? Worried? I look at the agent knocked out in my car. "What am I supposed to do with him?"

"Get rid of him."

I gasp. "I'm not killing him!"

"What? No!" Athena groans. "Why is that your first thought?"

"I don't know! You said it so casually!"

"Cybil, I meant *move* him. You need to get him out of your car."

My breathing shallows. I look around the neighborhood. I haven't seen a car, which is good but also bad. "I think it's illegal to dump a body on the side of the road, even if they aren't dead. Not to mention I threw up my DNA all over the place."

Athena sighs, and I can practically hear her pinching the bridge of her nose. "I have an idea, but I need you to stop hyperventilating."

"I'm not hyperventilating." But I am. I take a long, deep breath and exhale slowly. "Okay, I'm good. Please tell me your idea doesn't involve me committing any more felonies tonight."

Fifteen minutes later, I'm back in my car, back in downtown Dallas, and pulling into the half-circle drive of the Merius Hotel. A valet makes eye contact and hustles over.

"Are you sure this is a good idea?"

"It'll work so long as you sell it," Athena assures me. "Call me when it's done."

"Sounds just like a mob boss ordering a hit."

Athena laughs and I end the call as the valet reaches for my door.

I open it before he can. "Hi, hey, um, I'm just pulling up to help my husband." I thumb toward the back seat. The valet peeks inside, then looks back at me, eyes subtly scanning over my dress. Is that *puke* on my hem? I fight the urge to recoil and instead force a sheepish smile. "He had a little too much to drink."

The valet, young—maybe in his mid-twenties—nods knowingly,

like this is just another Saturday night. Do unconscious federal agents *frequent* five-star hotels?

"I'm just going to get him to our room and then move my car to public parking, if that's okay. Won't take long."

"Sure. Just pull up over there."

"Thanks."

I park, get out, and immediately realize I have *no idea* how to move an unconscious man into the hotel without drawing attention. As understanding as the valet seems, there are definitely people inside who might be more . . . curious.

"Hey, honey," I jostle the agent's leg, not sure if I want him awake or not. Awake would make it easier to move him but assure he could identify me. Arrest me. "We're at the hotel now."

He moans, and I startle. His glassy green eyes flutter open, unfocused. "Ssssssick."

"Me too," I mutter. I reach for his hand and pull him upright. His head lolls to the side, then back to me. I shift, angling so he can't get a clear view of my face. "Let's get inside."

The second he slides out of the car, his legs buckle, and his full weight crashes onto me. My knees nearly give out.

"Ma'am, do you need some help?" The valet—bless his Southern soul—is back at my side. "My dad and Jack Daniels are close friends," he says with a grin. "I've got a little experience with this."

The *last* thing I want to do is involve someone else in . . . whatever crime this technically is—no matter what Athena says. But there's no way I can move the agent alone.

"Yes," I say, feigning exasperation. "If we can get him to the lobby, I'll order us some coffee, get him sobered up enough to make it to our room."

With the valet's help, we half walk, half drag the agent through the lobby. To my shock, no one seems remotely concerned—which is, honestly, concerning. The second he hits the plush club chair, his eyes slide shut with a loud, unceremonious snore.

"Thank you."

"No problem." The valet turns to leave, then hesitates, glancing between me and the agent. My heart stalls. *I'm caught.*

Then he sighs, shakes his head. "Ma'am, if you don't mind me saying . . . you can do better."

Relief and unexpected sympathy twist in my chest. "Thanks," I say, and he turns to leave, but I stop him. "You wouldn't happen to have a piece of paper and pen on you?"

"No, but there's hotel stationery and pens near the lobby phone."

I thank him again, hurry over, and scribble a quick note. After a glance around, I slip it into the agent's hand. Back at my car, I dig out a twenty, hand it to the helpful valet, and begin to drive away, only to catch sight of a security camera mounted on the corner of the hotel.

My stomach plummets. *Cameras!* I duck my chin like the dozens of cameras I can assume are all over the Merius Hotel didn't just capture me drag-walking a *federal agent* into a luxury hotel from ten different angles.

I hit the gas like I can outrun the poor life choices that got me here. But the truth is, not all of them were mine. Some were made for me, some were forced on me, and some—like this one—felt less like a choice and more like survival. I've spent years trying to do the right thing in a world that doesn't play fair, trying to tip the scales just enough to protect people like my mom—people who don't stand a chance against the ones with the money and power to make the rules.

I yank out my phone and dial Athena, and the second she picks up I hiss, "There are cameras! All over the hotel."

"Relax," she says, unfazed. "We'll take care of that."

I don't ask what that means because I'm not sure I want to know. Instead, I let out a shaky breath and turn onto the highway. "What do I do now?"

"Will you feel safe at your apartment until I can figure out if you've been compromised?"

Safe. The word feels foreign and dangerous. Hours ago, my heart believed Ben could make me feel that way, but that was a mistake. The only place I've ever felt truly safe is—

"Cypress Creek. I can go to my uncle Buddy and aunt Renee's place. It's his birthday this weekend, so it won't be unexpected, but if you think I'm in real danger—if my cover is blown—I don't want to bring that to my family."

Athena doesn't respond right away, and I imagine she's running through every possible scenario in that calculating brain of hers, weighing risks and outcomes in real time.

"What did you tell Edmond when you left the restaurant?" she asks.

"That I wasn't feeling well."

"Good. Go to your family's ranch. Stay put until I can figure out if your cover is blown. And *don't* do anything reckless like pick up federal agents."

She's joking, trying to lighten the mood, but the word *reckless* lands like a gut punch. Is she wrong though? I let old feelings for Ben distract me, and now I'm in a tangled mess of my own making. My voice is quiet when I ask, "Do you really think Ben sold me out?"

Athena exhales. "I don't know," she admits, but there's concern in her voice—real concern. "Stay with your family until I find out."

I should feel relief at having a plan. Instead, uncertainty grips me cold and tight. My eyes flick to the rearview mirror, half expecting to see Ramirez's headlights closing in. If my cover is blown, my recklessness might be following me straight to my family.

CHAPTER 29

Ben

Dallas, Texas
Saturday night

The Bureau drilled it into us from day one—always have a way out. Always know your exits, your alibis, your cover stories. Have contingencies stacked like poker chips in case the house burns down.

But no one ever talks about the moment before it all implodes—the half second when you realize it's already too late.

"That broker Ramirez asked you about—Samuel Baird?" Ruby's voice comes through my comms, low but sharp. "He's bad news. Really bad."

Around me firefighters move in controlled chaos, barking orders, their gear clanking as they move in and out of the restaurant to put out the kitchen fire I started. Condo residents linger in the parking lot, griping about the disruption to their evening, while others hold up their phones, recording.

I slow my pace through the parking lot, my jaw tightening. "Define *bad*."

"Oh, you know, just your everyday black-market facilitator, mostly arms and high-tech material sales with a stellar client list ranging from terrorist organizations to enemy states. The kind of guy who doesn't do business unless it comes with a body count."

I stop midstep, my blood running cold—a suffocating contrast to the stifling Texas heat clinging to my skin despite the late hour. My mind races, recalibrating. "Why would someone like that be interested in Ramirez's deal?"

Ruby snorts. "Maybe Ramirez is hoping for Businessman of the Year in the 'Most Likely to Start an International Incident' category."

Ruby's dry wit lands like a gut punch. If Ramirez wants to open the deal to someone like Baird, then the stakes just skyrocketed. Up until now, my focus wasn't on the deal Ramirez was putting together with Earl Edmond. Shadow Broker's mission focused on the financials of the deal—tracking the transactions, gaining access to his accounts, and gathering enough RICO evidence to lock up Ramirez.

But this? If Ramirez wants to work with Baird, then whatever he's auctioning off isn't just valuable—it poses a possible direct threat to national security.

And that would guarantee a life sentence.

"I need to talk to Katherine," I say. "If Baird's involved, we need to reassess."

Crossing through the parking lot, I get to the street and begin walking down the block to where the surveillance van is parked. Traffic is slow as drivers rubberneck the scene, their headlights fighting with the red lights still flashing from the fire trucks. I loosen my tie and lengthen my stride until I turn the corner and the van comes into view.

"You're sure that's the only thing you need to reassess?"

Something in her tone puts me on edge. I don't think I need to ask what she means, but I do anyway. "Meaning?"

"Your *friend*."

My body goes rigid, but I'm unsure if it's because I feel called out or because I immediately want to defend Cybil as more than just my friend—which is probably the last thing I need to be admitting to anyone, including myself, considering I set a small kitchen fire to protect her.

I get to the van, step inside, and shut the door behind me, cutting off the noise from the street. The dim glow of the monitors greets me, the only light in the cramped space. Ruby puts down her cell phone and swivels in her chair to face me, her expression telling me she's waiting for an answer.

I rake a hand through my hair and collapse on the bench seat at the back of the van. "You don't just decide to spy on a crime boss like Ramirez, Ruby."

"That's my point," she says. "You think she's just some innocent girl in over her head?"

Innocence is not what I saw in Cybil's eyes when I caught her in the hallway, but am I ready to admit she's tangled up in a mess that now might have international terror implications? No.

"I don't think—"

"Hold that thought." Ruby swivels to face the screens. She looks at her phone again and then sets it down to begin typing on the keyboard. "I was running facial recognition on the guests at the cocktail party tonight with anyone who attended the museum gala fundraiser a few weeks ago. Ramirez thinks someone is going behind his back to get access to his deal, and since you had a little run-in with someone trying to break into the museum library, I thought maybe they might be here too."

I sit forward. "That's smart. Anyone attend both events?"

"Yes." Ruby continues typing and shifts so I can see the monitor. It's divided into a grid with faces on it. "The images on the right are from the museum. Left is from tonight."

I stand to look over her shoulder. My gaze immediately goes to Cybil, and the shock of seeing her that night rushes through me all over again. *What are you doing, Cybil?*

"Aside from the usual suspects like Ramirez, his attorney Rook, Earl and Sebastian Edmond, and Cybil Langford, you've got a handful of crossovers." She taps different faces on the screen. "Elena Cross, wealthy philanthropist and real estate investor. Adrian Whitmore, media mogul in music and television. Quentin Hayes, former tech entrepreneur turned financier. All shady."

I study each one, trying to imagine them as the figure in black trying to break into the library. Adrian Whitmore has the kind of broad shoulders

I'd recognize even in the shadows. He's not my guy. Which leaves Elena and Quentin. "It could be either of them."

Ruby's fingers fly over the keyboard, and the screen changes from the still images to the surveillance footage from the night at the museum. "I had tech send me video from the time you go upstairs to the library until the time you get back." On the screen, I watch myself exit a door and nearly crash into the server. "Then I asked them to cross-check all the footage to see who disappears at the same time you do."

"That's brilliant, Ruby." I clap her on the shoulder.

"Again, hold that thought," she says, her voice ominous. The screen splits into grids again, only this time it's video footage of . . . Cybil. She's mingling with guests, sticking by Mr. Edmond's side until she's . . . not. I search different camera angles, but with each passing second that turns into minutes, it's clear what Ruby's trying to show me. "The only person who seems to disappear from the gala at the exact same time as you is—"

"Cybil." Her name escapes in a whisper, disbelief tightening my throat. Could she have been the figure in black? Was she the one trying to break into the museum library? The timing is too perfect—too coincidental. I watch her step into the gala seconds before I do, her expression unsettled, like she'd been caught off guard.

Like someone unexpectedly got in the way of her mission.

I can't unsee it. Suddenly, the shadowy figure has a face and it's Cybil. "I thought tech said the surveillance footage from that night was glitchy."

Ruby pauses the video and looks over her shoulder at me. I hate the pity I see in her gaze—like she thinks I've let myself be duped by a woman I once had feelings for and am desperate for an excuse. "Our techs wiped the footage so no one would see *you* up there, but they didn't scrub the entire feed. The other cameras in the museum were still working, which makes it look less like a glitch and more like someone *else* deliberately tampered with the footage."

Someone like Cybil . . .

My gut twists. Cybil, a corporate spy? Even with the evidence right in front of my face, it still doesn't track. "Maybe she's not innocent," I admit. "But she's not—"

"What if she's *not* the person you think she is anymore?"

Ruby checks her cell phone again, and irritation flares in me at her distraction.

"Expecting a call?" My question comes out sharper than I mean.

"Yeah." Her brows pinch. "Seth hasn't checked in yet."

My pulse kicks up. "What do you mean?"

Her eyes meet mine, and the look in them makes my blood run cold. "He hasn't checked in yet," she repeats.

I'm already out of the van and heading to the restaurant. The last time I saw Seth, he looked terrible—pale and unsteady. Using my comms, I ask, "When was the last time you saw him?"

"Not since he walked inside the restaurant."

I check my watch and do the math from the last time I saw Seth.

Twenty-five minutes. Not such a long time unless you're being waterboarded or electrocuted—or you're missing an FBI agent among a den of criminals. Given the high-stakes nature of the cocktail party and the presence of dangerous individuals, my immediate concern is that Seth—who isn't trained for undercover fieldwork—might have blown his cover.

Twenty-five minutes could be a matter of life and death.

My gut twists like a live wire. Seth Jackson has a family—a wife and two little girls who are expecting him to walk through the door tonight. *Danny Morales never made it home.*

I grit my teeth, pushing the thought away. I won't let that happen to Seth.

The back of the restaurant comes into view. It's mostly empty except for a few stragglers and the last of the firefighters rolling their hoses and putting their gear away. Seth's not among them.

When we briefed him on his role tonight, we expected the party to last a lot longer and for Seth to simply call an Uber and leave at the end of the night. Once he was on his way home, he was supposed to check in and let us know. "Did he exit out the front?"

"I've searched through the footage I was able to get before the fire trucks showed up, but I didn't see him leave."

Ruby doesn't worry—at least, that's what she wants everyone to believe. She fights anxiety with sarcasm, but I hear the concern threading through her voice. Seth isn't trained for this kind of thing, but he's not stupid, and if she's worried, it's for good reason.

I sidestep a hose and approach a broad-shouldered firefighter, his uniform smelling of smoke and cooking oil. He glances up as I approach.

"You with the restaurant?" he asks.

I shake my head. "Is anyone left inside?"

"It's all clear."

I nod, clenching my jaw. Not the answer I wanted.

"Only the owner and staff are allowed back inside, but if you left anything, you can talk to that guy over there."

He points to a server standing by the back door.

"Thanks." My pulse is jackhammering with every second I can't find Seth. I look around again and my eye catches on a camera mounted on the back of the building. I'm already jogging back to the van. "Ruby, can we pull footage from the adjacent buildings?"

"Already working on it," she says, her voice clipped. "But it's gonna require a call to OTD."

I exhale sharply. The FBI's Operational Technology Division can tap into remote surveillance, but it requires authorization neither Ruby nor I have. The moment we make that call, the Bureau will pull the trigger on a Critical Response Team, and our entire operation will go up in smoke. Ramirez won't just hear about the FBI swarming the restaurant—he'll know exactly who they're after.

It doesn't matter.

Nothing matters more than finding Seth and getting him home to his family.

I pull open the van door, but Ruby holds a finger up, phone pressed to her ear. My gut clenches, and I pray with everything in me that it's Seth.

"Yes, ma'am, he's here," she says, her expression unreadable.

I step inside, shutting the door behind me as she sets the phone on the desk and mouths, *Katherine*.

My stomach tightens. "We have a problem."

"I'll say we do," Katherine's voice snaps through the speaker. "Would you like to explain why the hotel manager of the Merius just called to report a snoring man matching my forensic accountant's description passed out in their lobby with a note instructing them to 'Call the FBI'?"

CHAPTER 30

Ben

Dallas, Texas
Saturday night

It's been an hour and a half, and I haven't stopped pacing since Ruby and I got back to the office. My head is pounding, my shirt is stiff with dried sweat, though I've unbuttoned the collar and rolled up the sleeves, and I know my pulse won't slow down until Seth Jackson walks through the door.

Katherine assured us Seth was fine—confused, but a team was bringing him back here to be debriefed. Then it's our turn. The weight of the night is circling my brain like vultures. Every decision, every risk, every close call that has me second-guessing myself.

Tonight's operation was supposed to be airtight. Every angle covered, the risks calculated, but the events of this evening proved how quickly things can all fall apart.

Ruby's phone vibrates on the desk for the third time in five minutes. She picks it up, frowns, and flips it over, silencing it.

"Who is it?" I ask.

"No idea." She shrugs. "I don't recognize the number."

"I know I'm the new guy on the team, but is letting me get kidnapped part of the initiation? Do I at least get a T-shirt?"

My attention jerks to the doorway where Seth is standing, coffee in hand, looking as calm as someone who regularly gets kidnapped on a Saturday night.

He sips his coffee. "One minute I'm a trusted member of this organization, and the next the Dallas PD is giving me a field sobriety test and running my name through *our* most wanted list."

Ruby rolls her eyes, but I can see she's relieved to see Seth unharmed.

I rise to meet him, and my throat is tight with the apology he deserves. Tonight was a disaster, but it could've gone absolutely sideways in ways I've been trying not to imagine. "Man, I—"

"It's my fault." Seth holds up a hand, shaking his head and looking sheepish. "I thought I grabbed the cold and flu medicine but accidentally took my wife's anti-nausea medicine instead. Knocked me out cold."

"What's it called?" Ruby reaches across the desk for a pen. "I've got a neighbor who won't stop leaving notes on my door about my recycling habits, and I feel like a well-timed nap might make her rethink her life choices."

I send her a sharp look.

"What?" She shrugs. "Too soon?"

Seth gives a tired laugh and drops into the seat next to hers. His eyes are still a little glassy, but I'll take that over the alternative.

"You should've told me. I would've pulled you from the mission."

"I didn't realize what I had done until I went into the men's room and saw three of me in the mirror. Then the fire alarm went off and the last thing I remember is getting into the back of an Uber."

"Not an Uber," Katherine says, stepping into the office and closing the door behind her. She sits at the desk and logs into her computer, typing as Seth, Ruby, and I exchange quick glances. She turns her screen so we can see the paused video image. "This is from an ATM machine inside of the Merius Hotel."

Katherine hits a button and the video plays. A man is withdrawing cash at an ATM, blissfully unaware that in the background Seth is being escorted into the lobby like a washed-up rock star who pregamed too hard. He's stumbling, his arms slung around their shoulders, but that doesn't stop him from kicking one leg out at an odd angle.

Ruby leans closer to the screen. "Are you . . . dancing?"

Seth squints at the footage. "I think avoiding a potted fern. Or celebrating it. Hard to say."

My gaze locks onto the man and woman with Seth. The man is wearing a hotel uniform and looks disturbingly at ease guiding Seth. But the woman . . .

My jaw clenches.

"You recognize the woman," Katherine says, and I know she knows I do.

"Yes," I say, my voice rough. "It's Cybil Langford."

"I was kidnapped by your ex-girlfriend?" Seth nails the mock indignation, but it doesn't relieve the pressure weighing down on me. *Does he realize how lucky he is that it was Cybil and not Ramirez?*

"She's not my ex-girlfriend," I mutter, but I catch Ruby's pointed look. I press on. "There are some new developments."

Katherine folds her arms. "Let me guess. Ms. Langford might be our elusive interceptor at the museum? Edmond might have a more nefarious purpose for investing in Ramirez's deal?" She leans forward. "Or maybe Ms. Langford isn't *just* the unassuming assistant?"

Those didn't sound like guesses to me. I swing a look at Ruby, but she gives a tiny shake of her head. I face Katherine, trying to find an explanation for how bad it looks, because it looks *really* bad. But for the first time since running into Cybil, I'm feeling like maybe the rose-colored glasses have slipped and I'm seeing her as . . . Nope. *I can't.*

"I know how it looks, ma'am, but—"

"Don't get formal on me, Ben." She sits back in her chair and folds her arms again. "Save that for the report. What I want right now is an explanation for what happened tonight."

Taking a breath, I recount the events of the night. I don't leave out anything, including Seth's unsteady posture and glazed expression, my conversation with Cybil, and then the way I found her in the hallway, which led to the fire I started and the terrifying moments when we couldn't find Seth.

"I'm sorry." I face Seth, because this apology is as much to him as it is to Katherine. "I should've recognized you were sick and called the operation right then."

"I'm good, man." Seth shrugs. "Your girl didn't get too frisky with me."

The room falls silent, and I slide a sideways glance at Katherine. She's expressionless, unlike Ruby, who is biting her lip.

Seth, still woozy, blinks. "Wait."

Another second passes in his medicine-induced state until he realizes what he said.

His eyes widen. "Too soon?"

Ruby full-on cackles, and for the first time all night there's a tiny break in the tension.

"We're all grateful for your safe return," Katherine says, her tone deep and genuine, but I know she's not looking for an apology—she's looking for the truth about how our mission tonight imploded. And her next words confirm that. "Let's go back to the conversation you had with Rook and Ramirez."

"I know they saw me talking with Cybil, so I assumed they were going to ask me about our conversation, but instead, they wanted to know if I thought she might be willing to give me information on Edmond's accounts."

Katherine frowns. "Why?"

"One of Edmond's offshore accounts has been flagged. Ramirez is worried it'll draw attention to any large transactions."

"By whom?" Seth asks, a little more alert now.

"They didn't say," I admit. "But any new transaction—especially a large one—will likely lead back to Ramirez. And after tonight, I think he might be willing to cut Edmond out of the deal completely, but it will come at the cost of bringing in a more concerning investor."

"Like Sam Baird," Ruby offers.

"Or Milosh Kamarov," I add. "I know tonight didn't go as planned, but in a way, I think it's revealed a bigger threat. I'm not sure getting the RICO evidence is our priority anymore. It's the deal. We need to figure out what Ramirez is selling and why an ex-KGB member like Kamarov and an international broker like Baird are interested in it."

"*And* Ms. Langford."

I swing my gaze to Ruby, and she looks unapologetic. "What?"

"If she's gathering intel on Ramirez, it might not be for Edmond. We might need to consider she has her own agenda."

"Like what?" My question comes out like a demand, but Ruby doesn't flinch.

"I know you want to rule her out," Ruby continues. "But we know that *someone* was trying to get into the museum library before the meeting with Ramirez and Edmond. A meeting where they were supposed to discuss the deal and where Ms. Langford disappeared from the gala at the same time. In Italy you were concerned you were being followed, and I don't know if you noticed, but Cybil was nearby in every instance. Tonight you caught her eavesdropping in the hallway, and that was after she was talking with Kamarov, right?"

I don't like the direction this is going. "What are you saying?"

"Maybe Cybil's a pawn. Maybe she's not. But she's gathering information, if not for herself, then for someone, and if we're going to change the scope of this mission, then we have to assume everyone involved is a potential threat."

I run a hand through my hair, gripping the back of my neck. My brain can't find an argument with what Ruby is saying, but my heart? My heart doesn't want to accept it. Not when it's *her*. I know Cybil's been lying to me. But the weight in my chest doesn't come from betrayal—it comes from the terrifying realization that I might love her anyway.

Falling for the woman who kidnaps FBI agents? Yeah, I think I skipped straight to advanced-level Stockholm syndrome.

"I'm not saying she's innocent in all of this," I concede. "But Cybil Langford is the kind of girl who would go out of her way to protect others. People don't just wake up one morning and decide to spy on a dangerous crime boss like Ramirez. If she's involved—*truly* involved—there must be a good reason."

"Then we find out what it is," Katherine says, finally speaking. "While I don't condone setting restaurants on fire, I think it's important we determine Ms. Langford's intentions—and possibly how we can use them."

"Use them?"

"We need to uncover information about Ramirez's deal, correct? As Edmond's assistant, she has better access than we do, and something's motivating her to go up against Ramirez. If we find out what that is, what she knows, we might be able to use that information to take him down."

I know she's assessing this situation through a level of experience I can't begin to comprehend, but I want to make sure I'm hearing her clearly. "You want to turn Cybil into an informant?"

"Given the outcome of tonight, I don't think you're going to get anywhere near the YubiKey or Ramirez's accounts. Nobody wants him to pay for what he did to Danny Morales more than we do, and Ms. Langford might be our best and only chance to do that."

I'm about to argue when a knock on the door stops me. Katherine rises to answer it. A man on the other side whispers something to her, then hands her a cell phone. She turns, locking eyes with me.

"Your grandmother."

Every muscle in my body tenses. Gran wouldn't call at this time of night unless something was *really* wrong. I stand and take the phone. "Gran? Is everything okay?"

"Yes, of course, honey," she says lightly, oblivious to the near heart attack she just gave me. "But I have a question."

"Gran, it's late," I say, glancing over my shoulder to find the team watching me with barely restrained amusement. "And I'm working. Can it wait?"

"How exactly does one perform a citizen's arrest?"

I pinch the bridge of my nose. "Gran—"

"There's this new fella, just moved in, and I don't think he's *just* here for the shuffleboard and early-bird specials, if you know what I mean."

I don't.

"Bernie and I saw him sneaking out the back gate with a suspiciously heavy duffel bag. We would've followed him, but Bernie just had hip surgery and—"

"Gran, you *have* to stop spying on your neighbors," I whisper-hiss, and Ruby outright snickers behind me. "I have to go, but I'll call you later."

"Fine," she sighs. "I'll see you tomorrow, then."

I frown. "Tomorrow?"

"Don't tell me you're not coming to Buddy's birthday. Everyone will be there."

I groan. I completely forgot about the invitation Rex sent for his dad's birthday. The man is like a second father to me, but with everything going on, there's no way I'll be able to make it. "I've got work."

"Bennett Bradley, work isn't everything."

"I know, Gran. I'll see what I can do."

"Good. And if you happen to have any night-vision goggles, bring those with you."

I hang up before she can ask for wiretapping equipment and hand the phone back to Katherine.

"Instead of Bring Your Kid to Work Day, can we have a Bring Your Grandma to Work Day?" Ruby grins.

I return to my seat. "I love her, but I'm pretty sure she was responsible for the Chicken Coup of '92."

Katherine's brows lift. "I don't know what that is, but I'm curious how your grandmother got access to my assistant's personal cell phone number."

My lips part because I don't know either. "Um, do you want me to call her back and find out?"

"No," Katherine says. "How fast can you get in touch with Ms. Langford?"

The thought of calling Cybil sends my pulse into overdrive. I don't like the idea of turning her into an informant—*especially* when my whole plan was to keep her off Ramirez's radar, not paint a bigger target on her back.

"I don't have her number, but I can try to reach her tomorrow by calling Edmond's office."

Katherine's lips press into a thin line. "That's not soon enough."

"Not to pour fuel on the fire," Ruby chimes in, "but have we considered how Ms. Langford knew who to call about Agent Sleeping Beauty over here?"

"Hey," Seth protests, then grimaces. "That's going to stick, isn't it?"

I ignore him because, one, yes, that nickname is officially permanent, and two, I don't think he's fully alert to realize where Ruby's question is leading.

"There was a note on Seth to contact the FBI, right?" She looks to him for confirmation, and he nods. "So how did she know he was with us?"

The question slams into my chest, leaving a gnawing pit of unease.

How *did* she know?

Katherine's gaze sharpens. "We need to get ahold of Cybil Langford—*now*."

I take a deep breath, dread already pooling in my stomach. I know exactly where to find her.

Holt Ranch—where I first fell for her, where she used to drive me crazy in more ways than one, and where every teenage ounce of my pride got tangled up in wanting her attention. Only this time, it's not just teasing and adolescent pranks. This time, the stakes are real, and more than my heart is on the line.

"Looks like I'm headed to a birthday party."

CHAPTER 31

Cybil

I-35 Texas
Sunday morning

Is this what it feels like to be on the run? It's nearly two in the morning, and the only signs of life on I-35 are a convoy of semis, a couple of night-owl drivers who are probably chugging gas station coffee to stay alert, and me—paranoid, exhausted, and trying not to look like someone who just dumped a barely conscious FBI agent at a hotel like he was last night's leftovers.

Athena directed me to go straight home and pack a bag—"But don't make it look like you're running away." So, obviously, I panic-packed and overanalyzed whether taking a duffel bag or carry-on looked less like a person running away. Or if taking my lucky hoodie, extra cash, and six pairs of underwear for a two-day trip screamed "normal weekend" or "witness protection starter kit."

I strategically left my bed unmade, marked my calendar with a dentist appointment I don't have for Monday, and left a half-eaten granola bar on the counter, hoping it looked like I just stepped out for a quick trip and *not* because I was afraid I'd end up in an unmarked van.

My stomach grumbles. I made the wise decision to stop at Buc-ee's and grab my favorite pecan praline coffee and the family-size bag of peanut butter M&M's to keep me company on the drive to my aunt and uncle's ranch. The caffeine and sugar are definitely not helping me with my nerves.

I clench the wheel, checking my mirrors again. The route to Cypress Creek is second nature, but I've still switched roads, made unnecessary turns, and doubled back twice to check for a tail. No one has followed me. At least, not that I can see. Every set of headlights in my rearview feels like a possible threat, but unless Ramirez or the FBI has resorted to using rusted-out Camrys or lifted trucks with bumper stickers about fishing, I'm probably okay. For now.

My cell phone rings through the car speakers, and I *jump*. Nope, definitely not okay. Totally fine though. Super chill.

I answer. "Hello."

"Hey, how are you doing?" Athena's voice is as calm as ever—which is easy to be when you're not the one whose face is about to be plastered all over the news for discarding an FBI agent at a hotel. I'm sure he's okay. Right? If he's unharmed, then it's a lesser charge, right?

"Oh, you know, just an ordinary Saturday night—kidnapping an FBI agent, spying on crime bosses, wondering if peanut butter M&M's were the right choice for my last meal."

"First, you're funny when you're dramatic. Second, is there a better last meal than chocolate and peanut butter?"

I can't argue with that logic.

But am I really being dramatic?

"I kidnapped an FBI agent and left him nearly unconscious on a hotel chair." I track a suspicious-looking minivan that's been keeping pace with me for a few miles. "Pretty sure I'm not being dramatic enough—oh, wait, Lorenzo Ramirez might know I've been spying on him."

"You didn't kidnap an FBI agent. We pulled the video footage, and he got into your car all on his own."

I slow down and breathe easier when the van cruises past me. "Will that hold up in court?"

"You watch way too many crime shows."

"I watch enough to know that circumstantial evidence can get you twenty to life in an orange jumpsuit, and orange is *not* in my color palette."

"Cybil, I need you to take a breath and listen to what I'm going to tell you."

The shift in her tone causes me to straighten in my seat. "I'm listening."

"And breathing?"

"I'd be dead if I wasn't."

Silence.

"Yes." I blow out an exhale that's loud enough for her to hear. "I'm breathing."

"Good, because what I'm about to tell you might make you panic a tiny little bit."

"We've really got to work on your calming techniques."

"When we were checking to see how the FBI agent got into your car, we spotted your boyfriend, Craig Miller."

I wrinkle my nose. "He's not my—never mind. What was he doing?"

"You said he pulled the fire alarm, giving you a chance to get away from Rook, but if he's working for Rook and they suspect you, why would he let you go?"

I've been trying to work that out too. My brain wants to explain it as nothing more than coincidence, but my heart is holding out for the more romantic notion that he did it to protect me because he has feelings for me.

"So we tracked Craig's movements after the fire. He leaves the parking lot and heads down the street. There's one camera that gives us a partial view of him walking toward some vehicles, but we can't see which one is his. Then several minutes later, he comes back to the restaurant and seems to be looking for someone."

"Me?"

"Sorry to burst your bubble, but I don't think so."

"Then who?" I didn't see him with anyone else at the cocktail party.

"Don't know. He never met up with anyone, just walked back down the street again. So we started running the license plates on all of the vehicles we could see and any that drove away around the same time we can't see him anymore."

Something big is coming. I can feel it and I'm not sure my nerves can handle it. "What is it, Athena?"

"Just trying to match your dramatics."

I grip the steering wheel. "I've had enough drama tonight to last me a lifetime."

"*Well* . . . we pulled a plate from a van. It took some effort, but we confirmed—it's the FBI."

It's way too late—or is it early?—for my brain to compute what this means. "Right. He's the one I kidnapped, remember?"

"You really have to stop saying you kidnapped him," Athena says. "We expected that if an FBI agent is at the cocktail party for Ramirez, he'd be there undercover and would have a team nearby—though a fat lot of good that did. But it's interesting that Ben is near the van. We don't know if he's under surveillance or if he's . . . working for them."

My heart stalls in my chest. "What do you mean?"

"Our team is very good at finding information on people, Cybil. Exceptionally good. We have a cyber expert who trains the government's cyber experts. So when *he* can't dig up anything on Ben—or Craig—it sets off alarms."

"How could you find out that the man I kidnapped was FBI so quickly, but you can't find out anything about Ben after all this time? Don't y'all have them on speed dial or something? Can you just call them and ask?"

"We try very hard not to interfere with other agencies' work."

"If there's ever a time to interfere, Athena, I think it might be to find out if my old childhood friend, the man who's made it very difficult for me to do my job for you"—*the man I might've imagined a whole Disney moment with hours ago*—"is a possible FBI agent."

"Or under their surveillance," Athena adds solemnly. "Given who Ben's working for, the easy answer is that he's on the FBI's radar. But here's the bigger concern—if he *is* working *with* the FBI, they've buried it deep. We can trace the Bureau's involvement, but we don't know the what or why."

"I don't understand," I say. "You found out the guy I kidnapped was FBI, but you can't find out if Ben is?"

"We did get a name for the man you *briefly detained*. His records were partially sealed, but there were remnants in financial crimes task force logs, older training rosters, and a blacked-out case file out of DC."

I blink. "So the FBI didn't fully wipe him?"

"They wiped enough to keep him off *Ramirez's* radar. But our clearance goes deeper. And they didn't expect us to be looking."

"But Ben?"

"Nothing. No agency logs. No case mentions. No digital fingerprints. It's like his name was scrubbed from every channel that could confirm his identity. And that kind of silence doesn't happen by accident. It's deliberate. Protective. And very, very good."

The implication of what Athena just said lands with all the weight of a grenade—blowing up any idea that Ben might have feelings for me. If he's an FBI agent, he lied. If the FBI is watching him, then he's not who I thought he was, and I need to stay as far away from him as possible.

I see the exit for Cypress Creek, and like magic, a restfulness settles over me, drawing me like a magnet to the long country road.

"What do you want me to do?"

"Sit tight at your aunt and uncle's house and let us figure out how the FBI's involved."

"And what about Ramirez?"

"We'll keep an eye on him this weekend, and if I get any indication that you've been compromised, we'll intervene."

"How?"

"Let's not worry about that now."

I flip on my blinker and take the exit. "What about my family? Am I putting them in danger by coming here?"

"Your uncle is a former Texas Ranger, right?"

"Yes."

"You'll be fine."

And deep down, I know I will be. Uncle Buddy would never let anything happen to me, but I can't squash the anxiousness that I'm bringing trouble to the only place I've ever felt completely safe.

The route to the ranch is second nature. With my mom's ADHD, I didn't have a lot of constants in my life growing up, but Buddy and Renee, my cousin Rex, and their beautiful ranch kept me anchored.

I pull into the long dirt driveway, the sky an inky black, the house dark and peaceful against the Texas night. I feel bad I'm arriving so late, but Athena told me to take my time getting here so they could monitor if Rook or Ramirez was looking for me. *Or the FBI.*

Ben in the FBI? Is that really so far-fetched? I mean, probably less far-fetched than thinking he's in cahoots with Ramirez. Unless he is.

But if only one of them could be true . . . obviously I'd want him to be FBI. Right?

Unless—oh, crap.

My brain does a full, panicked highlight reel of all the times I thought I was being slick, and suddenly it's more of a blooper reel. The museum library, where I oh-so-casually tried to plant a listening device? He was *right there.* The balcony in Italy, where I almost died? He only flinched when I fed him the line about the cat because he knew I was lying. Oh, *sweet mercy,* the ring excuse. He knew I'd been in Ramirez's office and saw right through my line before I even finished making it up.

The whole time I was suspicious of him working for Ramirez, and the whole time it had to look like I was neck-deep in his criminal operation.

But if he isn't FBI, then I've been playing spy with someone who already knows the game and knows how to beat me.

When I see the main house ahead, I cut my car's headlights and circle around the gravel drive toward the guesthouse in the back. I park near a large pecan tree and smile when I see the tire swing still hanging from its thick branch. Getting out of the car, I stretch my back where tightness has seeped into my muscles. I take a deep inhale of the sweet country air, and it's impossible not to feel the tug of yearning deep in my soul.

This is what security and stability are supposed to feel like.

Crickets serenade me as I quietly pull my overnight bag out of the back seat along with the grocery bag holding the ingredients for peach cobbler. In my effort not to look like I was a fleeing fugitive, I swung by the only open grocery store on my way out of town to grab ingredients for cobbler. It's my uncle Buddy's favorite and the one thing he requested when I asked him what he wanted for his birthday. A familiar request from a simple man in a place that hasn't changed in years. Which is exactly why I've come here—to pretend that my life still makes sense.

The guesthouse is a cookie-cutter version of the main house. Hand-hewn oak beams and reclaimed barn siding complement the creamy natural stone of both residences, even though the guesthouse was built just a few years ago.

Adjusting the load in my arms, I squat down to retrieve the key tucked under the edge of the mat. Set a few miles from the interstate and deep into the hills of Cypress Creek, there isn't much need for security—at least none Uncle Buddy and his family can't provide given they own nearly a hundred acres of riverfront property in all directions from here. I unlock the door and step in, breathing in the familiar scent of lavender and cedar. *Home.* Or at least the closest I've ever known.

The second I step inside, I feel it.

Something is off.

Then I hear it—the faintest creak of a floorboard.

My stomach drops.

Someone is here.

My heart slams into my ribs. Rook? Ramirez? Have I led them straight to my family? I hold my breath, waiting for the next sound so I can pinpoint where it's coming from. Uncle Buddy keeps rifles near the back door of the main house, but the last thing I want to do is make a run for it and lead whoever is in here with me straight to my aunt and uncle.

A shadow passes and without thinking, I grab the first thing in my grocery bag I can wrap my fingers around—a five-pound sack of flour—and hurl it at the shadow moving in the corner.

I'm rewarded with a grunt. Then a muffled curse.

The moonlight reflects on the cloud of white floating in the air, coating the intruder like a ghostly specter.

"Son of a—"

A cough muffles the rest of his words, but . . . that voice.

You have got to be kidding me.

CHAPTER 32

Ben

Cypress Creek, Texas
Sunday morning

My nose is throbbing and I'm choking on the cascade of smooth powder covering my face, when across the kitchen I catch Cybil moving toward the island. I open my mouth to let her know it's me, but I suck in another lungful of . . . What is this? The tasteless powder turns into a paste on my tongue—flour. *She hit me with a bag of flour?*

Oof. I'm hit in the stomach by something hard and round. Through the moonlight I see Cybil clutching a bowl of fruit, her arm ready to lob—

An apple. I dodge to the left and the fruit smacks the refrigerator with enough force I know she's not playing around. She means to harm me.

"Cyb—"

"What are you doing here?"

She doesn't wait for an answer and throws more fruit at me, one after another, forcing me to dodge and weave like I'm fighting a fruit ninja. When I think she's run out, I rise to my full height. "Uncle Buddy's birthday."

"Liar!"

I don't see the banana until she's released it like a boomerang and it nails my arm hard enough it splits, splattering banana guts all over me.

"I'm not—"

Cybil darts around the island and I dart the other way. She opens a drawer and whips out a wooden spoon and chucks it at my head with a painful thwack.

I rub the spot and glare at her. "Dang it, Cybil, would you stop attacking me?"

"Not until you tell me why you're lying."

She doesn't give me a chance to answer before she lifts another bowl, and I shake my head at her.

"Don't you dare!"

Her hand wraps around an egg. "Tell me why you're lying."

"I'm *not*."

An egg flies at me, and I duck right. It cracks against the cabinet. The moonlight glints against the spark in her eyes and her lips tug into a wicked smile. *Oh, this is war.*

I growl and her gaze widens, and she immediately throws another egg. I duck left and it cracks against the counter. She tries again and I make a grab for it but miss. It breaks against my hand, sending a stream of slimy yolk through my fingers. She throws three more in rapid succession, and I bob and weave around the island to avoid them.

I go left, she goes left—another egg flies at my head. I go right, she goes right, and she takes aim again. At some point, she has to run out of eggs, right? Faking left, I go right and she's within grasp. She arches her arm back, releases an egg, but this time I catch it—unbroken.

It takes a second, but I'm close enough to see the realization flash in her eyes that I'm the armed one now. She backs away and I toss the egg in my hand and catch it, smiling.

I stalk her with slow steps, enjoying the game. My heart is thrumming against my chest because there's a current of attraction I can no longer ignore. I close the space and Cybil backs into the counter with an abrupt stop, her eyes locked on mine.

But there's no fear in them. "I dare you."

"Aw, Billy, have you forgotten how much I love a good dare?"

A blast of cold water hits my face, and I throw my hand up to block it. Cybil has the sink's sprayer aimed in front of her.

"Stop," I sputter. The flour on my face is turning into something like a papier mâché mixture. I lunge for her, and she screams, dropping the hose. She darts around the island, but I'm quick and I round the other way and capture her in my arms. "Got y—"

The wind is knocked out of me as Cybil lands a blow into my gut, forcing me to release her. I do and she pivots, swinging her leg around to kick the back of my knee, causing my leg to buckle. She takes advantage of my unsteady footing and locks her arm in mine, and with impressive speed and strength, she uses my body weight to take me to the ground.

But I don't go alone.

I manage to slip my arms around her waist and pull her with me. She face-plants against my chest, her scream muffled as we both hit the ground. Something weighty and squishy is seeping into my shirt and my chest is heaving with every breath, but I can't ignore how good it feels to have her in my arms.

This should be my suave secret agent moment. Instead, I'm breathless, egg yolk dripping down the side of my face, and being subdued by a woman half my size. Bond would be ashamed.

If I think the game is over, I'm wrong. Cybil shoves off me and attempts to lock my arms down to my side with her legs.

"I don't think so," I huff, lifting her off me with ease. She writhes against my grip and twists, trying to get free, but I'm about to show off all my hours at the gy—

She does some kind of ninja move and breaks free of my grip, and I twist to my side, narrowly escaping an elbow to the liver. I have no choice but to fight back, not enough to hurt her or anything, because I'm having more fun than I've had in a long time, but a man's gotta keep his dignity here. I get ahold of her hand and she's pulling back trying to get me to release it and I'm shocked at how strong she is. Suddenly, she releases the tension so that my own hand flies back in my face and I end up punching myself in the lip. *So much for self-dignity.*

"Will . . . you . . ." I talk between gasps and my stinging lip. "Please . . . stop . . ." I'm about to go for her wrists again but think better of it, and instead scoop up a handful of flour off the floor and drop it over her head.

She rears back, wiping at the white powder raining over her face. This time I take advantage, wrapping my legs around her waist and bringing her back to the floor next to me. She tries to pull away, but I have her arms pinned to her chest and I ignore the teasing floral scent and the problematically attractive position we're currently in to distract me from getting answers.

"Why were you listening to my conversation with Rook and Ramirez at the restaurant tonight?"

"Let me go," she says, sending a puff of flour into the air with each fiery word.

I stare at her ghostly face and—dang it—even looking like an angry baker, she's beautiful. "I think you gave me a concussion with that bag of flour."

Releasing her, I lay my head back on the floor and regret it when I land in something sticky and wet.

"Good." She shoves away from me. "Next time you won't break into houses and sneak up on people."

I run a finger gently over my nose. Then my lip. Both are tender and throbbing. "I think you gave me a fat lip."

"Refer back to my previous statement."

"You don't feel a little bit sorry you might've broken my nose with a bag of flour?"

"No."

But the softness in her voice tells me she does. A little.

Rolling to my side, Cybil immediately scoots backward away from me, her body rigid like she's ready for round two. I hold up one hand and use the other to push myself up to a seated position. "Stand down, Billy."

"Stop calling me—" she snaps, but her words are cut off as she shifts and slips on the mess beneath us. I reach out instinctively, trying to steady her, but it's no use—my knee slips and we both slide, tangled in the chaos. She ends up flat on her back, and I end up above her—one hand cradling the back of her head, the other braced against the floor to keep from crushing her. Her eyes lock on mine.

"Billy," she finishes on a whisper.

Our flour-covered faces are inches away from each other. I search her face, my eyes dropping to her lips for a second before I find her eyes again, our breathing rough and unsteady. It would be one of those romantic movie moments, except with each breath we exhale a plume of flour into the other's face like we're trying to seduce each other and suffocate each other at the same time.

Cybil's eyes narrow. "You're breathing flour into my eyeballs."

"You're returning the favor."

She blinks, eyes crossing slightly as another flour puff hits her nose.

"Don't," I whisper.

"I'm—"

"Don't do it."

"I'm gonna—*Achoo!*"

The sneeze blasts straight into my face.

We both freeze, staring at each other through a new, even thicker haze.

I blink. "That might've been the most intimate thing I've ever experienced."

She blinks at me and then bursts into laughter, her body shaking beneath me. The sound is glorious. *This* is the Cybil I remember. The one I—

The rest of my thought is interrupted by a bright light that temporarily blinds me and cuts Cybil's laughter off instantly.

I blink a few times, trying to focus—and then I see them. A pair of boots I know all too well. There stands Cybil's uncle Buddy. Plaid pajama pants. White T-shirt. Rifle in hand. And that look on his face that says, *One wrong move and I'll bury you behind the barn.*

I shove myself off the floor, Cybil and I untangling ourselves as fast as humanly possible.

"What in the— Oh my."

Cybil's aunt Renee's voice cuts through the tension, and I glance up just in time to see her cover her mouth with her hand. But it's the smile peeking through her fingers that throws me.

Wait . . . is she horrified? Or amused?

I flick my eyes back to Buddy, still standing there with his rifle—but not pointing it at me, which feels like a small miracle. He's helping Cybil to her feet and someone behind him is belly laughing.

Rex steps around his dad, grinning. "Bro." He stretches down his hand to help me. "You both look ridiculous."

"No thanks to you!" Cybil shoves her cousin in the shoulder. "You didn't tell me"—her eyes land on me—"he was going to be in the house."

"You didn't ask." Rex chuckles unapologetically. "I thought it would be a nice way for you to reunite after all these years."

If he only knew.

I catch Cybil's sideways glance, and I know she's thinking the same thing. It feels like we have a shared secret, and if it weren't so freaking dangerous, I might've enjoyed the moment more. She quickly throws her arms around her aunt and uncle. She exchanged her cocktail dress from earlier tonight for a tank top and a pair of joggers, and my eyes—traitors that they are—lock on the lean muscles across her back and sculpting her arms. No wonder she managed to drop me. She's solid.

"Ahem."

My gaze jerks up. Buddy's watching me like a man who knows *exactly* what I'm thinking—and is daring me to keep thinking it. The man practically raised me, but the warning in his blue-gray eyes tells me he won't think twice about putting a boot where the sun doesn't shine.

I open my mouth to explain, to say it's not what it looks like . . . but yeah. It's *exactly* what it looks like. My lip throbs. I touch it and wince—it's already swelling. I've taken hits from fists before. But never from a bag of flour.

"I'm sorry about the mess," Cybil says, already gathering the groceries that spilled from her bag. She picks up a can of something dented, and I silently thank the Lord that *wasn't* the first thing she grabbed when she came at me like a ninja. "I didn't know anyone else was going to be in the house," she adds, glancing at me, "and he startled me." She gestures at the battlefield of bruised fruit, leaking eggs, and flour-dusted everything. "I'll clean it all up. And I'll replace the food before the party tomorrow."

"Don't you worry about it," Renee says, taking the can from Cybil's hand and setting it on the counter with a soft smile. "Rex can help Ben clean up in here."

"But I didn't make the mess," Rex grumbles.

We're nearly thirty, full-grown adults, but one look from Buddy is all it takes to remind us respect isn't optional.

"Don't argue with your mom, son," Buddy grunts, then pivots on his heel, following Renee and Cybil back to the main house. "G'night."

With Cybil gone, the space feels oddly empty. I turn on Rex. "What were you thinking?"

"What?" Rex is all fake innocence. "Cyb always stays in the guesthouse when she visits."

I find a broom, toss it to Rex, and grab a rag to start wiping the counters. "How often does she come back to visit?"

Rex begins sweeping, but I catch the sideways look he sends me. "Why?"

Because ever since I saw her again, I've been starving for pieces of her life—who she became, what she's been through, and what led her down a path that ends with Edmond, Ramirez, and her life in danger.

But I just shrug and keep wiping. "Just wondering."

"Give me a break." He stops sweeping. "I saw the way Dad caught you ogling my cousin. He's probably sleeping with his rifle tucked in his arms."

"I wasn't ogling." I hope the flour caked on my face is thick enough to hide the heat growing in my cheeks. "I had flour in my eyes. I could barely see."

"Sure." Rex's eyes flick to the main house before locking back on me. "Remember, my dad likes you, but he definitely likes Cybil more."

I keep cleaning, wasting time I don't have.

Rex isn't wrong—Buddy's always had a soft spot for his niece. Once my feelings for her started to shift into something real, I was careful. Cautious. Never crossed a line.

But now? With Rook and Ramirez closing in, I can't afford caution. I need to know what she knows—where she stands in all this—so I can figure out how to keep her safe.

I glance toward the main house. The kitchen light flicks off.

The probability Buddy has his rifle within arm's reach is high. And he'll do whatever it takes to keep Cybil safe—even from me. I'm pretty sure he wouldn't shoot me . . .

Still, if I'm going to talk to Cybil, for my safety, it'll have to wait until tomorrow.

CHAPTER 33

Cybil

Cypress Creek, Texas
Sunday morning

There's a terrifying moment, maybe a second or two, when you realize you're being watched. The fight, flight, or freeze instinct kicks in, and as I lie in bed, eyes still closed, every nerve in my body snaps to attention.

If I fight, there'll be blood. If I run, I might not make it. If I freeze . . . well, that rarely ends well.

A weight shifts beside me on the bed, and a whisper of movement tells me I'm not alone. My heart pounds. I was supposed to be safe here.

I crack one eye open.

Beak. Feathers. Murderous eyes.

Kentucky Fried.

My aunt and uncle's devil rooster with the personality of Jack the Ripper.

How is he still alive?

I inhale a sharp breath as the oversized ball of feathers pecks at a loose thread on the bedspread like it's plotting my slow demise. The window's open—of course it is—and with it comes the scent of honeysuckle and betrayal. Kentucky Fried didn't just waltz in. He had help.

And if I make it out alive, I'm going to kill them.

Keeping the covers tight around me, I wiggle my foot under the blanket just enough to nudge Kentucky Fried. He growls. Actually growls. I didn't even know roosters could do that.

Nope. Not today, Satan.

With a battle cry worthy of a horror movie heroine, I fling the covers over the rooster's head and leap out of bed. My foot catches in the sheet, and I crash to the floor in a tangle of cotton and panic. I scramble for the door, arms flailing, just as Kentucky Fried explodes from the bedding like a heat-seeking missile. I slam the door behind me and press my back to it, chest heaving.

On the other side of the door there's scratching. Claws. A low, judgmental cluck.

Kentucky Fried survives another day.

Ben and Rex? Maybe not.

As I pound down the stairs two at a time, the memories of the pranks Ben and Rex played on me every summer come roaring back. But using the feathered, demented freak of nature named Kentucky Fried was extra low.

At the door, I shove my feet into Aunt Renee's garden boots and yank a sweatshirt off a hook, pulling it over my pajamas as I march toward the guesthouse. Crossing the yard, I find Uncle Buddy by the smoker. He tosses me the UTV keys before I can say a word.

"They're in the west field," he hollers.

"Kentucky Fried's in my room," I say, swinging into the Gator. "If you turn him into stew, make it spicy."

Uncle Buddy gives a sharp nod. "Light 'em up."

Two shotgun blasts crack in the distance.

"You know I will."

Less than five minutes and one deeply cathartic fantasy about strangling Ben and Rex with a boa made of Kentucky Fried's feathers later, I crest the hill to the west field and spot them—Rex on the railing and Ben loading a shotgun like he's posing for the cover of a rugged outdoorsman calendar. Both have their backs turned and ear protection on, and I'm smart enough to know not to sneak up on them. I hang back, cover my ears, and wait until Rex presses the release.

Two orange disks soar through the air. Ben hits the first and clips the second. When he opens the shotgun to discharge the shells, I make my entrance by shoving Rex off the rail. He disappears into a bush with a yell.

Ben turns and I notice it. A fat lip. Oh, that is *satisfying*.

He flashes a smug grin that only highlights the swollen curve of his lower lip. "Morning, sunshine."

I cock my head. "Looks like someone ran into a door."

Ben touches his lip lightly, eyes locked on mine. "More like a right hook with trust issues."

"Trust issues?" I scoff. "Maybe I thought you were someone else."

Our gazes are locked in a battle—and this isn't just banter. It's reconnaissance. If Ben's working for Ramirez, his presence here after catching me at the restaurant might not be so innocent. I don't know what Rook wanted to talk to me about last night, but it's possible they sent Ben to get to me instead. But if he's FBI, that doesn't make me safe—it makes me a liability. I've lied. Snooped. Crossed enough lines that if Ben connects the wrong dots, I won't just lose the mission. I'll lose my cover, my job . . . maybe worse. His expression doesn't flinch, which tells me he's watching me as closely as I'm watching him—like we're both waiting to see who's gonna break first.

"Oh, I think you knew exactly who you were hitting," Ben says deadpan. "You definitely hit me like someone who's been waiting a long time."

For the first time I feel a twinge of guilt. Partly because I hurt him, but mostly because under all the secrets and lies before any of this got complicated, once upon a time I wanted to give my heart to Bennett Bradley, and only hours ago, dancing with him, I was reminded I'd do it again.

This is exactly how spies like James Bond get into trouble. Only instead of a femme fatale in heels, my version just happens to be a man with a busted lip, a shotgun in hand, and a grin that could unravel years of resolve in a single glance.

Ben smirks—his gaze landing on my uncle's oversized Carhartt sweatshirt I'm wearing. "My sweatshirt looks good on you."

It's only then that I realize the warm, masculine scent—cedar and spice, familiar and comforting—is his.

I tug down the hem, flustered despite myself. The urge to peel off his sweatshirt and toss it on the ground wars with my confidence in my bedtime attire. There's nothing scandalous about my tank top and sleep shorts, but the sweatshirt feels like a shield against the heat blooming in my cheeks. It's not embarrassment—that would be easier to handle. No, this is something slower. Sharper. That inevitable awareness that his smile still has the power to hijack my pulse.

Stay focused, Langford. You're here to find out if Ben is a criminal or a federal agent—not give in to flirtatious feelings.

"I wouldn't be in your stupid shirt if you hadn't put that demon rooster in my room."

Rex climbs back onto the platform, brushing leaves off his jeans. "It was Ben's idea."

Ben shrugs, loading another round. "Figured you could handle a rooster. Not like it's the first time you've had something dangerous coming at you."

My gaze sharpens. "I don't have any problem facing down danger, especially when I know who I'm dealing with."

Rex freezes halfway through wiping dirt off his sleeve. "Wait, are you still talking about a rooster?"

Ben ignores Rex and stares me down. "And you know *who* you're dealing with?"

"Yes, *Craig*, I do."

He doesn't flinch, but I see a flicker. Barely there, but it tells me I caught him off guard.

Rex blinks, looking between us. "Who's Craig?"

"Oh, you didn't know?" I keep my tone light, teasing. "Your best buddy goes by different identities these days." I tip my head up like I'm thinking. "Thought I'd double-check which one showed up this morning. Is it Craig Miller?"

Ben's hand pauses over the shells just long enough to confirm I've struck a nerve. Then he slides back into his easy swagger like it means nothing. "Guess it depends on who's asking."

Rex squints. "Wait—Craig Miller? Cybil's boyfriend from high school?" Recollection lights his eyes, and he grins. "The one we convinced to use deer attractant as a bug spray?"

Ben's lip quirks. "I think it was an improvement."

I narrow my eyes. "What are you, twelve?"

"Just needed a throwaway name for some business stuff."

"Business stuff," I echo. "Sounds legit."

Ben counters smoothly, "What about you? Any interesting deals lately? Work trips?" He closes the shotgun with a soft click, his smile still in place but his voice quieter. "Russian oligarchs?"

He's watching me now. Closely. Too closely.

Since I don't know whose side he's on, I can't tell whether his question is a warning or bait. Either way, I need to tread carefully.

"You're not *hiding* anything?"

"Are *you*?"

"Nope," he says, with just enough ease to make it suspicious. "Just doing my job."

"Me too."

Rex glances between us like he's missed the start of a movie. "Am I missing something here? Cybil's a secretary for some developer, right?"

"Yep, just a secretary." I smile, slow and sharp. "Although you can't take people at face value these days."

Ben steps closer, lowering his voice. "No. You really can't."

The way he looks at me—it's not teasing anymore. It's layered. Like he's trying to decide if I'm friend or foe. And I'm doing the exact same thing.

I look over his shoulder at the open field, grasping for clarity, for the steady ground I used to feel under my feet whenever I was here on the ranch. But nothing feels simple anymore. There's no good reason for Ben's smolder to affect me the way it does. None. And I know just how to wipe that smug look off his face.

"Though with the way you're shooting, you might need more practice."

"Ooh." He rests the shotgun on his shoulder in the safety position. "That sounds like a challenge."

"The only challenge I see is you hitting your target."

I don't know why I'm engaging in this. Maybe it's exhaustion. Maybe it's old habits. But there's something in the way he's looking at me that makes it impossible for me to walk away. I want to go toe to toe with him if only to prove I can. To prove I'm not the girl he spoke about to Rex all those years ago.

He sets his shotgun on the table, picks up another from the case, and checks the barrel like he's done it a hundred times. "Tell you what," he says, sliding a glance my way. "Since you're *so* curious about my job, how about a bet?"

I arch a brow. "A bet?"

Ben leans a hip against the table, all confidence. "First one to hit two clean shots gets to ask the other a question and they *have* to answer it."

"Ben—"

"Truthfully," I add, cutting Rex off.

His grin ticks up as he hands me the shotgun. "Of course."

Rex groans. "You two are exhausting."

I step to the firing line. "You're sure?"

Ben cocks his head, studying me. "Scared?"

I load two shells and snap the shotgun closed. "Guests go first."

We shake on it—brief, electric, and laced with enough unspoken history to blow up a small building.

"Hey, Ben, you don't have to—" Rex starts.

"Bet's made, Rex," I say. He throws his hands up and heads for the control panel.

Ben takes his stance and glances my way. He doesn't look worried. Not even a little bit. *He should be.*

"You can still back out if you want," he says far too smugly.

"Nope." I pull on a pair of safety glasses and ear protection. "I like to know who's on my team. Or . . . who's about to shoot me in the back."

Ben gives me a look that's equal parts amused and assessing, like he's playing along but also reading between every word I say. Calculating. Wondering how much I know—and how much I'm hiding.

Rex presses the button and the machine releases the clay pigeons. Ben fires. First one—clean hit.

My turn. I track the disk, pull the trigger. It shatters.

Next round. Ben aims, fires—just a graze.

Mine explodes in midair.

Ben pulls off his ear protection, and I can't help the smug smile stretching across my face as I eject the empty shells and set the shotgun down with a little flair.

He eyes me, equal parts suspicious and impressed. "You hustled me."

"Don't hate the player," I say with a casual shrug. "Hate your aim."

He shakes his head, but his smile causes my heart to flutter in my chest. I immediately shut it down.

Focus.

I move closer, arms crossed, pulse skittering under the surface because this is the moment I've been waiting for since my conversation with Athena last night. "Ready to answer my question?"

Ben shifts, and for a second, I think I catch something—nervousness. My mouth opens to ask the question that's been burning in my brain—*Are you FBI?*—but his phone buzzes.

He pulls it out, glances at the screen. And then immediately answers. "Gran?"

If he thinks a phone call is going to distract me from getting to the truth, he's—

"Whoa, Gran, wait." His voice sharpens, concerned now. "Slow down. What do you mean you're in a dumpster?"

I freeze. My gaze slides to Rex. He shakes his head.

"What do you mean you were tailing—" Ben stops short, rubbing his temple. "Gran, where's Bernie?"

Rex starts packing up the shotguns, still shaking his head like this isn't new.

"Who's he talking to?" I whisper.

"His grandmother."

I frown. "His grandmother is in a dumpster?"

Rex shrugs. "Not as strange as it sounds."

Ben turns, pacing now. "Gran, do *not* use the flare gun. Tell Bernie to stay put— Wait, what?" He presses a palm to his forehead before resignation washes over his face. "If Bernie's walker is stolen, I will replace it," he says through gritted teeth. "Don't move." He shakes his head. "Yes, Gran, I know you wouldn't be calling me if you could move. Just . . . just don't use the flare gun. I'm on my way."

He hangs up and turns to me. "I have to go."

I stare at him. "Your grandmother's in a dumpster?"

"Yes," he says on a sigh. "Can I ride back in the Gator?"

I nod, following him to the UTV. "Is she okay?"

"For now, yes." He climbs into the passenger seat. "But the last time Gran did this, it ended in a restraining order and three citations for public disturbance."

"The last time?" I get into the driver's seat and start heading back to the house. "So this is a regular thing, your grandmother in a dumpster?"

Ben glances over with that trademark smirk. "Some grandmothers crochet—mine organizes unlicensed stakeouts."

CHAPTER 34

Ben

Cypress Creek, Texas
Sunday morning

The Gator rattles up to the ranch house, a plume of dust trailing behind us as Cybil pulls up to the barn and parks. She's out of the UTV and inside the house before I can get a word in. If I weren't picturing my grandmother knee-deep in trash with a flare gun and an itchy trigger finger, I'd chase after her.

The ride back was quiet and quick. I know at least twice, Cybil hit the ruts in the road extra hard, causing me to tighten my grip on my seat. *"You think you know me, but you absolutely don't."*

And maybe she's right. Mostly. We've both grown up and changed, but that doesn't mean I don't see the girl I once knew. The way she dodged my questions wasn't just clever; it was impressive. A two-step of lies that made me respect the game—if only that's what it was.

Unfortunately, it got me no closer to knowing the truth about who she's really working for and what her interest is in Ramirez's deal.

And now I have to deal with my grandmother and—I'm halfway to my truck when I hear it.

A low, menacing cluck from inside the cab.

I swing open my truck door and freeze.

There, strutting across the bench seat like he owns the place, is

Kentucky Fried. His beady eye turns on me. I don't blink. I don't move. I don't even breathe.

Good play, Cybil.

Behind me, a low chuckle rumbles. I glance over to see Buddy standing near the porch with one of his ranch hands, arms crossed, his Stetson low against the morning sun.

"What's going on?" Cybil strolls out of the house, already dressed, eyes locking onto the standoff between me and the demon rooster.

"Like you don't know," I hiss.

Kentucky Fried swivels his head and lets out a growl. I slam the door shut and jump back. He puffs out his chest and crows like he just won a turf war.

I whirl around and point at Cybil. "Nice payback."

Her eyes widen. "I didn't do that. You think I'd touch that deranged menace?"

"You?" I ask, turning to Buddy.

He shrugs and wraps a protective arm around Cybil. "No idea how he got in there."

Cybil kisses her uncle on the cheek. "Need anything else at the store while I'm gone?"

"I'm good, honey." Buddy and the ranch hand head over to his truck.

"Wait—I need someone to help me get this rooster out of my truck. Gran's gotten herself in trouble again."

Buddy squints. "She safe?"

"She's . . . in a dumpster, sir. With a flare gun."

He just nods. "You'd better get that rooster outta your truck, son. You don't want Dorothy Bradley on the evening news."

"That's the last thing I want," I mutter, then call out louder, "Yes, sir."

"Good luck, Craig," Cybil says as she walks past me toward her car.

I step into her path. "I need your help."

"I'm not going anywhere near that rooster."

"Just take me into town. Let me get to Gran before she causes a literal dumpster fire. She's old. And feeble."

Cybil glances at my truck. Kentucky Fried pecks at the window like a dementor. She sighs. "Fine."

I give the rooster one last look, unsure if I should thank him for giving me the perfect excuse to spend more time with Cybil or worry that he's going to turn the interior of my truck into shredded cheese.

I climb into the passenger seat of her car and force myself not to examine everything too closely. At the academy, they taught us a vehicle can tell you a lot about a person. And being in hers feels . . . personal.

An air freshener shaped like a chocolate bar is attached to her vent.

"I thought you didn't like chocolate."

She snatches it and tosses it into the door pocket. "It was a gift." Then, side-eyeing me, adds, "Stop assessing my car."

"I'm not," I lie, hands raised.

Glancing over my shoulder at the back seat, I fight a grin. Imagining Seth knocked out back there . . . It's not funny, I know. But the look on her face when she discovered him must've been priceless.

"Nice back seat space. Looks roomy."

Her eyes flash to mine. "How about we don't talk."

I let a few seconds pass and then turn in my seat. "Don't you want to ask me a question? You did best me—even if it was a hustle."

"It wasn't a hustle."

"You didn't shoot like that when we were kids."

"We're not kids anymore."

"No, we're not," I say quietly.

Cybil's gaze slides to me and then back to the country road leading us into town.

"Come on, Billy. Don't you want to know something? Curious about my souvenir spoon collection? Where I get my Bond tuxedos? What shampoo brand I use to keep my hair so shiny?" I run a hand through my hair. "My dating life?"

"What?" She jerks her head toward me. "No. I don't care about your dating life."

I grin. "Good. Because I don't have one."

"Not surprising."

"Ouch." I clutch my chest. "What about you?"

"I don't collect spoons, and I use whatever shampoo is on sale."

"And your dating life?"

"None of your business."

"Right, just like you sneaking around on the ledge outside of my room in Italy wasn't my business?"

Cybil remains focused on the road. "I wasn't sneaking around."

"No?"

"There was a cat."

She hits a pothole—definitely on purpose. My seat belt digs into my hips.

"You'll ruin your struts like that. Not good if you need to haul anything . . . unusual."

She shoots me a look but doesn't take the bait. "Where's your grandmother at?"

"Butter My Biscuits."

Five silent minutes later, we arrive at the breakfast joint. We walk around back and take a quick peek into the dumpster, but all I find is enough bacon grease to summon Paula Deen.

"She's not here." I pull out my phone and dial Gran's number. No answer. "Maybe we should check the police station."

Cybil scoffs. "She's your grandmother, not a fugitive."

"You haven't met my Gran."

We're crossing the parking lot back to Cybil's car when something catches my attention. Across the street, I spot a small hedge bordering the Baptist church. Behind it, in a folding chair under a sign that reads "Jesus Sees You—Smile!" sits my grandmother in a pink track suit with binoculars pressed to her face. Beside her, Bernie—her seventy-something partner in crime—is perched on her walker, holding a notepad and a walkie-talkie.

"Oh, good grief."

I cross the street with Cybil close behind. Not until my shadow falls over Gran does she look up and grin. "Took you long enough, Benny."

Cybil snorts.

Gran's eyes brighten when she sees her. "You brought a friend?"

I make a quick introduction. "This is Cybil. Buddy's granddaughter. Cybil, this is my gran and her friend Bernice."

Gran squints up at me, lips pursing. "Benny, who'd you get in a scrap with? Your nose looks like it lost a bet."

Beside her, Bernie hums. "Lip's puffy too. Did you deserve it?"

Cybil doesn't bother to hide her smirk.

"Long story," I mutter and then redirect my grandmother. "You told me you were in a dumpster."

"Imagine if I was!" Gran looks offended. "Long as it took you to come to my rescue, I might've had raccoons for roommates."

"Better than cellmates," I mutter. "Which is where you're headed if you keep spying on people."

Bernie shushes me and speaks into her walkie-talkie. "Subject exiting front door. Still has the black bag. Looks smug."

"Copy that," Gran replies, despite both devices being off. She yanks at my T-shirt to pull me down just as the pastor peeks from a church window. He waves. I wave back. Yep. Real covert.

The "subject" in question is a man wearing gym clothes and, indeed, carrying a duffel bag.

"Gran—"

Cybil squats beside her. "What are we watching him for?"

"Do not encourage—"

"We think he's tampering with the tapioca," Gran says proudly, handing Cybil the binoculars. "He started working at the restaurant and, suddenly, no more tapioca."

"Gran," I sigh. "Why would he be tampering with the pudding?"

"Maybe he's juicing it. Putting the 'roids in it."

I blink. "What?"

"Mm-hmm," Bernie fans herself with her notebook. "He *does* have nice calves."

"You're right." Cybil hands the binoculars back. "He does have nice calves."

Before I can respond, the man notices us.

Gran hisses, "Abort mission, Bernie. Code peach cobbler. Code *peach cobbler*!"

"Wait—I thought peach cobbler meant he's got a weapon," Bernie whispers urgently, wobbling as she tries to stand. I remember she's recently had hip surgery and help her.

"No, that's banana pudding."

The man crosses the parking lot. "Dorothy? Bernice? Everything okay?"

"We're just enjoying the weather," Gran says sweetly.

"With binoculars?"

"Bird-watching," Cybil chimes in. She stretches a hand to him. "I'm Cybil."

He smiles and it lingers too long for my liking. "Chad Wexler."

Bernie squints at Chad. "What'd you do with our tapioca pudding?"

"Bernie!" Gran shakes her head. "Way to be discreet!"

Chad looks between them, utterly baffled. "Tapioca pudding?" Something dawns in his expression. "Wait . . . are you the one who keeps leaving the anonymous notes in my locker?"

"I don't know what you're talking about!" Gran shoots back.

"You wrote, 'We know what you did,' with letters clipped from a magazine."

Gran lifts her chin. "That was for dramatic effect."

I look skyward, like maybe divine intervention will deliver me from this moment. The answer to my prayer comes in the grin the pastor sends me from the church, like he's glad it's me and not him.

"Ladies, I had nothing to do with the pudding," Chad says. "The kitchen manager wants me to bring in some healthier options."

Gran narrows her eyes. "Like 'roids?"

"Nobody says 'roids, Gran."

Chad laughs. "I promise, no 'roids and I'll talk to the kitchen. Maybe I can bring in something better."

Bernie scowls. "None of that low-fat stuff."

"I apologize for my grandmother and her friend," I say.

"Honey, don't apologize for me." Gran waves me off. "Someone's gotta keep order."

Chad chuckles, backing away. "Stay out of trouble, you two."

When he's out of earshot, Gran turns to Cybil, eyes gleaming. "I like you."

"I like you too," Cybil says, smiling—and my traitorous heart skips a beat.

Gran links arms with her. "If you were older, I'd invite you to join our Pearls and Pistols club. 'Course, you'd have to be a resident, but we know how to clear openings when needed, right, Bernie?"

"Sure do," Bernie says, carefully navigating her walker over the asphalt.

"Gran, that kind of talk makes it premeditated." I use her keys and open the car door for them.

"Actually, under Texas law, you need intent *and* an overt act for it to be premeditated." Cybil winks. "And unless your gran's got a taser stashed in that floral purse, she's safe."

"Ooh, she's dangerous *and* smart." Gran beams. "I'm glad my Benny has finally found a good girl."

"Gran," I warn.

"Poor boy was never the same after that girl broke his heart."

"Gran," I repeat, sharper.

"It was pitiful. My boy moped around for ages. What was her name?" She frowns. "Something odd, wasn't it, Benny?"

I meet Cybil's gaze and my chest tightens. "Billy. I called her Billy."

Cybil swallows and an emotion flashes in her eyes so fast I can't name it. She turns to Gran. "It was lovely meeting you both, but I need to get to the grocery store to pick up some items."

"Of course." Gran pats her arm. "I'll see you at your uncle's birthday, right?"

"Yes," Cybil says before leaving.

"Gran, you shouldn't have said that," I murmur after Bernie gets settled into the passenger seat and I fold her walker into the back seat.

"Whyever not?" Gran touches my cheek. "The romantic tension nearly knocked me down when the two of you walked over. Besides"—she points at me—"she needs to know you still love her. And you should know she does too."

"I don't know, Gran." I glance across the street and see Cybil's car still in the parking lot. "Things are . . . different now."

Gran pats my cheek—*hard*. "Don't give me that nonsense. Take it from me, life's short. If you find a girl who knows your worst secrets and still splits a biscuit with you in public? You marry that girl."

I blink. "That's your benchmark for love? Sharing biscuits in public?"

"You wouldn't be here if it weren't for biscuits and benches." She grins.

Bernie cackles. I groan.

Gran gets into her car and starts her engine. "Go get your girl."

I watch them drive off, then cross the street. Cybil's car is still idling.

"You waited?"

"I know what I want to ask you."

The air shifts, bringing reality crashing right over me. If she's digging for information on Ramirez for Edmond or someone else, I have to protect the mission and it will confirm what Ruby and Katherine already suspect. Cybil is part of the crime. And that will effectively shut down any hope I—or my gran—might have about biscuits and benches. Unless, of course, they have those in the federal penitentiary.

"Ben?"

My heart stutters. "You said my name."

She looks at me, confused and a little frustrated. "Are we still doing this? Craig?"

"No, it's just . . . I'd forgotten how nice it is to hear you say my name."

She exhales. "Were you going to show up at the tree that day?"

My stomach drops. "What?"

"The day we were supposed to meet—"

"I know the day you're talking about," I say, cutting her off. "I waited. You didn't come." The hurt rushes over me and I feel like that vulnerable teen boy all over again. "Why?"

Cybil stares at her hands gripping the steering wheel. "I was going to. But I heard you talking to Rex. You told him I was a risk. That I was different and would never end up"—she gestures around her—"here."

I frown, trying to recollect the conversation she's referring to, and then it hits me. "Wait, that's why you didn't show up?"

She turns to me. "Why would I if you thought I had no intention of sticking around? I was too big a risk, right?"

"No," I say softly, reaching through her window to tilt her chin up. "I was eighteen. Insecure. And wildly terrified that the girl I'd loved since she put frogs in my boots might not love me back."

She's staring at me. I want to kiss her. Hold her. But I still have a job to do.

"Cybil—"

My phone rings.

She leans back. "It's fine."

It's not, but when I see Ruby's name on the screen, I don't have a choice.

"Yeah?" I answer, turning slightly away.

"Where are you?" Ruby's voice is tight, no preamble.

My eyes flick to Cybil. "With family."

"You need to come in."

"Now?" I step away from the car. "I haven't gotten any information yet."

"It's too late," she cuts in. "Bring her with you."

My pulse kicks hard. "What's happened?"

A pause.

Then Ruby says quietly, "They're looking for her."

Every nerve in my body goes on alert, and I search the area around me for Ramirez or Rook.

"You need to get her here—"

"I have permission to tell her the truth?"

"Just get her here."

My fat lip and bruised nose tell me Cybil might be more dangerous than Kentucky Fried if I try to get her to Dallas without telling her why. *And she can shoot.* "She's not going to get into the car to go with me to Dallas without knowing why."

"You don't have to get her to Dallas." The line crackles. "There's an abandoned property at the end of Highway 39. I'll send you the address."

Highway 39? "You're here?"

"Take the back road to pull in," Ruby answers without answering. "See you soon."

The line goes dead.

I stare at the phone, then at Cybil.

If Ruby's here in Cypress Creek, it's not a check-in—it's because something went wrong, and fast. And all I need to do is get Cybil to the edge of town without her asking any questions I can't answer.

Sure, no problem. *I should've taken my chance with Kentucky Fried.*

CHAPTER 35

Cybil

Cypress Creek, Texas
Sunday afternoon

This is how I die. By the man who broke my heart and then in some weird way just randomly confessed to his pistol-toting grandmother that *I* was the one who broke *his* heart. The car ride is silent except for Ben giving me directions.

"You'll take the next left."

It's a dirt road in the middle of farmland and my gut is telling me to yank the wheel around and go back to town where there are witnesses. But do I do that? *Noooo.* Like every solid damsel in a horror movie, I just keep driving to the destination of my murder and simply ask, "Where are we going again?"

Ben shifts in his seat next to me. Whoever called him on the phone shifted his easygoing demeanor into tight ridges and hard lines across his face. I should be freaked out. I still don't know if Ben is working for the FBI or if his illegal activities working for Ramirez have put the FBI's spotlight on him. If it's the former, I should survive. If it's the latter, then I'm praying there are federal agents watching us from the tree line a few miles away.

"My parents wanted me to pick up Buddy's gift."

His voice is tight, and he doesn't look at me. Instead, his eyes are tracking the landscape around us with each passing mile like he's watching for someone. The FBI? Or Ramirez?

This is the part where the narrator from *Dateline* explains, "She had no idea that the danger wasn't in front of her—it was riding shotgun." Why am I not pulling over and demanding that Ben get out of my car? I'm the one driving. I see a ditch ahead. Maybe I can convince him to unbuckle his seat belt and then hit the gas so fast it knocks his head into the dash?

My heart pinches. *Ugh.* The first rule in avoiding murder is not to feel sorry for the murderer. I don't want to hurt him. I don't want to die. I want . . . answers.

Yes. This is how women survive murder, right? Get the killer talking, distract him, then run like the last deviled egg just hit the church's potluck table.

"Is it true?"

"What?"

"You showed up at the oak tree and waited for me?"

Ben sighs. "Until Buddy came to get me." He looks over at me. "The whole time I was waiting I thought maybe I went to the wrong tree or that you were still getting ready and I kept thinking how silly that was because you were already so pretty."

Do not get weepy, Cybil Renee Langford, I scold myself when my eyes start to water and my heart begins to swoon. This is exactly how Stockholm syndrome works.

"But you left." His voice is soft and tender. "And now I know it's because of me."

I blow out a shaky breath. "It wasn't your fault. I mean, yeah, your words hurt, but I was young and clearly had my own insecurities."

"Cybil, you have to know that I would never, ever try to hurt you. Then. Or now."

Now? Would someone say that if they were leading me to my death? If they did, that's extra cruel, and nothing about who I know Ben to be is cruel. Even when he filled my shower with worms. Ben was a prankster, annoying, a pest worse than a fly at a barbecue, but he was also kind, gentle, and, yes, ridiculously good looking and charming. But there was nothing cruel about him.

"Please believe me."

The pleading in his voice causes me to slow down my vehicle so I can face him. And maybe make a run for it if I need to. Deep down, I don't think he would ever hurt me, but the men he might work for certainly could.

I put the car in Park and Ben doesn't object. *So he's not in a hurry to see me harmed.* That's gotta be good, right? "I want to believe you."

Ben's hand reaches across the console and takes mine. "I was a dumb kid trying not to let his best friend know I was head over heels gaga for his cousin. You were smart. Driven. And way too good for a boy like me with dirt on his boots and no real plan. I watched you grow into someone who carried the weight of your family and made something out of the chaos. I never stopped seeing you as the strongest person I knew." His thumb runs over my knuckles and I'm hanging on to every word as if it's a balm to my soul. "You didn't settle. You persevered and I wanted to be someone worthy of standing next to you."

His eyes are soft but serious.

"What you heard that night? What I said to Rex . . . it wasn't about you. It was about me. I was scared. Scared that I was going to give you my whole heart, and you'd leave—because I knew you were meant for big things. You were always going to make the world bend to your will. And I thought I'd be left behind, proud but watching from a distance."

I stare at our hands, trying to wrap my head around what he's saying. It sounds real. Too real. And for a second, I forget I'm supposed to be suspicious. For a second, I just want to believe every word like it's gospel.

"I don't know what to do with that," I whisper, my voice tighter than I want it to be. "You're saying those things . . . It's what I always wanted to hear. Back then. Maybe even now."

I finally look at him. Really look at him. The charming Ben who lives life like it's a joke is a lot easier to handle than the one sitting across from me now. His eyes are steady, full of quiet intensity that feels more dangerous to me than any lie.

But in the end, there are lies. Between both of us.

"The problem is, I don't know if that's you talking, or Craig Miller." I take my hand back gently. "I need the truth, Ben. And if you care about me the way you say you do, you'll stop hiding behind whatever or whoever you're trying to protect."

Ben turns away from me and looks out the window. I don't know what he's thinking, and for the first time I feel like I want to take it back. Like the tides have shifted and no matter what he says, it's going to change everything.

"Do you trust me?"

I swallow. "What?"

He faces me, reaches for my hand, and squeezes it with gentle strength. "Do you trust me?"

I don't want to be the kind of woman who gets swept away by feelings alone. I know better than that. Trust is earned—it's steady and proven, not just felt. So I've held it close, like armor. Treating it like precious currency, knowing that once it's lost, it's almost impossible to earn back.

It's ironic. Here I am, worried about Ben's trustworthiness, when I'm fully engaged in my own web of lies. But it's different, right? I spy on bad men. Dangerous, corrupt men. They're not people I love. They're not people who can shatter me with a single broken promise. I know the risks and I accept them.

Betrayal from a stranger is a transaction. Betrayal from someone you love is a wound.

I didn't go to the oak tree that night because I was afraid. Afraid that if I gave Ben my trust, I'd end up like my mom—heartbroken and betrayed. But if I had gone, I would've heard the truth. That he cared. That he was afraid too.

And now I'm sitting in this car, holding the hand of the boy I once ran from and the man I don't know if I can run toward, wondering if I can trust him now.

Exhaustion weighs on me. No one tells you how heavy the burden is to protect yourself. And maybe that's the problem. Maybe trust is like love, not something you guard, but something you offer. Grounded not in certainty but in faith.

"Yes," I whisper, and I'm surprised by how much I mean it.

A second of silence passes, and Ben's expression shifts from surprise to relief. He gives my hand another squeeze before releasing it and pointing ahead.

"See that barn? That's where we're headed."

The barn he's indicating is a dilapidated structure with peeling paint and half a roof. There's a tractor on the side that's nearly buried by overgrown grass and weeds. And the kind of place the *Dateline* narrator would call *"remote, eerily quiet . . . and the last place she was seen alive."*

"Trust me, Cybil."

I take a steadying breath and accelerate toward the barn. My tires bump over the cattle crossing bars and I'm surprised to see a small farmhouse tucked behind the barn. It's invisible from the road. It looks dark and empty. Have I just made the worst mistake of my life?

"She was blinded by old attraction and a charming jawline."

I shut off the *Dateline* narration and park. Ben unbuckles his seat belt, but I stay where I am. If he's telling the truth, I don't need to go inside, right?

"You coming?"

"Nah, I'll just wait here."

Ben's lip quirks. "Cybil, it's going to be okay."

"I'm sure that's what every murderer tells his victim right before he strangles her."

"You think I'm going to kill you?" Ben laughs, but when he sees I'm not laughing, he stops. "You're serious."

"You haven't exactly been honest with me, Craig." I look at the farmhouse and frown. Was that movement in the window? My heart drops into my stomach. Is Ramirez there? Rook? "What are we doing here, because I know it's not to pick up a gift for my uncle."

Ben looks back at the farmhouse and I'm pretty sure gives a shake of his head. The front door opens, and my jaw unhinges when Athena walks out.

"What in the world?"

"Stay here."

Ben gets out of the car and closes the door behind him. He takes a step toward Athena and then stops, his posture rigid like he's preparing for a fight. I quickly unbuckle my seat belt and get out too.

"I said to stay in the car," he calls over his shoulder.

"What are you doing here?" I ask Athena.

"Come inside, Cybil."

"You know her?" Ben asks, confused.

"Yes, but I don't know why she's—"

I stop when I see another woman appear in the doorway behind Athena.

"It'd probably be safer if you two come inside now."

Ben waits for me, and together we walk up to the old farmhouse. The floorboards groan under our steps. The scent of mildew and old wood is thick in the air as we step inside. Sunlight filters in through the broken slats and filthy windows.

Another woman stands just behind a table—tall, blond, and serious, with the kind of posture that says she's not here for polite conversation. I flick a look toward Athena. She gives me a small, reassuring nod—the kind that says, *"You're safe—or at least, not dying today."*

"Hello, Cybil," the blonde says, her voice crisp enough to chill a glass of sweet tea. "It's nice to meet you finally."

I don't respond. I just move to stand beside Athena, like my body has decided who it trusts before my brain can catch up. Ben notices. There's a flicker of hurt in his eyes, and then it's gone so fast I wonder if anyone else saw it.

And someone did. The dark-haired woman standing between Ben and the blonde. She looks vaguely familiar, but I can't place how I know her. What I do notice is how carefully she's watching me. Not with open suspicion, but with some kind of quiet scrutiny that reads like a warning.

"Cybil." Athena gestures to the woman staring at me. "This is Ruby Knight." Ruby barely gives me a nod. "And this is Katherine Scott, Special Agent in Charge, Organized Crime and Counterintelligence with the FBI."

My stomach tightens. I glance at Ben, who's watching me. So. FBI. I don't even have a chance to react to the relief rushing through me or the emotion building in my chest, because Ben shifts his attention to Athena.

He steps forward, his posture tight, voice low and controlled. "And you are?"

There's no charm, no grin.

Athena doesn't flinch. She meets his gaze with that unbothered calm that makes people either trust her or want to run. "It's not necessary for our purposes here."

Ben doesn't blink. "That's not a name."

Athena arches a brow, then finally says, "You can call me Athena."

The look on his face reveals he knows she's not being honest. "And you work for?"

She lets a second pass. "The Strategic Neutralization and Protection Agency—Global Division."

Ben exhales sharply, but it's not relief—it's wariness. "You're private sector?"

"Yes, but we also do work for the government when necessary." She holds his gaze. "Sometimes we're contracted by agencies, sometimes by individuals or corporations." She pauses, then adds, "It depends on the mission, but our objective is the same. Keep people safe and strategically neutralize threats."

"And you?" He turns to me. "You're a spy?"

"And you're FBI."

His brown eyes narrow on me, but they're not accusatory. There's a flash of amusement shining in them when he says, "It was you in the museum."

"It was *you* in the museum," I answer back.

"You've been undercover this whole time?"

"Only when you're around, *Craig Miller*," I say sweetly.

"Well, this feels like a weird first date," Ruby says, swishing her hand at a fly. "But can we get back to why we're here?"

"Yes," Katherine Scott says. "Let's talk about how the two of you are going to work together to protect national security—without letting your complicated history turn it into a classified disaster."

CHAPTER 36

Ben

Cypress Creek, Texas
Sunday afternoon

I stare at the tablet Athena is reading from like it's a loaded gun. In a way, it is. Russian KGB. International arms broker. Multiple encrypted calls. An expedited auction happening sometime in the next forty-eight hours. All of it tied to the reason I'm standing in a farmhouse on the edge of town reconciling the truth that Cybil Langford is a spy.

Or, as Athena described her, a *cover asset*.

Forget protecting her—what I should've been worried about was how many ways she could kill me with a nail file and still make it look like an accident.

If there was any relief in learning Cybil wasn't spying for Edmond or a former Russian KGB member, it was short-lived when Athena and Katherine explained why SNAP Global was now involved in Operation Shadow Broker—or rather taking it over.

"Ramirez has an operation in Brazil called PetroSul. It's a subsidiary of Enzo Coal & Oil and works with a local energy consortium to explore for natural gas deposits in underdeveloped parts of the Amazon basin," Athena explains. "While there, his team discovered a naturally occurring but incredibly rare mineral called Aurelite-X. On its own, it's not much more than a shimmering metallic ore. But once it's refined and combined with certain reactive elements—think niobium, scandium, even trace amounts of enriched boron—it becomes something else entirely. It's lightweight, nearly indestructible, and can withstand extreme heat and energy output without structural failure, making it ideal for weapons casings, missile guidance systems, stealth drone components . . . even hypersonic delivery systems." Athena pauses. "Because it's new and unregulated, Aurelite-X isn't on any export control lists. No watchdogs. No oversight. If Ramirez can get it out of the country and into the wrong hands, it's not just a weapon. It's an arms race shortcut."

"And why we've decided to bring you both in today," Katherine says. "Now that we're dealing with a national security threat, we've hit a point where compartmentalization is no longer an asset—it's a liability. Both of you have ingrained yourselves into a position we can use to effectively take down Lorenzo Ramirez and stop an international security threat before it's weaponized."

I glance between Katherine and Athena. Off to the side, Cybil is leaning against the wall, spinning her father's gold ring on her thumb. She's anxious. And rightfully so. If a global threat isn't bad enough, if I understand what was just said, the situation isn't just bad—it's escalating. And Katherine and Athena are dropping us deeper into it.

Which—sure. Fine. I've worked hard missions. High stakes, ugly targets. But none of those involved someone I care about standing in the line of fire.

"What do you want us to do?"

Cybil's question doesn't seem to surprise Katherine. Or Athena. And Ruby looks almost amused. I am not.

I glance at Cybil. She meets my eyes—steady, stubborn. And I know she's not going to back down.

"You're both going to do exactly what you've been doing," Katherine says. "*Craig Miller* will continue to serve Ramirez's financial needs regarding the deal. We know of two interested parties, Kamarov and Samuel Baird. The unknown is who Baird might be brokering the deal on behalf of. We need names in case the deal goes through."

I frown. "In case?"

"Our goal is to prevent the auction altogether," Athena says. "But we expect Ramirez's growing suspicion will push him to accelerate the deal, leaving us without much time to intervene. If we have the names of the buyers, we can pursue them post-auction."

Cybil pushes off the wall. "What do you need me to do?"

For the first time, Athena's confident posture shifts. "Earl Edmond has been invited to the auction. You'll go with him as expected. We need you to get close enough to Ramirez's laptop to access the evidence for the mineral deal."

"You expect her to break into his laptop?" I say, my voice wavering with incredulity and anger. Frustration slices through me. This is my fault. This was my mission and because I failed, Cybil's life is on the line. "Ramirez is already suspicious of her. If she gets anywhere near his laptop, you might as well hand him the gun and tell him to shoot."

"We need the proof," Katherine says calmly. "If Cybil disappears now, it confirms Ramirez's suspicion and accelerates his response. But if she reappears as expected, acting as if nothing has changed, it creates doubt. He'll question whether he misread her, whether he overreacted. That uncertainty works in our favor. Her presence is the variable that destabilizes him." She looks at Ruby. "And she only needs to get close enough for the PhantomKey to extract the information, right?"

"Yes." Ruby slides a matte-black case out of her pocket and opens it with a quiet click. Nestled inside is a sleek, dime-sized disc the color of gunmetal, with a faint ring of light pulsing at its center. "This is a PhantomKey. It's a zero-latency proximity breach device. Think of it like a Trojan horse, but sexy. Get it close enough to Ramirez's laptop and it hijacks the laptop's biometric input—fingerprint, face ID, retinal scan, whatever he uses—and creates a synthetic credential that unlocks the system long enough for us to access the encrypted directories."

Cybil blinks. "So I just walk up to his laptop with this in my pocket?"

"No." Ruby snaps the case closed. "It'll be embedded in custom housing to look like a brooch. To anyone else, it's jewelry, but it's going to require you to get close. We're talking elbow-on-the-table, lean-in-for-a-whisper close. It's the only way to bypass the YubiKey encryption."

"So get within kissing distance of a laptop owned by a war criminal and pray he doesn't notice my jewelry is cloning his hard drive. Honestly"—Cybil swallows—"still not the worst date I've ever been on."

"Sure, because nothing screams subtle espionage like leaning in close to a paranoid crime boss with a weaponized brooch." I don't know if her nonchalance is covering nerves, but I'm not okay with this. "Why not give her a pair of exploding earrings too?"

"It's the only shot we have." Ruby gives me a look that reads *trust me*. And I want to, but this is Cybil we're talking about. "She doesn't have to get close to Ramirez. Just his laptop—within ten inches to activate." Ruby looks at Cybil. "Once it locks onto his laptop, you'll feel a single vibration. That means the device has found a viable connection. It'll take about twenty seconds. When you feel a double vibration, that means the scan's complete and the data has been transmitted to our secure server." Ruby meets Cybil's gaze. "You'll only get one shot. Once the scan completes, the device disables itself."

"Twenty seconds." Cybil nods. "I can do that."

"You say it like it'll be easy." I cross my arms. "Ramirez is spooked. His suspicion is already directed at Edmond and everyone"—I glance at Cybil—"working with him. He'll be *looking* for any abnormal behavior. You so much as blink wrong, and he won't ask questions before reacting. Not only are we putting her in danger, but we're also putting the entire operation in danger."

"Well, guess I'd better practice my blinking then." She gives a little laugh. "Wouldn't want to accidentally launch World War III with a side-eye."

I exhale sharply through my nose. "That's not funny."

"Maybe not." She shrugs. "But if I don't laugh, I'll start panicking. And then I'll blink weird. And we're back to a nuclear fallout."

Ruby snorts. "I like you."

"Listen." Katherine's focus turns to me. "This isn't about RICO charges anymore. National security threats supersede RICO crimes. SNAP Global has jurisdiction now."

I look between her and Athena. "What do you mean?"

"Our agency is going to work with the FBI," Athena says, "but we have the green light to neutralize the threat with or without your help."

I stiffen. "So we cooperate or get benched."

Katherine nods. "Exactly."

There's a beat of silence before Athena adds, "But Cybil will stay."

I watch Cybil. There's a flicker of nerves behind her resolve, the way she presses her thumb against her father's ring like it's armor. She's ready to do this. Of course she is. But she isn't going to do it alone.

I exhale, my jaw tight. "Fine." I glance at both Katherine and Athena. "But let me be clear—if anything feels off, if I even suspect her life is in danger, I'll pull her out myself. I don't care whose jurisdiction this falls within." My voice sharpens. "She's not disposable. And if protecting her costs me my badge, then so be it."

Athena studies me, unreadable. Katherine doesn't blink. Cybil's trying to look steady, but I can see it—the flicker of emotion behind her eyes. She meets my gaze, and I nod. Just once. Not approval. Not agreement. A promise.

We don't say much after we leave the farmhouse. Cybil spoke with Athena for a few minutes after we were told we needed to get back to Dallas this afternoon. We're going to miss Buddy's birthday party, but the fact that Cybil didn't argue tells me she's taking this seriously. She doesn't want any trouble coming to find her or her family. So we're going to it instead.

We're halfway down the winding back road leading back to the ranch, tires humming beneath us, Texas sunlight pouring gold across the dashboard, when she looks over at me.

I look over at her. "So you spy on powerful criminals in your free time."

"Mostly corrupt CEOs, the occasional smuggler with a yacht fetish, or an ex-boyfriend who lies about what he does for a living." She tilts her head. "My résumé is very versatile."

"Anything else you want to confess?"

Cybil stares out the windshield, unbothered. "Define 'confess.'"

I let out a sharp breath. "Let's start with something simple. Do you hate chocolate?"

A pause.

"Open my glove box."

I do and it's stuffed with bags of M&M's. I swing a look at her. "Did you eat the chocolate cake in Italy?"

She shrugs. "You said you didn't want it."

"You said you didn't like chocolate."

She turns, a slow smile forming. "And you believed me. That's on you, *Miller*."

"And the cat you risked your life trying to rescue in Lagoverde?"

She shrugs, not even bothering to look apologetic.

"Unbelievable." I sit back in my seat. "It was you in the museum that night, wasn't it?"

"You saw me, didn't you?"

"I mean, upstairs. Trying to break in. You were the one in black."

"If you're asking if I was the one who gave you the slip"—her lips tip up—"then yes, that was me."

"I think I remember you not getting inside," I say smugly, but then I sit up. "Wait, was the bike crash on purpose? Were you following me?"

"It was not on purpose."

"Remind me to reach out to our international operations division and pull a video of that moment," I say teasingly. "Might be my favorite memory."

"Mine was the wolf with the hunky six-pack," Cybil says with a sigh, and jealousy flares in my chest.

"Was it boredom?" I ask, wanting to forget that particular moment in Italy. "Or some deep-seated desire to tangle with arms dealers and egomaniacs?"

"What?"

"The reason you work for SNAP."

She smiles, barely. "It's the money."

I wait.

"And the whole justice thing," she adds after a beat. "But yeah. The money doesn't hurt when you have a mountain of student loans and a mom with ADHD who treats impulse shopping like a coping mechanism. One bad day and suddenly we owned six Himalayan salt lamps and a Texas-shaped waffle maker."

I laugh. I shouldn't. But it's her delivery. Dry. Perfect.

She sighs and finally looks at me. "When I left for college, my mom spiraled. I think she relied on me to keep her life on track—bills, work, all of it. Without me, things slipped. I used my student loans to cover her bills, worked two jobs just to stay afloat, and by the time I graduated, the debt was unmanageable. I mean, canned soup by candlelight wasn't exactly the goal I had for myself."

I know that. Cybil was going places, and it crushes me to hear how much she's struggled.

"I needed a job that paid the bills, allowed me to heat my soup." She smiles. "SNAP offered to pay me well and I get to help take down bad people."

"And it doesn't bother you? Lying to people?"

"Does it bother you?"

I take a slow breath because she has me there. But . . . "I'm trained."

"To lie?"

"To do what's necessary to take down the bad guy. I know the risk going up against criminals like Lorenzo Ramirez. Did you?"

Her silence is my answer, and my earlier concern comes roaring back.

"Cybil, you don't have to do this."

"Yes, I do," she says. "Ever since my dad's settlement was stolen, I've felt helpless. It's a horrible feeling. SNAP has given me two things I've never had: control and stability. I grew up waiting for the next eviction notice or to see if my mom remembered to buy groceries. But this? I get to lie to bad people for a living. I no longer feel helpless. I feel like I can do something to help protect others from becoming a victim like my mom and I were."

It's probably a good thing Cybil's driving, because if she weren't, I'd be unable to resist pulling her into my arms and doing something reckless. Like tell her I haven't stopped loving her since the day she shoved me into cow manure. Or that I've wanted to kiss her ever since she busted my lip with a bag of flour.

The car rolls to a stop in front of her uncle's ranch house, dust pluming across the front porch. Birds are chirping like nothing's wrong in the world, like we didn't just get handed a mission that could end badly in more ways than I can count.

Cybil kills the engine and rests her hands on the wheel. I know she doesn't want to leave, and I hate that she has to.

"Hey," I say, voice low. "I'm sorry."

She glances at me, brow furrowed. "For what?"

"For lying to you. For not figuring out a way to protect you from Ramirez. I never wanted you to get caught up in this."

She huffs, a dry laugh escaping as she settles her hand on the steering wheel. "I chose this mess. It pays well. And supports my chocolate addiction, which, frankly, is more committed to me than most men."

I shake my head, lips twitching. "So my competition is chocolate. That's tough."

She grins, the kind that's quick and sharp and completely unfair to my ability to think straight. "You're not responsible for me, Ben."

I lean back against the seat, watching her profile in the afternoon sun. "Well, I can't rely on Craig Miller, can I? Dude's such a loser."

"I don't know," she says with a shrug. "He's kind of endeared himself to me."

That gets me. Right in the chest. I turn to look at her fully, but she's already halfway smirking, not giving me an inch.

Then her gaze drops to my still-swollen lip, and she clicks her tongue. "But his fighting skills are abysmal."

"He's not skilled in food combat," I say solemnly. "Especially not when ambushed by a five-pound bag of flour and a woman with excellent aim."

She leans her head back, eyes closed, and lets out a laugh. A real one. And as much as I want to kiss her—bruised lip and all—I realize that this moment is more than that. It's the moment I know. I want this woman in my life. The sharp, stubborn, justice-fueled firecracker who lies for good reasons and keeps secret stashes of M&M's for stress, stakeouts, and emotional sabotage.

Cybil believes she has to protect herself. But I want to change that.

"I promise you, if Craig Miller doesn't do his part in this mission, I will."

She turns to me, and there's something steady in her eyes now—something honest.

"That's good." She opens the door and steps out into the warm afternoon air. Looking back over her shoulder, she says, "Because it would be really embarrassing if I have to save both of you."

The door shuts behind her with a soft thud, and I'm left sitting there, head spinning. I know she's joking. I know she's guarding herself—with sass and sarcasm, her favorite kind of armor. And maybe she doesn't need protecting. She might've bested me last night with a fruit bowl, but I've got skills. Actual federally certified ones.

Still. I've never felt more outmatched—or more determined to keep someone safe.

Cybil disappears inside the house, and I pull out my phone and call Katherine.

She picks up on the second ring. "Please tell me you haven't been taken hostage with a bobby pin and a glare."

"Not yet," I mutter, glancing at the house. "But the day's not over and she's terrifyingly resourceful."

"What's going on?"

I exhale, shifting against the seat. "Ramirez's paranoia isn't going away. I'm concerned about the plan working."

Katherine is quiet for a beat. "What do you suggest?"

"We stop trying to cover our tracks. We let Ramirez think he's figured it out, let him believe he's found the leak."

"You have a plan?"

"Yeah," I say, a grin tugging at the corner of my mouth.

"Will she go along with it?"

I run my thumb across my fat lip. "Yeah, she'll go along with it." And likely love every second of it.

CHAPTER 37

Cybil

I-35 Texas
Sunday evening

If I had a dollar for every time I told myself, "This is probably fine," before doing something wildly not-fine, I could pay off my student loan. At least one of them. Okay, maybe half of one.

Still. Way too many times. But all those other times, I was the only one at risk. This time, it's more than my life at risk.

I take a curve a little too fast, my tires skimming the gravel. A mile marker blurs by, followed by the smear of what remains of an armadillo that clearly didn't make a great decision today.

"You're sure this will work?" I ask, voice low.

Ben's answer comes too fast. Too sure. "I trust you."

I grip the wheel tighter, knuckles paling. The plan *should* work. Ben's confident tone assures me it has all the makings of a covert success, but there's one problem.

Me.

Two weeks ago, when Ben's smug face came back into my life, I would have had no problem with the plan. Nine days ago, when Ben found me in Italian velour splattered with smashed fruit and tried to cover up his laughter at my expense, I might've hesitated, but today?

Today, after Ben's confession, my heart hasn't stopped doing this swoopy, fluttery thing. Romantic in theory. Completely inconvenient when you need to fake confidence in front of a mobster.

"You're sure I'm the right person for this?" I ask. "Because there's a fine line between brilliantly unhinged and 'Please notify next of kin.'"

Ben's laugh crackles over the line. "You're the one I want."

My heart swoops even though he's not saying it in the way my heart wants to believe. "That's brave considering you could probably pick someone who doesn't still daydream about payback involving hot sauce and duct tape."

"You dream about me?"

His voice is teasing, rich, and far too smug for someone who's trusting me with his life. I roll my eyes and will my heartbeat back to normal. "Not in a 'you'd enjoy it' kind of way."

He laughs, low and pleased with himself. "That sounds like denial, Langford."

"That sounds like ego, *Miller*."

"You wound me."

"Not yet," I say, but I'm smiling now. The tension in my chest eases—not gone, but quieter.

It's crazy how easy it is to fall under his charm, but this time it feels different. I have more information. I have the truth. Bennett Bradley cared about me—still does. And now he's asking me to—

"Hey, I'm getting a call from the office. Text me when you make it home."

"Sure."

"It's going to be okay, Billy."

The call ends and now I'm just . . . alone. In a car. With a bag full of food my aunt Renee insisted I take with me because nothing solves all your problems like ten pounds of smoked meat coupled with three pounds of potato salad. I promised Uncle Buddy I'd be back to make his peach cobbler, but my promise felt hollow after the secret meeting at the farmhouse. Kind of hard to commit to dessert when you might not live to see Sunday.

Am I really just supposed to go home, turn on a rom-com, and pretend like I'm not neck-deep in a national security threat and unresolved feelings? There should be a manual for this part: *So You've Just Fallen for a Spy—Now What?*

It would certainly include chapters like:

- *Chapter 1: Weaponize Flirting—When Winking Is a Tactical Risk*
- *Chapter 2: How to Hold a Gun and a Grudge Simultaneously*
- *Chapter 3: Always Have an Exit Strategy—For Your Mission, Your Alias, and Your Stupid, Stupid Heart*

I reach for the radio—anything to drown out the spiral—when my phone rings.

My heart stutters when I see the name on the screen. Earl Edmond.

Why is he calling me?

Do I answer?

Do I not answer?

I thought I was ready for the plan, but *this* was not part of the plan. I'm not supposed to talk to my boss until tomorrow. When I've had a chance to rehearse what I'm going to say.

- *Chapter 4: How to Answer a Call from Your Crime-Suspect Boss Without Sounding Like You're Actively Having a Panic Attack*

I answer. "Hello?"

"Cybil?"

"Mr. Edmond, yes, sir."

My voice sounds way too calm for someone sweating through her tank top at a red light.

"I apologize for calling you on the weekend, and I do hope you're feeling better."

Lie. Tell him you're still not feeling good and HANG UP! "I'm better."

Ugh.

- *Chapter 5: When Your Southern Manners Override Your Survival Instincts*

"Good. I need you to come by the lake house."

The lake house? Before tonight, this wouldn't be an absurd request. I've been to Edmond's home, his lake house, his country club, all in the name of collecting intel for Athena. But . . . "Tonight?"

"Yes."

The way he says it—steady, expectant—makes my skin prickle.

Still, I try to keep my tone light. Unbothered, when internally I'm screaming, *This is not part of the plan!* "I—I'm actually just heading home now. I'm pretty tired, so if we can discuss this tomorrow or maybe at work on Monday—"

"No. This conversation needs to happen tonight. Between you and me."

The words land like a fist to the gut. I grip the wheel tighter, heart thudding in my ears. I have to get out of this. "What about tomorrow?" I try, weaker this time. "I can come by in the morning."

"Cybil."

That's all he says. Just my name. Flat. Heavy. Like a warning and a test rolled into one. "You've worked hard to earn my trust. I'd hate for that to change."

My breath catches. Not loud, but enough.

This isn't a request. This is a line in the sand. I don't want to exaggerate my role, but the only way SNAP or the FBI gets access to the evidence on Ramirez's laptop is if I show up at that auction. I kind of need to be alive for that to happen.

I don't know why Mr. Edmond wants me at his lake house or what the conversation's about. If Ramirez is suspicious of me, it's possible Mr. Edmond is too. But the only way I can find out is to go.

Edmond's lake house sits tucked along the wooded shoreline of Cedar Creek Lake, just over an hour southeast of Dallas. A long gravel drive winds through iron gates and towering pines before revealing a sleek, low-slung structure that's less cozy lakeside cabin and more architectural flex. Steel, glass, and money, perched with enough space between neighbors to bury secrets—or bodies—without anyone noticing.

It's beautiful.

And eerily quiet.

My car crunches across the gravel drive as I try calling Ben again, but the cell signal is useless out here—too many trees, too middle of nowhere. I cut the engine and scan the front of the house. The sunlight is blocked by the canopy of trees, filtering down in patches that shimmer across the house's floor-to-ceiling windows. I can see into the home's curated modern aesthetic, and even though I don't see anyone, I can't shake the feeling that someone can see me.

Before I get out of the car, I send a message to Joy and Marcos telling them where I'm at, because if this is where it ends for me—alone, unarmed, and one bad choice away from a shallow grave—I at least want them to know where to look for my body.

I knock once and a light flicks on right before the door swings open.

"Come in," Mr. Edmond says, stepping aside.

He's in jeans and a linen button-down, sleeves rolled. Casual. Relaxed. The perfect uniform for someone who wants you to feel safe right before you disappear.

Get a grip, Cybil. You're not starring in a Netflix docuseries. Yet.

With that little self–pep talk, I follow him through the glass-paneled entryway into a sprawling open-concept living room that blends seamlessly into a chef's kitchen straight out of a luxury magazine. No matter how many times I've been here, I can't help admiring the place. For whatever reason, my eyes catch on a bowl of lemons sitting dead center on the marble island—so ordinary, so bright, so aggressively cheerful.

He opens the refrigerator and pulls out a pitcher of lemonade, then takes two glasses from a cabinet. "Just made this today."

I stay on my side of the kitchen island, counting how many steps it would take to get to the front door. Twenty-five at a normal pace. Ten if I sprint. A thousand slow, dragging ones if I'm poisoned.

My heart stutters when he reaches for a knife from the butcher block.

"I apologize for calling you over here unexpectedly," he says, taking a lemon from the bowl and slicing it in half, then again. "But I'm afraid we've run out of time."

He drops a lemon wedge into each glass before filling them with lemonade.

I don't touch mine.

He takes his to the living room, settles into a chair, and waits for me to follow. I do, carefully, noting that the closest exit now is the set of French doors leading to the lake.

"What can I do for you, Mr. Edmond?"

"Are you sure you're feeling better, Cybil?"

It's the look in his eyes that always undoes me—genuine concern, calm and steady. Mr. Edmond might work with unsavory business partners, and while I don't know the extent of his own criminal entanglements, he's always taken a fatherly interest in me.

That's what makes him dangerous. Not the power. Not the money. The kindness that feels real enough to make me forget who he is.

"I'm tired, sir. Ready to get home."

He sips his lemonade and then sets the glass on the side table. It's then I notice a very sharp letter opener lying on a stack of opened envelopes. *It was Mr. Edmond in the lake house with the letter opener.*

"You look nervous."

Do I? Do I look like I'm not thrilled to be featured in a true crime documentary? "I'm fine." *Will that be what goes on my tombstone? "Cybil Langford—She's fine."*

"I won't waste your time. You aren't who I thought you were."

The room seems to tilt.

My pulse jackhammers against my rib cage. I don't move. I don't blink.

"You've been working for me long enough for me to notice your behavior. The way you handle my business. Your discretion. Commitment. You've never given me reason to question your loyalty."

I keep my expression smooth. Measured. Internally, I'm halfway to planning an escape route that ends with me diving into the lake and faking my death just to stay alive.

He's still looking at me. Waiting. Letting the silence get to me.

It's working.

"But I have to let you go," he finally says.

I flinch. "You're firing me?"

"Yes, effective immediately."

If I wasn't already sitting, I'm pretty sure my knees would've buckled from underneath me. I should be relieved, jumping for joy, but this has thrown a giant wrench in the plan to get to Ramirez's laptop. "May I ask what I did?"

"I have paid you for the rest of the year." He reaches for a piece of paper and hands it to me. "If there's anything else you need, a recommendation, I will help you in any way I can."

I look at the amount written on the check. My breath catches. "Sir, that's double my salary."

"Take that and go on a long vacation or start fresh somewhere new. It doesn't matter, but you need to leave, Cybil. Disappear. Tonight, if you can."

I raise my chin. "Excuse me?"

He takes a breath like it's heavier than the words he's about to say. "It's my fault. I should've seen it coming. Should've shielded you. But I failed. I couldn't even protect my own son."

"Sebastian?"

Mr. Edmond nods, bitterness edging his voice. "He launched a crypto venture two years ago. Thought he'd landed the perfect investor with Lorenzo, but what he found was a viper in a tailored suit. I didn't know how dangerous Ramirez was until it was too late. I should've done more to keep Sebastian safe."

"What's happened?"

Mr. Edmond's gaze drifts toward the lake, eyes shadowed with regret. "Lorenzo preyed on Sebastian's ambition—on his need to succeed without me looking over his shoulder. He's always been so determined to break free of the label put on him. That he'll never be more than my shadow."

It's not the emotion in Mr. Edmond's voice that hooks me—it's the words.

Break free of the label.

That small, loaded phrase cuts deeper than I expect. Because I know exactly what it feels like to wear a label that sticks no matter how hard you try to scrub it off.

All my life, I've believed I had to prove I wasn't unstable. That I wasn't reckless or irresponsible or doomed to fall apart like the mother I grew up raising. That the only way anyone would take me seriously—or love me—was if I could show them I was built on control, structure, success.

And worse, I believed Ben thought that too. Just a few careless words, but they wrapped around me like a second skin. Until today. When Ben didn't just tell me I was wrong, but showed me. With his actions. His faith. The way he looked at me like I was already everything I kept trying to prove. The whole time I blamed him for a label he never gave me—but one I gave myself.

The thought barely has time to settle before Mr. Edmond's voice pulls me back to the present.

"Lorenzo used Sebastian's company as a front to wash cartel funds—millions. By the time I uncovered the truth, it was too late." He turns back to me, and for the first time, I see Earl Edmond the father—not the CEO, not the strategist, just a man carrying the weight of watching his son get played. "I've been trying to fix it. Quietly. Liquidating my own assets, looking for someone else to step in and take over the deal so I can get Sebastian as far away from Lorenzo and his crimes as possible. But I wasn't careful enough. Ramirez noticed. And now he's watching everyone more closely"—his eyes settle on me—"including you."

It hits me then. Mr. Edmond didn't bring me here to confront me. Or kill me. He doesn't know who I am. Not really. Or what I've been doing. I should be relieved, but for one brief, disorienting second, I feel guilty.

He's trying to shield me from the dumpster fire I'm already neck-deep in because he thinks I'm just collateral. He has no idea I'm one of the people holding the matches.

"Do you understand what I'm saying?" His voice sharpens, heavier now. "If you stay, he won't give you a warning. He'll just . . . make the problem disappear."

"I can't leave."

"Cybil, this isn't pride." Urgency is etched into the lines of his face. "I will pay whatever you ask if you'll take it and disappear. This is your life I'm talking about."

"What about you and Sebastian?"

He exhales slowly, like he's been carrying the answer for too long. "There are things I did in the early years when I was building my company. Things I'm not proud of." He looks out toward the lake again, voice rough with memory. "Cut corners. Looked the other way. Told myself it was survival, not ambition. And I justified it because I wanted a future for my son. Something better than what I had."

A pause. His gaze lowers.

"But you don't build something clean by burying the dirty parts deeper. I've tried to be different these last few years. Tried to make it right—cut ties, change the culture, protect what matters. But Ramirez . . ." His jaw clenches. "He doesn't let go. And now Sebastian is in the middle of it, and so are you."

I swallow hard. The guilt from earlier creeps in again, curling under my ribs like a wire pulled too tight. He doesn't know the whole truth. Doesn't know I'm here because I made myself part of this mess.

"I can't leave," I say again, quieter this time. Not defiant, just . . . resolute.

"Cybil—"

"You said it yourself—Mr. Ramirez notices everything." I meet his eyes, steady now. "If he suspects me and I suddenly just vanish, it'll confirm every doubt he has. I have to stay."

He's silent for a beat. Thinking. And then his expression falls. He doesn't have a way out of this. Except through me and the plan Ben and I have to take Ramirez down.

"I'm so sorry, Cybil." His voice is raw. "I'll do whatever I can to get you out of this—to protect you. You have my word."

I nod, throat tight. I want to believe him. And part of me does.

But the other part of me knows better. My pulse hammers beneath layers of lies, each one heavier than the last. I take a deep breath and steady my voice, because the truth is, the only person I've ever trusted to fight for me . . . is the boy who once promised to meet me under an oak tree. And the man who showed up anyway—even when I never did.

I don't think twice. I just say it. "Sir, I need to tell you about Craig Miller."

CHAPTER 38

Ben

Dallas, Texas
Monday evening

Another day, another felon with too much money and not enough imagination. Lucky for him, I've plenty of both.

I'm sitting at a table on the rooftop of Stirling and Vine. The steaks are dry-aged, the waiters can moonlight as bodyguards, and private deals are as abundant as the lies whispered over seared scallops and bourbon.

"If you're happy with everything we discussed"—I slide the contract across the table between us—"sign here and your money'll be *cleaning* itself through five countries and a church donation box before you finish that glass of scotch."

Marshall Dade doesn't even blink. The Texas oil tycoon made his first billion handling land rights, drilling contracts, and a wide network of senators on speed dial. As far as I can tell, he's conducted his business legally—until now. Now he's trying to keep the IRS out of his pocket and his name off any list that ends in "sanctions."

He picks up the glass, swirling it like it's a vintage truth serum. "I never rush through a scotch, son."

I smile. "Then I'll make sure the first wire hits before the ice melts."

He smiles appreciatively. "I didn't think anyone wore those anymore."

"What?"

"Tie tacks."

I glance down and adjust the silver oak tree pinned to my tie. "A friend gave it to me."

Marshall finishes his scotch, signs the last page, and slides the contract back across the table with the kind of smug satisfaction you only earn after a lifetime of stepping on necks in handmade boots.

"Pleasure doing business," he says.

"You have my number if you need anything else," I reply, tucking the document into a folder. *Nothing says capitalism like laundering your morals before the sun sets.*

He shakes my hand and then leaves me to take care of the check. I ask the server to add a steak sandwich to my bill and hand him my credit card. I pull out my personal phone. I shouldn't have it with me, but I missed three calls from Cybil last night and I haven't stopped worrying about her.

I try calling her number. No answer. Straight to voicemail.

The rooftop wind hits stronger now, like the air's trying to shake loose the tension crawling up my spine.

Cybil's probably fine. She's smart. Capable. But she's not trained. Not like I am.

And she's under serious pressure. I have no idea of the extent of her role in collecting intel for SNAP, but going toe to toe with a mobster like Lorenzo Ramirez is a lot different than stealing meeting notes.

I shove the phone back in my jacket and exhale, tight and sharp.

I told her I'd protect her. That she wasn't alone in this. But now, standing here with a rooftop wind whipping against my collar and a contract full of fake promises, all I've got is radio silence and a clock ticking louder than I like.

This whole thing was supposed to be about justice. About taking Ramirez down for what he did to Danny Morales. And I understand the stakes now—the mineral deal, the international buyers, the fallout if it all goes through. But if I'd done my job in the first place—if I'd gotten access to his laptop—this would already be over.

And I'd be living a different version of my life—the kind where I'm not paying for overpriced scotch for another person trying to cheat on his taxes, but instead I'm with Cybil, locked in a standoff over whether or not she knew it was me when she punched me in the face with a bag of flour—or if she'd just been waiting for the perfect opportunity to give it to me.

In that version, we're arguing over pancakes at her kitchen table, pretending the biggest threat in our lives is that rogue rooster on her uncle's ranch—not this.

But I'm not living in that version.

I'm in the one where Cybil thinks I didn't show up all those years ago. I can't shake the way she looked at me back at the ranch. When she said she heard me, years ago. That she thought I didn't like her. That I'd said something awful about her.

I've carried a lot of regret in my life, but that one—that she *believed* it, that she *lived* like it was true all these years—that one cracked me.

And now? I'd do anything to make up for it.

My phone buzzes in my jacket pocket.

It's my work phone. Ruby.

I answer just as the server sets down my sandwich and returns my credit card. I sign the receipt. "Where is she?"

"With Edmond."

"Is she safe?"

A pause. "Define *safe*?"

My grip tightens around the phone. "Is she *okay*?"

"She's with her boss and the plan is moving forward." There's a bite to her tone before she exhales. "Are you sure you're up for this?"

I crack open the to-go container and hit it with some special *seasoning* I brought just for the occasion. I close it up and head toward the elevator, grateful it's empty. "You know I am."

"Do I?" she asks, her tone softer now. "Look, I'm not trying to give you a hard time. I've seen the way you work and how dedicated you've been to get to Ramirez."

"I'm still dedicated."

"But there's more at risk now. You have feelings for her. Strong ones."

I'm not going to lie. I'm tired of it. "I do. I always have." I lean against the elevator wall and run a hand down my neck. "I wasn't expecting this."

"Yeah, falling in love in the middle of a mission has never worked out for James Bond either." Her teasing eases some of the pressure building in my chest. "But here we are, and I want to make sure you don't do anything dumb like give her the door while you freeze in the water."

I frown. "Did you just identify me with Jack and Rose from the *Titanic*?"

"Movie night with my mom and aunts."

"Don't you hate sappy romance movies?"

"It's a tragic maritime accident. I blame the director and Leo for making it all . . . human."

"You know people di—never mind." The elevator doors open. "I promise I won't do anything dumb."

"Or heroic," she deadpans.

"Heroic?"

"You know what I'm talking about. That whole alpha male chest puffing," she says. "You know, 'Let me fight the bad guy in a dumb heroic way that only works in the movies and never in real life.'"

I start for the parking garage. "No idea what you're talking about."

"Just stick to the plan, *Miller*."

Calling me by my alias is Ruby's way of reminding me that I'm still playing a part. One that needs to be Oscar worthy. Did Bond ever win an Oscar?

"Do you trust her?" she asks, quieter now. "I mean really trust her—not just the part of you that's eighteen and still hung up on her, but the part that knows Earl Edmond might make her talk if he pushes hard enough?"

My throat tightens and I loosen my tie and unbutton my top button. "She's not trained."

"She's not," Ruby agrees.

"But she'd never let down the people she cares about," I say. And that's exactly what scares me. Because I *know* Cybil. I know the girl with steel beneath the sarcasm. The girl who carried the weight of her mom's condition like it was her personal responsibility—still does. Cybil won't let anyone down. Not even if it costs her. And that's the part that kept me up all night.

My personal phone vibrates in my pocket.

"I have to go," I tell Ruby. I'm not going to miss another call from Cybil. "I'll see you soon."

I end the call, anxious to speak to Cybil, but it's not her number on my phone. "If you're calling me to bail you out of jail, I'm a little busy right now."

"Well, hello to you, too, grandson. And you don't have to worry about that. Bernie handles all the bail bonds for our group."

I don't even know where to go with that. "I don't mean to rush you, but I'm working. Is there something you need that doesn't require a background check or permit?"

"Not today, honey. I just wanted to check in on you and your sweet friend, Cybil. Such a nice girl, and I've talked to our members and we've agreed to make an exception if she wants to join. An honorary member of Pistols and Pearls."

It's both sweet and scary that my grandmother has already taken to Cybil. Or maybe it was the fact that Cybil was so willing to commit felonies with Gran that won her over. Either way, I probably need to keep expectations low for Gran's newest recruit until I know what a future with Cybil looks like. Or at least get us through this mission.

A black SUV drives by, slow enough that it immediately catches my attention. "Gran, I need to call you back later."

"Don't you lie to me."

"I won't. Love you." I hang up on my grandmother and drop the phone into the nearest trash can just as the SUV pulls up to the curb and jerks to a stop. The back door opens and out steps Rook.

The hair on the back of my neck rises.

"I need you to come with me," Rook says, glancing around like he's suddenly a Bond villain on retainer—minus the charm and the British accent.

"Unfortunately, I've got to get back to the office." I hold up the folder. "Trying to catch up on work before Mr. Ramirez's auction."

"Marshall Dade can wait a few hours for his paperwork to go through." His eyes lock with mine and I stay silent. "We should go."

It was a flex, Rook admitting that he knew who I was meeting with, and I have to keep my nerves in check because this can only go one way.

"I really don't have time today."

Behind Rook, the driver circles the front and it's none other than Sammy Pawson. His suit jacket opens to give me a not-so-subtle flash of the gun tucked into his waistband.

"What's going on?"

"Lorenzo wants to talk."

I glance back at the parking garage, weighing my options, and sigh. "Well, I wouldn't want to keep him waiting."

"No, you wouldn't."

Pawson eyes my bag of food, and I shake my head and just hand it to him before I slide into the back seat, Rook behind me.

The ride is silent except for Pawson's noisy enjoyment of my steak sandwich. No one talks. No music. Just the low hum of tires on pavement as Rook stares out the window like this is some kind of scenic drive.

If I'm headed to an early grave, I might as well dig for intel. "Is this about the auction?"

Rook doesn't blink.

"If Mr. Ramirez is still looking for interested investors, I might have a few clients with money to spend."

Nothing. I've got to hand it to Rook—this is the quietest he's ever been. No conversational narcissism. Normally, someone like Rook wouldn't bother me, but today? By the time we pull through a chain-link gate and up to a half-finished construction site, my nerves are fried.

Dust swirls through the afternoon sunlight, scaffolding clings to skeletal concrete walls, and a metal crane looms overhead like a guillotine waiting to drop. Rebar juts from unfinished flat work and pallets of lumber are lined up like a dangerous maze.

Rook gets out, sharp and composed. Sammy trails behind me, but some of the color has drained from his face, and that "I don't need a weapon, I am one" swagger is noticeably gone. Either the plan is going to work or this is the part where I disappear quietly.

I walk with Rook toward a trailer where I notice a single security camera mounted. I have no expectation that it works or, if it does, that it'll have any record of this visit.

Lorenzo Ramirez steps out of the jobsite trailer, every inch the man pulling the strings. His dark eyes scan me like I'm a spreadsheet with too many inconsistencies. He walks over and I reach out my hand to him. He shakes it, but his grip is tight.

"Glad you could meet me on such short notice."

I flash a look at Rook like I had any choice in the matter. "I'm here for whatever you need, sir."

"Good," Ramirez says, his tone serious. He releases my hand and walks away. "Let's talk."

I follow with Rook falling into step behind me. We step deeper into the construction site—sunlight catching on exposed steel, the air thick with dust. There's a sign reminding workers this is a hard hat area, but the way Ramirez strolls ahead says that he's not concerned about OSHA fining him. Or safety.

"I'm afraid I don't have my laptop with me, but if there's anything you need me to have ready before the auction tomorrow, I can—"

We round a corner and my words dry up on my tongue when I see them.

Cybil's eyes lock with mine. Barely a flicker of recognition. She's standing stiffly beside Mr. Edmond and Sebastian. In front of them is a table where Ramirez's laptop is open, the screen angled just enough to catch the light—and my attention. Rook walks over to it and gives Ramirez a nod.

Ramirez sweeps his gaze across all four of us—slow, deliberate, like he's choosing which fuse to light first.

Then he says it.

Calm. Cold. Deadly.

"One of you has been playing me. And it's time to find out who."

CHAPTER 39

Cybil

Dallas, Texas
Monday evening

The silence after the accusation is heavy enough to crush bone. Which, with the crusher parked twenty feet away, might actually be a possibility.

Ramirez stares at us, and I force myself not to look at Ben. I can't. If I meet his eyes, I might lose whatever clarity I need to hold on to. Mr. Edmond reminded me last night how easy it is to be swayed by hopes and dreams and just how dangerous it is to give trust away.

"What is the meaning of this, Lorenzo?" Mr. Edmond asks, and I hear the slight tremor in his voice. Sebastian watches his father. He heard it too.

After last night's conversation with Mr. Edmond, things shifted. I can't help but see Sebastian differently. Not as the arrogant, aloof son of a wealthy developer, but as someone who, like my mom, trusted the wrong people. Who didn't see the trap until it was already closed.

My mom didn't trust herself to handle the settlement after my dad died—didn't think she was stable enough, smart enough, strong enough to take care of me. Sebastian thought ambition was enough to keep him in control of the empire he was trying to build to prove he was capable of living outside of his father's shadow. Both trusted someone who had the right credentials, the right words, the right promises. But it was all a lie.

Lies are what have led all of us here.

Ramirez isn't here to build something. He's here to tear *someone* down.

"I agreed to a meeting to finalize the auction terms—not a field trip," Edmond says, offering a tight smile. "What exactly are we doing here, Lorenzo?"

Ramirez paces slowly, his boots crunching over gravel, hands folded behind his back like a teacher about to assign someone detention. Except instead of spending hours bored to death in a room, the punishment here involves bullets.

"You know," he says, pausing in front of Mr. Edmond, "when I brought you into this deal, I expected a certain level of . . . loyalty."

Mr. Edmond shifts beside me, but he does not cower. "Your version of an invitation reads much more like extortion."

Ramirez smiles. Callous. Cruel. He looks at Sebastian. "Your son wanted investors. I gave him an opportunity—"

"You tricked him!" Mr. Edmond growls. "You made him complicit to *your* crimes."

Rook starts for him, but Ramirez holds up a hand. "I've got this, James."

An audible *ding* pulls my attention to the laptop. Rook's focus returns to it. He taps the keyboard and smiles, causing something in my gut to twist.

"My crimes?" Ramirez replies simply. "One shouldn't throw stones." His cold gaze swings to me. "Right, Ms. Langford?"

My heart drops into my stomach. Next to me, Sebastian shifts, but a sharp glance from Ramirez keeps him still.

A sudden noise breaks the tension—a low groan from the far side of the construction site. I glance over and spot Sammy Pawson, hunched near a cement mixer, hand braced on his knee.

Rook notices too. "You good?" he calls.

Pawson waves him off, but his face is pale, and he's sweating like it's a hundred degrees hotter than it is. He curses under his breath. "I need to . . . go."

Without waiting for permission, he staggers toward the path leading down from the site, one hand pressed to his stomach. Nobody follows.

Rook watches him go, then mutters, "I told him he eats too much crap."

"Shouldn't we be focusing on the auction?" Ben asks, his voice calm, strong. The sound of it nearly undoes me.

Ramirez doesn't look at him right away. He takes his time, eyes lingering on me a second too long before turning back to the laptop. Walking over, he twists it so that we can all see the lines of data flicker and shift on the screen. "The auction is already underway."

My pulse races. The auction has started? No. That's not how this was supposed to unfold. Not yet. Ben glances toward the laptop, too, the smallest flicker of alarm breaking through his mask. That wasn't part of the script.

"So you see," Mr. Ramirez continues and turns, his gaze landing back on me, "we can now focus on what's in front of us."

I stiffen.

"You," he says with a thin smile. "I almost didn't notice. Quiet. Polite. Efficient. The kind of person no one watches too closely." He takes a step toward me. "But it's always the ones we least expect."

I say nothing. I don't trust my voice not to shake.

"Lorenzo, leave her alone." Mr. Edmond steps to my side. "She's got nothing to do with this."

It should make me feel safe. But there's only one person here I've ever *wanted* to trust—and naturally, he comes with alibis and a badge.

Ramirez waves him off. "Don't insult me, Earl. I've known from the beginning that you'd try to protect your son. I even respected it at first. But that's not why we're here." His gaze pierces me. "I expect betrayal from the loud ones. The obvious threats. But you? You were a surprise."

Edmond turns to me, confused. "What's he talking about, Cybil?"

Ramirez doesn't wait. "Italy. You were in my office, going through my paperwork. Your mishap in the village. Maybe it was an innocent accident or maybe you were somewhere you weren't supposed to be. The roads and traffic can be so dangerous. But then you decided to leave dinner early. And search my office."

I feel the blood drain from my face.

"And let's not forget the cocktail party." His eyes narrow. "It was another surprise to see you talking with a member of the Russian military. Tell me, do you and Milosh Kamarov have a lot in common?"

I keep my eyes on him, my heartbeat loud enough to be its own soundtrack. But I don't answer. I can't. Because I don't know which version of the lie he'll kill me for first.

Ramirez waits a beat and then sighs. He pulls out a gun with the kind of nonchalance that tells me he's used it before. "That's disappointing."

Nobody moves. The only sound is coming from the clicking of Rook at the laptop as he monitors the bids from criminals ready to buy a war weapon.

The barrel of the gun tilts toward me and I can barely swallow over the tightness in my throat. But I'm not going to let my fear keep me silent. I'm not going to be the victim of anyone else's betrayal.

"You're not wrong," I say. Cool. Or as cool as someone who has a gun pointed at them by a man who thinks selling a mineral to warlords is totally awesome. "Sometimes it's an unassuming pebble in your shoe that slows your step. A single spark that brings down the house. Or the tiniest tremble in the ocean that becomes a tsunami."

Ramirez pauses, clearly caught off guard.

I step forward, slow and deliberate. "But you're aiming at the wrong traitor."

All eyes snap to me. Including Ben's.

And I let my gaze slide to him like I've connected every last dot. Like I've been played—and now I'm done.

"I was trying to dig for information because I knew something was off," I say, pitching my voice low. Bitter. "He was too perfect. Too polished. The kind of man who knows exactly what to say to make you feel like you're the only one in the room—until you realize he's been lying the whole time."

Ben's brows pinch. "Cybil—"

"It's true," I say, cutting off him off. "I was in your office in Italy. In the village I was following him to find out who he was meeting with, and at the cocktail party I spoke to Milosh Kamarov to find out why Craig Miller was meeting with Olek Radin."

Mr. Edmond reaches into his pocket, causing Ramirez to swing the gun his direction. He holds up a hand while the other pulls out a folded printout from his coat and tosses it on the table next to the laptop. The photo is grainy, time-stamped, but clear enough.

Craig Miller—Ben—sitting across from Olek Radin.

"Olek Radin is a tech broker tied to dark-net financial platforms," Mr. Edmond explains. "He's got a knack for accessing and rerouting digital funds, making money in shell corporations disappear."

Ramirez frowns and picks up the photo for closer inspection.

"That man"—Mr. Edmond points at the photo—"is talking to the one person standing here with direct access to your crypto wallet. The person who's been betraying you the whole time."

Ben looks between us, shock playing out on his features. "This is insane. You're being fed lies—"

"Then why were you there?" I ask, eyes hard, voice low. "Why did you ask me to meet you in Mr. Ramirez's office in Italy? You never showed up—because you wanted me to take the fall. You wanted a distraction. You set me up so Mr. Ramirez would watch me—while you slipped out the back with everything."

A muscle in Ben's jaw twitches. Just once. He doesn't speak. Doesn't defend himself.

But his eyes narrow just enough.

"Show me my accounts," Ramirez barks at Ben, lowering the gun just slightly.

"I assure you all of your accounts are in order," Ben says, his hands rising defensively.

"I don't want your assurance," Ramirez seethes. "I want you to pull up my accounts."

Ben hesitates, his gaze flicking to the laptop, then to Ramirez . . . and finally to me. The fear on his face looks real—too real. For a split second, doubt slips in. Was this a mistake? He takes slow steps toward the laptop. Rook backs away and gives him access.

With several keystrokes, Ben logs in, fingers gliding over the keyboard with the kind of precision that comes from practice. The loading bar inches across the screen—slowly.

Ramirez's gaze sharpens. "Why is it taking so long?" he asks, voice low and dangerous.

Ben doesn't flinch. "Encrypted server. Takes a second to sync across regions."

Ramirez steps closer, eyes narrowing at the screen, then at Ben.

"A second's up," he growls. "If you've touched anything in those accounts—if what she says is true—"

Ben's jaw flexes, but he keeps his eyes fixed on the screen. I've only seen him angry once before—when we were kids and his friend crushed a butterfly just to see it break. He didn't yell. Didn't even raise his voice. Just stood there, still and quiet, like fury was something he kept under lock and key.

He looks like that now.

His fingers still over the keyboard for half a second too long, like he's weighing something. A pause that doesn't go unnoticed.

Ramirez's eyes narrow. "Problem?"

Ben clears his throat. "No," he says firmly. "No problem. But you might find this interesting." He turns the laptop toward Ramirez, fingers gliding across the track pad to open the most recent transaction history. "There has been unauthorized activity on one of your offshore accounts." He points at the screen. "That transfer is marked two days ago. Not from me. It was authorized using Sebastian Edmond's credentials."

The air goes still.

Ramirez shifts his gaze toward Sebastian.

He's staring at the screen like it just slapped him. "I—I didn't—That's not—"

My breath snags—sharp and involuntary—as the accusation lands.

Ramirez takes a step forward. "You stole from me?"

Mr. Edmond spins on Sebastian. "Lies!"

Sebastian backs up. "No—this isn't what it looks like. I would never—"

But it's too late.

Sebastian lunges at Ben.

CHAPTER 40

Ben

Dallas, Texas
Monday night

I take the hit square in the ribs, and I don't know if the cracking noise is the sound of my bones or the chair Rook was sitting in. Sebastian's shoulder drives into me like a battering ram—fury, panic, and pure adrenaline wrapped in a designer button-down.

Ramirez shouts. Cybil screams. Rook draws his weapon.

I stumble back, catching myself against the table—just in time to see the laptop slide off the edge and hit the concrete hard. It slides across the floor and crashes against a steel beam.

Not good.

Somewhere in cyberspace, there's a bidding war over a mineral that could destabilize global security. And that laptop is the only thing keeping us in the game.

Sebastian's fists fly—wild, furious. More panic than precision. I've got newfound respect for Cybil's combat skills. I catch his arm before his knuckles land again, twist, and shove him off me—hard—just as Rook barrels in from the side.

Ramirez barks something sharp in Spanish—too fast to track—but it's already too late.

Earl Edmond moves. He grabs a rusted pipe from the scaffolding and slams it into Ramirez's arm with a crack that echoes off the concrete. The gun goes flying. It arcs once, lands with a metallic thud, and skitters across the dusty floor, landing out of reach.

For a second, everything holds.

Then . . . chaos.

The pipe clangs to the ground. Ramirez stumbles back, clutching his arm. My gaze flies to where the gun is sitting a few feet away—closer to Sebastian than anyone else.

My pulse spikes.

Sebastian scrambles up from where I shoved him, eyes locking on the weapon. He can't really fight, but you don't need skills to pull the trigger.

Don't go for it. Don't go for it—

He goes for it.

Cybil lunges for it at the same time.

No—

It's a split-second collision course, a tangle of limbs and gravel and fear. Dust kicks up. Someone coughs, Ramirez shouts again, but it's a blur now. I'm not sure who he's yelling at—maybe all of us.

Cybil reaches the gun first.

She rises slowly, gun in both hands, eyes hard and unblinking. Ramirez freezes. Rook stops short. Even Edmond, his breaths heaving, comes to a standstill.

My chest rises and falls in sharp jerks. Sweat stings my eyes, but I try—I try to get her to look at me. Just a flicker. Something to let me know she's okay.

"Cybil," Mr. Edmond tries.

Her grip on the gun doesn't waver. But her eyes—they're not as steady. They flick to Ramirez, then to me. Like she's calculating. Cornered and . . . deciding.

"You don't have to do this," I say, stepping toward her. Slowly. Hands up. "He'll turn on you, too, Cybil. You think you're safe with him? You're not."

She doesn't move. Doesn't blink.

"You're pointing that at the wrong man."

Ramirez chuckles low in his throat. "She's not as stupid as you thought, Craig."

My jaw clenches. "They're only in this for themselves. Edmond won't protect you. He can't. His hands are tied, and even if he could . . . you're in this mess because of him."

That lands.

Her eyes flash. But I don't know if it's fury or guilt.

"Cybil," Mr. Edmond says, "don't listen to him."

I take another step. "He used you. Just like Ramirez used his son. You're on the wrong side."

She raises the gun slightly. Not at Ramirez. Not at Edmond.

At me.

"Cybil . . ."

My gaze jumps from her to Rook, who's tracking my movement. Ramirez hasn't moved. He's quiet—watching her like a wolf circling a doe.

Edmond takes a slow step. "Cybil." She shakes her head once. "You don't want to do this."

"I don't *want* any of this," she snaps, loud enough that Sebastian flinches. "But I'm tired of being played. I'm tired of people using me. I'm done being the collateral damage in someone else's war."

Her words hit hard. Hearing them, hearing the pain behind every syllable—it feels too real. *This was a mistake.* She's right. She's being used—by me. By the FBI. By SNAP.

I want to take it from her, but one wrong move now could get us both killed.

Edmond takes another step, voice calm but weighted. "Cybil, you don't want this on your conscience," he says. "You're not like us. Don't cross that line. There's no coming back."

Cybil's grip falters—just slightly. A flicker of something crosses her face. But it's gone in an instant.

Rook moves.

He raises his weapon. Points it straight at me.

And then Cybil does the one thing no one expects.

She pulls the trigger.

The shot cracks across the open air.

Something hits me—hard.

My body jerks. The world tilts. And then I'm falling.

CHAPTER 41

Cybil

Dallas, Texas
Monday night

The sound of the gunshot rings in my ears. Or maybe that's the blood rushing to my head. Ben's body disappears over the edge of the elevated slab floor—half built and open to the drop below—and the silence that follows is worse than the blast itself.

I shot him. I shot Ben.

I don't breathe. I can't.

The gun is heavy in my hand, the smell of cordite clinging to the air like static. This is not okay. This was not part of the plan. This was—

"Dad!"

Sebastian's scream cuts through the fog in my brain. I spin just in time to see him dive for his father—a blur of motion—and then another shot cracks the air. Mr. Edmond falls backward, a thud against concrete. Sebastian collapses over him with a sharp guttural sound.

Rook whips the gun toward me. I don't blink. I run.

I dart behind a pallet stacked with drywall—splinters and dust blooming around me as another bullet ricochets off the steel beam overhead. My foot catches on a stray length of rebar, and I go down hard, hands scraping against the concrete. The gun skitters out of my grip, sliding somewhere behind me. I twist to grab it, but another shot cracks through the air, too close.

I scramble the rest of the way behind cover, heart slamming, lungs burning, fingers still twitching from the weapon I no longer have. *Am I really in a freaking shootout?*

A grunt pulls my attention. I peek around the corner and am relieved to see Sebastian moving. He's clutching his arm, blood darkening his sleeve. Ramirez is nowhere in sight, but Rook is closing in, gun raised. He's going to finish them off and I have nothing. No gun. No plan. Just a whole lot of adrenaline and very questionable judgment.

My gaze skims the construction site. Scattered tools. Buckets of nails. PVC pipe. And there—a bright red fire extinguisher, still strapped to a column a few feet away. Close enough to reach if I'm fast.

I take a breath. "Please don't die, please don't die," I whisper to myself.

Then I run.

I vault over a coil of extension cords, grab the extinguisher with both hands, and yank. It comes loose with a jerk that nearly dislocates my shoulder. Rook doesn't see me until it's too late. I swing the extinguisher like a bat and catch him full force in the ribs. The impact rings through my arms. He cries out, stumbles—gun dropping to the concrete.

Rook staggers, clutching his side. "You little—"

I yank the pin from the extinguisher and squeeze the handle. A blast of white foam hits him square in the face. He chokes, swears, stumbles back—temporarily blinded.

"Come on." I drop the extinguisher with a clatter. "We have to move. Now."

Mr. Edmond is conscious—stunned, wide-eyed, but not hurt. I reach for him.

Sebastian groans, trying to push upright, his good hand pressing hard against his bleeding arm. He's pale, sweating, but his jaw is set with sheer determination.

"I've got him," he grits out, shifting to help his father.

"*Now* is not the time for your ego," I mutter, looping an arm under Edmond's shoulder as Sebastian does the same on the other side. Together we hustle him toward a stack of concrete blocks.

I spot the gun, tucked against a cracked paint bucket and someone's abandoned thermos.

Then Rook hits me. I don't see him, just *feel* him, a wall of rage and limbs as we go down hard against the concrete. My shoulder slams into the ground, the gun skidding out of reach *again*. We grapple, elbows and fists and gritted teeth. I manage to land a knee in his stomach, but he recovers fast, slamming me back against a steel beam.

"You're not going to win this one," he snarls.

I glare up at him. "You'd be amazed what I can accomplish when I'm ticked off."

He tries to wrap his fingers around my throat. I claw at his hands, fighting against his grip. Sebastian charges into view, swinging a pipe like a one-armed knight. The blow knocks Rook sideways, long enough for me to suck in a breath.

But Rook is like a cockroach that won't die. He grabs Sebastian's injured arm and slams him into a support post. Sebastian groans, slumps.

I crawl toward the gun and twist just in time to see Rook looming toward me. My eyes flick up. A rope is tied haphazardly around a bundle of metal framing bars suspended from a crane hook about fifteen feet above him. I aim and pull the trigger. The pulley snaps, sending the bars crashing down and burying Rook in a tangle of steel and dust.

I wait to see if he stays down because, you know, cockroaches. When he doesn't move, I scramble to Sebastian. He's groaning but conscious.

"I'm okay," he rasps. "The laptop?"

I spin to check. "It's gone."

So is Ramirez.

Sebastian slumps against the beam, chest heaving. "Go."

I apply pressure to his wound. "I'm not leaving you—"

"We'll be fine." Mr. Edmond is at my side now, and he takes my place, gently pressing his hand on his son's injury. Sebastian winces but continues. "If he gets away with that laptop, none of this matters."

"He's right," Mr. Edmond says. "Go—I've got him."

I give them a tight smile, then spin toward the stairwell. And run.

CHAPTER 42

Cybil

Dallas, Texas
Monday night

My shoes scrape against loose gravel, heart pounding against my ribs as I fight the adrenaline coursing through me. I round the corner of the half-built retaining wall where I watched Ben fall—and stop cold. He's not there.

I didn't shoot to kill him. I know that. I *know* where I aimed. But still—he should be here. Panic pricks at the edges of my thoughts.

There's a mess of rigid foam insulation sheets leaning at an awkward angle—cracked and dented. It takes me a second to register the streak of blood trailing across them. My stomach knots.

I search the open floor slab, heart hammering harder now. My eyes dart across the exposed concrete and jagged debris. Nothing. No sign of him.

Just—blood.

A faint trail of it, smeared across the cement. Not enough to say fatal. But enough to make my skin crawl. *I know where I aimed . . .*

"Ben?" My voice catches. Breaks.

No answer—just the lonely thwapping of a torn tarp flapping in the wind.

I back up a step, nearly tripping over a snapped rebar. *This isn't how it ends. It can't be.*

I blink hard, willing my vision to sharpen through the haze of dust and fear. Nothing moves. No groan, no cough, no smart-aleck quip rising from the shadows to tell me I'm overreacting.

Only that blood.

A soft *ding* cuts through the silence. I freeze. Another *ding*. It's faint but distinct—the sound of a notification. An alert. From a cell phone?

Or laptop.

I follow the sound, heart in my throat, creeping past a low partition wall partially framed with exposed beams and bent conduit. The jagged outline of scaffolding looms overhead as I walk deeper into the site, like I'm walking into the belly of the beast.

I keep going until I see it. The laptop. Perched on a stack of paint buckets. It's open, the screen lit, and . . . My eyes scan the area around it. Unattended? Where's Ramirez?

Another *ding* draws me to it. The auction window is open and showing a live feed of bids still rolling in. A timer is ticking down as numbers continue to climb. Bank account strings. Transaction IDs. Countries I can't even pronounce.

The auction is still happening. I glance around, half expecting Ramirez to jump out from behind a support column, gun drawn. Nothing. If he ran, why didn't he take this with him? I think about the empty spot where Ben's body should've been. Did something happen?

It gives me hope that Ben's alive—wounded—but maybe he's subdued Ramirez somewhere, which means it's my job to stop the auction.

But how?

I begin jabbing at keys. Try to close windows. Hit the escape button several times, harder with each hit. Nothing works. It's encrypted, locked tight behind layers of code. What if I smash it? Would that stop it? I don't know but I have to try.

I look around and spot a broken brick a few feet away. I run to it, but before my fingers can latch onto the rough edge, I hear it.

A scuffling noise.

I freeze.

Then his voice slithers out from the shadows behind me—low, quiet, and ice-cold. "You should've stayed the assistant. You're better at coffee than betrayal."

I turn slowly. Ramirez steps out of the shadows, gun in hand. Dust streaks his jacket, his expression unbothered, like he's walking into a meeting and not pointing a gun at my head.

"I'd love to get you a latte laced with arsenic," I say, meeting his gaze. "Or do you prefer antifreeze?"

His lips twitch, a flicker of amusement as he starts to circle me—slow, deliberate, like a vulture with a Rolex. "You really don't know what you've walked into, do you?"

"I know enough to suggest adding 'violent narcissist' to your dating profile."

Is it wise to joke with a guy with a God complex who's holding a gun? Probably not. But until I find a way out of this, I use what I've got—sarcasm and nerve. Unfortunately, neither is bulletproof.

"It's a shame." Ramirez pauses. "You almost got past my defenses." His eyes narrow. "Almost. You're smart, resourceful. A waste with someone like Earl, but with me, with a little mentoring, you might prove useful."

I blink. Then laugh—sharp and humorless. "You always try to shoot your employees before hiring them?"

He lifts a shoulder. Not quite apologetic. "Shows me what they're made of."

"Not really the employee benefits I'm looking for."

He actually chuckles, the sound dark and easy. It's unnerving how calm he is. "Loyalty is overrated. Fear motivates people."

"Well, I'm not looking to work for a psychopath willing to sell out his own country."

"You think I'm selling out my country?" He clicks his tongue against his teeth. "My dear, you think I'm the villain? I'm leveling the playing field. You don't think our government won't do the exact same thing I'm doing when they get their hands on my mineral?"

I look at the laptop. "Uncle Sam's bidding right now?"

He smiles. Slow. Sinister. "No." He tilts his head. "They weren't invited to the sale. Too much red-tape bureaucracy to dip into America's pockets. But you're not seeing the bigger picture."

He's talking too much. Explaining his plan like I should be impressed. But men like Ramirez don't narrate their strategy unless they're planning to bury the witness. If I don't do something now, I'm not walking out of here.

My gaze flicks to the brick. It's too far. Running for cover would just give him a moving target. I track his position, the way his finger rests against the trigger. I need to stall. *Buy time so he won't see it coming.* "Global warfare not big enough?"

A flicker of annoyance crosses his face before his expression smooths back into that eerie calm. "This auction?" he says, taking a step closer. "It's history in the making. And every name on that ledger—the buyers, the countries, the clients—they're mine now. I own them. They—"

I move. Fast. My elbow snaps up and knocks his wrist to the side. The gun goes off—*crack!*—and the shot slams into the steel column behind me. I drive my knee into his leg, reach for the gun, anything—

But he's stronger. Faster.

He slams into me and I go flying, landing hard on the uneven slab. My palms scrape across crumbled mortar and loose gravel, the sting blooming instantly. My breath punches out of my lungs. My ears are ringing, my vision swimming, but I force myself to focus—on him.

Ramirez barrels forward, gun leveled at my chest, his steps deliberate, intent evident. "Such a shame."

Thwack.

The sound makes me flinch—sharp and quick—but it takes a second to register it wasn't a gunshot. Ramirez's body lurches forward and collapses face-first into the concrete. Behind him, shovel in hand, stands Ben. Dirt-smeared. Bloodied. And wearing the kind of smug grin that could probably be weaponized by the Department of Defense.

I exhale, breath catching in my throat. "About time you showed up."

Ben drops the shovel with a clunk. "You shot me."

It's then that I notice the dark bloom of blood on his left arm, staining his shirt.

"He was going to shoot you first," I say, brushing my hands against my pants. "I just . . . sped up the timeline."

Ben raises a brow, offering his uninjured arm to pull me up. "So you did it to save me?" he asks, voice low and warm, wrapping around my spine and daring my knees to hold me steady.

I bite my lip, not bothering to hide the grin. "Absolutely."

"Seems like you enjoyed it."

"I'm not saying I didn't."

His brow lifts in amusement. "What *are* you saying, Billy?"

I lean in, whispering like it's classified. "That it gave me immense satisfaction to shoot Craig. *Freaking.* Miller."

CHAPTER 43

Ben

Dallas, Texas
Monday night

I've had a lot of firsts. First undercover op. First time laundering a million dollars for the FBI. First almost full-body cavity search courtesy of a cartel. But being shot by the girl I like? That's one for the books.

And definitely not part of the plan.

Pawson was easy—he stole the food, as predicted, and got a crash course in digestive karma courtesy of a heavy dose of laxatives.

Getting Edmond to arrange a meeting with Ramirez so I could get the PhantomKey close enough to his laptop? Unexpected.

Ramirez pulling a gun? Expected.

But Cybil grabbing the gun . . . aiming it at me? Pulling the trigger?

That was never part of the script.

According to the paramedic, the bullet grazed just beneath the deltoid—bloody, painful, but not life-threatening. Which is great for my survival but terrible for the sympathy angle I'm trying to work.

I let out a groan—loud enough to be heard over the blur of police radios and shouted commands. The paramedic gives me a side-eye as she winds another strip of gauze around my upper arm.

Cybil's head snaps toward me, eyes narrowing in that way that usually precedes either concern or an insult. "Is he going to be okay?"

The paramedic nods. "Bullet missed the bone and artery. Whoever fired it knew exactly where to aim to make a statement without causing permanent damage."

I lift my brows to Cybil.

She presses her lips together, but her eyes flash with something that looks suspiciously like pride. "Don't be dramatic. I had to wrestle a psychopath and his lawyer."

"I got shot."

"You got *clipped*."

"I'm emotionally wounded."

She leans closer, voice low and dry. "You want a lollipop or a Purple Heart?"

What I want is to kiss her. What I say is, "I want you to admit you were worried."

Cybil crouches beside me, expression softening just enough to give me hope—or mess with my head. Her lips twitch and she crosses her arms and speaks to the paramedic. "I aimed for his ego, but apparently it's bulletproof."

The paramedic snorts.

"It's like you don't even feel bad," I murmur.

Around us is chaos. The FBI's mobile units are parked alongside police vehicles. Beyond the gates, the media is already setting up to report the news of Lorenzo Ramirez's and his attorney's arrest. Ruby and Athena are geared up, earbuds blinking with comms chatter as agents sweep the scene for loose ends, and Katherine is standing in the middle of it all, issuing orders with the kind of calm that could silence a riot with a single arched brow.

But I only see her.

Cybil Langford.

"Do you two need a couples therapist or a tactical debrief?"

I glance over to see Ruby striding toward us, sleeves rolled and expression set to amused but slightly exasperated. Katherine and Athena trail behind her, both looking far too composed considering what just went down.

"Nice of y'all to show up," I grumble, shifting on the metal bumper of the ambulance. The surface is hard and completely unsympathetic—kind of like the mood I'm cultivating right now.

Katherine ignores the jab. "You two okay?"

"I was *shot*," I remind them, lifting my gauze-wrapped arm like a tragic show-and-tell.

"We're fine," Cybil answers. "What about Sebastian?"

Athena steps forward, thumbs hooking into the tactical vest she's wearing. "Stable. The bullet missed anything vital, and he's already on his way to the hospital. Edmond's following with federal agents."

"They're both willing to testify. Edmond knows the layout of the Aurelite-X deal better than anyone, and Sebastian has access to the crypto shell corporations being used to launder money. Between that and the laptop"—she nods toward me—"we've got enough to bury Ramirez under a mountain of federal charges."

Ruby snorts. "Oh, and in case anyone's wondering, Pawson was found curled up in a porta-john behind the crane. Terrible bout of food poisoning."

I shrug. "Some people have to learn the hard way not to mess with another man's food."

The tension in my shoulders eases, and for the first time, Cybil looks relieved.

"You both played your roles perfectly," Athena adds. "You fed Edmond just enough false intel about Craig Miller to put pressure on Ramirez—forcing him to move the auction and keep you close to that laptop."

"Speaking of"—Katherine turns to me—"how's our evidence?"

"Safe." I reach for my tie, now wrinkled and bloody, and hold it up. The silver tie tack gleams in the light. I glance sideways, unable to stop the smirk. "Good thing I know how to take a bullet."

Cybil meets my smirk with one of her own. "Good thing I have great aim."

"And smart enough to keep Ramirez talking," Athena said, giving Cybil a nod that, frankly, felt a little too much like approval of her *shooting* me. "It took our team a little longer to clone the data from the laptop."

"Might be time to upgrade your system," I mutter, shifting on the bumper. "Or at least program it to move a little faster before someone else has to take a bullet."

Cybil's lips twitch like she's trying not to smile.

I grin, despite the throb and the possibility I'm concussed. Which explains the mix of emotions rushing through me. I shouldn't be disappointed this is over. I should be relieved. And I am. Maybe it's the painkillers, or maybe it's just her—dust on her cheek, blood on her knuckles, and fire in her eyes—but a part of me would do it all over again.

With her.

For her.

Because these last few weeks have made me feel something I hadn't in a long time. Not adrenaline. Not duty. Hope.

"It bought us time," Athena says, cutting into my thoughts.

"I don't understand why Ramirez didn't just run," Cybil says. "He had the laptop."

"Because he couldn't," Athena replies. "His laptop was the auction's central node—tied to an encrypted satellite uplink, bouncing through servers in Croatia. Once the auction went live, pulling the laptop would've killed the connection and taken the whole operation offline. No bids. No money. No buyers."

Cybil's eyes drift to Ramirez now being loaded into a police vehicle. "And the buyers?"

"Still in the virtual auction room," Athena says. "Blissfully unaware that their last bids are being logged directly into an FBI database."

Ruby grins. "A digital takedown. Less blood. More felony."

"We'll be sorting through the ledger for weeks," Athena says, brushing a strand of windblown hair from her face. "Buyers, shell companies, sovereign entities—enough evidence to get sanctions approved on Aurelite-X."

"And put Ramirez away for the rest of his life," Katherine adds. "The district attorney is very happy."

Athena checks her watch. "I hate to break up the fun, but I've got to get back to the airport for a debrief in DC."

I tilt my head toward her. "Do you have it?"

She smiles. The kind that *almost* makes me believe she feels bad about my gunshot wound. "The info's already on your phone." She reaches into her pocket and hands it over. It's my personal phone, the one I tossed in the trash can when Rook came to collect me.

Cybil's eyes flick between us, curiosity drawing a fine crease between her brows.

When the others drift off, giving us a moment, I ask, "Are you okay?"

"A few scratches and bruises, but I'm good." She hesitates. "What was that about?"

I unlock the phone and open the message already waiting—sent from an encrypted line. "I had Katherine do some digging with the Bureau's Financial Crimes division. They found the original transfer from your mom's account when she transferred your father's settlement money to Celeste Harlowe."

Cybil's eyes widen.

"Athena helped, but they've found her. It's all there."

I hand her the phone. Her fingers tremble just slightly as she scrolls, scanning through the details, absorbing the information.

She looks up. Her voice is soft but sure. "She's here. In Dallas."

"Katherine already spoke with the DA. You're not just closing one case today, Cybil." I pause. "You're opening the next."

Her gaze meets mine. There's something electric behind it—relief and fire and purpose all tangled into one perfect storm. The wind catches a strand of her hair and brushes it across her cheek. I reach up, gently tuck it behind her ear.

"I meant what I said," I murmur. "Back at the ranch. About you."

Her expression falters slightly—just enough for me to see the walls she always keeps up start to lower.

"You're the strongest person I've ever met, Billy. Not because you don't get scared. But because you do—and you still show up anyway. For everyone else. For the truth. For justice. Even when no one's fighting for you."

She doesn't speak, but her eyes shine—like maybe she's letting herself believe it.

"But it's my turn. To show up for you. To fight for you. To be your backup. Your partner. Your target practice who's still trying to figure out how to do the right things at the right time."

A long beat stretches between us. She doesn't pull her hand away.

"I know chasing down Celeste Harlowe isn't going to be easy. It might get messy. You might want to shoot me again." She smiles and my heart flips. "But if you want to go after her"—I reach for her hand, my voice quiet but certain—"then I'm with you. Every step of the way. If you want that."

Something flickers behind her eyes—something raw and unguarded. "I spent a long time believing my life was too messy to share with someone. That I didn't deserve anything good unless I had my life together." She pauses, eyes searching mine like she's still not sure how I got past her defenses. "But you, you saw the cracks. Even as a kid, my mess never seemed to scare you. You oddly seemed to enjoy getting messy with me." She gives me a smile. "I want that. I want someone who runs toward the fire with me."

I take a half step closer. Her breath hitches but she doesn't back away.

The world goes quiet around us—the sirens, the voices, the buzz of activity fading into background noise.

Her hand brushes my arm—barely there. But it's enough to anchor me.

She looks up, and I see it all in her eyes—the weight she's carried, the lies she's outlived, the hope she's still scared to hold. I see the fire, the fight, and, for the first time, a sliver of peace trying to break through.

Neither of us speaks.

She leans in, eyes flicking to my lips, then back to my eyes—as if asking permission or maybe daring me to cross the space between us.

So I do.

I kiss her.

Just once. Just long enough to taste the adrenaline still humming through her, to feel the way her breath stutters against mine, to know this isn't a maybe anymore. It's a beginning—raw and real and entirely ours.

Her hand curls lightly around the collar of my shirt, fingers tightening like she's afraid the moment might slip away if she lets go. Like maybe she's holding on not because she needs me to steady her, but because—for the first time—she doesn't want to stand alone. And I won't let her.

Then—of course—my phone rings.

Cybil pulls back just enough to breathe, her forehead brushing mine, lips barely a breath away. "Are you going to answer that?"

"Do I have to?" My hand stays at her waist, unwilling to let the warmth of her go just yet. Her cheeks are flushed, her breathing shallow, and all I want is to chase that kiss a little longer.

"Might be important," she says.

I glance at the screen and groan. "It's Gran."

Cybil bites back a smile. "You should probably answer that."

"I'll call her back," I whisper, already leaning in again. "Eventually."

"What if she's"—Cybil raises a brow, voice teasing—"holding the bingo caller hostage?"

I sigh. "You're right." I press a quick kiss to her forehead and answer the call, putting it on speaker as I brace for impact.

"Gran, you'd better not be calling me from a jail cell."

Her voice crackles through the line, full of indignation and zero remorse.

"It's not a jail cell—it's a holding room. And I told them if there was a limit on the wine samples"—she hiccups—"they should've said that in the first place."

CHAPTER 44

Cybil

Dallas, Texas
One month later

The city slips past in a blur of headlights and heat shimmer, the kind of thick summer night that clings to your skin even with the windows up. Downtown Dallas glows ahead of us, skyscrapers lit like someone strung stars through steel. The hum of cicadas follows us even here, muffled by the hum of the car's AC and the low, rhythmic thud of tires over warm pavement.

Joy fans herself dramatically with the gala invite. "Remind me again why these things can't be held in January?"

I adjust the clasp on my necklace, the AC doing its best against the sticky Dallas heat. "Because if the rich don't have to suffer for fashion, they don't earn their philanthropic street cred."

She smirks. "Right. Nothing says 'selfless humanitarian' like pit stains on a Versace tux."

She leans forward, peering out the tinted windows as the city lights flicker across her dress. "Hey—wasn't it somewhere around here you almost tossed out the FBI agent you kidnapped?"

I see the driver glance at me in the rearview mirror, brows raised just slightly.

"Maybe we *don't* talk about me kidnapping a federal agent," I whisper, though I can't help smiling. It wasn't funny then, but now? Now I can find the humor in it. Mostly.

Joy leans in, stage-whispering with a grin, "Okay, what about the FBI agent you *shot?*"

The car jerks slightly to the left, sending Joy tumbling into my shoulder with a startled squeak. The driver mutters an apology in a tone that says he *very much* regrets picking up this ride.

We burst into laughter.

I can't believe it's only been a month. It's felt like both a lifetime and a long weekend with apocalyptic vibes.

The news over the last week has been a carousel of headlines. It's only been three weeks since the incident at the construction site, but the federal indictment dropped faster than anyone expected. Wire fraud. Racketeering. Economic espionage. Illegal export of strategic resources. Jimmy Rook's name was all over the indictments too—along with a somber little paragraph announcing the untimely death of financial consultant Craig Miller. *RIP, buddy.*

There's no mention of Earl or Sebastian Edmond. Not publicly. Not yet. Maybe there won't be—because their testimony helped seal the case against Ramirez. I don't know what kind of deal they made, but I hope the second chance given to them reminds them that doing the right thing isn't weakness. It's the hardest kind of strength.

When our laughter finally dies down, Joy leans back against the cool leather seat and sighs. "Remember the last time you got dressed up for a gala?"

I snort, adjusting the clasp on my necklace. "Yeah. I ended up stepping in a public toilet and nearly got caught spying on my childhood nemesis."

Joy grins. "Do you think he actually would've arrested you?"

"Yes," I say deadpan. "And he would've loved every second of it."

The car slows as we near the Stratmore Pavilion, a glass-and-granite landmark tucked just off the Arts District. Spotlights sweep across the façade, catching on the crystal fixtures that glitter like stardust above the main entrance.

The driver pulls up and valets in black tuxedos open our doors. Joy and I step out and into a crowd of guests in evening gowns and sharp suits making their way up the front steps, their laughter and camera flashes echoing into the warm summer air.

Suddenly, I feel like my dress is too tight.

Joy straightens her neckline. "You ready for this?"

"Not even a little," I admit, but I smile anyway. "But I've got backup. And slightly better shoes than last time."

"Speaking of backup—"

Marcos meets us at the bottom of the steps, all charm in a navy suit that probably cost more than my rent. He spins Joy once, grinning like they've been doing this their whole lives, but they still call themselves just friends. The kind who share inside jokes and pretend they're not perfect together.

Then he turns to me and offers a hand. "You two are dressed to kill—and I'm pretty sure one of you might actually do it."

"Don't forget it," I tease.

"Billy." The name hits like a tremor. I turn—and there he is.

Ben. Tuxedo. Five o'clock shadow. That dangerous, crooked smile that hasn't stopped giving me heart palpitations since we first locked horns in the museum not even a block away. His eyes sweep over me in a way that makes me feel seen. Beautiful. Worthy.

He takes my hand and spins me slowly. "You're stunning."

The dress I chose tonight clings in all the right places. Black silk, low back, high slit, and just enough elegance to make me feel a little invincible. Like I'll be able to pull this off tonight.

Then Ben kisses me, soft and certain, and suddenly I'm wondering why we're not back on my couch watching *Survivor* and arguing over tribal alliances.

"We'll meet you inside," Joy calls as she and Marcos disappear into the crowd.

Ben pulls me aside to a quiet corner near a hedge-lined path. The music is muffled here, the air warm and honey-sweet with night-blooming jasmine. "Did you get it?"

I grip my clutch tighter, nerves thrumming. "It came an hour ago."

His hands brush down my arms, steadying me. "What did it say?"

"I don't know," I admit. "I wanted to wait. I wanted to open it with you."

Ben's whole expression softens, and I know I made the right choice. "You ready?"

"I don't know." My heart is pounding. I haven't wanted to think about this email or the results or what it might mean for me and my future. "It feels like there's a hoedown happening in my stomach."

"A what?"

"My nerves are line dancing all over my stomach. 'Cotton-Eyed Joe' kind of energy."

He laughs, then tips my chin up so I meet his eyes. "Billy, you helped take down a crime boss. Wrestled his sleazy lawyer. Whatever that email says, it doesn't define you or your future. But I have every hope you're going to have the future you deserve."

I pull out my phone, fingers shaking. I don't know why I thought it was a good idea to take the LSAT two weeks after everything that happened. But I was already registered before I knew I was going to be involved in an international anti-terrorism mission. And Ben helped me study. In between kissing breaks, which—honestly—were a better reward system than anything Kaplan ever designed.

I breathe. Click the link. Find my name. Click again. I stare.

Ben shifts beside me. "Well?"

"I passed." The words come out on a stunned whisper. "I actually passed."

"Of course you did." He pulls me into a hug, lifts me right off the ground, then peppers kiss after kiss along my jaw, my cheek, until he finally meets my lips.

I return the kiss—deep, grateful, and filled with all the promises of everything we survived to get here.

When he pulls back, he's breathless. His cheeks are tinged pink and the longing in his eyes tells me he wants more. But his expression is shifting—his smile fading into something sharp. Focused. It's his federal agent pose and it's stupidly attractive.

He checks his watch and then looks at me. "Everything's ready. Are you?"

The Solace Summit Gala, an annual black-tie affair dedicated to "honoring those who make the world a better place." Which, in tonight's case, includes one very polished con artist who's minutes away from a very public undoing.

Celeste Harlowe stole millions under the guise of helping families invest in their future—then vanished with their money. But tonight, with the help of the FBI, the charade ends.

She thinks she's getting an award, but it'll be a shiny pair of handcuffs instead.

This won't undo what's already been lost. Won't bring back the money. Won't erase the heartbreak she's caused. But if no one else becomes one of her victims, then that's a win you can measure in dollars.

I look at Ben—my partner, my beginning—and nod. "Let's finish it."

I take his offered arm and we ascend the marble steps. Tonight the pavilion is bathed in warm amber light, its dramatic floor-to-ceiling windows revealing flashes of crystal chandeliers, sculptural floral displays, and the city's most polished socialites drifting past white-gloved waiters with flutes of champagne. Strings play something sweeping and rich.

Only a month ago, I walked into a gala like this thinking control was the only thing that kept me safe. That if I wasn't composed and capable and two steps ahead, I'd become the girl people whispered about. The risk. The chaos. The one who couldn't be counted on.

I built my life proving I wasn't like my mom. That what I'd overheard Ben say years ago—even if he didn't mean it—wasn't true.

Control isn't the same thing as security. And perfection doesn't equal worth.

That voice in my head still fights dirty, still tells me if I'm not managing everything perfectly, I'm not enough. But I'm not fighting it alone anymore. Not when I have people who show up. Who stay when things get messy. Risky.

Ben. Joy. Marcos. Even Earl. Not because I made them—but because they chose to. Each of them a reminder that maybe I'm not the risk I thought I was.

Unless, of course, I choose to be . . .

At the entryway, a hostess flashes us a rehearsed smile. "Names?"

Ben and I glance at each other. A shared look. A silent pact that says we're on this adventure together.

I smile back at the hostess and say, without missing a beat, "Mr. and Mrs. Smith."

Acknowledgments

Writing a book is an adventure, and by adventure, I mean a slightly chaotic operation fueled by chocolate, prayer, and questionable Google searches that inevitably have landed me on federal watchlists. For this I have plenty of ~~accomplices~~ friends I need to thank:

To my amazing agent, Tamela Hancock-Murray, you always steer me toward wisdom, and I'm so grateful for your continued support and encouragement to chase my dreams.

To Becky Monds, my brilliant editor, and the entire editing team at HCCP, thank you for wrangling my words, sharpening my chaos, and never once asking how I know what I know. My lawyer says that's smart defense. Y'all have helped me turn my fictional felonies into a polished story that'll keep the authorities wondering how much of this is actually fiction.

To my fellow co-conspirators, Ashley, Joy, Rachel, Christen, Emilie, Crissy, Steffani, and Amy, thank you for standing by me through the chaos and cheering me on when I want to quit.

Jessica Patch, my partner in crime and the one who lit the match under the chaos that started the fire that landed me here—this whole Sweet & Stabby blaze is partly your fault. I owe you tea, chocolate, and possibly bail money.

Words would not have made it on the page without the kind baristas at the Woodway Starbucks. You kept me caffeinated, made sure I had a table, and never once judged me for the number of hours I've spent muttering about murder. That's alibi-level loyalty right there.

GIJOE, thanks for never blinking when I say things like, "Do you think this body could fit in a trunk?", for being a good sport when I need to research something felonious on a victim, and for keeping some money set aside for bail. And for my kiddos, no matter what I do, I'm the proudest of each of you.

To every reader who picks up this story—thank you. You're the reason I get to write about chaos, courage, and love with a little side of felony. You're my favorite kind of unhinged.

Most of all, I give thanks to my Lord and Savior. Every good thing in my life is a gift from Him. This story, this opportunity, the people who cheer me on, and the joy of creating something I love. I am grateful beyond words for His guidance, His grace, and the blessings He has poured into my family, friendships, and work. And even if all of this were to disappear tomorrow, I would remain richly blessed because He is always enough.

Discussion Questions

1. Cybil takes on an undercover job in order to pay her bills. Do you think you could ever do a job like Cybil or Ben, even if you were in a desperate situation and required the work?

2. Do you think Cybil was too harsh with Ben when she wouldn't forgive him for the past? Why or why not?

3. The book holds many humorous moments in spite of its seriousness. Which lighter moment is your favorite?

4. Have you ever felt the burden to care for a family member who made unwise choices (whether their fault or not)? If you're comfortable, share some of the challenges resulting from that.

5. Ben and Cybil were both in difficult positions, not being able to tell one another about their jobs or the danger in the people each were working for. Considering the complicated situation, do you think they handled their secrecy appropriately, or should they have told each other sooner?

6. Cybil says, "That voice in my head still fights dirty, still tells me if I'm not managing everything perfectly, I'm not enough. But I'm not fighting it alone anymore. Not when I have people who show up. Who stay when things get messy. Risky." Who are the people in your life who stick around even when you might feel like your life is messy?

7. Cybil also says, "Control isn't the same thing as security. And perfection doesn't equal worth." Is perfection something you struggle with? How can you remind yourself that control or perfection aren't how you achieve worth?

8. Ben says, "You're the strongest person I've ever met, Billy. Not because you don't get scared. But because you do—and you still show up anyway." Can you think of a situation in your life where you were scared but had to show up anyway? How did you get through that time?

9. Cybil carries Ben's words from the past with her and says, "I know exactly what it feels like to wear a label that sticks no matter how hard you try to scrub it off. All my life, I've believed I had to prove I wasn't unstable." Words can be very powerful. Have you ever had a hard time letting go of words that were said to you?

10. Later in the book, Cybil realizes, "I no longer feel helpless. I feel like I can do something to help protect others from becoming a victim like my mom and I were." Can you think of a situation in your life where something bad happened and you were able to use it for good?

11. Who is your favorite character, and why is it Ben's grandma?

About the Author

Emilie Haney @ EAH Creative

Natalie Walters is a bestselling and award-winning author who loves thrilling adventure, quick-witted characters, fun banter, and romantic tension with all the sizzling chemistry. She writes sweet and stabby suspense for readers who crave plot twists, emotional stakes, and just enough mischief to make you wonder if that shovel in the trunk is for gardening . . . or something else.

Connect with her online at nataliewalterswriter.com.
Instagram: @nataliewalters_writer
BookBub: @nataliewalters